SEVEN BROTHERS

A Novel

SEVEN
BROTHERS
by ALEKSIS KIVI, pseud.

Aleksis Stenvall

Translated
by Alex. Matson

THE AMERICAN-SCANDINAVIAN FOUNDATION
New York
1962

Illustrated by
Akseli Gallen-Kallela

With the permission of Tammi Publishers, Helsinki,
this special printing of "SEVEN BROTHERS"
by Aleksis Kivi has been photo-offset
from the English-language edition issued
in Finland, by Tammi Publishers in 1959

TRANSLATOR'S FOREWORD

"Seven Brothers", for three quarters of a century the most widely circulated book in Finland next to the Bible, can be read as a simple tale of adventure and humour, as it is read and enjoyed by Finns of all ages who ask of a book solely that it shall engross and entertain them. For the non-Finnish reader it can be something more. Entertainment certainly, but at the same time a key to the Finnish national character and the country by which that character was moulded.

The face of Finland has of course altered greatly since Kivi wrote his novel in the 1860's, drawing even then on his memories of earlier times. It might be difficult to recognize in the Finnish farmer of to-day the children of nature Kivi drew. Yet for all that, national character does not easily change, and Kivi's "brothers" are still typical of the nation. The traits of character that determined the course of their lives — stubbornness, hardy individualism, endurance, independence, love of liberty — are those which have determined the course of Finland's history in our times.

Nor has the character of the Finnish landscape changed for all the local transformations brought about by industrialization and a growing population. If it is the spirit of the nation a stranger to Finland wishes to know, there is still no better introduction than Kivi's novel.

*

Aleksis Kivi, to-day Finland's best-known author, unanimously acclaimed as the greatest genius in the history of Finnish literature, suffered the fate of most original artists. His gifts did not go unrecognized in his lifetime, but his greatness was divined only by a slow process of discovery that still continues as successive generations of critics study his work. The farther back he recedes in time, the higher he is seen to tower not only over his contemporaries, but over those who came after him.

The son of a poor village tailor, he was able with the fitful aid of a brother and at the cost of privations that now seem almost incredible to prepare himself for the university, only to find systematic study made impossible by extreme poverty. And even in the country, to which he was forced to retire, his existence was dependent largely on charity. A successful literary career seemed to open for him when his first major work "Kullervo", a tragedy on a theme from the Kalevala ,was awarded a State prize. Later, too, his full-length comedy "The Heath Cobblers" and a shorter comedy "The Betrothal", the first works in which he gave expression to his profound love and understanding of the unspoiled Finnish rustic, were highly praised by a discerning critic of authority. His short lyrical drama "Lea" was the first serious play ever to be staged in Finnish. The public, however, for a writer in Finnish was small in those days, when as a result of the long connection with Sweden the Swedish language still dominated in cultural matters, and Kivi never earned enough by his pen even for the merest subsistence.

The wonder is that there is no taint of bitterness in his work, no railing against fate, only joy in the richness and beauty of the universe: the illumined idealism of a Shelley coupled with warm human feeling and a delicious humour. Even his melancholy is the unearthly melancholy that is sister to rapture. A heroic soul, if ever there was one. Only, no human frame could long endure the combination of physical suffering and the intense concentration of the inspired poet. The strain was too great, and in 1871 Kivi, born in 1834 and thus only 38, died, the mental collapse that preceded his death hastened on by a cruel criticism of "The Seven Brothers"

6

accusing him of coarseness and of dishonouring the calling of an author. He himself never saw his belief in his "brothers" vindicated.

*

Kivi began his "Seven Brothers" with no further intention than that of narrating in a humorous vein the adventures of seven brothers in the Finnish wilds. The theme, however, aroused the artist in him so thoroughly that instead of carrying out his plan of publishing the work in serial parts — that he might earn as he wrote — he toiled at it for nine years.

This genesis of the work accounts in part for its unusual character, but not altogether. Thus, the original plan is evident in the absence of a central plot beyond that provided by the brothers' revolt against civilization and their ultimate return to its fold, and in a certain outward picaresque quality. This aspect of the novel doubtless also owes something to the fact that instead of studying the works of contemporary novelists, Kivi derived his conception of literary art from Cervantes and Shakespeare. The influence of both of these can be traced in his work, that of Shakespeare in Aapo's speeches and the stories he tells, in which the language rises on occasion to a poetry exceeding the speaker's own powers of expression as in the Shakespearen monologue. Kivi was however an original genius, and in the novel there is something else that is peculiarly his own: an instinctive feeling for form in the strictest sense of the word.

It is to this instinct, to a powerful striving for balanced architectural form, that every element in the structure of his novel can ultimately be traced back. Close study of the structure of "The Seven Brothers" reveals the work to be something more than narrative; it is seen to be an ordered work of art, perfectly integrated, a composition in which each word plays the part of a note in a symphony — hence Kivi's economical old-fashioned notation of dialogue. Behind the outward irregularity, the shapelessness characteristic of the true novel-form, structural principles can be disc-

7

erned too consequently applied to be accidental. Thus, each important event grows out of a previous similar theme in miniature. The flight of the brothers into the wilds on which the main action hangs, is a development on a grand scale of the incident from the brothers' childhood Kivi describes in his opening pages, and similar parallels can be detected all along. No turn occurs in the narrative that is not heralded by words or sentences sounding at first unobtrusively, then ever more insistently, so that when the new theme opens, the reader's ear is prepared for a change in key, tempo and mood.

The equivalent of modulation and variation can be seen in the manner in which the legends in which Kivi gives rein to his poetical imagination are followed by a burlesque version, either action or direct parody. Here, the swing from poetry and romance to the comic restores the balace of the novel on that plane of naturalism, of truth to everyday life, from which the novelist departs at his peril. Musical structure is apparent also in the manner in which Kivi alternates solo passages with a full orchestra working up to a crescendo. Kivi's stage-setting, too, his grouping of stars and chorus and manipulation of sound effects, can be curiously reminiscent of opera. Even his choice of words, the construction of his sentences, his prose rythms, are analogous to music, though for this the reader must take the translator's word, for a translator, compelled to stick to an author's meaning, can but rarely reproduce the cadences and beats of the original sentences in which sound, stress and meaning were created simultaneously.

In all this there is nothing deliberate, no laboured theory; the structure never obtrudes as it does when an author works consciously to a theory of form. Indeed, the form of Kivi's novel is doubly interesting for the very reason that it was arrived at unconsciously in the course of a search for perfection in what Kivi to the end regarded as a story, for it points to hidden affinities between the novel and the other arts, to the element of art in the novel-form that aesthetic research has so far failed to pin down. Kivi knew nothing of the theory of music and his opportunities for

8

hearing good music were few, yet led solely by feeling, by his sense of the beautiful, he arrived through endless rewriting, recasting, adding and eliminating at thematic, or better still, symphonic structure. By sheer natural genius he anticipated findings in regard to the novel only diffidently expressed by Henry James and E. M. Forster.

And not for a moment did he forget the claims of the realistic story that was his material. That provided the stuff which the artist in him moulded into a form that was to become the complete expression of his own personality, yet a picture to be looked at and judged on its own merits as a composition. Ever in the forefront of his mind was his desire to communicate his own intense delight in the simple country people among whom most of his life was spent, and to open the eyes of his fellow-Finns to the beauty of the country it was their privilege to inhabit. Hence, partly, the care with which he modelled his characters until each of the brothers stands out in the round, all individualized, yet each a facet of a larger personality, that of a race. Hence, also, the lovingness with which he depicts landscape.

*

For appreciation of Kivi's novel, it is by no means necessary that the reader should pay attention to its structural merits. Such matters are for the professional student of literature. Like all other novels, Kivi's novel was written to be read as a story. It was to that end that Kivi's art was directed, and the layman is advised to ignore all that has been said herein about thematic structure and simply to read.

The effect at which an artist aims is the main thing, and the struggles of the artist to achieve the desired effect are no matter for the public. Yet one remark should perhaps still be added on the subject of structure. The result of Kivi's labours to satisfy his sense of form is an unusual solidity that becomes apparent only after repeated re-readings in an increased vividness and reality in the scenes depicted. As for perfect pleasure in great music some acquaintance with its pattern is necessary, so too Kivi's novel reads best after its contents have become familiar. Experience has shown this to be the case in Finland, where people talk not of having read the book, but of the number of times they have read it. Indeed, there are Kivi-enthusiasts who know the novel by heart and can at any time summon to memory favorite pages precisely as a music-lover will recall to mind passages from a musical composition. One might say that what drives them to re-read to the point of memorizing need not be so much any excellence the book may possess, as their own pleasure in it. But how many novels will bear memorizing and still continue to enchant?

SEVEN
BROTHERS

JUKOLA Farm, in the southern part of Häme, lies on the northern slope of a hill not far from a village called Toukola. Around the house the ground is studded with boulders, but farther down the slope are fields, where once, before the farm fell into decay, heavy-eared crops used to wave. Below the fields is a meadow, clover-rimmed and cleft by a winding brook; and richly it yielded hay before it became grazing ground for the village cattle. Attached to the farm are also immense forests, swamps and backwoods, acquired mostly at the great enclosure of lands long ago, thanks to the admirable sense of the founder of the farm. For it was then that the master of Jukola, looking more to the advantage of his descendants than his own, accepted for his share forest ravaged by fire and for this was given seven times the area allotted to his neighbours. Now, however, all traces of fire had vanished from his holding, and dense forest covered the site. — Such is the home of the seven brothers, whose fortunes I am about to relate.

The names of the brothers, from the eldest downward, are: Juhani, Tuomas, Aapo, Simeoni, Timo, Lauri and Eero. Tuomas and Aapo are twins, likewise Timo and·Lauri. Juhani, the eldest, is twenty-five; Eero, the youngest, has barely seen eighteen circuits of the sun. In build, they are stocky and broad-shouldered, of middling height, except Eero, who is still very short. Tallest is

13

Aapo, though by far not the broadest across the shoulders. That advantage and honour falls to Tuomas, who is actually famous for the breadth of his shoulders. Peculiar to them all is the brownness of their skin and their stiff, hemplike hair, the coarseness of which is especially striking in Juhani.

Their father, a passionate hunter, met a sudden death in the prime of his life in an encounter with an enraged bear. Both were found dead, the shaggy king of the wilds and the man, lying side by side on the bloodstained ground. Sorely was the man mangled, but the brute too was seen to have been gashed with a knife and to have had its breast pierced by the keen bullet of a musket. So perished a sturdy fellow who in his time had killed more than fifty bears. — For love of the hunt, however, he neglected to work on his farm, which gradually, with no master watching over it, fell into decay. Nor were his sons either enamoured of sowing and ploughing; from their father they had inherited the same powerful eagerness to hunt game in the forests. They laid traps, set gins and snares and dug grouse-pits, to the undoing of wildfowl and hares. In such pursuits they passed their boyhood until they were able to use fire-arms and dared seek out Bruin in his wilds.

Their mother tried, indeed, with tongue and rod to turn them into the path of work and diligence, but the boys stubbornly resisted all her efforts. She was in every respect a deserving woman, known for her straightforward and honest, though perhaps a trifle over-harsh character. A fine fellow was her brother, too, the boys' greatly admired uncle, who in his youth had sailed the distant seas, a stalwart sailor, and seen many peoples and cities; until having lost his sight and become stone-blind, he spent the dark days of his old age at Jukola. There, as he carved by touch dippers, spoons, axeshafts and other household articles, he would tell his nephews stories and describe to them strange events that had happened in their own country or alien kingdoms, or relate to them miracles and other things from the Bible. To these talks of his the boys listened attentively, impressing them for all time on their memories. With less pleasure they listened to their mother's commands and scoldings, turning to them a deaf ear in spite of repeated thrashings. All too often, perceiving the imminence of a whipping, the gang of brothers would decamp, causing their mother and others acute anxiety and trouble and thereby making their own case worse.

May one such episode from the brothers' childhood be recorded here. They were aware of the existence, under their barn, of a hen's nest belonging to an old woman known as Granny Pinewood, her little cabin being situated in a clump of pines near Jukola. One day, a fancy for baked eggs having entered their minds, they decided to plunder this nest and then enjoy their spoil in the forest. They carried out this decision, emptied the nest and made off in a body for the woods, six brothers; Eero still clung at that time to his mother's skirts. Reaching a purling brook in a dark sprucewood, they made a fire on the bank, wrapped the eggs in rags, and having dipped them in water, set them to bake in the hissing ashes. And when their titbits were cooked, they ate a tasty meal and set off contentedly home again. But no sooner had they reached the home rise, than a storm broke over their heads; their misdeed had been discovered. Granny Pinewood raged and scolded, and fierce of countenance their mother hastened to meet them, a whining rod in her hand. The boys, however, were not of a mind to encounter such a squall, but turned back and fled to the forest for shelter, heedless of their mother's cries.

A day now passed, and then a second, but of the truants there was no sign; and at last their absence became a cause of great disquietude to the mother; her anger soon gave way to grief and tears of pity. She set out to look for them, scoured the woods in all directions, but in vain. The matter then began to take on an ever more dreadful aspect and finally to call for action by the Crown's servants. Word was sent to the beadle, who at once alarmed the whole of Toukola and the outlying farms. And now a search-party of old and young, women as well as men, set out, headed by the beadle, to comb the forests. The first day they searched the vicinity, but without the result hoped for; the next day

15

they moved farther way, and now, as they breasted a high hill, they saw in the distance, on the margin of a swamp, a blue pillar of smoke corkscrewing up into the sky. Carefully marking the direction, they pushed on towards the smoke. And at last, approaching nearer, they heard a voice sing these words:

'Well fared the men of olden days,
The wilds did not dismay 'em.
Driftwood kept their fire ablaze,
Their ale the river gave 'em.'

On hearing this song the mistress of Jukola was mightily cheered, for she recognized the voice as that of her son Juhani. And the forest also ringing with the crashes of a firehammer, the searchers knew that they were heading for the truants' camp. The beadle gave an order for the boys to be surrounded, after which the party was to close in silently and then halt some distance away.

His order was obeyed. And when the yarty, closing in on all sides, had approached to within fifty paces, it came to a halt; and now the following sight met their gaze: built of spruce-branches at the foot of a rock was a tiny shelter, in the doorway of which Juhani reclined on a mossy couch, staring up at the clouds and singing. A few yards away from the shelter a camp-fire blazed merrily, and in its embers Simeoni was roasting a grouse the brothers had snared for dinner. Aapo and Timo, both with sooty faces after playing at being brownies, were baking turnips in hot ashes. Beside a little clay-pit Lauri was silently busy modelling clay whistles, bulls and spirited foals; he already had a long row of these set to dry on the moss-clad trunk of a fallen tree. Tuomas banged away with a fire-hammer: spit frothily on an embedded rock, laid a live coal on the saliva and then brought down with all his might a second rock on the coal, whereupon a crash, often as sharp as the report of a rifle, would echo around, and a sooty smoke issue from between the rocks.

16

Juhani: 'Well fared the men of olden days,
  The wilds did not dismay 'em,'
but the Devil will get us yet out here. It's as good as in our hands,
ye sons of beavers.

Aapo: Isn't that what I said when we took the hare's path.
What fools we were! Let robbers and gypsies wallow like this
with only the sky for roof.

Timo: God's sky, anyhow.

Aapo: Living here with wolves and bears.

Tuomas: And with God.

Juhani: Right, Tuomas! With God and his angels. Ah, if we
only had the eyes of a soul in Heaven, we'd see as plainly as anything a whole host of sheltering angels with wings in a ring around
us, and God himself, like a grey old gaffer, sitting right in our
midst as a loving father.

Simeoni: Ay, but what will poor mother be thinking?

Tuomas: She'll be wanting to hammer us tender the minute
she can lay her hands on us.

Juhani: Ay, boy, that would be a basting!

Tuomas: A basting. A good basting.

Juhani: A fire-spitting basting. We know that.

Aapo: We've got to take it some time.

Simeoni: That's true. So best go and get the basting over and
end this bullock's holiday.

Juhani: A bullock doesn't exactly go of its own free will,
brother, to be slaughtered.

Aapo: Don't talk rubbish, boy. Winter's coming, and we were-
n't born with a pelt to our backs.

Simeoni: So there's nothing for it but homeward march for our
hiding, and a well-earned one.

Juhani: Brothers, brothers, let our backs be spared a little while
yet. How do we know what way out God may find for us in the
next two or three days. Ay, let's still romp here, our days yonder
around our tree-stump fireplace, our nights in our spruce hut,
grunting side by side in a row like sucking-pigs in a stye. — What

dost thou say, Lauri boy, in thy claypit? What? Shall we go meekly and take our hiding?

Lauri: Let's stay here yet.

Juhani: That's what I think's best. Just that. — But that's a mighty herd of cattle thou hast there.

Tuomas: Cattle and poultry, that boy has.

Juhani: A mighty flock. There's the makings of a real whistle-maker in thee.

Tuomas: A real plasterer.

Juhani: A grand plasterer. — What's that Russian doll just out of thy paws?

Lauri: This is only a kind of a little boy.

Juhani: See the rascal!

Tuomas. Makes boys like a man.

Juhani: Boys stout as tree-stumps; and feeds his boys and cattle like a man. — But say, brothers, brothers, hurry up with the dinner, my stomach's beginning to grumble. More ashes, boiling hot ashes, on that roasting turnip, that one there. — Whose turn is it to steal turnips?

Simeoni: My turn for that work of sin.

Juhani: We're forced to do a little pinching to keep body and soul together. If that's a sin, 'tis one of the smallest done in this maggotty world. See ye, if I die with no other black mark in my books, that little crow'sfoot'll hardly stop me from entering on a better life. I'd soon be chased out of the real bridal chamber, that I know, but there'd always be some doorkeeper's job for this lad, and even that would be terrible fun. — Ay, let's stick to that belief and cheerfully take as much as our gizzards will hold at a time.

Aapo: But I believe we'd do well to leava Kuokkala's turnip-field in peace now and find us another. When a crop gets smaller day by day, a farmer soon starts watching his land night and day.

The Beadle: No need to worry about that, boys, no need at all. Well, well, why this flurry? Look, see how a host of guardian angels has ringed ye round right smartly.

In such wise the beadle addressed the brothers, who, greatly scared, dashed up and scuttled off in all directions, but soon saw their escape cut off everywhere. Whereupon the beadle said: "You're in the net now, ye rascals, safe in a net where you'll stay until you've been scaled a little as a reminder, a little reminder, of the footsoreness you've caused us, ye rascals. Here with your birch, mother, and lay on them with a warm hand. And if there should be any resistance, there's plenty of helpwomen." Followed a thrashing from a mother's hand, boy after boy down the line of brothers; and loud was the outcry in Kuokkala's woods. Lustily the woman wielded her rod, yet the beadle averred that the hiding had been too mild.

And after her task had been completed, they all set off home, so too the mother and her sons. All the way she stormed, scolding the truants; nor did the tempest abate even after they had reached their home. Even while laying a meal for the boys on a stool the housewife continued to rage, threatening them with a new thrashing. But seeing the ravenous hunger with which they dug their teeth into the bread and pickled sprats, she turned her face away, wiping in secret a tear from her brown coarse cheek.

So ended the brothers' escapade. And this was the incident from the days of their childhood I interrupted my story to describe.

Another favourite pastime of the brothers was hitting the disc, a game they still loved to play in their manhood. Divided into two sides, they competed eagerly, each side trying to bat the disc across the other's goal line. Furiously they shouted, ran and jostled, and sweat poured in streams down their faces. The disc danced humming along the ground, often rebounding from a bat on to a player's face, so that on their return from a game one or more of the brothers would be nursing a tremendous bump on the forehead or a mussel-like bruise on the cheek. So passed the days of their youth: the summers in the forest or on the road, hitting the disc, the winters on top of the huge stove in perspiring heat.

But even the brothers could not help seeing the changes brought by time. Events occurred which forced them to take more heed of the morrow than they were wont to do, and to alter in some measure the direction of their lives. — Their mother had died, and one of them had now to take charge to avoid letting the farm go to utter ruin and see to the payment of the Crown tax, which, compared with the large area of land and forest belonging to Jukola, was certainly small. But on a neglected farm, there are work and duties in plenty. And to crown all, the new Vicar of the parish turned out to be terribly strict in all that pertained to his office. Especially towards backward readers was he without mercy, harrying them in every way, even confining them in the stocks. Thus, his sharp eye had fallen also on the Jukola brothers. He had already delivered to them a stern command, actually through a writserver, to hie them at more than their usual speed to the hymnleader for teaching in reading. — Remembering these circumstances, sitting one late summer evening in the living-room of their home, the brothers held the following conversation.

Aapo: I say that this wild life won't do, and can only end in ruin and destruction. Brothers! other habits and works, if happiness and peace is to be ours.

Juhani: Thou speakest truth, no denying that.

Simeoni: God ha' mercy! unbridled, wild has our life been unto this day.

Timo: There's life enough in this life, and world in the world. It's all right, hard as it is. Ohoo!

Juhani: We have lived too wildly, or to put the matter rightly, too carelessly, that can't be denied. Still, let us not forget: "youth and wildness, old age and wisdom".

Aapo: Well, it's time now for us to grow wiser, time to bring our lusts and passions under the yoke of our brains, and in the first place do that which profits us, not that which tastes sweetest. Up now to setting our farm without delay into respectable shape again!

Juhani: Well spoken! Let's get busy first on the manure like dungbeetles, and may the axe echo from morning to eve around Jukola's walls chopping pine-twigs for the midden; the cattle, our

21

grand cattle, let them too do their best to raise the pile; and may
the dunghills in our yard rise high as the golden walls of a king's
castle. Next Monday we'll begin, starting from the roots.

Aapo: Why not to-morrow?

Juhani: Monday, and not before. No harm in letting a matter
ripen a bit first. Ay, let that be settled, next Monday.

Aapo: One thing, however, we must do now. The case is this:
if we wish for order and a firm foundation for our household, let
one of us be leader and master. This right and duty, we know,
is Juhani's both as his birthright and by our mother's command.

Juhani: Ay, mine's the right, the power and the strength.

Aapo: See then that thou usest them mildly for the common
good.

Juhani: I'll try my best. If you'll only obey me without a clout
in the face or the whip. However, I'll do my best.

Aapo: The whip?

Juhani: Sithee, if so be needed.

Tuomas: Speak to thy dogs of the whip.

Timo: Thou'lt not warm my withers, never; let the rod of law
and justice do that if my back ever itches with cause.

Juhani: Why pounce on an idle word. There's room here for
all of us to be happy, if only harmony reigns and each of us
draws in his horns.

Eero: Let's make it quite plain, however, how we stand to each
other.

Aapo: And let's hear everybody's opinion.

Juhani: What sayest thou, Lauri, always a man of few words?

Lauri: I'll say something. Let's move into the forest, and to
Hell with the din of the world.

Juhani: Eigh?

Aapo: The man's raving again.

Juhani: Move into the forest? What madness would that be?

Aapo: Take no notice. — See this is what I've thought out.
Thou, Juhani, hast the first right to become master, if it is thy
wish.

22

Juhani: It is my wish.

Aapo: We others, so long as we stay in this dear home of ours and are unmarried, will work on the farm, eat the farm's food and receive our clothing from the farm. The first Monday of the month, except at sowing and reaping time, will always be ours to spend as we like, while still getting our meals from the farm. The farm will also give each of us a half barrel of oats for sowing every year, and every year we are to have the right to clear a patch of land of not less than three acres for the lot of us to grow our oats on. That is my idea for as long as we stay at home and are unmarried. But I know that not one of us would willingly part from the dear soil of Jukola, nor is there any reason why we should, for there's plenty of room here for seven brothers. Yet suppose in the course of time one of us should feel like founding a home and family of his own without having to call in the law and pay the cost of a surveyor to cut up the farm, mightn't he agree to the following terms. Let him receive in heritage a piece of land on which he can build his house and lay out his fields. And let him also be given a section of meadow and the right to clear for himself in the forest as much grazing land as would keep a couple of horses and four or five cows. Let him then farm his land and enjoy its fruits free of tax and rent, and his children after him, living in peace on his own soil. — That is how I have thought matters out. What say you others?

Juhani: Pretty sensibly thought out. Let's take thy points under consideration.

Lauri: We can do differently and even even more sensibly. Let's move into the bosom of the forest and sell wretched Jukola, or let's rent it to the tanner at Rajaportti. He has sent word to us of his willingness to close a bargain; only he wants possession for at least ten years. Let's do as I say and move with our horse, dogs and guns to the foot of Impivaara's steep height. There we can build ourselves a jolly cabin on a southward looking clearing and live in peace far away from the bustle of the world and touchy people, hunting game in the forests. — That's what I've been thinking day and night for years.

Juhani: Has the Devil bewitched thy brains, boy?

Eero: If not the Devil, then a wood-nymph.

Lauri: It's what I think, and it's what I'll one day do. There we'd be living like lords, hunting wildfowl, squirrels, hares, foxes, wolves, badgers and bushy bears.

Juhani: Well, I'll be — Go on right through Noah's Ark, from mouse to moose.

Eero: There's an idea: say farewell to salt and bread and suck blood, gorge on flesh like mosquitoes and Lapland wizards. Would we eat fox and wolf, too, in Impivaara's caves, like the hairy mountain ogres?

Lauri: Foxes and wolves would give us pelts, pelts money, money salt and bread.

Eero: Pelts would make us clothes, but let our only food be flesh, bloody steaming flesh; apes and baboons in woods don't need salt and bread.

Lauri: It's what I think, and it's what I'll one day do.

Timo: Let's weigh the matter carefully from every side. Why shouldn't we be able to munch salt and bread in the forest as well? Why? Eero's a mocker, always in our way, always the stone in our path. Who's to forbid a man of the forests from coming out now and then to the edge of a village, every once in a while according to his needs? Or wouldst thou bash me on the head with a stick, Eero?

Eero: No, brother, no. I'd even "salt give to him who berries doth bring". — Move, boys, move, I won't forbid ye, I'll cart you there, whisk you off from here at a wolf's trot.

Juhani: The forest spirits would soon whisk them back again, I'll lay.

Lauri: The home threshold is high for him who would come back, I know that, so don't think that I'll ever knock at thy door once I've closed it behind me. — On May-day I'm off.

Timo: Maybe I'll go with thee.

24

Lauri: I neither invite nor forbid thee: do as thy heart says is best. — I'm moving on May-day to Impivaara clearing. At first, until my own snug little cabin is ready, I'll live in the mossy hut grandfather used while he was burning charcoal. Ah then, when my day's work is over, I'll rest in a real abode of peace, hearing the bear whistle in the wilds and the grouse calling on Sompio Bog.

Timo: I'm coming too, Lauri. It's settled, Lauri.

Tuomas: If the times don't improve, I'll come too.

Juhani: Tuomas too! Wouldst thou too move there?

Tuomas: If the times don't improve.

Lauri: I'm moving on May-day even though days of milk and honey were to dawn for Jukola.

Timo: Thou and I, we two, we'll move from here to Sompio Bog like two cranes in spring-time; and won't wind and weather ring as we go!

Juhani: Mercy on us! But sithee, to tell the truth, there's a secret spell in Lauri's plan. The forest draws us. Dammit, I seem to see the bright plain of sky beyond those woods.

Aapo: Ye madmen, what can you be thinking? — Move into the forest? Why? Haven't we a farm and a farmhouse, a golden roof over our heads?

Juhani: True, we have a farm to which we'll cling tooth and nail so long as it smells at all of bread. But hark ye, suppose hard luck were to turn everything here topsey-turvey, contrary to a man's best plans, let the forest be my backwoods farm, whither I'll quickly betake myself when the last grains rattle in the hopper. — But now we'll pounce with terrific punch on work and husbandry, and let's get back to the point that was our real question. — According to my stupid skull Aapo has on the whole thought out matters fairly sensibly; and all will go well, if only each of us does his own best to maintain harmony and agreement in our midst. For sithee, if it's trouble we seek, we can always find some cause to set our neck hairs bristling.

Simeoni: Where cannot we find that so long as the Old Adam itches and tickles in us, between our skin and our bones.

Timo: I always think of Old Adam as a solemn old fellow in a felt hat, a long black coat, knee-breeches and a red waistcoat reaching to the pit of his belly. In my thoughts I see him just like that, plodding along and driving a team of oxen.

Simeoni: When we say Old Adam, we mean the root of sin, original sin.

Timo: I know he's the mark and sign of original sin, the horny Satan of Hell, but that's the kind of old boy I see him as, marching on behind a pair of oxen. I can't help it.

Juhani: Leave that matter of religion, and let's stick to the point. — Aapo, what is our idea of those two crofts of ours, Vuohenkalma and Kekkuri?

Aapo: We must not forget that both tenants once cleared their land from what used to be raw dismal forest, and that they may not therefore be evicted from their soil — which would indeed be wrong — so long as they are able to keep their fields growing, and even then the law expects the farm to make some provision for their old age. These are the facts in that case. — But let us glance at another matter, which to my belief is a ticklish one. For it is our most important step down here on earth; it either turns our hair grey too early or brings us the sunshine of life and ends our days in a golden sunset glow. And it is thee, Juhani, it first concerns. Mark therefore what I say: a mastership without a mistress is lopsided and lame; a farm without a mistress on its storehouse path...

Timo: Is like a wolf's den without the she-wolf, or like a topboot without the other topboot; verily it is lame, as Aapo says.

Aapo: A farm without a mistress on its storehouse path is like a cloudy day, and gloom sits at the head of the family table like a dying autumn evening. Whereas a good mistress is the bright sun of a house, spreading light and warmth. — Lo! she is first in the morning out of bed; mixes her dough, sets breakfast for her husband on the table, packs food in knapsacks for the forest and then hastens pail in hand to milk her mottled cows. Now she kneads the loaves, hustles and bustles, now beside the table, now tripping,

26

a loaf on her palm, to the back bench, and now like a tempest she stirs the fire until the oven's gaping maw spews flames and smoke. Then, while the loaves rise, she has time at last, babe at breast, to break her own fast, eat a hunk of bread and a broiled sprat and wash it down with curdled milk from the bowl. Nor does she forget the dog, the farm's faithful guardian on the step, nor the cat, which peers down sleepily from the top of the stove. — And now again she hustles and bustles, trips and turns, mixes a second dough in her tub to rise, kneads the loaves and bakes them, and sweat pours in streams from her brow. And lo! when the day is spent her loaves are under the rafters, row upon row, wafting downward a sweet breath of life. And when the menfolk return from the forest, a steaming supper awaits them on the newly scrubbed table. But where is she, the mistress? Yonder in the cattleyard she milks again her curly-horned cows, and in the pail the foamy crest rises high. — So she hustles and bustles, so she trips and turns, and not until all others snore already fast asleep does she sink down praying on her own bed. And even now her labours are not over. Uncomplainingly she rises from her bed in the night for a moment, for an hour, rises to soothe her tiny infant that lies whimpering in its cradle. — Such, brothers, is a good housewife.

Juhani: Well spoken, Aapo, and I understand the purpose of thy speech. It aims, namely, at persuading me to get married. A wife, sayest thou, is a necessary article in a household. True! But don't worry. Thy hope, to my belief, will be fulfilled, and soon. Ay, ay, that's so. I confess that my mind is already set in earnest on a maid, who'll make me a wife and a good one, if the old signs don't lead me astray. — Ay, brothers, new days and new tricks lie ahead of us, and the mastership I must take on myself is a heavy burden on my mind. A terrible load rests on the shoulders of a master here on earth, and he has much to answer for on Judgment Day. I am now responsible for the whole lot of you; remember that.

Tuomas: Thou? Why?

Juhani: I am your master; my fingers will once be bled for your sakes.

Tuomas: I answer myself for my body and soul.

Timo: I too answer for myself, hey!

Aapo: Brother Juhani, note that such remarks create bad blood.

Juhani: Bad blood was no more my meaning than bad flesh; you only pounce like fury on an idle, meaningless word and stick to it like tar, like burrs in a hot summer, though you know me to the bottom of my heart. I'll lose my temper!

Aapo: Leave that, and tell us now, if thou wilt, who is the girl who has drawn thy heart to her.

Juhani: That I will say without flinching. The wench with whom I am ruthlessly in love is Granny Pinewood's Venla.

Aapo: Hm.

Juhani: What dost thou say?

Aapo: Hm, was what I said.

Tuomas: An awkward business.

Simeoni: Venla. Well, well! But let the Heavenly Father decide.

Aapo: Hm, so it's Venla.

Juhani: What are you all muttering? Ah! I suspect something; and may the Son of the Lord protect us! What? Speak out!

Aapo: Listen: for years now my mind has been earnestly set on that girl.

Simeoni: If the Creator has granted her to me, why should I repine?

Eero: Don't then. She was granted to thee, while I take her.

Juhani: What says Tuomas?

Tuomas: An awkward business; the girl pleases me greatly, that I confess.

Juhani: So, so. Good! What about Timo?

Timo: I make the same confession.

Juhani: "Son of the Lord!" What about thee, Eero?

Eero: I make the same simple confession, the same simple confession.

Juhani: Good, very good! Ha-haa! — Even Timo, even Timo!

Timo: The girl is greatly dear to me, that I confess. I admit she

29

once whacked me like anything, pounded poor little me right hard, and I still remember that beating; ah well!

Juhani: Shut up about that. The question now is dost thou love her?

Timo: A-ay, a-ay, I do, and mightily, that is, if she loves me back.

Juhani: Well, well. So thou too wouldst get in my way?

Timo: Not at all, not at all, unless thou really canst not control thyself, thy mind and thy tongue. Still, I like the wench very much and will also do my best to make her my wife.

Juhani: Good, good! But what says Lauri?

Lauri: What have I to do with the girl?

Juhani: Whose side art thou on?

Lauri: I'll have naught to do with the matter, on this side or yon.

Juhani: There's going to be a fine stew, all the same.

Lauri: I'll keep my spoon out of it, I.

Juhani: All, therefore, except Lauri. Boys, boys, sons of Jukola and clansmen all! Now for a clash, and earth and heaven will quake! Now, darling brothers, the knife, the axe or the club, and one against all and all against one like seven bulls! I'm agreed. A club's my weapon; I seize this curlygrained billet, and whoever's skull gets a splinter of it, he has himself to blame for it. — Seize your billets, boys, and step forth if you can stand up to a man.

Eero: Here I stand armed, though a bit shorter than you others.

Juhani: Thou, whippersnapper. But sithee, I note on thy face that mocking, that sly, that damnable grin, and it seems thou makest fun of the matter. But I'll teach thee.

Eero: What is it to thee so long as my billet is in earnest?

Juhani: I'll soon teach thee. Take hold of your billets, boys, your billets!

Timo: Here I am, and here's my billet, if it has to be. I don't want anger and a quarrel, but if it has to be.

Juhani: Thy billet, Tuomas!

Tuomas: Go to Hades with thy billet, owl.

Juhani: Fire and lightning!

Simeoni: Terrible, heathenish and Turkish, this brawling. I'm out of the game and leave my marriage business in the Lord's hands.

Lauri: I'm out of it too.

Juhani: Step aside, then, you two, step out of our way. — At thy billet, Aapo, and let Jukola's walls echo to the splitting of skulls. Fire and horny devils!

Aapo: O wretched child of earth. I'm horrified, Juhani, when I look on thee now, seeing how thine eyes roll and thy hair sticks up on end like a tussock of hay.

Juhani: Let it stick, let it stick; it's just what an ordinary Jack's hair should rightly do.

Eero: I'm minded to dust it a little.

Juhani: Thou hop-o-my-thumb! Best keep nicely in a corner. Away! I pity thee.

Eero: Take that dreadful jaw of thine into a corner in good time. I pity that, for it's quaking and shaking like a beggar.

Juhani: Look how this billet's quaking, look!

Aapo: Juhani!

Eero: Strike! And I believe it'll rain back from here, maybe rain back real hailstones, big as billets. Strike!

Juhani: I will.

Aapo: Thou wilt not, Juhani.

Juhani: Go to the dunghill, thou, or seize thy billet and defend thyself, or I'll pound thy head into a jelly. Seize thy billet!

Aapo: Where are thy brains?

Juhani: In this tough billet; look, now it'll whisper a word.

Aapo: Wait, brother, wait, until I too have grabbed a weapon. — Now then, here I stand with a wooden sausage in my hand. But first a couple of words, my Christian band of brothers, and then let's fight like mad wolves. — Note: a man in a fury of rage is a bloodthirsty beast and no human being; too blind to see what is just and proper; least of all can he carry out works of love in the grip of anger. Nevertheless, if we were now to try to look in the

31

light of commonsense on the matter that has brought brothers to the verge of blows, I believe we shall find the case to be this. The girl cannot love all of us, but only one, if so be she would accept any of us as the one in whose company she would be willing to wander hand in hand over the thorny hill of life. I therefore think it best that we should go to her in a body, all at the same time, to inform her solemnly of our matter and with pious heart and tongue ask whether she could bestow her heart on one of us and on whom. Then if the girl is willing, may the one who draws the happy lot thank his luck, and the others accept their fate without murmuring. He who is left without must swallow his disappointment, hoping that he too will still meet the spouse ordained for him down here. If we act thus, we shall be acting like men and true brothers. And then the bright shades of our father and mother will step forth from the glowing gate of Heaven and standing on the rim of a shining cloud look down on us, crying to us in a loud voice: "Just so, Juhani, just so, Tuomas and Aapo, just so, Simeoni, Timo and Lauri, that's the way, my little Eero! Ye are sons in whom we are well pleased."

Juhani: Man, thou speakest, Devil take it, like an angel from Heaven and very nearly hadst me weeping.

Simeoni: We thank thee, Aapo.

Juhani: Yes, thanks. There goes my billet.

Timo: And there goes mine. And this quarrel ends as I wanted it to from the start.

Simeoni: Aapo holds up a mirror to us, and for that let us thank him.

Eero: Let us thank him, let us sing him a Simon's thanksgiving hymn.

Simeoni: Mockery, mockery and impudence again.

Timo: Don't make a mock of God's word, Eero, of Simon's thanksgiving hymn.

Aapo: So young and ah! so hardened!

Simeoni: So young and so hardened. Eero, Eero! Ay, I'll say no more, only sigh on thy behalf.

32

Juhani: I prophesy, Eero, that once or twice we shall have to lay on thee with a father's hand. Mother brought thee up too gently.

Simeoni: We must punish him while his heart is still pliant with the softness of youth; only let us do it with a loving hand and not in wrath. The hand of wrath drives devils in, not out.

Eero: Take that from a real loving hand.

Simeoni: Oh the godless: He hit me!

Eero: Square on the snout. Bile can overflow for less.

Juhani: Come here, my boy. Timo, give me that stick from yon corner.

Simeoni: That's right, Juhani. Hold him nicely across thy knee, I'll let his trousers down.

Eero: Stop! Hell!

Juhani: Vainly thou wrigglest, shrimp.

Simeoni: Don't let go of him.

Juhani: See the wildcat! But thou wilt not escape, no.

Eero: Hit me, ye accursed, and I'll set the house on fire. I'll raise fire and smoke, I will in earnest, fire and smoke!

Juhani: What gall! Wouldst set fire to the house? Ah what gall!

Simeoni: God protect us, what gall!

Juhani: Hither with the stick, Timo.

Timo: I can't find it.

Juhani: Blind, canst not see it in yon corner?

Timo: Oh, this one? This birch?

Juhani: Just that. Pass it here.

Simeoni: Lay on, but sensibly, not quite with all thy might.

Juhani: I know how.

Lauri: Not a single stroke, say I.

Tuomas: Leave the boy alone.

Juhani: He needs his tail warming.

Lauri: Thou'lt not lay a finger on him.

Tuomas: Set the boy free! At once!

Timo: Let him be forgiven, Eero-lad, still this once, anyhow.

Simeoni: Forgiven, forgiven, until tares and weeds have choked the wheat.

Lauri: Don't touch him.

Aapo: Let us forgive him and try in that way to heap glowing coals on his head.

Juhani: Go then and thank thy stars.

Simeoni: And pray to God to grant thee a new heart, mind and tongue.

Timo: I'm off to bed.

Aapo: Let's still cast a glance at one matter.

Timo: I'm off to bed. Come along, Eero, let's go to bed and forget this ant-heap of a world, this miserable pile that steams and smokes in the rain. Come, Eero.

Juhani: What is the matter thou wouldst have us thrash out?

Aapo: God ha mercy! isn't it a fact that we don't even know our 'a', the first letter of the alphabet, and yet the art of reading is an essential duty of a Christian citizen. But we can be forced to it by the power of the law, the power of church law. And you know what Crown contraption waits for us, eager to gets its teeth into us, if we don't dutifully learn to read. The stocks await us, brothers, the black stocks, which, with its round holes sternly gaping, squats in the church porch like a black boar. With these Hell's pincers our Vicar has already threatened us, and he might carry out his threat if he doesn't see us busily practising every day, that's certain.

Juhani: Impossible to learn to read.

Aapo: It's a trick people have learned to do before.

Tuomas: 'Twould set a fellow sweating.

Juhani: And puffing. I have such a hard head.

Aapo: A strong will can take a man through grey granite. Let's get to work, send to Hämeenlinna for a-b-c books and go to the hymnleader's to school, as was our Vicar's order. Let's do it before we are rushed there at Crown speed.

Juhani: I'm afraid that that's what we have to do, I'm afraid so. God have mercy upon us! But let's leave the matter until to-morrow and go to bed now.

34

A CALM September morning. Dew glitters in the fields; mist swirls around the branches of the yellowing trees, to fade at last into the upper air. This morning the brothers rose very ill-tempered and silent, washed their faces, combed their hair and dressed in their Sunday best. For to-day they mean to go to the hymnleader's to school.

They sit now at breakfast around Jukola's long pine table, and the brown peas seem to taste well to them, though instead of merriment a dark frown of resentment has settled on their brows; the thought of the school-trip on which they must soon depart has caused this scowl. Yet, having eaten, they do not hasten at once on their way, but linger on resting. They sit in silence, some gazing moodily down at the floor, some staring at their red-backed a-b-c books as they finger the stout leaves. Beside the southern window of the living-room sits Juhani, his glance on the stony hillside and the dense pine-wood with its glimpse of the old woman's cabin and its red-framed door.

Juhani: There's Venla tripping along the path, and nimbly she skips too.

Aapo: And it was yesterday that both mother and daughter were to go to their kinsfolk at Tikkala to dig turnips and pick lingonberries, meaning to stay there until late autumn.

Juhani: Until late autumn? It makes me very uneasy. Happen they'll go, but there's a farmhand at Tikkala this year, a bonny lad and a great rogue, and that'd soon be the end of all our hopes. Best do the great deed, therefore, right now; put the question, of all questions the question. So let's go and ask the wench if her mind can be persuaded and her heart catch fire.

Tuomas: I, too, think that's best.

Timo: And I too.

Juhani: Ay, ay, there's nothing for it now but a-marrying, all together and at the same moment like true lads. Ay, ay! The Lord protect us! But it can't be helped, so a-marrying, a-marrying! Here we are in our best clother, washed and brushed, our whole outward appearance that of a Christian being: tidy and as though born again. — I feel very uneasy. — But on to Venla! Now is an acceptable time.

Eero: And may it be also a day of bliss.

Juhani: Whose day of bliss, whose? Ahaa! whose dost thou think, lad?

Eero: Why not all of ours?

Juhani: In other words, that she would become the wife of all of us?

Eero: I'm willing.

Juhani: What?

Simeoni: How in God's name would that be possible?

Eero: Nothing is impossible before God. Let's all trust, hope and love with one accord.

Juhani: Shut up, Eero! For now we're off a-marrying and the same road to school, bag on back.

Aapo: But in order to do the job properly, one of us ought to act as a kind of spokesman in the cabin.

Juhani: An important point. But thou thyself art as though fashioned for the part. Thou hast goodly gifts; thy speech has always lit fire and lightning in a man's bosom. Verily! thou wert born to be a parson.

Aapo: What do I know? And why speak of gifts. Here in the

woods they are lost in the mists of ignorance, fade away like a tinkling brook into sand.

Juhani: Hard luck has kept thee from school.

Aapo: Where would our farm have got the means to send me to school? Remember: many's the foodbag that dances between home and school before a boy's in the wooden tub. — But back to our business, our marrying business. Be it as ye wish. I'll step forward as the common spokesman and try to speak like a wise man.

Juhani: Le't get to work. — Holy Lord! But it can't be helped, so let's get to work in earnest. We'll leave our bags outside the cabin, and Lauri, who has no cows in this well, can guard them from the pigs. Let's go now. And let's enter the bridal chamber a-b-c book in fist; it lends us a kind of solemnity.

Eero: Especially if we turn the last page with the cockerel on outside.

Juhani: At it again? But the cock reminds me of the horrid dream that upset me last night.

Simeoni: Tell us it; maybe it was sent as a healthy warning.

Juhani: I dreamed that on yon stove there was a hen's nest with seven eggs in it.

Simeoni: Jukola's seven sons!

Juhani: But one of the eggs was ridiculously small.

Simeoni: Eero!

Juhani: The cock died.

Simeoni: Our father!

Juhani: The hen died.

Simeoni: Our mother!

Juhani: Then suddenly all the world's mice, rats and weasels attacked the nest. — What would these animals mean?

Simeoni: Our sinful passions and the lusts of the world.

Juhani: Likely that. — The weasels, rats and mice came and turned and rolled, tapped and rattled the eggs, which soon broke, and from the tiny egg burst a very bitter stink.

Simeoni: Mark that, Eero.

Juhani: The eggs were broken, and from the stove top an awful voice, as the roar of many waters, shouted in my ear: "All is broken, and great was the breakage thereof!" That's what it shouted, but we began at last to collect the mess and cook it, and in the end we got what are called scrambled eggs; and we ate it with great pleasure and gave some to our neighbours too.

Eero: A good dream.

Juhani: Bitter, bitter; thou stankest in it like hell. It was a very bitter dream I had of thee, lad.

Eero: But I dreamed right sweetly of thee. I saw the cockerel in the a-b-c book lay thee, in reward for thy diligence and wisdom, a big heap of sweets and lumps of sugar. Thou wert greatly pleased, champing at thy goodies; thou gavest some to me.

Juhani: Did I give thee some? That was a good deed.

Eero: When is it evil to give?

Juhani: Never; especially if I were to give thee a little taste of the stick.

Eero: Why only a little?

Juhani: Hold thy jaw, bull-calf!

Tuomas: Do that both of you, and let us start.

Aapo: Let each take his bag and his a-b-c book.

So they set forth to woo their neighbour's daughter. In Indian file, silent, they crossed the mound in which their potato-cellar lay, marched up the stony hill and stood at last before Granny Pinewood's cabin.

Juhani: Here we are and here we leave our bags; do thou, Lauri, keep faithful watch until we return from the bridal chamber.

Lauri: Will you be there long?

Juhani: As long as the shaping of our errand demands. — Has anyone a ring?

Eero: It isn't needed.

Juhani: Has anyone a ring in his pocket?

Timo: Not I, nor as far as I know have the others. There you are now: a bachelor ought always to have a glittering ring in his pocket when he goes out.

Juhani: The Devil! Here we stand now. And pedlar Isak was at our place yesterday, who could have sold me both the ring and the shawl. But I, pig that I am, never thought of that.

Aapo: Such instruments we can buy ourselves later. Indeed it is best to know first for certain whether any of us, and which, is to make these joyful purchases.

Juhani: Who opened the door? Was it Venla?

Timo: It was the old woman, the long-chinned hag.

Juhani: Venla's spinning-wheel hums in there like a merry dung-beetle on a summer evening, foretelling fine weather. Let's go in now. Where's my a-b-c?

Aapo: In thy fist, brother. Why, God's creation, thou art as though a little mixed in thy head.

Juhani: Nothing to be afraid of, brother. I'm not smutty in the face, am I?

Eero: Not in the least, thou art as clean and warm as a new-laid egg.

Juhani: Let's go in now!

Eero: Wait! I am the youngest and will open the door for you and come in last. Walk in.

They entered the old woman's low-roofed cabin, Juhani first, eyes staring and hair upright like the spikes of a hedgehog, and faithfully, gravely the others followed at his heels. They entered, and Eero quickly closed the door behind them, but himself stayed outside and sat down on the grass, a knowing grin on his lips.

The old woman in whose cabin five brothers now stand as wooers, is a nimble and vigorous woman; she makes a living by keeping hens and gathering berries. All the summer and autumn she bobs about the stump-bestrewn clearings, the mounds where grow the alpine strawberries and lingonberries, bobs and sweats with her daughter Venla. The maiden is said to be beautiful. Her hair is the colour of rust, her glance cunning and sharp, her mouth melting, though perhaps a little too wide. She is short in stature, but broad-shouldered and plump, and is said to be strong. Such was the brothers' love-bird in the pinewood's shelter.

39

But suddenly the cabin door squeaked and Juhani came excitedly out, angrily exclaiming to the others who still lingered within: "Come away, boys!" And soon they were all outside, with annoyance writ large on their faces, and began walking towards the village. But when they had come some fifty paces from the cabin, Juhani picked up a stone about as big as a man's fist and, snorting with rage, cast it at the cabin door. The cabin shook, and inside, the old woman shrieked; then, throwing open the door, she cursed and raged, shaking her fist at the retreating brothers. With their a-b-c's in their hands and bags on their shoulders the brothers marched on in file along the road to church, without exchanging a word. At a furious speed born of anger they marched: the sand hissed and the bags danced; nor did they notice how quickly they fared.

Eero: How did the matter succeed?

Juhani: Ah, indeed! How did it succeed? Didst thou come in with us, thou magpie, thou young crow? But thou didst not dare, truly thou durst not. What good is a young crow like thee! Venla could hide thee in her skirts. But sithee how much I have dreamed of thee. I had, as I now remember, another dream of thee last night. Funny! There in the pine-grove thou didst sit with Venla, billing and cooing, as I drew near, creeping stealthily. But oh, when you saw me, what did Venla do? Hid thee, Devil take me, in her skirts. "What hast thou wrapped up in thy skirts?" asks I. "Only a young crow", answered the wench. He-he-he! And this was no dream at all, no, dog take it, it wasn't! But 'twas made up altogether, out of his own head, by Juhani-boy. Ah, indeed! He isn't quite as stupid as folk think.

Eero: Funny how we have dreamed of each other. This is what I dreamed of thee: among the pines over there thou and Venla stood, lovingly hugging each other and looking solemnly up at the clouds. From there, from the heights of the sky, you craved some sign, something to show that your love had found favour. The heavens listened, the forests, fields and even the little birds listened, and you yourselves waited in deepest silence for what would befall.

40

Came at last an old crow, flying stiffly through the calm air, and when he reached the place where you were standing he cast down one glance at you, but soon turned his gaze elsewhere, and spreading out his legs squirted something white that fell with a splosh on the two young foreheads, splashed right over your faces. — But don't let this annoy thee; for I dreamed all this and have not made up anything out of my own head.

Juhani: Thou devil-possessed, I'll...

And he charged furiously at Eero, who fled swiftly before his enraged brother. With one spring he was off the road and scuttling like a hare over the clearing, with Juhani shambling after him like a maddened bear. Their bags danced, the dry ground rang beneath them; and from afar the voices of the other brothers entreated them to goodwill and forbearance. Then back to the road hastened Eero again, and the others rushed forward to save him from the dread clutch of Juhani, who ran already at the heels of his youngest brother.

Tuomas: Stop now and be quiet, Juhani.

Juhani: I'll lay him out.

Tuomas: Quietly, my boy.

Juhani: Thunder and lightning!

Aapo: He only returned honour for honour.

Juhani: Accursed be his tongue, accursed be this day! Were we not, in God's name, refused by Venla! Hornyheaded goblins and Hosts of High Heaven! My eyes can scarce see a fathom before me, so black is the earth and sky, black on my heart's account. Thunder and lightning!

Simeoni: Don't curse, man.

Juhani: I'll curse till the world spins round and falls into pieces like an old log-sleigh under a heavy tree trunk.

Simeoni: What can we do?

Juhani: Do? If this a-b-c were not the Word of God, God's own book, I'd dash it into bits at once! But see here: I will dash my dinner-bag to bits against the hillside! Would you like to see?

41

Simeoni: For the Lord's sake not the gift of God. Think of the Maid of Paimio.

Juhani: In the torment of my heart!

Simeoni: "Pain and torment on earth, manna in Heaven."

Juhani: A fig for manna in Heaven when I couldn't get Granny Pinewood's Venla. Oh brothers and kinsmen! If you knew, you would understand that my thoughts have circled daftly round that wench for years. But now my hopes are gone, gone like ashes before the wind.

Timo: We were refused in the early morning.

Juhani: Every one of us!

Timo: No mercy for anyone, not even the least among us. We all got the same.

Juhani: All, all! But even that was better than that one of you should have won her for his better half. Devil take me! I'd thrash the lad who'd had that luck, that I would.

Tuomas: We were quite out of the question. That the girl's mocking grin showed when Aapo had mentioned our errand.

Juhani: She deserves to be beaten, the slut. To make a mock of us! Wait, thou jade. — Aapo did his best, that can't be denied, but even the tongue of a cherub wouldn't have helped here.

Timo: But if we had stepped before the girl in a black broadcloth coat, and a watch like a big turnip had bulged out our waistcoat pocket, the key clinked on a chain and a silverbound pipe smoked between our teeth, there'd have been, dog take it, both eggs and chickens hatched out of our errand.

Juhani: Women and magpies have the same fierce desire for shiny things. — But Aapo's as silent as a frozen lake.

Aapo: Our voice cannot carry in a storm. Or are the wild whirlwinds of thy mind beginning to calm down in thy bosom?

Juhani: The bloody pool of my heart still storms, and will storm for long. But say a word, anyhow.

Aapo: Two, if needed. So listen. Take thy heart in thy hand, and whisper this in its ear with the voice of common-sense: Venla would not have thee because she does not love thee, and that she

42

does not love thee is nothing to lose thy temper over; for the flame of love is lit at Heaven's and not at man's command. A beggar-girl falls in love with a king, a queen falls madly in love with a chimney-sweep's boy. So flies the spirit of love around down here, and thou knowest not whence it cometh.

Timo: Love bloweth where it listeth, thou hearest the voice thereof, but thou knowest not whence it cometh and whither it goeth. So I often used to hear the old pensioned widow say. But it was the love of God she meant, I'll lay.

Aapo: Go on, Juhani, to thy heart thus, stop kicking! Venla did right in refusing thee; for to enter into marriage without the spur of love doesn't seem to end well, but brings trouble and often leads to works of eternal regret, as, more's the pity, we so often see and hear nowadays. Ay, brothers, may Venla take the one set apart for her, we'll do the same.

Timo: The girl who was made out of my rib will be mine in the end, though the Devil were to scream. I know another thing: a man's heart lies on the left, and a woman's on the right of her breast.

Juhani: My heart doesn't lie anywhere, but jumps and rages like a heathen. — Oh thou hussy, thou gypsy jade! Why didst thou refuse me, a farmer, the eldest son of a real clay-soil farm?

Aapo: Nothing to wonder at in that. Our farm is in crying need, and the girl hopes, though to my belief vainly, to become mistress of a much better farm. I have heard that that good-for-nothing Juhani Sorvari cuddles her.

Juhani: Thou spiky-chinned Juhani! If I had thee in these hands now, I'd wipe thee down a little. Tricking a wench to her everlasting shame.

Aapo: Ay, ay, the world is mad and treacherous all at the same time. Venla is not lacking in beauty, nor Jussi in cunning. Sorvari is a well-known farm and that entices, while Jukola, this beggarly nest, is in a very sad state, and we ourselves, its seven heirs, in a still sadder state, at least in the eyes of the world. Remembering the idle and often wild life of our youth, people hardly expect anything good to come of us. And I know that even ten years of good and in every way respectable behaviour would scarcely be enough to raise us again in the sight of our fellows. So hard is it to free ourselves from the dirt of a bad name, once it has stuck to a man. Yet it's better to rise late than to sink for ever in the mudpool of our misery. So now, improvement with all our might!

Juhani: We're on the road to improvement now. But this unlucky wooing-trip has given my heart a blow that it will suffer from dreadfully for days and weeks; it caused a wound.

Aapo: A wound, ay, that it did; but time, I know, will cover the wound with the scab and skin of forgetfulness. — What hubbub is that on the road?

Timo: A merry crowd of lads from Toukola.

Aapo: Enjoying an idle Monday with a big spree, the scamps.

Timo: And greatly want us too to join them.

Juhani: Temptation draws nigh.

Timo: They're having such a good time.

Juhani: But we? What lies before us? A thousand horned heads! A fiery wigging is what awaits us poor wretches.

Eero: What a difference: to jabber the a-b-c in the hymnleader's corner, or to enjoy an idle Monday, cheering and singing with jolly comrades.

Juhani: The difference is terribly big, big as the depth between a well and Heaven. Brothers, which shall we choose?

Eero: Let's choose Heaven.

Aapo: The well, the well! To guzzle ourselves full of the water of life. Let's push on into the jungle of learning, skill and wisdom.

Tuomas: To the hymnleader's!

Juhani: Well, let's plod on then.

Eero: Hark at Aapeli Kíssala's clarinet.

Juhani: Lovely!

Timo: Rings out like a head-angel's bassoon.

Juhani: When the hosts of Heaven exercise and march till the dust flies. Lovely!

Timo: They are greatly keen on us joining them.

Juhani: That's well known. Temptation draws nigh, truly it does.

While the brothers thus conversed, a number of lads from Tou-kola village approached them, though not in quite as polite and good-natured a spirit as the brothers supposed. They were a little drunk, and being minded to jest with the brothers, sang as they came along a song newly made up, to which they had given the name "Seven Men Strong." Thus, to Aapeli Kissala's accompaniment they sang:

Set, my lads, your throats a-squealing,
Here's a song will set you reeling;
Seven Men Strong is the ditty.

Like the Great Bear up in Heaven,
Jukola has brothers seven,
Lubberly, hulking joskins.

Juho roars, the cabin quivers,
That's a lad gives me the shivers;
Jussi, a lad high and mighty.

Tuomas stands, an oak unbending,
Hearing Aapo's gab unending, —
Hearken to Solomon spouting.

Simeon, his whiskers quaking,
Mourns for man in accents shaking —
"Sinful, sorrowful, Satan."

Simeon works, the peas preparing,
Timo adds the fat, and stirring,
Spits in the pot to clear it.

Lauri-lad the forest searches
With an eye to twisted birches,
Nosing the woods like a weasel.

Last of all the brothers hearty,
Little Eero, slippery party,
Jukola's snappy-tongued puppy.

There's a band to go to battle,
Stout and hale as full-blood cattle,
Here's to the health of the seven!

In silence, though grinding their teeth, the brothers listened
to this song. But when the mockery of their tormentors ceased
not at this, and endless gibes rained on them from every side,
especially with regard to the cockerel on the back of their a-b-c
books and its fancied power of laying eggs for the brothers, their
gorge began to rise and their eyes grow small, small and sharp
as the eyes of a mink, as it looks out from beneath its tree-stump
in the wilds at the light of day. And now a wag from the ranks
of the Toukola men, in passing Juhani, suddenly snatched the a-b-c
book from his hand and made off with it at top speed. Mad with
rage, Juhani instantly thundered after him: whereupon the other
brothers charged with equal fury at their mockers, and a general
fight began. At first only slaps resounded on either side, but soon
they were at each other's throats and began — blindly, with whist-
ling breath — tearing and gorging and laying about them with
flail-like fists. Fiercely the Toukola lads hit back, but with greater
ferocity the men of Jukola laid on; and heavily as sledgehammers
the brothers' fists fell on the heads of their enemies. In dust and
sand they wrestled; dust rose from the dry road in rolling clouds;
sand and gravel rattled around them in the bushes. So for a space
the fight went noisily on, and the brothers, on the point of victory,
already cried in a loud voice: "Will you beg, Devil's spawn, for
mercy?" and an echo from the clouds answered "Mercy!" But for

46

long the men of Toukola resisted, till at last they sank nerveless to the ground. There, with torn lapels to their coats and swollen faces, they lay, greedily swallowing the cool air into their heated, gasping bowels. And as victors the brothers stood, but their appearance too showed that they had had their fill, and that a moment's rest was welcome. Especially with Eero had it gone hardly in the fight; the shortness of his stature had been a great advantage to his opponents. Often while the combat raged, he had rolled like a little beagle under the feet of the other heroes, and only swift assistance from the brothers had saved him from a thorough beating. With ruffled hair he now sat on the edge of the ditch and gathered new strength, meanwhile puffing mightily.

But just as the others ceased fighting, Juhani approached with his man, dragging him by the collar, and now and again squeezing him by the throat. Fear-inspiring, terrible, was now the visage of the eldest Jukola. Fury flashed like fire from his always smallish eyes, which, bloodshot now with rage, rolled wildly in his head; an acrid sweat poured down his cheeks, and he puffed and snorted like a war-horse.

Juhani: Fetch my a-b-c book, fetch it at once! Look, I'll squeeze thee till thy guts fly out if thou don't. Bring, for God's sake, that red-backed a-b-c of mine, thou knave. See this is what I'll give thee, see this!

The Man from Toukola: Don't hit me!

Juhani: The a-b-c book!

The Man from Toukola: I threw it over there in a bush.

Juhani: Give it into this hand like a good child, in thy best style, thou knave. Dost think thou art dancing here for thy pleasure, knave? Wilt thou not, accursed, give that a-b-c book into my hand?

The Man from Toukola: Thou'rt crushing my throat, my throat!

Juhani: The a-b-c book! The Lord preserve us! The a-b-c book!

The Man from Toukola: Here, thou terrible man.

Juhani: Give it a little kiss. Ay, kiss it nicely.

The Man from Toukola: What? Kiss it?

Juhani: Real nicely. And for God's sake do it, brother, if thy back itcheth and thy life is dear to thee. Do it, do it, or this very minute thy blood shall cry aloud for vengeance on me, like aforetime pious Abel's blood. Thou seest that I am black in the face as a bath-house brownie. So kiss my a-b-c. I beseech thee for both our sakes! — There.

The Man from Toukola: Art thou satisfied?

Juhani: Very satisfied. Go now and thank thy Creator for getting off so easily. And if thou shouldst feel, halfway between thy shoulders and that hammer-head of thine, a few marks tomorrow, like the marks of a toothed vice, and especially if thou shouldst feel a mump-like stiffness there, be not overmuch surprised. Ay, off with thee now. But one word more, one word, little brother. Who made up the song we were forced to listen to a while back with ears erect?

The Man from Toukola: That I don't know.

Juhani: Out with it!

The Man from Toukola: I don't know.

Juhani: Well, well, I can always find out. But greet Aapeli Kissala from me and tell him that next time I meet him his throat'll sing shriller than his clarinet did just now. Go now, for my presence is not the healthiest place for thee. — Leave off muttering about revenge. Take care I don't get it into my head to set off after thee, to give thee a little into the bargain.

Tuomas: Leave him in peace now, the miserable man.

Juhani: He's got his hiding, I'll warrant that. — But let's leave this dreadfully ploughed bit of road, all scratched over in every direction. It isn't wise to linger here, for a fight on the highway is a desperate business in the eyes of the law, and can land its man in a tight fix.

Aapo: Let us hurry on. — But that was a basting; I'd have been well plucked if Simeoni hadn't spread out the pile over me a little.

Simeoni: Why did we touch them? But man is weak and cannot control the strength of his anger and the power of sin. Ah! Seeing how Tuomas's fist felled men, I couldn't help thinking: now murder is near.

Tuomas: Perhaps I did hit out a bit unthinkingly, but men have been hit for less. — Let's walk a bit quicker, the day is getting on.

Swiftly they strode on, but resentment and indignation seemed loth to fade from their faces and stung painfully at their hearts, as they remembered the insulting song of the Toukola lads. Silent, Juhani marched on ahead, marched with the fierceness of an enraged man, spitting and now and again shaking his head. At last, however, turning towards the others, he opened his mouth.

Juhani: What accursed imp made up that song?

Eero: Aapeli Kissala.

Aapo: That's what I suspect too; for he is a spiteful mocker. It was he made up that cruel poem about our poor old curate, who — the Lord ha' mercy on him — happened to besmirch his nose a little at Bible Class.

Timo: If I had a span of brandy and were to whisper a couple of words in Ananias Nikula's ear, we'd soon hear a song a fathom long if we liked, which'd show plainly what kind of a man Aapeli is. A great scoundrel and a rogue; struts about the villages with his clarinet in his hand, getting the serving-wenches with child and living on his poor old mother. The man's a scoundrel.

Juhani: If the rubbishy song they call "Seven Men Strong" hails from his skull, lo and behold, next time I meet him, even if it is on the church rise, I'll flay the scalp off him from his neck to his eyebrows, may that be said. — But couldn't we set the law on him?

Aapo: The law won't sentence anyone without solemn witness.

Juhani: Well, let him take oath on his innocence; I believe he'd think twice before casting his soul into the valley of darkness. But if he were to do this miserable trick, well — goodnight, neighbour, sleep in peace for me.

Aapo: I don't think the law lets an accused man swear himself guiltless in a case like this.

Juhani: Then he'll get it from my own fist and that, I believe, will have the same sting for him that the salt of law and justice would have had.

Simeoni: Let's leave both the song and that brutelike brawl on the highway now. — There's the resiny stump at whose foot I once had a marvellous dream while tending the cattle, though hunger squealed in my stomach. I was as though in Heaven, sitting on a soft and springy sofa, with a heaped-up table steaming before me. Tasty, ah so tasty were those dishes, and so fat. I ate and drank, and little cherub boys waited on me like on some great person. Everything was matchlessly beautiful and solemn; nearby, in a golden hall, echoed the angel choir, and I heard them sing the new and wondrous song. This I dreamed, and it was there I got this spark in my bosom, which I hope will nevermore leave it.

Juhani: It was that Bible-reading old shepherd, that red-eyed, waggle-bearded Tuomas Tervakoski, thy companion that time at the herding, made thee slightly daft; and there's thy spark.

Simeoni: Ey, well, we'll see on the last day.

Tuomas: There's the spruce where our father once brought down a big lynx; and it was his last lynx.

Timo: So it was, after that time he never came striding home any more, but was dragged out of the forest, stiff.

Juhani: A brave and bonny man, but hard and unbending as a rock towards his sons. Yet it was seldom he walked the Jukola yard; he lived in the woods, while the rats and mice throve in our home.

Aapo: True he would forget his home for long on account of that craze of his for hunting, which was perhaps bewitchment, but he was a good father anyhow and died like a man. May he rest in peace!

Timo: And doubly so our mother.

Juhani: There was a good housewife and a pious woman for you, even though she could not read.

Simeoni: Yet she prayed on her knees every morning and evening.

Juhani: That she did. A matchless mother and housewife! I always remember how she strode after the plough, stout as a giantess.

50

Eero: She was a good mother, but why weren't we obedient children; why didn't we toil then in the fields like seven bears? Jukola would look different now. But what did I understand at that time, a little brat in a shift.

Juhani: Hold thy jaw now! I well remember thy wicked and impudent way with our poor mother. But she always forgave thee, as fathers and mothers usually do their youngest child; it's the eldest's fur is for ever being dusted, as I know best from myself. Haven't I, in the Devil's name, been beaten in my time like a cur? But I still hope all was for the best, with God's help.

Simeoni: Punishment surely does good, especially if thou blessest the rod and punishest in God's name.

Eero: Especially if thou warmest the rod as well.

Simeoni: I am deaf to thy miserable jokes, thou stone-blind, thou sparingly-punished child.

Timo: "A good child punishes itself", but that's a trick I'd like to see.

Simeoni: Here's the cross-roads under Sonnimäki Hill, where the ghost of a dead man followed that sinful glazier from Kiikkala all the way from the churchyard for having uttered, the godless man, a fearful oath while passing the church at night. Let this be a warning to you to beware of the sin of swearing.

Juhani: Now we're on Sonnimäki's summit; there's the church, and yonder the hymnleader's redpainted house glows like a flaming nest of devils. Hi! There's the whole glory of Hell, dreadful wisdom and awesome honour. Now all my limbs turn numb and my legs rise mercilessly against me. Ah! What shall I do in this hangman's hour, what shall I do, I, your miserable eldest brother?

Eero: As thou art the eldest, lead on with good example and turn back from the road to Hell. I'll follow thee.

Tuomas: Silence, Eero, not a step backward now.

Juhani: O horny bulls! The hymnleader's door is the gate of death to me.

Aapo: There lie the beginnings of our self-respect and our honour.

51

Juhani: A hot honour, a hot honour! Woe us! I see the hymn-leader's in all its glory and the fearful grandeur of the vicarage, and my nature rises against me — God help us! — rises against me. What dost thou say, Timo?

Timo: Strongly it rises.

Aapo: I believe that, but we can't always be dancing on flowers and roses down here.

Juhani: Flowers and roses? Have we danced on flowers and roses?

Aapo: We shall have many bitter pills to swallow yet, little brother.

Juhani: Bitter pills? Haven't we swallowed enough bitter pills? Oh poor Aapo! we've been boiled in many soups already, our hair ruffled in many winds. And why? Where is our victory? This world is a big dunghill, and nothing more. To Purgatory with hymnleaders and priests, Bible-classes and books and sheriffs with their piles of paper. The evil spirits of this world, all of them! I mentioned books, but of course I didn't mean the Bible, the hymn-book, the Catechism and the a-b-c book, nor the "Voice in the Wilderness" — that terrible book — I didn't mean any of these. But why was I born at all?

Simeoni: Do not curse thy days, the days of thy time of mercy.

Juhani: Why was I born at all, why was I born?

Timo: Into this world I was born a wretched wanderer. Why didn't I sooner open my eyes as a split-lipped young hare under that spruce yonder?

Juhani: Or as that squirrel, who chatters on the fork of yon pine with his tail bolt upright? His carefree bread is the pine-cone, and his blanket the beard of the spruce in his mossy cabin.

Timo: And he needn't learn to read.

Juhani: He needn't kuow how to read!

Aapo: Each was given his lot, and "a sword to match". And lamenting and sorrow won't help, but work and action will. Onward now, brother!

Tuomas: Onward, to the hymnleader's, though the way led over the foaming straits of the sea.

Juhani: What dost thou think, Eero-lad?

Eero: I'm thinking of going to the hymnleader's to school.

Juhani: Hm! Well, let's be going, let's march on. Ah, Son of the Lord! Sing, brother Timo, sing!

Timo: I'll sing of the squirrel in his little mossy chamber.

Juhani: Ay, do.

Timo: Cosily the little squirrel
        Cowers in his mossy chamber;
        There no hound, its white fangs baring
        Nor the cunning, guileful ranger
        Ever discovered the way.

        From his home on high he seeth
        All the earth in conflict riven,
        Strife and battles rage beneath him;
        O'er his head a branch, wind-driven,
        Flutters its pennant of peace.

        O the life of bliss untroubled
        In a swaying cradle-bower.
        In the spruce's mother-bosom
        Rocked through every happy hour;
        Forest, thy lullaby sing!

        There with tail aloft he dozes
        At his tiny casement lying;
        Songs of birds beneath the heavens
        Waft him when the day lies dying
        Into an Eden of dreams.

CHAPTER 3

TWO days have gone by. In the hymnleader's room the brothers sit round the table, chanting the alphabet as it is read out to them, now by the hymnleader himself, now by his little eight-year daughter. A-b-c books in hand, they pursue learning with perspiring brows. But only five of the sons of Jukola are to be seen on the benches round the table. Where can Juhani and Timo be? There, near the door, they stand in the corner of shame, and their hair, which has newly been coiled round the hymnleader's muscular fist, still sticks up in a high tangle.

Very slowly has the brothers' learning proceeded, the fear-inspiring strictness of their teacher tending rather to damp their zeal and their spirits than to carry them onward. Juhani and Timo hardly know more than the letter A; the others' knowledge has progressed a few letters further. Only Eero has proved a great exception to the rest, and having left the alphabet behind him, is practising spelling.

Evening drew nigh, but during the whole of that day the brothers had not yet broken their fast. For the hymnleader, who had laid an embargo on their provisions, was trying the effect of hunger on their willingness to learn. And so, nipped by a raging hunger, Juhani stood in his nook, shaking his round head, spitting and casting malevolent, bull-like glances at his teacher. At his side

Timo nodded, heedless of the way of the world. — At last, however, the hymnleader broke off the lesson, saying: "Stop now and
eat, you wooden horses, champ like browsing goats in a garden.
But remember, after this meal not a crumb of food shall pass your
lips until the alphabet is in your heads, you hard-headed bulls.
One hour I give you for your meal, but not a step shall you take
yet outside the door. I believe the healthiest thing is to prolong
your arrest until night, much the healthiest. Open your mouths
now, for your bags shall be in your hands this minute." Thus
saying he departed and sent the brothers their provisions by a serving maid, after which the door was firmly fastened.

Timo: Where's my bag?

Lauri: There's thine and here's mine. I could eat little stones.

Juhani: Now we shan't eat a single morsel!

Lauri: What? Aren't we to eat now?

Juhani: Not a morsel!

Lauri: As well hold back the sea with thy palm.

Juhani: Leave the bags sweetly in peace.

Aapo: What is thy idea?

Juhani: To spite the hymnleader. We won't eat now until
tomorrow has dawned. My blood boils, boys, and my head goes
round like Keitula's windmill. But spite against spite.

Aapo: Such spite would make the old man laugh heartily.

Juhani: Let him laugh! I'm not going to eat. — Eero spells
already, oh ay. — I'm not going to eat.

Tuomas: Neither am I here, but on Sonnimäki Heath yonder.
There I'll soon be sitting on a bolster of heather.

Juhani: Right! There we'll soon be tumbling.

Eero: I agree to your plan, boys.

Aapo: What madness now?

Juhani: Away out of captivity!

Aapo: Brains ahoy!

Juhani: Sonnimäki's pines ahoy!

Eero: Just so! And our brains answer: ahoy!

Juhani: Answer like a man.

55

Aapo: Simeoni, try thou thy best.

Simeoni: Behave yourselves, brothers! But I must say we weren't meant for readers, and so farewell to all work in that field. All the same, let our lives be blameless and decent; for we can live like Christian people without being able to read, if we only believe.

Aapo: Thou tearest down, confound it, instead of building up.

Juhani: Simeoni speaks the tongue of justice and fairness. Out of this, boys; my nature can stand no more.

Tuomas: It makes my heart ache to see Juhani being pounded. Out of this, boys!

Juhani: The matter's settled. But don't pity me, Tuomas; for vengeance is in my hand. Haven't I been put through the mill, torn like crab-bait, of a truth! And in my pocket I have a big handful of flax, flax heckled by the hymnleader. But if this bunch doesn't once stop up the hymnleader's gullet, it will be because I shall have made a machine or some sort of works of it. The hymnleader has a throat, ay, he has a throat; but I'll say no more.

Eero: I know another, perhaps a better, way of using it. We could twine the hair thou savest in thy pocket into a fine fishing-line, to give to the hymnleader as a present for his good teaching. But why do I incite thee to sin, when I know, as all of us are agreed, that punishment does a powerful lot of good.

Juhani: Eero spells already. Look at the good boy, look.

Eero: Shame enough to be learning spelling at my age.

Juhani: At thy age? What about our ages?

Simeoni: He's mocking us.

Juhani: Ay, go on mocking, thou tare in Jukola's wheatfield, thou bitter leavening in Jukola's Christian brother-dough, thou hedgehog, thou prickly little swine, thou frog!

Simeoni: Hush, for the hymnleader's sake, hush!

Juhani: Out of the dungeon, all with a single mind! Who argues with us now, it's a bang on the snout for him.

Tuomas: Off away, all of us!

Aapo: Timo, thou stout-willed brother, what sayest thou?

Timo: That "a coat can't be made of birch-bark, or a parson out of an old man", so let's be off, all with a single mind. I can clinch the matter with another proverb: "An axe is ground on both sides."

Aapo: Lauri, what art thou going to do?

Lauri: I'm off to Sonnimäki.

Aapo: Ah! Though the dead were to cry from their graves: ye truants, ye madmen!

Juhani: Even that wouldn't help, but off and away, lad. Art thou coming? Else — Lord Almighty! — there'll be a flash and a crash from here. Art thou coming?

Aapo: I'll come. But first a word.

Tuomas: A thousand words wouldn't help now.

Juhani: Not even if every word had a thousand swords.

Eero: And every sword a thousand blades.

Juhani: A thousand fire-spitting blades. Just so; it wouldn't help a bit. Away from Marstrand, away from Siberia, away from the dreadful jungle like seven balls out of the cannon's mouth! Here's both a ball and a cannon, a loaded cannon that gets hotter and hotter, that's red-hot now and'll soon go off. O beloved brothers and kinsmen and offspring of the same mother! You saw how he twisted this forelock round his fore-finger, then grabbed with all his fist like this, look, like this, and then shook me until my teeth rang. Grrh!

Tuomas: I saw it and my cheeks bulged with anger.

Eero: I heard Juhani's teeth ring and saw Tuomas's cheeks bulge and was terrified, but then I thanked God on your behalf, remembering all the good punishment can do.

Juhani: Don't, my dear brother, bring a fuse near the cannon's touch-pan, namely, into these two ears, don't do it.

Tuomas: Why wilt thou annoy him, Eero?

Juhani: Eero is the hymnleader's good boy. Well, that's good too, very good. But what harm have I done for the hymnleader to torture me like this? Is it a crime that I have such a hard head? It wouldn't take much to make me cry.

Timo: What have I done that my hair should be tugged so damned hard? Is it because I have the brains God in his wisdom once gave me?

Lauri: I too have had my hair pulled three times.

Juhani: All of us have sweet memories of this place. — The door open!

Aapo: Mark, we are behind closed doors.

Timo: There's a prop against the door, a strong prop.

Juhani: It'll break like a blade of grass; but on the other hand, there's the window. One swipe with my bag and you'll hear a musical tinkling and clinking.

Aapo: Is thy head altogether addled now?

Juhani: After two days' shaking, two days' shaking, my boy!

Simeoni: Don't let us break the window, anyhow, but let us speak nicely with the hymnleader.

Juhani: Go to Hell and speak nicely with the Devil! — The window to pieces and away out of prison. "Out the whole battalion!" shouted the captain in his anger.

Tuomas: Bolt the door, Eero.

Eero: Right; bolt the castle gate while the battalion marches out of the fort's back-door. — The door's bolted.

Aapo: I warn you!

Juhani: What's done is done. See that!

Aapo: Thou awful man, openly godless!

Simeoni: There now! It's done! There went the window.

Juhani: The window crashed and heaven flashed, at one swipe of Juhani's bag! That was a bang in Lazy-Jake's style.

Simeoni: Poor us!

Juhani: The road's open, wilt thou be off?

Simeoni: I'll come with thee, brother dear.

Juhani: Aapo, the road's open, art thou coming?

Aapo: Why lift thy fist, madman. I'll come, I'll come. What else can I do, with our sleigh provisioned?

Juhani: Fire and lighting!

Tuomas: Bags on back now and out of the window! The porch shakes with footsteps.

Juhani: Is it the hymnleader? I'll smack him.

Tuomas: Come!

Juhani: It's the hymnleader. I'll smack him a little.

Tuomas: Away! say I.

Juhani: Don't step in my way now. I love thee, brother Tuomas.

Tuomas: I won't let thee do deeds of terror. Hurry now with me out of the window; there go the others galloping across the potato-patch. Come!

Juhani: Let go! Why dost thou fear deeds of terror? I'll only take him gently across my knee, lift up the long skirts of his coat and smack him with my naked palm, and this palm will do the work well. Let go, dear brother, or my heart'll burst like Kork's bagpipes. Let go! thou seest how my head steams.

Tuomas: We are eternal enemies if thou dost not obey me now. Heed what I say.

Juhani: Let's go then. But I wouldn't agree to this if I didn't love thee with all my heart.

They ceased talking, cast themselves out of the window on to the hillside, and ran swifty across the parish clerk's potato-patch. The pebbles rattled in the rows, clumps of soil flew high into the air, and soon they had vanished after the others into a dense grove of alders. Then the hymnleader, the picture of awful rage, burst in, waving a stout bamboo stave. In a high-pitched, screaming voice he called the truants, but in vain. Out on the other side of the alder-grove dashed the brothers; onward over a stony, rock-bestrewn strip of ground they ran, onward through a thick belt of juniper, onward through the Vicar's big, reed-edged meadow, over a wide echoing clearing, until they stood on the sandy road under Sonnimäki's sloping side. Up the cobbly slope they strode, and reaching the ridge, decided to pitch their camp at the foot of some pines, on ground covered with heather; and soon the smoke of their fire was wafted among the tree-tops.

High was the site on which the brothers camped. Behind a hill they could see the mansard roof of the vicarage, and on the hill itself was the hymnleader's red building, the large village, and in a belt of spruce the grey stone parish church, magnificent, solemn. They saw, further, a lake dotted with rocks, now streaked by the northeast wind, which blew gently and swooningly under the clear sky, fanning the lake, the meadows and forests and the pines on Sonnimäki, beneath which the brothers now rested and baked turnips beside a blazing camp-fire.

Juhani: Now for a real royal meal.

Timo: A real gentleman's meal.

Juhani: Beef from our bags and stewed turnips from the ashes. They'll be ripe this minute.

> The wind it blows and the tree-tops sway,
> My love's voice echoes far away...

What ox-like daftness on our part to sit on the hymnleader's bench, a-b-c in hand, sit for two devilish days.

Eero: Ah, but to stand in the corner, that was another matter.

Juhani: Good, my Eero, my wise Eero, my six inch Eero, thou hop-o-my-thumb. — In the hymnleader's corner! I'll teach the little imp.

Aapo: Keep quiet, you heathens!

Tuomas: Sit in peace, Juhani, and take no notice of what he says.

Juhani: Take thy cap off while eating, thou dwarf.

Tuomas: Cap off, say I too.

Juhani: There then. Thou hadst to obey.

Simeoni: Always nagging, nothing but nagging. God light up your souls and hearts!

Juhani: He's always making trouble.

Eero: It's I am always in your accursed teeth — "that midge, that hop-o-my-thumb, that little button Eero". But that's why I'm tough.

60

Juhani: Thou art a snappy-tongued puppy, as it says in the song "Seven Men Strong".

Eero: I can bite back and hard.

Juhani: Thou art full of bile.

Aapo: May I say a word? Eero said something that I believe has a mite of truth in it. See, the bile he sometimes spreads around him, we ourselves have helped a lot in cooking. But let us remember that we are all creatures of the same Creator.

Timo: Quite so. "If I have two snouts, one like a boot-tree, the other like a loaf", what has that to do with others? I myself carry them. But let's drop noses and posies, Creators and creations now. Here, Juhani, here's a turnip, soft as a toadstool. Seize on that and never mind that scamp's remarks. He is young and without understanding. — Eat, brother mine.

Juhani: I'll eat all right.

Timo: Now we're like at a wedding on this high, echoing hill.

Juhani: Like at Heaven's wedding. But I must say we were tortured real cruelly down there in Hell a little while ago.

Timo: "Sometimes dashed down, sometimes uplifted", so it is with us in this world.

Juhani: That's it. What dost thou say, brother Aapo?

Aapo: I have tried my best, but all to no good. Now I too will let myself go for once and leave the tiller of our lives in fate's hand. Here I sit.

Juhani: Here we sit and there under our feet lies the whole world. The hymnleader's house glows there like a red cockerel, and yonder the spire of God's temple rises on high.

Aapo: At the foot of that temple we shall sit once in the black stocks of shame, sit with bent heads, like seven young crows on a fence, hearing people say, as they point to us: there sit the lazy Jukola brothers.

Juhani: The day will never dawn when the sons of Jukola, with heads bent like young crows on a fence, sit in the black stocks of shame, hearing people say, as they point to us: there sit the lazy Jukola brothers. That day will not dawn; I'd sooner hang myself, or march to the very end of the world, to the battalion at Heinola to swing a rifle. "What do I care, a scapegrace so young?" Now, brothers, now that we have eaten, let's sing, let's yell until the heath shakes.

Simeoni: Let's bless ourselves and go to sleep.
Juhani: First a song: "What do I care." Clear thy throat, Timo.
Timo: I'm ready.
Juhani: How about Eero-lad? Friends again?
Eero: Friends and brothers.
Juhani: All's well then. Screw up thy throat.
Eero: It's already in tune.
Juhani: Good! And listen you others to the pines quaking. — Now boys!

> What do I care, a scapegrace so young,
> Broad in the shoulder and lusty of lung?
> Fra-la ra-la ra-la ra-la ra-la ra-la-lah!
>
> Away to the ranks of the soldiers so grand
> At Heinola town I am off thro' the land.
> Fra-la ra-la ra-la ra-la ra-la ra-la-lah!
>
> For bishops and priests I care not a fig,
> Soon I'll be dressed in a hero's gay rig.
> Fra-la ra-la ra-la ra-la ra-la ra-la-lah!
>
> Swifter my bay horse, for soon we shall crack
> An Emperor's rations, the hardest of tack.
> Fra-la ra-la ra-la ra-la ra-la ra-la-lah!
>
> What do I care, a scapegrace so young,
> Broad in the shoulder and lusty of lung?
> Fra-la ra-la ra-la ra-la ra-la ra-la-lah!

Juhani: That's the way! Ah, this is a good place for us to be in.
Simeoni: Less noise, less noise! You're brawling like a legion of goblins. — Hush, hush! there are people coming.
Juhani: People! Look closer, and thou wilt see a pack of gypsies, the "Rajamäki Regiment".

The party which now approached was a certain nomad family whose only home was a little hut on a clearing on Rajamäki Hill, for which reason it was known to the world as the Rajamäki Regiment. Its leader and head is the Mikko known to everybody, a short lively fellow in a black felt hat. He hawks pitch on his journeys and flashes skilfully a gelder's sharp knife. He practises the fiddler's art as well, and at dances and bee-parties draws a squeaky music from his dark red instrument of joy, wetting his throat as often as hospitality is offered. — His wife Kaisa, a snuffy-chinned irascible hag, is a gentle hand at blood-letting. Rare the sauna* she fails to set warming when she passes by, for the women of the neighbourhood to be leeched by her. Then Kaisa's hands move deftly, her mouth champing and her snuffy face sweating, but her food-bag too quickly swells. — They have a number of children who follow them on their wanderings from village to village and farm to farm. Two of them travel on their own legs, skipping merrily along the road, now ahead, now in the rear of their parents. The three youngest ride in a little waggon, and always Kaisa is in the shafts, while Mikko pushes with his stick from behind. Loud is the hubbub wherever the Rajamäki family is on its way; and a certain wag had composed a long mocking ballad about it, calling it after the regiment. This was the noisy party that now came faring along the road below Sonnimäki Heath on its way to the church village, as the brothers, merry as goats, celebrated their freedom on the high spine of the wooded heath.

Juhani: Halloo! Well met, thou aforesaid regiment, well met!
Timo: 'Hustotaytill?' says the Swede.
Eero: 'Kappusiveye?' says the Russian.

---

* Sauna = Finnish bath and bath-house.

Kaisa: What do you want, you up there?

Eero: The old girl to come and suck a whopping horn from the brown thigh of Juhani here.

Juhani: The old woman to tap and suck while the old man plays, now wouldn't that go well together.

Mikko: I give the Devil to you, you Jukola bandits.

Eero: The old man doesn't want to play. Well then we'll sing, and a real rousing march.

Juhani: A rousing march as the Rajamäki Regiment marches past. Now boys, Timo and Eero!

> Now we're off a-wandering
> Round the land and back,
> Gelding and a-blood-letting
> Hawking pitch so black.
>
> At the shafts with snuffy face
> Kaisa you will find;
> Mikko, chewing, sets the pace,
> Pushing hard behind.

Juhani: Just so! This is a real jolly, rollicky bit of a song.

Kaisa: I'll let you know, you devil's food up there, that we always walk in honour, but you, you slink about other people's forests like robbers and beasts of prey. I let blood, I do, and bring health; Mikko gelds and makes fat swine, fine oxen and bonny geldings for the King of Kings to ride on; know that, you devils!

Juhani: A couple of verses on top of that sermon, boys! Timo and Eero, my stout lads! All together!

> Kaisa smacks her nether lip,
> Sets the blood a-running;
> Mother Jane in Kaisa's grip
> Tells her tales of cunning.

64

But yonder on the farmyard side
Why this sudden shrieking?
The boars and stallions try to hide,
The piglets fall a-squeaking.

Why this tumult 'mongst the boars?
What makes the piglets scream
See: as Mikko farmward soars
His knife is seen to gleam.

Juhani: Truly a jolly rollicking song. Can that be denied, Mikko?

Mikko: Close thy bread-trap and quickly, and know that I am Master Mikko himself, who nipped the Governor's stallion over a clean sheet without spilling a single drop of blood. And for that trick got a stifficate that the Emperor of Rome couldn't belittle. That's the sort of Mikko I am.

Eero: Oh thou double Boar-gelder Mikko with thy witch of a wife!

Kaisa: See that I don't turn you all into a pack of wolves, as my grandfather once did a proud wedding company.

Juhani: Here I still stand, the same old Juhani Jukola, in my own breeches, and so with God's help I hope to stand from now onward too. Thy witch' tricks, poor woman, can do no more than they did two years ago when thou foretoldest the end of the world and made many a wife beg her husband's pardon for past scoldings without the slightest need.

Kaisa: Hear what I prophesy now.

Eero: Thou prophesyest and wishest us a hot bath, with thou thyself to bleed us in the neck.

Juhani: But that's a vain prophecy and wish. True, I mean to heat the *sauna* when I come home and bathe right heartily, but I'm in no mind to have the Adam's pelt opened at my neck.

Kansa: Listen, listen! Fire shall eat up thy sauna and thy dwelling too, and in wretched state shalt thou wander forth through forests, bogs and marshes, seeking shelter for thy perishing body. Ah! bloodily wilt thou yet fight with men and the beasts of the forest, after which, puffing like a dying hare, thou wilt lay down thy accursed head in a bush. Hear me and remember.

Juhani: To Hell...

Tuomas: Shut up now, shut up!

Simeoni: Thou godless man, bewitched!

Juhani: Go to red-hot Hell! Go to the hymnleader and bewitch his throat with the everlasting mumps.

Eero: So that he'll sing like an old long-tusked hoar in Mikko's hands.

Juhani: Ay, and go to the Vicar, to that hypocritical and rich, fat and greasy Vicar... What shall we order him? Say, Eero.

Eero: May it happen to him at Bible meeting as it happened to the publican at Oulu's gate; may a big cat-pie appear in his sack.

Juhani: Ay, a Paltamo pasty, with a cat, a hairy, furry cat inside.

Eero: And let him make a sermon of it next Sunday so full of wrath and fury that his fatty stomach bursts of a sudden with a loud bang.

Juhani: Ay, and then may the Old 'Un take him up on his back and fly away with him as is the Devil's way with parsons.

Eero: Let him carry off the rich and mighty Vicar for company to the rich man.

Juhani: There's the greeting we bid thee carry to the hymnleader and the Vicar. And if thou dost this, thou canst turn me into a wolf, if thou likest, as thou hast threatened.

Eero: A wolf so fierce that it eats up the whole Rajamäki Regiment at one gulp.

Juhani: Ay! And the bag of horns into the bargain.

Eero: And the pitch-sack for savoury.

Juhani: Just so, thou son of a hammer.

Kaisa: Good! The Vicar and the hymnleader shall hear your message, and you'll find this same soup in your bowls yet, you accursed! Send 'em a parting greeting with a stone, Mikko; split open their skulls.

Mikko: Here's a good pebble, as though made to order. — Take that, you squinting goats! — Quick march, Kaisa! now we're off.

Juhani: The scoundrel! Threw a stone, and it was a near thing I didn't get it on the head.

Eero: Let's send the ball back.

Juhani: Make the old fellow's hat rattle!

Tuomas: Don't throw, lad, if thou wouldst spare thy poll.

Aapo: Can't you see, rascals, that there are children there.

Juhani: Hold thy stone; they're galloping off already so the heath thunders.

Simeoni: Oh you wicked wretches, you Calmucks and savages! Even a peaceful traveller can't pass you in peace. Oh you bandits!

Juhani: What, I, who wouldn't hurt a hair of their heads? But sithee, when a man feels real mad and mighty spasms run through his bonny carcase, he — thou knowest what. Two days and two nights this lad has been shut up in a tower. But I sent a grand greeting to the hymnleader to ease my mind a little.

Aapo: And still more foolish ones to the Vicar. We shall have cause to rue these greetings yet.

Juhani: "What do I care, a scapegrace so young." Life, a young man's life is just like this roaring, echoing heath. Yonder in the northeast Impivaara's steep side shows, and yonder in the northwest the lake by the village gleams, and I can even see other lakes, there on the edge of the air as though in eternal distance. I can see the three lakes of Kolistin.

> It can't be helped, it can't be helped,
> I'll jump into the lake;
> My sweetheart is so mad today
> And hisses like a snake.

On the surface of that lake our old hymnleader often sits with a fishing-rod in his hand. Ah! if he only squatted there now and

I were a fierce gust of wind, a raving squall from the southeast, I know well where I'd charge with a roar, and the hymnleader's punt would soon be upset.

Simeoni: What a sinful wish!

Juhani: It's what I'd do; I'd upset the punt so that the water boiled around him like gruel.

Timo: To the wolves for their dinner, a man like him!

Juhani: I'd dash him into a wolf-pit and then walk blissfully round it.

Aapo: Once the fox, bearing a grudge against the bear, tricked poor Bruin into a pit. And then he laughed heartily and walked round the gaping pit, talking mockingly. After that he got on to a wild-cat's back, and the wild-cat took him up into a big spruce that grew close by. The fox then began to sing for joy and to call together the winds from the four quarters of the earth, commanding them to play the harp of the spruce to his song. Came the east, west and south winds, and the spruce roared and crackled loudly. Came the north wind, charging across the mossy, gloomy forests, humming loudly and crashing. Then the spruce stormed, quivered and bowed down deeply, until at last it broke and fell down over the pit, throwing as it fell the fox into the bear's arms down in the pit.

Timo: The Devil! What then?

Juhani: Thou canst guess what happened then. I bet the bear grabbed the fox firmly by the scruff and shook him until his teeth rattled, like the kind hymnleader did me. — But I understand what Aapo means. He wants to remind me that he who digs a pit for others can fall into it himself. That may be, but I'd like to see the hymnleader fall into a pit all the same.

Timo: My heart either wouldn't be against seeing the hymnleader stumble into a pit. But I wouldn't torture the old beggar too long by keeping him in a stuffy hole. Two hours, only two hours. But enough. May he live in peace without even falling into the pit of my angry heart. Only, one thing surprises me. How can you believe such rubbish about a fox and a bear. Why, brothers, a fox can't even talk nonsense, let alone call together all the four winds. You believe this, but I make it out a downright lie.

Juhani: We all know that Timo's head is not one of the sharpest in this world.

Timo: Maybe not. But with this head I walk through the world as honourably as thou or anyone eles, man or woman.

Aapo: Timo doesn't understand a fable.

Juhani: Not a bit does the poor boy understand it. But if I were to explain it to thee. This matter between the bear and the fox happened, I guess, in those days when all the animals and even the trees could speak, as it says in the Old Testament; and this I heard from our old blind uncle.

Aapo: Even thou dost not understand a fable and its purpose.

Timo: And yet "the kettle mocks the pot, black in the ribs the two."

Juhani: Art trying to be clever, man? Believe me, I thank God that I am not as stupid as thou, poor Timo.

Timo: What if thou'rt not; I see no harm in it.

Eero: Do thou, Timo, as the publican once did; only smite thy breast, and we'll see which of you marches home the better man.

Juhani: Ai, did it touch Little-Eero, publican thyself?

Eero: It touched the chief publican, that Little-Zacchaeus, on a sore spot.

Juhani: I give a fig for thy jests, and lay me down to slumber sweet. I'll turn my back on all of you and sleep like an ant's nest under the snow. — But God help us! this is an awful place we have settled in.

Aapo: How so?

Juhani: Why, there lies that strange, terrifying rock that always answers so mournfully to the sound of the church bells. And look at those eyes in it that stare so unwinkingly at us. I'm scared! Let's leave this spot in the Lord's name.

Tuomas: Let's sit here in peace.

Juhani: But the forest-spirit is stern and angry here.

Aapo: Only towards those who swear or do other godless deeds. So take care. The tale of those images on the rock-side is a story of far-off days.

Lauri: Wilt thou tell us this tale?

Aapo: Look carefully at the rock first. You'll see there something that looks like four shining golden spots. These are the melting eyes of two lovers, a fair maiden and a gallant youth; you'll see their images graven in the rock. Look at them, with your eyes half-shut. There they sit, entwined in the most loving embrace. Lower down, at the young people's feet, is an old warrior, bowed down and pierced by a sword.

Timo: It's just as thou sayest.

Lauri: I too believe I can see something of the sort there. But go on with the tale.

And Aapo told them this tale:

A grand castle once stood hereabouts, and the lord of this castle was a rich and mighty man. He had a step-daughter, a motherless girl, sweet and fair as the morn. A youth loved the maiden, but the castle's terrible master, in whose heart love had never found room, hated both the youth and the maiden. The girl too loved the noble youth, and they would often meet on this echoing heath. And it was just the foot of this rock that was their trysting-place. But the father found out the young people's secret and once uttered a fearful vow in the maiden's ear. "Daughter", he said, "see that I don't catch you two embracing in the forest's night. Know that my sword will then be swift to wed you in bloody death. This I promise and swear by all that is holy." This he said, and fear gripped the maiden as she heard the vow. Nevertheless, she forgot not the friend of her heart, and the flame of her love only burned the brighter.

It was a calm summer night. In the maiden's breast a feeling awoke that the youth was pacing the heath, awaiting his own true love. So at last, when she believed everyone in the castle was asleep, she set forth, wrapped in a big, finely-woven shawl; set forth on her love-adventure, and creeping out like a shadow, was soon lost to view in the forest, and a blue shawl flickered once in a dewy thicket. But everyone in the castle was not asleep; there behind a window stood the master of the castle himself, spying on the maiden, who like a ghost of night faded from his view Whereupon he girt on his sword, seized a spear, and hastening after the maiden was also soon lost to sight among the trees. A bloodthirsty beast hunting a meek-eyed lamb.

Up towards the heath hurried the panting maiden and there met her friend, at the grey rocks's base. There they stood, lovingly embracing each other and whispering the language of love in a rapturous hour. They stood no longer on the face of this earth; their spirits wandered in Heaven's flowery meadows. — So passed a few short moments; then all of a sudden the terrible lord dashed forth and thrust his sharp spear in the maiden's left side with such force that its point came out of the young man's right, thus joining them together in death. They drooped towards the rock, and their blood gushed forth in a single stream, dyeing the cheeks of the heather-blossoms. There, united in bonds of steel, they sat on their rocky throne, silent, yet all the time lovingly embracing each other. And ravishingly, like four golden stars, their eyes shone upon the castle's mighty master, who looked in wonder upon this strange calm picture in the very jaws of death. Suddenly a thunderstorm arose, the heavens flashed and rumbled, but in the lightning's bluish glare the young people's eyes still shone blissfully, as four candles might burn in the holy air of Heaven. Upon all this the murderer looked while the wrath on high raged around and above him. Powerfully the beautifully fading eyes of the lovers spoke to his soul, equally powerfully the foaming torrent of their blood and the crashing sky. And for the first time his mind was moved, as with cold and black regret in his heart he gazed upon the wondrous eyes of the dying, which smiled without cease at him. His heart knew fear and he trembled as the lightning flashed and eternity thundered, and spirits of terror assailed him from every side. A boundless fury overcame his soul.

Once more he looked upon the youthful lovers: and still the

71

same shining eyes, though dimmer now, looked smiling back at him. Then, folding his arms across his breast, he began, with frozen glance, staring eastward; and thus he stood for long, dumb in the gloomy night. But at last and suddenly his bosom swelled and he shouted a long shout, long and terrifically loud, a shout that echoed roaring through the neighbourhood. Then for a space he was silent again, listening carefully, until the last echo of his cry had sunk into the bosom of the farthest hill. And when this had come to pass, he shouted terrifically again, still staring towards the east, and the forest heard the echoes for long, while he closely followed their passage from hill to hill. But at last the distant trembling voice died down, the lightning rested, and the shining eyes were extinguished; and only a heavy rain sighed in the forest. Then suddenly, as though waking from a dream, the castle's master snatched the sword from his scabbard, pierced his breast with it, and fell at the lover's feet. And once more the heavens flashed, flashed and thundered; but silence soon reigned everywhere again.

Morning came, and the dead were found on the heath at the foot of a grey rock; they were borne away and room was made for them side by side in the same grave. But afterwards their images were seen in the rock; one saw a youth and a maiden, embracing each other, and under them, on his knees, a grim, bearded warrior. And four marvellous studs, like four golden stars, shone in the rock by night and by day, reminding men of the rapture in the fainting eyes of the lovers. And it was a thunderbolt, so runs the tale, that carved these images in the rock in its flight. And as in this picture, the youth and maiden sit in happiness on a throne on high; and as the warrior is seen cowering there, so must he cower on a bed of punishment in parching air. Whenever the church bells ring, he bends his ear carefully to catch the sound, listening to the echo given out by the rock; but up to now its sound has been mournful. Once, however, a wondrously gentle and joyous sound will issue from the rock, and then the hour of the man's atonement and forgiveness will have come, but the day of all the world will also then be nigh. And that's why people always listen with such unrest

72

to the echo from this rock when the church-bells ring. Gladly would they welcome the dawn of the man's day of release, but remember with terror that the end of the world will then have come.

This was the tale Aapo told his brothers on Sonnimäki Heath.

Timo: The old boy has to sweat. Right to the Day of Judgment! Oho!

Simeoni: Thou dolt, see that the trumpet of judgment doesn't bray this very minute.

Eero: No fear of the world ending so long as there are heathens on the face of the earth. Why, God ha' mercy! here are seven benighted heathens right in the midst of Christendom. There's nothing so bad but that there's something good in it. We are pillars of this world, we are.

Juhani: Thou a pillar of the world? Six-inch!

Simeoni: Thou'lt tremble, Eero, tremble like the Devil, when the day approaches which thou now mockest.

Timo: That he won't, I'll stand for that. Oho! there'll be a din and rumpus then. There's been two big upheavals, the third is still to come. And then the great sign of bliss will appear; then the world'll fall to dust and ashes like an old birch-bark slipper. Then the cattle in the clearings will bellow and the pigs squeak fearfully in the lanes, that is, if this ruin comes upon us in summer-time; but if it comes in winter, then the cattle will go mad and bellow in the sheds and the poor pigs squeal in their styes. There'll be a row then, boys. Oho! Two upheavals have been, the third is still to come, as our blind uncle said.

Simeoni: Ay, ay, let us remember that day.

Juhani: Shut up, will you, brothers. God preserve us! You quite turn a man's heart inside-out with such talk. Let's go to sleep, let's go to sleep.

So they conversed, but at last their conversation died down, and sleep overcame them, one after the other. Last of all Simeoni sat awake, leaning against the bulging root of a pine. He sat and pondered gravely over those final moments of the world and the great day of judgment. His eyes burned with a reddish, moist, mild fire, while the ruddy flush of his coarse cheek shone afar. But at last he too slept. And so they all lay sleeping beside their campfire, which blazed for a while, then sank gradually and was extinguished.

The day declined and twilight deepened into night. The air was muggy and hot; an occasional flash lit up the northeast as an angry thunderstorm climbed up the sky. With the speed of an eagle it drew near to the village, casting down fire from its womb, until it suddenly set ablaze the vicar's barn, which, being full of dry straw, soon burst into mighty flames. The bells began to clamour and the village awoke into activity; people hurried from all directions to the raging fire, a stream of men and women, but in vain. Luridly the barn blazed, and blood-red shone the bowl of the sky. But the storm now hastened on towards Sonnimäki, where the brothers slept sweetly, the heath resounding with their snores. A terrible crash is now to awaken them in a terror greater than any they have known in their lives. Their dream-delirious minds will stand aghast as, with all nature raging around them in the cheerless night, the gloomy tale and the accounts of the end of the world recur to them. And all the light they will see in the night will be the flashing of thunderclouds and the reflection of the fire billowing in the village.

The flash came, and on its heels followed a burst of thunder so loud that it instantly woke up the sleeping brothers. Shouting loudly in shrill voices, they sprang up from the ground as one man, and with the hair upright on their heads like rustling reeds and their eyes like rings in their heads, stared at each other for a moment or two.

Simeoni: The Day of Judgment!

Juhani: Where are we, where are we?

Simeoni: Are we going already?

Juhani: Save us, mercy!

Aapo: Terrible, terrible!

Tuomas: Indeed terrible.

74

Timo: The Lord preserve us poor lads!

Simeoni: How the bells are ringing!

Juhani: And the rock jangles and dances! Hii! Ha!

Simeoni: "The bells of Heaven are ringing!"

Juhani: "And strength forsakes my limbs!"

Simeoni: Is this how we go?

Juhani: Help us, Mild and Merciful!

Aapo: Oh terror!

Juhani: Tuomas, Tuomas, grab hold of the tail of my coat. Hii! Ha!

Simeoni: Hii! Haa! Now we're off, we're off!

Juhani: Tuomas, my brother in Christ!

Tuomas: Here I am. What dost thou want?

Juhani: Pray!

Tuomas: Ay, try to pray now.

Juhani: Pray, Timo, if thou canst!

Timo: I'll try.

Juhani: Do it soon!

Timo: O Lord, O sorrow great, O merciful throne of Bethlehem!

Juhani: What does Lauri say?

Lauri: I don't know what to say in this misery.

Juhani: Ay, misery, bottomless misery! But I'm beginning to think the end is not just yet.

Simeoni: Oh if we were granted even a single day!

Juhani: Or a week, a precious week! But what are we to make of this ghastly light and the clatter of bells?

Aapo: There's a fire in the village, good people.

Juhani: Ay, Aapo, and that's the warning bell ringing.

Eero: The Vicar's barn's afire.

Juhani: A thousand barns can burn down so long as this maggotty world still stands and we seven of its sinful children on it. Lord help us! My whole body's swimming in a stream of cold sweat.

Timo: I won't say my own trousers aren't shaking.

Juhani: A matchless moment!

Simeoni: So God punishes us for our sins.

Juhani: True! Why did we sing that nasty song about the Raja-mäki Regiment.

Simeoni: You mocked shamelessly at Mikko and Kaisa.

Juhani: Why say it! But God bless them! God bless us all, every one, even the hymnleader.

Simeoni: That prayer found favour in Heaven.

Juhani: Let's leave this dreadful place. The fire shows here like the fiery furnace of the damned, and there those eyes shine so mournfully at us from the rock-side. Know that it was Aapo's tale of those cat's-eyes that caused this shaking in our backbones. Let's be off, and don't any of you forget your bags and a-b-c-books. Away, brothers! Let's march to Tammisto to see Kyösti; to Kyösti's with God's help, and then home tomorrow, if we're still alive. Come.

Lauri: We'll soon have the rain pouring down our necks and will be wet as rats.

Juhani: Let it rain, let it rain! We were still spared. Come on now!

They hurried off at a rapid march in file and soon came to a sandy road, where they turned off towards Tammisto Farm. To the flashing of fire and the roll of thunder they marched on for a while, until a drenching rain poured down. At that they increased their pace to a run until they arrived at the "Kulomäki spruce", a tree famous for its height and the denseness of its branches, which stood by the roadside, a shelter for many a wanderer in the rain. At the foot of this spruce the brothers sat until the rain abated, and the great spruce roared above them. And when the weather cleared, they continued their journey. And nature calmed down again, the wind died, the clouds fled and the moon rose palely out of the tree-tops. Leisurely and without a care the brothers then strode along the splashing road.

Tuomas: I've often wondered where the thunder comes from and what it can be, those flashes and that noise.

Aapo: Our blind uncle told us this mutiny in the heavens comes

76

when dry sand gets borne by the wind between masses of cloud.

Tuomas: Would it be that?

Juhani: A child's mind can fancy anything. How was it I, a little brat in my shift, pictured the thunder. It was God driving rattling along the streets of Heaven, and fire flashed from the stony road and the iron rim of his wheels. Ha-ha! A child has a child's mind.

Timo: What about me! I too imagined something of the sort when, a tiny imp, I toddled along the lane while the thunder rumbled, toddled there with a little bit of a shirt on me. God's ploughing his field, thinks I, and cracking his ox-tail whip, and each swipe makes the round flanks of his fat bay strike sparks, as we see the sparks fly from a horse's withers when we wipe it down. Ay, what ideas.

Simeoni: I thought as a child and still think: the heaven's flash and thunder proclaim God's wrath at the sinners on earth; for the sins of men are great, countless as the sands of the sea.

Juhani: Sins are committed down here, that can't be denied, but a sinner is well boiled down here too in salt and pepper. Think, my boy, of our trip to school and what we had to bear there. The hymnleader clawed and shook us like a hawk; I feel it yet and grind my teeth, my boy.

Soon the sandy road ended and Tammisto Farm drew nigh, and the brothers gravely entered and were given comfortable beds by Kyösti. This Kyösti, a man sturdy as an oak, was the only son of the house, but had never cared to take over the management of the farm, preferring always to keep to himself, to follow his own bent. At one time he had wandered as in a fever through the villages, preaching and shouting; and it was said that much thinking about religion had brought him to this pass. And when at last he recovered from this state, he was otherwise the same as before, but he never smiled again. And one curious thing came to pass, that ever afterwards he regarded the Jukola brothers as his best friends, though he had hardly known them before. This was the man with whom the brothers sought shelter for the night.

CHAPTER 4

THE following day, the Jukolas approached their home, stepping out one behind the other. But woebegone was their appearance: their garments hung in shreds and their faces were mottled with bruises and wounds. Juhani, who led the way, had his left eye almost closed up, Aapo's lips were badly swollen, a mighty bump protruded from Timo's forehead, and Simeoni, limping, brought up the rear. Their heads had been thoroughly pummeled and were now wrapped round with empty food-bags or with strips of rag torn from a coat. In such condition they returned from their trip to school. The dogs, Killi and Kiiski, rushed forth to meet them, leaping with joy; but the brothers had little strength left to respond to the caresses of their faithful house-guards.

Who then had used them so cruelly? Who had succeeded so well in crushing the doughty Jukola brothers? Who else but the men of Toukola, whose revenge it was. Having heard that the brothers were at Tammisto, they had banded themselves together, twenty men strong, and hidden in the bushes by the wayside to await their enemies. There, with stout staves in their hands, they had dozed and bided their time. Then, as the school-goers drew nigh, the villagers fell swiftly upon them, charging from both sides of the road, and a terrific cudgelling began in which the brothers were badly beaten. But neither did the Toukola men escape whole-skinned from the affray; many of them turned faint on acquaintance with the brothers' fists. And two were borne swooning to their homes: Kuninkala's Eenokki and Kissala's Aapeli. And on this occasion Aapeli's skull shone bare from neck to brow, shone like the bottom of a pewter mug. The hand of Juhani had done its fell work.

At last, however, the brothers sat in the large living-room of their home, terribly tired.

Juhani: Whose turn is it to heat the sauna?

Timo: It'll be mine now.

Juhani: Then heat it till the oven rattles.

Timo: I'll try my best.

Juhani: Do it like a man, for truly, our wounds need a steaming. And do thou, Eero, hasten and bring a can of brandy from Routio, for which they can have the stoutest log in our forest. A can of brandy!

Simeoni: Isn't that too much, a can?

Juhani: Why, it's hardly enough as grease for seven men. God knows, we have as many wounds between us as there are stars in the sky. But though this eye of mine aches and kicks right fiercely, the bile and heart in my innards ache fiercer still. But all's well, all's well! Jussi Jukola is not dead yet.

Evening fell, a melancholy September evening; Eero brought the spirits from Routio and Timo word that the bath was ready; and the men's sullen temper revived a little. They set out to their bath, and Timo threw water on the heated oven until the blackened stones heaped over it cracked with a noise like riflefire and a cloud of hot steam was wafted round the bath-house. Eeach plied now with all his strength the feathery bunches of leafy birch-twigs, so grateful to the skin; they bathed and washed their wounds, and the furious beating of the twigs was heard afar without the building.

Juhani: Our wounds are getting a real Turkish polka. Hot steam in the sauna, that's the best physic for soul and body. But my eye stings like Satan. Well, itch away and sting, all the hotter will I make it for thee. How is thy muzzle, Aapo?

Aapo: It's beginning to melt.

Juhani: Swipe away at it and beat it like a Russian hammers his nag, and it'll soon be softer. But more steam, Timo, seeing it is thy job tonight to wait on us. That's it, my boy! Let it come. Oh, but it's hot there, it's hot there! That's the way, my broth of a brother!

Lauri: It fair bites at my finger-nails.

Juhani: Let our nails get a basting, too.

Aapo: Stop throwing water now, boy; or we'll soon have to climb down from here, every man of us.

Eero: Go on praising him and we shall soon be roasted to cinders.

Juhani: That's enough, Timo. Don't throw any more. For Hell's sake stop throwing water on that oven! Art coming down from the platform, Simeoni?

Simeoni: I'm coming, wretch that I am. And ah, if ye only knew why!

Juhani: Tell us.

Simeoni: Man, remember the furnace of the lost and pray night and day.

Juhani: Stuff! Let the body have it if it wants; for the hotter the sauna the greater its healing-power. That thou knowest.

Simeoni: Whose hot water is this in the bucket near the oven?

Juhani: It's mine, as the smith said of his house. Don't touch it.

Simeoni: I'm going to take a drop of it, anyway.

Juhani: Don't do it, brother mine, or there'll be trouble. Why didst thou not warm some for thyself?

Tuomas: Why be so snappy without cause? Take a little from my tub, Simeoni.

Timo: Or from mine, under the platform steps there.

Juhani: Have some of mine then, too, but see thou leavest me at least half.

Lauri: Eero! Thou imp, take care I don't throw thee off the platform.

Aapo: What trick are you two up to in the corner?

80

Juhani: What's the squabbling about? Eigh?

Lauri: Blowing on a fellow's back.

Aapo: Softly, Eero!

Juhani: Hey, troublemonger.

Simeoni: Eero, Eero, can't even the stewing heat of the bath remind thee of the fires of Hell? Remember Juho Hemmola, remember him!

Juhani: He saw when he was stretched on a sickbed the fiery lake, from which he was saved that time, and all because, as it was then said to him, he had always thought of Hell when he was on the sauna platform. But can that be daylight shining through yon corner?

Lauri: Bright daylight.

Juhani: Oh the beast! the sauna sings its last note. So let the first aim of my mastership be a new sauna.

Aapo: A new one's needed, it's true.

Juhani: Ay, no gainsaying that. A farm without a sauna is no good either from the standpoint of baths or the babies a wife or the farm-hands' women might have. Ay, a smoking sauna, a barking hound, a crowing cock and a mewing pussy, these are the signs of a good farm. Ay, there's plenty to do for the one who takes over our home. A little more steam, Timo.

Timo: It shall be given thee.

Simeoni: Don't let us forget that it is Saturday night.

Juhani: And let us take care our skins aren't soon hanging from the rafters, like the former servingmaid's.

Simeoni: That was the maid who never had time to take her bath with the others, but dillied and dallied in the sauna long after all the others had gone to bed. Then one Saturday night she stayed longer than usual. And what did they find when they went to look for her? Only a skin hanging from the rafters. But it was a master-hand had done the flaying, for the hair, eyes, ears and even the nails had been left in the skin.

Juhani: Let this be a warning... Hi-hi, how skittishly this back of mine takes its steam! As though thou hadst not tasted a birch-twig since New Year's Day.

Lauri: But who had skinned her?

Timo: Who, thou askest. Who else but the . . .

Juhani: Old 'Un himself.

Timo: Ay, he who goes around like a roaring lion. A horrible story!

Juhani: Timo-lad, stick that shirt of mine from the rafters there into this fist.

Timo: What, this one?

Juhani: Ho! 'Tis Eero's little rag he offers to a full-grown man. Ah thee! That middle one there.

Timo: What, this one?

Juhani: That's a man's shirt. Ta, brother. A horrible story, say I too, to go back to what we were speaking of. Let it be a reminder to us that "the eve is the height of a feast-day." Now let's wash ourselves as clean as though we had just come from the midwife's nimble paws; and then shirt under arm to the house, so that our over-heated bodies can get a skinful of cool air on the way. But I do believe this beloved eye of mine is getting better.

Simeoni: My leg isn't better yet, but aches and burns as though it were wrapped round with hot ashes. What's to be come of poor me with it?

Eero: Go nicely to bed when we reach the house and pray for leg-salve, and then thank thy Creator who has not suffered thee today to "dash thy foot against a stone", as it says in evening prayer.

Simeoni: I do not hear thee, I do not hear.

Eero: Then pray for ear-salve as well. But start moving, or thou'lt be left here a prey to Old Nick.

Simeoni: My ears are closed to thee, closed in a spiritual sense. Understand me, man!

Eero: Come on, or thy skin will soon be hanging from the rafters, and that in a bodily sense.

Naked and hot, they went from the sauna to the livingroom,

82

their bodies glowing like the sunlit stem of a birch-tree. Arrived within, they sat down to rest a while, sweating copiously. Then little by little they dressed themselves. And now Juhani began concocting an ointment for the whole wounded brotherhood. Into an old handleless saucepan, which he placed on the fire, he poured the can of spirits, stirring into it two spans of gunpowder, one of ground sulphur and a like measure of salt. And when this had boiled for an hour, he set the mixture to cool, and the ointment, which resembled a pitchblack gruel, was ready. With this salve they anointed their wounds, paying particular attention to those in their heads, and then covered the whole with fresh, golden tar. Whereafter their teeth met fiercely and a dark flush overspread their faces; so burned the potent ointment in their wounds. But Simeoni set forth supper; seven ring-shaped loaves, the smoked haunch of a cow and a heaped-up platter of stewed turnips soon lay on the table. Food, however, was little to their taste that evening, and after a few moments they rose from table and having undressed, lay down on their beds.

The night was dark, peace and silence reigned everywhere. But suddenly the air around Jukola was illumined: the sauna had caught fire. So hot had Timo heated the grey stone oven that after smouldering a while the wall burst into flames. And in deepest peace the building burned to ashes, unseen of a single eye. And when morning dawned, there was left of the Jukola sauna only a few glowing cinders and the whitehot ruins of the oven. At last, at midday, the brothers woke, feeling a good deal fresher than on the previous day, and dressing themselves, sat down to breakfast; and food now tasted well to them. For long they ate without uttering a word, until at last a conversation arose about the scene of violence on the road between Tammisto and Toukola.

Juhani: True, it was a fair beating for us; but then they fell on us like robbers with staves and cudgels. Ah! if we too had had weapons in our hands and a hint of the danger beforehand, they'd be sawing coffin-boards in Toukola village today, and there'd be work for the grave-digger. However, I gave Kissala's Aapeli his due.

Tuomas: A white, hairless path ran down from his forehead to his nape like the Milky way in an autumn sky.

Juhani: Thou sawest?

Tuomas: I saw it.

Juhani: He got his due, but the others, the others, O Lord!

Eero: We'll be revenged on them down to their marrows.

Juhani: Let's lay our heads together; and it may be we can hit on an idea for a matchless revenge.

Aapo: Why should we work everlasting ruin? Let's seek the law and justice, and not revenge by our own hands.

Juhani: The first Toukola man I lay hands on, I'll eat alive, skin and hair; there's the law and justice.

Simeoni: Wretched brother! Dost ever intend to be heir to Heaven?

Juhani: What do I care for Heaven, if I can't see Matti Tuhkala's blood and guts!

Simeoni: Oh what a monster thou art, what a monster! I must weep.

Juhani: Weep thou for the cat's death, but not for my sake. Grrh! I'll make sausages of them.

Tuomas: I'll be revenged for this beating, I stake my word and oath on it. Only a wolf would treat a man so.

Juhani: A wild wolf. I swear the same oath.

Aapo: That revenge would only rebound on to our own backs. But the law would punish them and reward us.

Juhani: The law won't make their backs smart with these wounds of ours.

Aapo: All the worse will their purse and good name smart.

Simeoni: Let us put bloody revenge out of our minds; let us appeal to the law. I'm ready for that, even though the noise and bustle of a court-room is greatly scaring to me.

Juhani: If it comes to that, here's a lad who wouldn't flinch even there. True, a fellow's heart beats a bit faster the first time he stands before the table of high justice, but a real man soon bucks up. I still remember that time when I was witness for poor Kaisa Koivula, who applied for maintenance for her child. I remember how the Serjeant shouted: "Juhani, son of Juhani Jukola. of the village of Toukola!"

Timo: "And his younger brother Timotheus!" And, dog take it, Kaisa got a father for her child.

Juhani: That she did.

Timo: Even though we weren't allowed to take oath.

Juhani: We weren't, that's true. But our frank and honest witness helped a lot.

Timo: And our names have gone up in deeds and dockets right to the Emperor himself, hey!

Juhani: That's well known. Ay, so the Serjeant shouted, and there was a kind of jump in the cockles of this lad's heart, but he was soon at home and pouring out of his mouth the unwavering language of truth like he'd been an apostle, without heeding the laughter and giggling of all those in court.

Timo: That's how we're treated in court, and all goes well. But there's more than one noose cast there and many a foot put slyly out for a man to trip over.

Juhani: That's so, but truth and justice snatch the victory in the end for all their tricks.

Timo: For all their tricks and wiles; ay, unless the very devil is lawyer and makes out night to be day and day night and black tar to be skim-milk. But one thing can be as good as two. Why didn't God place justice on a firmer, ay, a downright firm footing? Why witnesses, long questionings and lawyers tricks? To my mind, the quickest road to truth and justice, if a matter seems doubtful and can't be settled, would be this: all the court, with the judge himself in the lead, would step out into the yard, where the Serjeant or hunt-bailiff would blow a big birchbark horn, that could be called the court-horn; with this he'd blow a few toots, holding its mouth towards God's Heaven. And then Heaven would open and the angel of the Lord appear to all the people, asking in a loud

85

voice: "What does the Serjeant want", and then the Serjeant would ask back in a high crying voice: "Is the accused man guilty or innocent?" Then the bright angel would give an answer the truth of which no one could doubt, and according to which the man would be let go, or get a thorough hiding. In this way I believe everything would go well.

Juhani: Why even that much shouting and fashing. See how I have thought the matter out. As the Creator I'd have arranged it so: the accused man would have to confirm his words by a vow, a sacred oath, and if he swore truly, let him toddle off home a free man again, but if he felt like loosing off a lie, let the solid earth open beneath him and Hell swallow him. That's the straightest road to truth.

Aapo: It might be done that way, but best perhaps as it was once ordained by the Father of Wisdom himself.

Juhani: Best! Here we sit, battered, scabby and one-eyed like tom-cats in March. Is this jolly? Marry, this world is the daftest thing under the sun!

Simeoni: So He hath arranged it, for He wishes to try His children's firmness in belief.

Juhani: Firmness in belief. He tries and weighs us, but through these trials of his souls go down to that everlasting sauna like midges; there, where I wouldn't wish a snake, although I'm only a sinful human being.

Tuomas: A hard game, this life and this world. Little is the hope for any of us of as small a chance as Joshua's and Caleb's amongst six hundred thousand men.

Juhani: You're right! What is this life then? The porch of Hell.

Simeoni: Juhani, Juhani, keep watch over thy thoughts and language!

Juhani: Hell itself, say I, if I take on my worst temper. I'm the suffering soul down here and the Toukola lads devils, with pitchforks in their fists. All men are like evil spirits towards us.

Aapo: Now, now, let us enter into our own bosoms a little. The wrath of mankind towards us has perhaps been lit and kept alive in great part by our own deeds. Let us not forget how we have sported in their turnip-fields and peastacks, how we have trampled their water-meadows on our fishing-trips and often shot the bears they had ringed in, and done many other such tricks, heedless of the law's warnings or the voice of conscience.

Simeoni: We have aroused the anger of Heaven and earth. Often when I lay me down to sleep and think of the wicked deeds of our youth, the fiery sword of conscience pricks real painfully at my wretched bosom and I seem to hear, like the sound of rain far away, a curious murmuring, and another dismal voice seems to whisper in my ear: "The sigh of God and Man for the seven sons of Jukola." Ruin threatens us, brothers, and the star of happiness will not shine for us until we are on better terms with our follow-men. Why shouldn't we then go and beg for forgiveness, promising to live differently hereafter?

Eero: I would weep if I could. Simeoni, Simeoni! "with but little more persuasion thou wouldest fain"... yea, there wasn't much lacking. "But go thy way this time."

Simeoni: Ay, ay, we'll see on the last day.

Timo: Would I be brought round to ask for forgiveness? I won't believe it.

Tuomas: Not while the raven is black.

Eero: We'll see it done then when we come to Judgment. Then the raven will be white as snow, as it says in the song of the merry lad and the loving old mother. Gladly for me the last grains in the hopper before we begin to pray.

Juhani: Believe me, Simeoni, it's no use always watching the state of our souls, for ever thinking of the fiery pit, the Devil and all the little devils. Such ideas either addle a man's brains altogether or tie a halter round his neck. Those former mad pranks of ours are to be looked upon rather as the foolishness of youth than as sins in the strictest sense. And secondly, I have come to the belief and conviction that we have sometimes to close our eyes down here, and pretend not to see what we see, or to know what we know. A man's got to do that if he wants to escape whole-skinned from the mortar of life. Don't stare at me like owls, there's no call for any staring. What I mean are those smaller sins against God, not against my neighbour. My neighbour and nearest has a skin to his nose and is as touchy as I am, and wants his best as I do mine; but God is a man slow to anger and plenteous in mercy, and always forgives us in the end, if we only pray from an earnest heart. Ay, ay, I mean that it is no use in season and out comparing to a hair our own works and the commandments, but best to stand half-way. Big sins we must keep from, by all means, say I, and pray for eye-salve, but the smaller ones, namely, smaller ones against God, we needn't for ever be weighing on the hooks of conscience, but stand half-way, half-way.

Simeoni: Good God! That's what Satan whispers in our ears.

Timo: Like Olli's old woman feeding Mäkelä's wife with lies when she's thirsting for a drink.

Aapo: Juhani uttered a few words that I heard with wonder and dismay. Brother, is that what God's commandments teach us? Is that what our mother taught us? Never! One is with the Lord as a thousand and a thousand as one. How canst thou then babble of smaller sins, of standing half-way, defending the serving of two masters? Say, Juhani, what is sin?

Juhani: What is truth? thou Jukola's Solomon, thou wise old man from Savo? "What is sin?" Ha! "What is sin?" Oh what wisdom, what marvellous wisdom. "There's a head for you on our little boy", verily there is. Ay, what's the good of speaking. "What is sin?" Ha-ha! What is truth, ask I.

Tuomas: Why wriggle out of it, lad? Know that the doctrine thou proclaimest is the Devil's doctrine.

Juhani: Let me give you a living example that strongly bears out my belief. Recall to your minds the former tanner in the village. The man got strange ideas about his soul, sin and wordly mammon, and began altering his former ways ways greatly. Thus he suddenly stopped taking in and giving out hides on Sunday, without looking to how important one road and two errands are to the farmer. His friends warned him in vain when they saw his business shrink from day to day, while that of the other tanner next door grew and grew. The madman always replied: "God will surely bless the work of my hands though there be less of it, but as for him who now thinks he is snatching the bread out of my mouth, he will reap curses in the end in the sweat of his brow for not having honoured the Lord's Sabbath." So he would spout, walking about staring on Sundays with a hymnbook in his fist, the eyes in his head round as marbles and his hair sticking up like Bomb-Peter's wig. And what happened to the man in the end? We know what. It wasn't long before he had the heaviest piece of wood in his hand, a beggar's staff, and his path became the endless highway. Now he wanders from village to village, emptying a glass wherever he can. I met him once at the road-side over yonder on Kanamäki Ridge; there he sat on the crossbar of his sledge, and royally drunk was the miserable man. "How fare you, tanner?'" asks I. "I fare as I fare" answers he, with one stiff look at me. But I asked him again: "How are matters with you, master?" "They are as they are" he answers again and went his way, bleating some foolish kind of song. That was his end. But the other tanner? He became rich as anything, and rich and happy he died.

Aapo: Narrow-minded belief and spiritual pride ruined the tanner, and so it will be with all of his ilk. However that may be, thy doctrine is false doctrine and belief.

Simeoni: False prophets and the last days of the world.

Timo: He wants to tempt us over to the Turk's religion. But thou canst not shake me; for I am sure and steadfast, sure and steadfast as the eye of an axe.

Juhani: Hand me, Tuomas, that half-loaf from the end of the table there. "False prophets." I tempt no man to sin and evildoing, and I myself wouldn't steal a bradawl from a cobbler or the eye of a needle from a tailor. But my heart strikes sparks when my meaning is always twisted to its worst, made out black as pitch, when a dark brown would be enough.

Aapo: Thou spokest so plainly, weighed the matter so from

point to point and chapter to chapter, that we couldn't have mis-understood it.

Timo: My head on it, he wanted to tempt us over to the Turk's religion.

Simeoni: God have mercy on him!

Juhani: Shut your mouths, and quickly. Pray to God for me, scold me like meek-eyed parsons, I tell you it won't do. I have just enough wisdom, even if I'm not pure unmixed wisdom like, for example, our Aapo there.

Aapo: God forbid! I'm not even as wise as I should be.

Juhani: Pure wisdom, pure wisdom! And keep thy breadtrap shut, or thou'lt get this paw against thy muzzle and a bit harder than yesterday. This I say and my paunch being full, leave off eating.

Timo: I'll lay that every man of us is as tight as a gad-fly.

Eero: But why do I see no sauna?

Juhani: What would a midget like thee be seeing? But — our sauna has gone to blazes!

Eero: No, but to Heaven in a fiery chariot.

Juhani: Can it have burned down?

Eero: How should I know, and what have I to do with it? It's the master of Jukola's sauna, not mine.

Juhani: Eero's body too, if I remember rightly, sweated there yesterday. Ay, Ay, everything on the master's back, that I well believe. But let's go and look. Where's my cap? Let's go and look, brothers. I know that our sauna is in ashes.

They went out to see what had befallen their sauna. But all that there was left to see was a blackened fireplace and a smoking chaos. The brothers gazed upon this scene of destruction for a while with annoyance, and at last returned to the living-room. Last came Juhani, in his fist two iron hinges which he cast angrily on the table.

Juhani: Ay, thé house of Jukola is now bathless.

Eero: "And a farm without a sauna is no good" said brother Juhani.

90

Juhani: Timo made the dear old oven too hot, and dust and ashes is all that's left of the beloved sooty rafters and walls, in whose shelter each of us entered into the light of the world. Timo heated the oven mightily, say I.

Timo: At thy bidding, at thy bidding; that thou knowest well.

Juhani: I give the Devil for "thy bidding" but that we are now bathless men, and that is an annoying thing. Building a new one won't add to our bread.

Aapo: An annoying matter; but still the sauna was old and its corners full of holes; and thou thyself didst decide yesterday to build a new one right soon.

Juhani: True it was old and its logs steamed through to their maarows, but it would have done at a pinch for a year or two. The farm has no strength yet to waste on building saunas; the fields, the fields are what we must pounce on first.

Tuomas: Thou'lt treat the fields as thou didst the big meadow last year, whose fine hay we let wither without a single stroke of the scythe. But it was thy wish. Whenever I reminded thee of the mowing, thou wouldst answer: "we won't go just yet, the hay is still growing so fast that you can hear it."

Juhani: That's something past and gone and thy jawing won't help it. The big meadow'll grow all the better in the coming summer. But who's that man coming towards the house in the field yonder?

Tuomas: Juryman Mäkelä. What can the man want?

Juhani: Now the Devil's loose. He comes in the Crown's name, and it's because of that accursed scrap with the Toukola lads.

Aapo: In the last fight the law is on our side, but in the first one we must look to ourselves. Let me explain matters to him.

Juhani: As the eldest, I too want the right to speak when our common good is being talked over.

Aapo: Then see thou dost not talk all of us into a trap, if so be we should have to wriggle a little.

Juhani: I know how.

Entered Mäkelä, an excellent and well-meaning juryman. He

came, however, on a different errand from that which the brothers had guessed.

Mäkelä: Good-day!

The Brothers: Good-day!

Mäkelä: What horrors do I see? Boys, how are matters here? Torn, bruised, scabby, dressed in rags! Miserable men!

Juhani: "Trust a dog to lick its wounds", but let the wolves look to themselves. Is this the reason you now stand in our house?

Mäkelä: What did I know of this? But can brothers have harried each other in this wise? Shame on you!

Juhani: You are mistaken, Mäkelä, we brothers have treated each other like angels. This is the work of neighbours.

Mäkelä: Who has done this?

Juhani: Kind neighbours. But may I ask why you have come to see us?

Mäkelä: For a grave reason. Boys, boys, the day of your ruin is upon you.

Juhani: What will that day be like?

Mäkelä: A day of .shame.

Juhani: When will it dawn?

Mäkelä: I have strict orders from the Vicar to bring you to church next Sunday.

Juhani: What does he want of us at church?.

Mäkelä: To put you in the stocks, to speak plainly.

Juhani: Why?

Mäkelä: For many reasons. You wild and maddened men! You broke the hymnleader's window and then fled like wolves.

Juhani: 'Twas the hymnleader worried us like the wildest wolf.

Mäkelä: But what has the Vicar done to you?

Juhani: Not the bite of a flea.

Mäkelä: And yet you mocked and insulted him through that foul-mouthed, brazen leech Kaisa. You sent, by Rajamäki's horrible regiment, the most filthy, really scoundrelly greetings to a well-born man, the shepherd of our parish; that was a barefaced insolence without like.

92

Juhani: "It's true enough, but prove it", said Kakkinen's Jake, but so say not I.

Mäkelä: But now, know that the Vicar's sternest vengeance will befall you. Now he is without pity for you.

Aapo: Sit down, Mäkelä, and let us talk over the matter a little more broadly and deeply. What do you say to this point: can the Vicar screw us down in the stocks for Rajamäki Kaisa's lies? Surely not! Let what we have said and in what way hurt his honour be legally proven.

Juhani: "First a matter must be weighed, ere the rod on back be laid", that's well known.

Mäkelä: But another thing, this matter of reading, gives him a fair amount of power, anyhow, under the church laws, which he is now sure in his anger to use against you.

Juhani: In the matter of reading we have God's own laws and regulations on our side, which stop anything in that line. Look you, already in our mother's womb He gave us such hard heads that it is impossible for us to learn to read. What are we to do, Mäkelä? The gifts of learning fall very unevenly on our heads down here.

Mäkelä: The hardness of your heads is only an empty fancy. Diligence and daily practice will overcome anything in the end. Your father was one of the best readers.

Aapo: But our mother never knew a single letter, and yet she was a true Christian.

Juhani: And brought up and chastised her sons in the fear of God. God bless the old woman.

Mäkelä: Did she try what the skill of others could do for you?

Juhani: Indeed she did her best; she tried what Old Granny Pinewood could do. But that hot-tempered beldame began at once hammering our backs, and her cabin became worse in our eyes than a cave of demons; and at last we never entered it, though they whipped us like a dying fire.

Mäkelä: In those days you were a thoughtless lot, but now you stand for yourselves as men; and a sensible, healthy man can do

93

what he wills; show the Vicar and the world, therefore, what manhood can do. As for thee, Aapo, who hast such a clever mind and lackest not a mite or two of knowledge, and whose sharp memory preserves all thou hearest or seest, at thee I must wonder that thou hast not already altered thy ways.

Aapo: 'Tis but little I know; oh well, I know a thing or two. Our blind uncle that was told us many things, things from the Bible, of his travels at sea and the build of the world, and then we always listened to him with pious hearts.

Juhani: We listened with ears erect as a hare's when the old man talked to us of Moses, the children of Israel, happenings from the Book of Kings and the miracles of Revelations. "And the sound of their wings was as the sound of chariots as they rush to war." Lord save us! we know many miracles and things, and aren't quite such black heathens as people think.

Mäkelä: But to become true members of the Christian Church you must begin from the a-b-c-book.

Aapo: Mäkelä, on that board you see seven a-b-c's, brought from Hämeenlinna, and may this sight prove to you our willingness to learn. Let the Vicar show a little more patience, and I think that something can take root, grow and prosper out of this matter.

Juhani: Let him be longsuffering towards us and I am willing to pay him his tithes twice over, and the flesh of young game won't be lacking from his bowl, at lawful times.

Mäkelä: Prayers and fine promises won't help here I'm afraid, when I think of his deep and righteous anger.

Juhani: What does he want of us then, and what do you want? Good! Come with seventy men, and blood shall squirt around us even then.

Mäkelä: Tell me, what steps do you mean to take to learn your alphabet and the lesser catechism, which is the chief concern of our Vicar.

Juhani: Try what the teaching of Granny Pinewood or her daughter can do for us here at home. Good reading women, both of them.

Mäkelä: I will tell the Vicar of your intention. But for the sake of your own peace go and beg his forgiveness for your insolent deed.

Juhani: We will think over that point.

Mäkelä: Do as I say; and note that unless he observes in you an honest and strenuous endeavour, you'll be in the stocks, nicely in the stocks one Sunday, under the church windows. This I say; and now fare ye well!

Juhani: Farewell, farewell!

Tuomas: Didst thou really mean what thou said'st about Old Granny Pinewood and her daughter? Was it in earnest thou half promised to go and crawl before the Vicar.

Juhani: There wasn't a mite of earnest in it, and of truth not a whit. To gain time was what this lad's prattle was meant for. Granny Pinewood or Venla to guide our reading-sticks! Why, even the Toukola pigs would laugh! You heard, we were threatened with the certain stocks, with the pillory of shame. A thousand flaming goblins! hasn't a man the right to live his own life as he likes in peace, when he stands in no one's way, tramples on no one's rights? Who'll forbid it? But I say once again: parsons and officials with their books and papers are the evil spirits of mankind. O thou black sow! O cursed day on earth! we're so knocked head over heels by the blows of hard fate and the cruelty of men, that I could dash my head against a wall. O thou black bull! Venla refused us; they've made a nasty, stinging song about us; the hymnleader tortured us like the Evil One himself; the Toukola lads hammered us like senseless earth, we were trounced like Christmas pigs and now strut here like real Christmas brownies, like one-eyed gnomes with rags round our heads. What more? Isn't our home now without the poor man's only treat, the roaring steam of the sauna? There the ruins of our sauna smoke and smoulder. And there's still the worst of devils left. Hrrh! With all its ten holes the stocks grins at us from the church porch. Bright lightning! If such a bunch of worries doesn't lift a razor to a man's throat, what will? O thou horned bull!

95

Eero: Now thy memory is a little weak; there aren't ten holes in the stocks.

Juhani: How many then?

Eero: How many stars in Charley's Wain, how many sons at Jukola?

Juhani: We are seven. Seven holes therefore and seven sons. Well, all the worse. Seven holes! Always worser and worser. See how men and hard fate are joined together against us. Seven holes like millstone-eyes! What mockery of hard fate! Well, let them shoot all the arrows of their rage at us, we'll clench our overgoaded hearts hard as sparkling steel. Let them blow poison at us from every side like snakes, and the heavens rain pure gall on us, we'll still, with eyes shut, grinding our teeth and roaring like mad bulls, charge at them. And if we are dragged at last by all the Crown's might to the stocks, why it's with blissful joy I'll sit in them, I.

Aapo: Why with joy?

Juhani: Thou dost not understand, brother, the awful power of anger. The thought of revenge would make this lad forget all shame; and it's shame is their purpose. A dream, that of bleeding our mister Vicar, it's that that would taste like honey-dew to my angry mind. And it wouldn't be a knife or a gun I'd use, like the former man from Karjaa, no, but with teeth and claws I'd fly at his throat like a she-wolf. I'd tear the man to bits, to a thousand bits, and taste my revenge to the last drop. I'd do this even if I had ten lives and each life were to be tortured ten years in a spiked barrel. It'd be nothing against the lust of my revenge.

Aapo: Thou stirrest up all thy being. Lave, miserable brother, the seething cauldron of thy heart with cool water from the rippling brook of patience, which flows onward through the meadows, gently winding.

Simeoni: Thy face is pitch-black, and thine eyes roll bloodshot, sharp as gimlets. Have mercy on thyself.

Tuomas: Truly, if we were made to sit in the stocks, we'd have revenge, but may our hearts beat in peace until that happens. All hope is not past yet.

96

Juhani: On one corner of the earth a day of peace still gleams for us. Ilvesjärvi Lake yonder, below Impivaara, is the harbour to which we can sail away from the storm. Now my mind is made up.

Lauri: Mine was made up last year already.

Eero: I'll follow you even into the deepest cave on Impivaara, where it is said the Old Man of the Mountain boils pitch, with a helmet made of a hundred sheep-skins on his head.

Tuomas: We'll all move there from here.

Juhani: Thither we'll move and build a new world.

Aapo: Cannot the hand of the law reach us there too?

Juhani: The forest shields its pups. There we are indeed on our own ground; deep as bleary-eyed moles we'll dig ourselves in, right to the bowels of the earth. And if they felt like meddling with us lads there, they'd be made to see what it feels like to disturb seven bears in their lair. Now to the tanner's to draw up a lease in writing. For ten years let the farm pass into other hands.

Simeoni: I too long for an abode of peace. Brothers, let us create ourselves a new home and a new heart in the depths of the forest.

Juhani: All with a single mind!

Aapo: What dost thou decide, Timo?

Timo: "Where all others, there I too", says the proverb.

Aapo: You would move, and I be left here, a lone pine in Jukola's yard? Ah, for that every root and fibre of my being is too firmly fast in your company. I'm agreed, then, and let's hope for the best from this trip. I'll come with you.

Juhani: Splendid! Now to the tanner's the lot of us, to draw up a proper lease. All with a single mind!

They set out in a body to draw up the lease, rented their farm to the tanner for ten years; and the following paragraphs were set down in writing. The tanner was to rule over and run the farm for ten years, the first three years without any rent, whereafter he was to pay the brothers seven barrels of rye each year and build a new sauna before the lease expired. Anywhere in the Jukola forests the brothers were at liberty to hunt, and any kind of game the law allowed. In the northern section of the farm's holding, around Impivaara, the brothers were free to do and live as they pleased, this applying both to the clearings and the forests. The tanner was to take over the farm on All Saints Day, but if they so wished, the brothers were to be given shelter in the home of their birth over the coming winter. These were the main conditions of the lease.

Came November, and the tanner stood with his loads in the Jukola yard and took over the management of the farm for the term of the lease. But to avoid the Vicar and his men, the brothers spent the winter mostly in the forest, ski-ing around and hunting; the charcoal-burner's hut on Impivaara did for camp. They did not, however, move altogether with horse and other belongings from the farm. This they had settled was to take place when spring had come. Nevertheless, they worked already at their coming abode, felled trees to dry during the spring and rolled stones for the foundations on to a stump-besprinkled clearing under the steep hill-side.

Thus passed the winter, and during the whole of its course no command or reminder reached the brothers from the Vicar. Was he merely biding his time, or had he left them to their fate?

CHAPTER 5

SPRING had come, the snowdrifts had melted; the winds blew mild; the earth began to blossom and the birchwoods to put on leaves.

The brothers toil on their removal from Jukola to Impivaara. They tramp along a stony, twisting forest path, guns on shoulders and birch-bark knapsacks with powder and shot in them on their backs. Juhani leads the way with Killi and Kiiski, the two big, fierce Jukola dogs. Behind them, drawing a springless cart, driven by Timo, walks the brothers' one-eyed horse, old Valko. The others, with their guns and knapsacks, follow the cart, helping Valko over the hardest stretches of the road. Last of all comes Eero, carrying in his arms Jukola's doughty cock, for the brothers were loth to part with it, and had decided to take it along to the wilds of Impivaara for a timepiece. On the cart were a coffer, traps for wolf and fox, an iron cauldron and in this two oaken bowls, a dipper, seven spoons and other instruments of the cook's art. A coarse sack filled with peas served as cover to the cauldron; and highest of all, the old farm cat squirmed and mewed in a little bag. Such was the brothers' departure from their home; silent and dejected, they trod the difficult, stony forest path. The sky was bright, the weather calm, and downhill to the west spun already the wheel of the sun.

Juhani: Man is a seafarer on the stormy sea of life. So we too now sail away from the dear haunts of our childhood, sail with our wheeled ship across the mazy forests towards the steep island of Impivaara. Ah!

Timo: It wouldn't take much for this poor frog, too, to be dabbing tears from his cheeks.

Juhani: That I scarce wonder at, having looked into my own bosom in this grievous hour. But there's no help for it in this world, a man's heart must always be hard as a flint. The child of man is born a wanderer on the face of the earth; here he has no abiding-place.

Timo: Here he wanders a little while, struts and prances, until at last he wilts and perishes like a rat at the foot of a wall.

Juhani: Rightly said, wisely uttered.

Simeoni: And if that were but all; but then's the point.

Juhani: Then comes the question of our pound, thou wouldst say. True.

Timo: Then we shall have to say without shift or guile: here am I and here, Lord, is thy pound.

Simeoni: A man ought always to remember his end; but his heart is hardened.

Juhani: Hardened, hardened, that can't be denied. But such, God knows, are all under this heaven. Yet we can earnestly try to live hereafter as befitteth true believers, once we have settled down and built ourselves a warm abode of peace. Let us join, brothers, in a strict league and cast away all works of sin, all anger, strife and hate in our bird's-nest here. Away anger, hate and pride.

Eero: And pomp.

Juhani: Ay!

Eero: Flaunting, sinful raiment.

Juhani: Ay!

Eero: Spring-carts and all such church-going vanities.

Juhani: Eigh? What art thou saying?

Simeoni: He's joking again.

Juhani: I notice that. See that I don't grab thee by the neck, that is, if I minded the babbling of a rogue; but I wouldn't be

100

a man if I did, that I wouldn't. How, thou twice damned imp, art thou holding that cock? Why is the poor brute squawking?

Eero: I only set its wing right; it hung down.

Juhani: I'll set thee right soon. See that I don't collar hold of thee. Know that that is the best cock in the whole of our province at his job. The first time he crows at two, the second at four o'clock, which is the best time for rising. We shall have much joy of that cock out here in the wilds. And the cat then up there on the load! Ah Matti-lad! There thou dancest and swayest and peerest out of thy sack, mewing quite pitifully. Poor old fellow, there aren't very many days left for thee to stalk about in. Thine eyes are turning very dark and thy mewing sounds hoarse. But perhaps thou wilt still pick up when thou startest on the fat forest mice. I hope so. But 'tis you, Killi and Kiiski, I love above everything. Like ourselves, you were born and bred on Jukola Farm, grew up with us like true brothers. Ah, how burningly you look into my eyes! Ay, Killi, ay, my Kiiski-lad, ay! And wagging your tails so merrily! Well, well, you can't know that we are now leaving our beautiful home. Oh you poor wretches! I can't help it, I must weep.

Timo: Look to thine own advice a moment ago. Keep a stout heart, a stout heart.

Juhani: I can't, I can't, leaving my golden home.

Tuomas: Truly a day to weigh on a man's heart; but up on Impivaara we shall soon have another home, soon perhaps as dear.

Juhani: What, brother? Not in heaven nor on earth is there a spot as dear to us as the place where we were born and bred and in whose fields we played as little, milk-bearded brats.

Aapo: The hour of parting crushes our hearts, 'tis true, for even to a hare the home-bush is dear.

Juhani: What was it the mother-hare once said, when feeling herself heavy again, she sent the little hare away, out of the way of a coming brood?

Timo: "Get thee on thy way, little son, little one, and remember always what I say: where the bush is there the trap is, where the leap is there the snare."

101

Juhani: So she said to her son and the lad went lolloping away; he lolloped, gaping, along the clearing and the edge of the heath, his split lip in a guileless grin. So he parted from his home, and mournfully shone the eve.

Eero: That was Jussi the Hare.

Juhani: If thou wilt. So he parted from his home, and so we too part from ours. Farewell, home! I could kiss thy threshold, even thy dunghill now.

Aapo: Ay, brother. But let us try to drive this gloom out of our minds. Soon we shall have a mighty task before us; soon the logs will thunder, the axes ring, and up on Impivaara clearing a stout cabin rise towards the heavens, set in the grandest forest. See, we are already in the wilds, amongst the roaring spruce.

Thus they spoke among themselves as they journeyed across a dark backwood. But soon the land began to rise, and their path wound upward to a tree-clad height, which was called Teerimäki. Here and there were mossy crags, shaped like the burial mounds of giants, round which the dwarfed, stout-rooted pines soughed and murmured. Severely were the cart and Valko's aged shoulder-blades shaken on the rocky road, where the eye could sometimes barely discern the marks of the trail. The path led over a hill, for bottomless quagmires stretched on either side. But the brothers did their utmost to lighten the toil of their one-eyed comrade. And at last the summit was reached, and granting Valko a short breathing-space, they looked down on the spreading earth. Their eye caught distant villages, meadows, fields, blue lakes, and on the edge of the forests in the west, the high steeple of a church. But in the south, on the slope of a knoll, Jukola glowed like a lost land of delight; and once again the brothers' bosoms filled with languishing thoughts. At last, however, they tore their glance away and looked north, and there saw lofty Impivaara, its steeply sloping sides, its darkling caves and the moss-bearded, storm-riven spruce that stood along the ribs of the height. But below the ridge they saw a pleasant stump-besprinkled clearing, their future dwelling-place, and below the clearing a copse to yield them sturdy logs wherewith to build their home. All this they saw: Lake Ilvesjärvi shine clear between the pines and a bright sun near to its setting beam from the northwest spur of the height; and once more a delicious flash of hope sparkled in their eves and caused their breasts to swell.

Onward they fared again and began with bolder speed to hasten to their new abode. The hill was passed and they came to a cloister of pines on a heath, where heather, mountain cranberry and withered tufts of grass in varied sequence hid the echoing ground. Across a sandy, man-built road, which led from Viertola Manor to the church, they marched, keeping to their forest track along the spine of the heath.

Aapo: This is the heath on which, so the old folk say, the court-room of the snakes used to be. The judge was their own king, that white snake so rarely seen of man, which has a crown of untold worth on its head. But once a gallant rider robbed them of the crown, as the story tells us.

And Aapo related the following tale to them as they trudged down the spine of the heath towards desolate Sompio Bog.

A rider came and on the heath saw the Snake King, which bore a glittering crown on its head. Riding towards it, he snatched the crown from the king's head with the point of his sword, dug the spurs into his horse and whirled away with his treasure as though borne on clouds and wind. But the snakes were as quick in setting out in furious pursuit of the brazen robber. Curled into rings, they sped hissing after him, and a thousand hoops whizzed on the rider's track like unto discs cast by playing boys on the road. Soon they caught up with the rider, swarmed already thickly round the horse's feet, bounding up along its flanks, and great was the man's danger. And in his distress he threw down his hat as a sop to them, which they at once tore into pieces and swallowed in the fury of their rage. But not for long did this trick help the man; soon the snakes sped on his track again and the sand whirled high on the road. And ever fiercer the rider spurred on his panting horse; blood ran in streams from the fiery stallion's ribs, and from its mouth a spumy lather spouted. The rider fled to the woods, but the trees did not hinder the speed of his pursuers. They came to a river, and with a mighty splash he rode headlong into its depths, and swiftly the stallion bore him over. The snakes too came to the river and with the thunder of many rapids dashed into the bosom of its waves, swimming across with the swiftness of a storm; and the white foam rose high in the sky. The man rode on, and still the maddened horde pursued him. Then far off, he saw a forest that burned fiercely, and now towards this he spurred his steed, and wrapping himself in the cloak that the river had wetted through, charged into the whirling flames; but the snakes never tarried a whit in following him. So might the mounted hero of Heaven cleave the golden clouds. Once more he struck his spurs into the stallion's sides, once more he was borne onward, and then the groaning stallion fell, forgetting for ever the heated game of life. But the man stood there free, saved from the fire and his awful enemy; for the fire had burned the numberless host of snakes. There the hero stood with rejoicing glance, the marvellous trinket in his hand.

Aapo: That is the tale of the white snake's crown on this same heath.

Juhani: A grand tale and still grander the man who snatched the crown from the snake's head and won it at last for himself. A bonny man!

Timo: Few have ever seen this snake, but he who sees it becomes matchlessly wise, old folk say.

Juhani: It is also said: "Whosoever catches this judge-snake in the spring before the cuckoo sings, and boils and eats it, that man will understand the speech of the ravens which tells him what is going to happen to him."

Eero: It is also said thus: "Whosoever dost as thou sayest after the cuckoo sings, that man will understand the raven's speech which tells him what has happened to him."

Juhani: Oh little brother, how daftly thou speakest! Doesn't every man know that without swallowing a crumb of snake's

104

meat? Look you, now Eero has shown us the man he really is in the matter of brains, an addled sheep. "Tell him what has happened to him." Can such a thought hail from a man's brain? Oh thou poor ninny!

Aapo: Not so fast, Juho. He spoke either in ignorance or else it was one of his jests; however that may be, in either case he cast down before us a thought worth marking. Let us try to weigh his words and I believe we can fish out the wisdom in them. To know what has happened is, one way of looking, great wisdom. If thou weighest over carefully what seed sown in byegone days gave profitable, what harmful fruit, and mappest out thy life, deeds and works thereafter, thou art a wise man. If our own eyes had opened earlier, we shouldn't be tramping here now like emigrants, I believe.

Juhani: Like wolves' cubs under the naked sky. But what's done is done.

Tuomas: What we lost in Jukola we can gain again on Impivaara clearing. Ho, hither the whole crowd of brothers, and let each man dig his claws into the load to help Valko until we're across the bog. Ho hither everybody! The wheels sink a whole span into the muddy ground.

Speaking thus among themselves they had wandered down from the heath, crossed Matti Seunala's wide clearing, passed through a close-growing sprucewood and now stood on the brink of Sompio Bog. Cheerless spread the bog, its surface showing in succession muddy, quaggy openings, mossy hummocks, and whortleberry bushes, while here and there stood a stunted dying birch, mournfully nodding its crown in the evening breeze. In the middle the bog was narrowest and there the earth was closer knit and firmer than elsewhere. Here stood short pines in mossy attire, and on the hummocks grew strong-scented bog-bilberry bushes. And over this stretch of land a wretched track reached over to the bog's farther shore, where the dark wilds began again. Along this road the brothers ventured out on the bog. Some pulled at the shafts beside Valko, the others pushed at the cart behind. And at last, after much exertion, the brink was reached and they fared again on dry land along a root-crossed forest track to the extent of some five hundred paces. And at last the stump-besprinkled level of the clearing shone before them and they had reached their goal, beneath the crannied ridge.

Where they now stood, the brothers' grandfather, a giant at toil, had once sown his clearings, and the smoke of his enormous charcoal-pits had risen like incense to the sky. Many were the forests around this hill that he had cut down and burned to clear and fructify the soil, many the black, sown fields he had harrowed with his clumsy, wooden-toothed harrow, to bear ultimately to his barn the grain-crowned sheaves. A tumbled ruin on the clearing's edge still marked the site of his barn, whence the precious grain had at once been carted home, leaving for winter's easier sledge-ways the straw and chaff. Some distance from the ruins of the barn, where forest and clearing met, the black cavity of a charcoalpit, immensely large, could still be seen, where he had burned the logs from his clearings for tinkling charcoal. In such tasks had the former sturdy master of Jukola toiled and laboured here beneath many scorching suns, wiping many a gush of pearly sweat from his brow. But his nights he rested in a turf-roofed hut, watching his kilns; and this hut the brothers had chosen for their temporary home.

Vast is the stump-filled clearing, yet beyond its edges thine eye cannot pierce; for in the east, the south and the west, forests limit the view and in the north the lofty height. But ascend the height, to its spine crowned by scattered spruce, and thy glance can range far on every side. Southward thou seest first, right beneath thy feet, the gently slanting clearing, a little beyond this a gloomy forest, beyond this again Sompio Bog, and yonder far on the verge of the sky rises Teerimäki, a fainting blue. On its northern side the height sinks gradually, its sloping side, burned of yore for tilling, now displaying to the eye a close-knit weft of growing birch, on whose grassless paths the heath-grouse strut and the ruff-grouse whistle mournfully. In the east is a level heath where the pines grow tall;

in the west a rocky country of mossy crags, with low, yet massive and thick-crowned pines set here and there on velvety ridges. Behind the pines Lake Ilvesjärvi glitters, limpid and teeming with fish, a thousand or so paces from the clearing. More thou wilt hardly see, though thy glance roam far indeed. The backwood's darkling sea looms round on every side. Thou canst catch, however, a dim gleam of Viertola Manor in the northeast, and far away on the distant southwest edge of the earth a grey church spire. Such with its surroundings was the spot the Jukola brothers had chosen for their home.

But this evening the brothers halted close to the charcoalburner's hut, and having freed the weary Valko from the shafts to seek, with a bell tied round its neck, its own pastures, they gathered stumps and faggots for a merry fire on the clearing. There Simeoni broiled sprats, turnips and beef for supper, while the others bustled round the cart, unpacking the load and bearing each tool and chattel to its appointed place. And when this was done and the food ready, they sat down to eat on the twilit clearing; and the sun had sunk behind the height.

Simeoni: This then is the first meal in our new home; may it bring luck and God's peace to all our other meals.

Juhani: May luck, a bounteous luck, be our only comrade here in all the works and deeds our hands can find to do.

Aapo: I have something important to say.

Juhani: Loosen it from the cockles of thy heart.

Aapo: A headless body is no use, say I.

Juhani: But bangs against walls like a beheaded hen.

Timo: Never mind beheaded, when the fit comes on it, a hen'll dash about like that and that, hither and thither. Old Granny Pinewood's hens often do, and then the old woman says that sorcerers' arrows are flying through the air.

Juhani: Empty thy mouth, brother Aapo.

Aapo: This is the idea in my mind: if we wish to get anything done here and done properly, one of us must be chief, leader of our councils, settler of our quarrels. In a word, let there be one among us whose voice shall always be foremost, for the sake of order.

Juhani: I am the eldest here.

Aapo: Thou art first-born in the row of Jukolas, so may the due right be thine.

Juhani: I am head of the row, and know how to demand obedience of you. If you would only obey me.

Aapo: That is fair and just. But still, let us hear everyone's voice in matters that concern us all.

Juhani: To thy advice in particular I shall always lend a willing ear. But I am chief.

Aapo: True. But what punishment shall we settle on for him who is always obstinate, always against the rest?

Juhani: I'll shut him up in one of the caves on yonder height, and carry a heavy pile of rocks to close up the cave's mouth. There he can sit a day or two, as matters and circumstances demand. Ay, there he can suck his nails and ponder over what belongs his peace.

Lauri: I won't agree to that for one.

Tuomas: Nor I.

Timo: Am I then a wrinkly-faced badger, whose home is a stuffy mountain cave? Far from it.

Juhani: You begin to mutiny?

Tuomas: That paragraph about punishment won't do, no.

Timo: Won't hold water, as the saying goes. I'm no badger, nor skunk either.

Juhani: Then behave thyself nicely and well, to escape the vengeful terror of my wrath.

Timo: But I'm no badger, nor wolf. Hey! I'm not even a bear, or a rat! Shame, for shame! Hey, hey!

Aapo: May I be allowed to say a word?

Juhani: Willingly. What didst thou wish to say?

Aapo: That neither do I approve of that punishment paragraph which thou wouldst lay down for us, but look upon it as too cruel, too savage amongst brothers.

Juhani: Oh, thou dost not approve? Thou dost not approve? Dost thou really not approve? Then tell us a wiser paragraph, as I never seem to know what is right, what wrong.

Aapo: That I won't do.

Juhani: Tell us the new, approved paragraph, thou Jukola's sage.

Aapo: Far from the honour of sage. But this ...

Juhani: The paragraph! The paragraph!

Aapo: This is ...

Juhani: The paragraph, the paragraph! Out with the wise paragraph!

Aapo: Art thou mad? Shouting there as though thy breeches were ablaze. What art thou shrieking and wagging thy head for like a garden-owl?

Juhani: The paragraph! I cry madly. The brand new and old wise paragraph! Say it and I'll listen speechless as a roach to a frog's croaking.

Aapo: This is my idea in the matter. He who scorns advice and warnings and always stirs up mischief, sowing the seed of discord among us, let him be removed from our midst, let him be driven far away.

Tuomas: Let this be the law.

Lauri: I agree to that.

Timo: I too.

Simeoni: We all agree to that together.

Juhani: Hm. That's settled then. And remember, the one who feels like getting frisky after this, it's a hare's passport in his fist, a kick in the buttocks and the open road for him. What work shall we start on tomorrow, you blackamoors? Oh I'll teach you yet.

Aapo: Still a little disgruntled; but that needn't dim our calm and bright spirits in this evening hour.

Juhani: What shall we begin on when the day dawns?

Aapo: The building of our cabin comes first of course.

Juhani: That's so. Early tomorrow let four men, each with an axe-shaft in his paw, start at their corners, these men being I myself, Tuomas, Simeoni and Aapo. The others can square the logs and roll them up to us. And as soon as the cabin and a tiny storehouse are ready, all hands to gathering grub on hunting and fishing trips. Remember that!

They finished at last their meal and lay down to rest in the shelter of the hut. Night came, a cloudy, yet calm May night. In the wilds the owl screeched hoarsely, the wild duck creaked on the lake, and now and again the sharp whistle of a bear was heard from afar. Else peace and a deep silence in nature. But to the brothers in their turf-roofed hut sleep seemed loth to come. Speechless, but tossing from side to side, they pondered over the way of the world and the instability of life.

Aapo: I believe not a single eye has closed yet.

Juhani: Timo's already asleep, but we others wriggle and twist here like sausages in a boiling cauldron. Why are we so wide-awake?

Aapo: The path of our lives has taken a sharp turn today.

Juhani: That's what makes me so uneasy, so very uneasy in my mind.

Simeoni: Dark is the state of my heart. What am I? A prodigal son.

Juhani: Hm. A lost sheep in the wilderness.

Simeoni: Leaving our neighbours and Christian fellows like this.

Tuomas: Here we are and here we stay as long as the forest yields fresh meat.

Aapo: All will turn out well if only we always set to with common-sense.

Simeoni: An owl's hooting yonder in the wilds and its cry never bodes any good. Doesn't it foretell fire, bloody battle and murder, like the old folks say.

Tuomas: To hoot in the forest is its job and has no meaning.

Eero: Here we are in our village, on Impivaara's turf-roofed farm.

Simeoni: Now the seer has changed his perch and hoots on the ridge of the height. There, once upon a time, as the tale tells us, the "Pale Maiden" used to pray forgiveness for her sins, all through the night, summer and winter.

Juhani: It was from her the place got the name Impivaara.* I once heard the story as a child, but most of it has already faded from my memory. Brother Aapo, tell us the tale again to wile away this dismal night.

Aapo: Timo snores like a man; but let him sleep in peace; I'll tell it to you others.

The following tale of the Pale Maiden was now told by Aapo to his brothers.

In the caverns of this hill there once dwelt a horrible monster, the terror and death of all humans. The two great lusts and passions of his life were: to gaze on and finger his treasures in the deepest corners of the caverns, and to drink human blood, for which he thirsted greatly. But his power to use violence ended nine paces away from the hill, and so he was forced to use trickery on his excursions. He could change himself into anything he liked; and he was seen wandering around now in the form of a beautiful youth, now in the form of a lovely maiden, according to whether it was male or female blood he wanted. Many were overcome by the hellish delight of his glance, many gave up their lives in his fearsome caverns. In this way the monster tempted victims into his power.

It was a mild summer night. A youth sat on the green sward, embracing his beloved, who rested on his bosom like a glowing rose. This was their farewell embrace, for the youth had to go on a journey and leave the friend of his heart for a time. "Maiden", said the youth, "I leave thee now, but hardly will a hundred suns have risen and set before I see thee again". And the maiden said: "Not the sun in its setting ever casts so loving a farewell glance at its world as I to my lover when he departs, nor the rising flame of day glow with a delight like to that in my eyes when I hasten to meet thee again. And all that the bright day can hold of my

---

* Impivaara — Maiden's Height.

soul is my thought of thee, and in the dim world of dreams I will walk with thee." Thus the maiden, but the youth said: "Sweetly thou speakest, but why does my soul scent evil? Maiden mine, let us swear eternal faithfulness to each other here under the face of Heaven." And they swore a sacred oath, swore before God and Heaven, and the forests and fells listened breathless to their words. And when the day broke they embraced for the last time and parted. Away hastened the youth, but the maiden roamed for long alone in the forest's twilight, remembering her beautiful lover.

As she thus wanders in the dense forest, what marvellous being is this that comes forth to meet her? She sees a young man, noble as a prince and fair as that golden morning. In his hat a plume gleams and changes colour like a flame. From his shoulders hangs a cloak, blue as the sky and like the sky, spattered with stars. His doublet is white as snow; round his waist a purple belt is tied. He looks at the maiden and from his glance streams a flaming love, and his voice echoes blissfully as he says to her: "Fear me not, sweet maid, for I am thy friend and will grant thee limitless joy if I may embrace thee but once. I am a mighty man, treasure and jewels without end are mine, and I could purchase the whole of this world. Be my bride and I will take thee to a splendid palace and seat thee beside me on a shining throne." This he said in an enticing tone and the maiden stood there dazed. She remembered the oath newly sworn and turned to go, but bent again towards the man, and a strange bewilderment possessed her mind. She turned towards the man, hiding her face with her hand as one who looks upon the sun; turned away, but looked once more upon the wondrous being. A mighty love shone thence to meet her, and suddenly the maiden sank in the prince's arms. But away sped the prince with his prey, who lay in his arms as in a swoon. Over steep hills, across deep valleys, they fled without resting, and darker and darker grew the forest around them. The maiden's heart beat uneasily and an anguished sweat ran down from her brow; for at last she noticed something beastlike, terrible, in the bewitching blaze of the being's eyes. She looked around her, and swiftly the

112

gloomy spruce hurtled past them as her bearer sped on; she looked in the youth's eyes and ghastly spasms shook her body, but a strange delight still gripped her soul.

They fared ever onward through the forests and at last saw a lofty hill pitted with dark caverns. And now, only a few paces from the hill, a horrible thing happened. The man in kingly attire suddenly became a hideous monster. Horns broke out upon his forehead, stiff bristles rustled on his neck, and the wretched maiden felt with pain his sharp claws at her breast. And there the hapless maiden shrieked, fought and struggled in her agony, but in vain. With an evil scream the monster dragged her to his deepest cave and sucked her blood to the very last drop. But now a miracle occurred; the life failed to leave the maiden's limbs; bloodless, white as snow, she went on living, like a mournful spectre of death from the land beyond. The monster saw this with amazement and used both teeth and claws to the best of his power against his victim, but to no avail. At last he decided to keep her for ever at his side in the bowels of the hill. But what service could she do him? What profit could he draw from her presence there? He put her to clean his treasures and precious stones and to pile them unceasingly before him, for he never tired of looking at them.

So for years the pallid bloodless maiden lived imprisoned in the height. But at night she was seen standing in silent prayer on its summit. Who gave her this freedom? Was it the power of Heaven? Through the nights, in storm, in rain and biting frost she stands on the brow of the hill, praying forgiveness for her sins. Bloodless, white as snow, like an image, so silent, moveless she stands, hands on breast, head bent down. Not once dares the wretched maiden lift her brow towards Heaven; but towards the church tower on the forest's distant edge her eyes are ever turned. For a secret voice still breathes hope in her ear, though no bigger than a distant spark, a thousand leagues away, does this hope gleam to her. Thus she spends her nights on the hill, and never a plaint falls from her lips, nor does her bosom ever rise or fall in sighs.

114

So wears the gloomy night, but at dawn she is snatched into the cavern by the pitiless monster.

Scarce had a hundred suns lit up the world before the maiden's lover returned merrily from his journey. But no sweet bride hastened to meet him. He asked where the fair one tarried, but no one could give him answer. He sought her everywhere by day and night, untiringly, but in vain; the maid had fled like the morning dew, leaving no trace. And at last hope left him; he forgot the joy of life, and walked yet a while on earth, a dumb shadow. Until one flaming morning the light of his eyes was dimmed in the night of death.

But the maiden lived through years of terrible length; the days in the monster's cavern, ceaselessly cleaning and piling up treasures under her cruel warder's eyes, the nights on the hill. Nor dare she raise her forehead to the heavens, but to the church tower on the forest's distant rim her eyes are ever strained. She makes no plaint, nor does her bosom ever rise or fall in sighs.

It is a light summer night. The maiden stands again on the hill, thinking of the time she has passed in cruel imprisonment; and a hundred years have gone by since she parted from her friend. Horror seizes her, her mind swoons and cold beads of sweat drop from her brow to the mossy ground as she pictures the length of those years. Then for the first time she dared to look up at the sky, and presently she saw a wondrous light approaching her like a star out of eternal distance. And it was no shooting star, but the transfigured youth, a gleaming sword in his hand. His face seemed deliciously familiar, and the maiden's heart beat quicker, for now she recognized her former bridegroom. But why the sword? It filled the maid with dread, and in a faint voice she uttered: "Is this the sword that ends at last my pain? Here is my breast, young hero, strike with thy gleaming sword and if thou canst, then grant me death, for which I have thirsted so long." Thus she spoke on the hill; but the youth brought her, not death, but the divine breath of life, which moved already round her like a perfumed morning wind. With loving glance he folded her in his arms, kissed her, and soon the bloodless maiden felt a thin stream of blood rush like the fairest torrent through her veins; her cheek glowed like a cloud at dawn and joy shone from her white forehead. Resting her curly head on her bridegroom's arm she looked up into the sunlit heights, purging her breast of a century's pain in a sigh; and the youth's fingers strayed in her curls, which fluttered prettily in the wind. Blissful was the hour of rescue and the morn of her day of deliverance. Birds warbled in the spruce on the sides of the mighty hill, and in the northeast rose the sun's glowing rim. Like to that other morning when the friends had parted on the green sward for a long time was this morn.

But now the fierce monster, his bristles wrathfully erect, clambered up the hill to drag the maiden down to his pit. But hardly had he stretched his claws towards her, when the youth's sword, swift as lightning, pierced his breast; and the black blood spouted on the hill. The maiden turned her head away at the sight and pressed her brow to the youth's breast as the monster, with a fearful cry, gave up his life and rolled off the hill. Thus was the world delivered from a terrible scourge. But in the bright embrace of a silver cloud the youth and maiden were wafted into the sky. On her bridegroom's knees the bride rested, and pressing her brow to his bosom, smiled happily. Through space they flew, and deep in the giddy depths the forest, hills and winding valleys were left behind. Until at last all faded from their sight as in a cloud of blue smoke.

Such was the tale of the Pale Maiden which Aapo told his brothers on that sleepless night in the turf-roofed hut on Impivaara clearing.

Juhani: Here's Timo waking just as our tale ends.

Timo: Why don't you sleep in peace, boys?

Juhani: Here's been a mighty telling of tales. Ay, that was the tale of the former maiden and the monster.

Simeoni: But they say this awful monster still lives. Hunters have seen him; he has only one eye that shines in the dark like a glowing cinder.

Juhani: What was it happened a few years ago to old man Kuokkala, now sleeping in the Lord? One spring, while he was out at the capercaillies' mating-time and awaited the passing of midnight by his camp-fire on this clearing, he saw over there at the foot of the hill that same glow and heard a voice that kept on asking endlessly: "Shall — a — chuck — it, shall — a — chuck — it?" It asked that many thousand times over, until the old man, one of the old sort whose heart didn't start beating for any little thing, got mad at last and answered in a fierce voice: "Chuck it then, thou Devil's food!"

Timo: But ah! no more was needed.

Juhani: Ay, tell us, Timo, what happened.

Timo: Why, in a minute a grinning skeleton comes crashing on to the old man's fire as though thrown by ten men and puts out the blaze to the very last spark. But at that the old man snatched up his rifle and toddled off out of sight of the whole hill, although, as Juhani here said, he was one of the old sort whose heart didn't start beating for every little thing.

Simeoni: We have come therefore to a town of trolls and devils.

Aapo: Here we have come and here we shall stay without fear. Even if he were still alive, the monster is now very weak, that is shown by his behaviour towards old man Kuokkala. All he could do in his spite was to put out the fire, even that only when the man gave him leave. His power was broken for ever by the young man's sword.

Juhani: I can't help feeling pity though for the maiden in the bowels of the earth, a girl with that accursed bristle-neck.

Simeoni: Why didn't she stand firm against temptation?

Juhani: Ai, my son, don't say that! How would it be, for instance, if in some flowery vale of peace a king's daughter were to meet thee, fair as a rose and flower, trip towards thee in silks, ribbons and the smell of pomades, in glittering golden frippery like a peacock, ay, a wench like that met thee and wanted to cuddle

117

and kiss thee, how would it be with thy miserable heart? I ask thee, Simeoni?

Simeoni: I'd pray for strength in belief.

Juhani: Hm.

Timo: I wouldn't let her come cuddling me and still less lip-smacking. Keep away from me, I'd say, keep, thou jade, at a distance, or I'll fetch a stick from yonder thicket and lay on until thy back is mottled tomorrow worse than a lady-bird's wing. That's what I'd do without any mercy. It'd show her.

Juhani: Oh little brother! I believe thou wouldst talk differently if thou hadst looked around thee a little more in this world, if thou hadst been, for instance, in Turku Town. That's what I've done when I drove the bulls there from Viertola Manor. I saw more than one thing to wonder at there, saw how pomp and glitter can turn the heads of sons of men. Ah thee, ah rowdy village, ah wordly life indeed! There rattles a carriage, here another, and in them sit the most fly-away fools with whiskery faces, and girls like porcelain dolls, spreading far around them a thick scent of costly oils and ointments. But look yonder! Help and save me! there, all in gilded feathers, minces a real jewel of a madam or miss, whatever she be. See her neck! White as curdled milk, cheeks red as the plague, and the eyes in her head burn like two bonfires in daylight as a true rapscallion of a lad sails up to her in a hat, shiny black tails, and peeps... well, may the Devil himself take thee! — peeps at her through a square bit of glass that gleams in the rascal's left eye. But now... by the Seven Smiths! — now they bob and bow on both sides, and see the woman purse up her mouth to a real strawberry of a mouth and twitter like a swallow on a sunlit roof, and the nob before her wag his hand and his tail, wave his hat and scrape his foot till the paving strikes sparks, ah, that was a game for you. Oh jays that ye are, thinks I to myself, a bit of a boy, standing there at the street corner, a bunch of raw hides on my shoulder and staring mouth agape at this billing.

Tuomas: Gentlefolk are fools.

118

Timo: And childish as milk-chinned brats. So they eat, too, with rags over their chests and without — dog take me — knowing enough to lick their spoons clean when they rise from table; that I have seen with my own eyes to my great surprise.

Simeoni: But at tricking and cheating a farmer they are man enough.

Juhani: True that among gentlefolk there is much that is womanish and silly, that I saw on my trip to Turku. But look you, when a simpering wench like that, in real scented oils and flying laces, comes near, it's not to say that the heart of a son of man doesn't begin to flutter. Ay, boys, the lusts of this world tempt strongly, that I noticed on my trip to Turku. And I say once again, that my heart bleeds for the maiden on yonder height. It was time for her to be saved from Hell and to sail with her friend to a haven of peace, to which may God help us also in His time. In this hope let's try to sleep now. There's still another marvellous tale about this hill, but it can keep for the present and let's all try to sleep. Go thou, however, Simeoni, and cover the glowing cinders with ashes, so that I needn't sit tinkling my fire-irons and waving a bunch of hay tomorrow, but can begin at once hammering at the end of a log like a redcrested woodpecker. Go now.

Simeoni went to do Juhani's bidding, but came quickly back with hair erect and eyes starting out of his head. Stutteringly he uttered something about a strange burning eye out there near the cart. At that the others too were startled, and with a blessing on their souls and bodies went out of the hut in a body; and their hair resembled a wind-gathered tangle in the crown of a birch. Moveless, dumb as statues they stood, staring in the direction shown by Simeoni's pointing finger. Without blinking they stared, and saw beyond mistake a weird gleam near the cart, which sometimes disappeared, but soon showed itself again. They might have deemed it the lone eye of their horse Valko, only no whiteness loomed around it, but rather something black, and there was no sound of the bell. Pondering thus, the brothers stood without moving; but at last Tuomas said in a fairly masterful voice:

Tuomas: What do you want?

Juhani: For God's sake don't talk so high and mighty to him. It's him! What shall we do now, brothers? It's him! What shall we say to him?

Aapo: I surely don't know.

Timo: Now a verse of a hymn would do good.

Juhani: Doesn't one of us know a single prayer by heart? Pray, dear brothers, out with something in God's name, whatever comes into your heads, without any bothering about suiting the text to the occasion. Read the Home Baptism Service, brothers dear, if you know nothing else.

Timo: I've known one and another stretch of the hymnbook in my time, but now it's as though a fearful prop were holding up the door of my brain.

Simeoni: The spirit won't allow thee to speak, any more than he will me.

Timo: Ay, he won't allow me.

Juhani: This is terrible!

Aapo: Terrible!

Timo: Truly terrible!

Juhani: What can we do?

Tuomas: A firm behaviour towards him is best, I believe. Let us ask him who he is and what he wants.

Juhani: Let me ask him. Who art thou? Who art thou? Who art thou and what dost want of us? — Not a word in answer.

Lauri: Lay hold of embers.

Juhani: We'll lay hold of embers from the fire and baste thee to a turn unless thou sayest thy name, thy family and thy errand.

Lauri: No, I meant let's grab the embers at once.

Juhani: If we dared.

Tuomas: One death we owe to the Lord.

Juhani: Ay, we owe the Lord one death! Embers in fist, boys!

Soon they stood in a row, burning brands for weapons in their hands. Foremost stood Juhani, his eyes round as an owl's, staring at the eye behind the cart, which with a fine glow stared back at

120

him. So stood the brothers with their fiery weapons on the nightly clearing; and a lapwing cried from the mountain spruce, the dismal wilds below them breathed heavily, and dark clouds covered the arch of the sky.

Juhani: When I say "Now, boys!" let the brands rain from our fists on to the devil's neck.

Simeoni: Let us try again if we can lay it first.

Juhani: Well thought! Let's try a little laying first. But what shall I say to him? Whisper thou to me, Simeoni, for I myself am oddly stupid just now. But whisper the words to me and I'll cast them in his face until the forest echoes.

Simeoni: Note then what I say. Here we stand.

Juhani: Here we stand!

Simeoni: Like heroes of the Faith, with flaming swords in our hands!

Juhani: Like heroes of the Faith, with flaming swords in our hands!

Simeoni: Go thy way.

Juhani: Go to thy Hell!

Simeoni: We are baptized Christians, warriors of the Lord.

Juhani: We are baptized Christians, warriors of the Lord, Christ's soldiers!

Simeoni: Even though we cannot read.

Juhani: Even though we cannot read.

Simeoni: But believe notwithstanding.

Juhani: But believe notwithstanding and trust firmly in it.

Simeoni: Go now.

Juhani: Go now!

Simeoni: Soon the cock croweth.

Juhani: Soon the cock croweth!

Simeoni: Proclaiming the light of the Lord.

Juhani: Proclaiming the light of the Lord Zebaoth!

Simeoni: But he doesn't seem to take any notice.

Juhani: But he doesn't seem to ... Ay, he doesn't care though

121

I bawl at him with the tongue of angels. May the Lord bless us, boys, for there's nothing left but to — Now, boys!

At that each threw his burning brand at the apparition, which, with the speed of lightning, dashed off at a run with a thunder of four hoofs, and the glowing cinders on its back flashed for long as it cleft the darkness. It fled the fiery skirmish, until, having reached the clearing's edge, it dared at last to stop, blowing once or twice noisily. And the brothers' ghost, the awe-inspiring monster, proved after all to be their one-eyed horse, which had lost for the time its whitish colour in the black mudpools of the morass, into which it had probably strayed and there splashed despairingly before regaining dry land. There, too, in its struggles it had loosened the bell from its neck, a matter which had greatly assisted to bewilder the brothers. This was the eye that had gleamed in the darkness behind the cart, as many an animal's eye can glow in the dark. But only after a moment or two had passed, and even then with caution, did the brothers dare to approach Valko and finally establish their error. They returned with wrathful faces to their hut, and at last as the night paled each lay in untroubled sleep.

CHAPTER 6

IT WAS ready at last, the brothers' cabin. Five fathoms was its length and three its breadth; one gable looked eastward, the other westward. Entering through the door at the cabin's eastern end, thou hadst on thy right a large bath-oven, on thy left a manger, built for Valko's use in the winter. From the threshold onward, almost to the middle of the room, a carpet of spruce branches hid the naked earth, but at the back of the room a stout floor had been made of broad planks and above this a roomy gallery. For the new cabin was to serve the brothers both as dwelling-place and sauna. About twenty paces from the house stood the store-room, joined together of small, round spruce-logs.

The brothers had thus a fine shelter against rain, storm and the frosts of winter, and an extra room for their provisions. And now they could devote their entire energies to hunting and all the divers forms of trapping. And then for the capercaillies, heath-grouse and partridges, hares, squirrels and stout-hearted badgers, and the wild duck and fish in Lake Ilvesjärvi, death was nigh. Then with the barking of the aroused Killi and Kiiski and the crash of guns, the hills and endless spruce-woods rang. The brother's guns felled too, now and again, a bushy-pelted bear; but the proper time for hunting bears had not yet come.

Came autumn with its frosty nights, and the grasshoppers, frogs and lizards died or fled to their deep hiding-places, and it was now time to trap the fox with shining irons; this art the brothers had learned from their father. Many a quickfooted Reynard then paid with his fine fur for a dainty tit-bit or two. Hares are known to tread paths in the soft snow of the forest, and across these paths the brothers stretched hundreds of brass-wire snares, to the doom of many a whitefurred denizen of the woods. They built as well a fine wolf-trap on the clearing's eastern edge. To catch wolves, they also dug a pit, enormously deep, some distance from the cabin on a dry sandy patch. A joint tempted many a hungry wolf into the strong trap; and then, when the brothers saw their prey in chancery, a din and crashing would arise in the trap on a dark autumn night. One of the brothers would stand on the slope of the fence, seeking, gun in hand, to fell the coarse-haired brute with a bullet; at his side another held a light, a blazing torch of resinous wood. The others helped Killi and Kiiski to drive the sombre-visaged, grinning beasts out of the bushes, flashing their resinous firebrands now here, now there. Great was the tumult, what with the shouting of the men, the raging of the hounds and the banging of guns, and the forest and Impivaara's pitted side rattled untiringly. Thus they would struggle; the snow would become stained, reddened more and more, fly around in a thousand directions, until the last wolf lay bleeding on the ground. And then the flaying of their prey provided work for the brothers; yet this labour was exceedingly pleasant to them. Into the pit, too, on the clearing's western edge, hastened more than one slant-eyed wolf.

It befell once that early in the morning, while the others still slept, Timo set out to examine the baited pit, whose half-fallen covering awakened hopes in him already at a distance. And having reached the pit, his joyful eye perceived indeed a grey object in the depths, a mighty wolf, which, with its muzzle pressed to the earth, lay moveless, peering up at the man. What did Timo now decide to do? Why, to kill the wolf singlehanded, and then, to the amazement of the others, enter the cabin with his hairy burden slung across his shoulder. Putting the idea into action, he fetched

124

the ladder from the cabin wall, lowered it cautiously into the pit, and with a heavy mallet in his hand stepped down the rungs, meaning to smash the brute's skull. For long he smote around him with his club, his teeth bared, but always at the empty air. The wolf's head darted nimbly right or left each time he brought down his clumsy weapon. At last he lost his club to the wolf, and could then think of nothing better than to climb up again and hurry to the cabin to report his find.

The brothers soon emerged, furnished with staves, ropes and nooses, to seize their prey. But when they reached the pit, it was empty. Along the ladder, which Timo had left behind him in the pit, their wolf had climbed neatly to safety and swiftly departed, thanking his lucky stars. This the brothers at once perceived, and, cursing and grinding their teeth, sought with enraged glance for Timo; but he was no longer present. He ran already in full flight at the forest's edge, where the pines soon hid him from view. He felt that it was unwise to stay and argue the matter. But the others howled after him, fists aloft, promising to bray him to a jelly from brow to heels, if he still dared to open the cabin door. So threatening, they left the pit ill-tempered and wroth and went back to the cabin. Meanwhile Timo wandered, a fugitive, in the forest, and soon the brothers began to regret their behaviour towards him, perceiving that the mischance was due more to his stupidity than to any evil intention. And so, already before evening, Juhani climbed to Impivaara's summit, and shouting in his mighty voice to all points of the compass, called Timo, assuring him on oath that he need not fear to return at once. He went on shouting, and after a time Timo returned, glowering angrily and rolling his eyes. Without a word he undressed, dropped down on his bed, and soon snored in deepest slumber.

Came, later, the best time for catching bears. Then the brothers took their spears, rammed huge bullets into their rifles and set out to waken the prince of the woods, where he already lay dreaming in his dark chamber deep under the snow-covered spruce. And to their rifles fell many a heavy-jowled bear, as it flung out, entraged, from its peaceful couch. Then a sharp tussle would often arise, the snow would whirl around and become stained by the flowing blood as wounds were dealt on either side. So they would fight on until at last the rough-visaged beast lay still. But the brothers, having cheerily reached home with their burden, anointed their wounds with the salve compounded of spirits, salt, powder and brimstone. They spread this over their wounds, covering the whole with yellow-brown tar.

Thus they garnered a living from the wilds and the thickets on the hills, filling their store-room with all kinds of game: wildfowl, hares, badgers and the flesh of bears. They had attended, too, to the winter provision of their old, faithful Valko. On the brink of the bog one saw a great hayrick, mown with sickles and roofed smoothly over, sufficient to tide over the winter. Nor had they forgotten to provide for the heating of their cabin during the cold period. A mighty stack of cordwood stood near the storeroom and a high pile of resinous roots, like a heap of fantastic elk-horns, rose to the cabin's eaves. Thus prepared they could look winter in its frosty beard unmoved.

It is Christmas Eve. A thaw has set in, grey clouds cover the sky and the new-fallen snow hides the hills and valleys. A faint rustling is heard from the forest; the heath-grouse sups in a catkin-covered birch, a flock of wax-wing in a glowing rowan, and a magpie, greedy maiden of the woods, carries twigs for a foundation for her coming nest. In hut and glittering manor joy and peace prevail, and so it was in the brothers' cabin on Impivaara clearing. Just outside the door is a load of straw, drawn by Valko from Viertola Manor to deck the floor in honour of Christmas. For even in the wilds the brothers would not forego that rustle of Christmas straw which was their most delightful memory from childhood's days.

From the cabin the hiss of water on the oven's heated stones is heard, and the slapping of soft bunches of birch twigs. The brothers are taking a stern Christmas bath. And when at last the scorching steam-bath was over, they stepped down from the platform, dressed themselves and rested on the beams which lined the walls in place of benches. There they sat, exuding perspiration and puffing. A blazing torch illumined the room; Valko champed oats at his manger, for his Christmas too had not been forgotten; dozing and yawning the cock sat on his rafter; Killi and Kiiski, chin on paw, slept near the oven, and on Juhani's knee the old, water-grey Jukola cat lay purring.

Timo and Simeoni began after a while to lay the supper; the others lifted in the sheaves. They opened the bindings and spead out the straw to the thickness of a span, but on the platform, where they usually spent their nights, they spread it thicker. Supper was ready at last: seven round loaves, two oaken trenchers of steaming bear's-meat and a pail of beer stood on the table. The beer they had brewed themselves, carefully recollecting their mother's methods of preparing the beverage. They had brewed it stronger, however, than ordinary peasant ale. Dark red it foamed in the pail; and wert thou to swallow a can of it, thou wouldst not fail to feel a slight dizziness in thy brain. But now they all sit at table, enjoying the meat and the foaming ale.

Aapo: Eh, but there's plenty of food piled up before us.

Juhani: Let's eat and drink, boys, for now it is Christmas, Christmas for all, for men and for beasts. Brother Timo, pour a little ale over Valko's oats. That's it, at least a whole can. No stinginess this evening, but may each get his, the horse, the dogs and the cat, as well as Jukola's merry brothers. The cock can sleep in peace and draw his rations tomorrow. Here's for you, Killi and Kiiski, a huge bit of bear's thigh, and here's thine, poor pussy. But first shake hands, narrow-eyes! Look! And now both hands! Look at our cat's tricks and admit that I'm a bit of a schoolmaster myself. He shakes hands already with both paws at once, and to do this he sits himself down like a solemn old man and shoves, the scamp, both fore-paws into my fist. Like that!

Aapo: Well, that is funny.

Tuomas: The things a man has to learn yet even in his old age.

Juhani: The learning took some time, I tell you. But I wouldn't leave the lad in peace until he could thank teacher with both paws.

127

Now he does it like a man, and schoolmaster's paid. There's a cat for you! Here! Get thy teeth into this lump of bear. And Killi and Kiiski there. Ay, ay! "Cast a stone at a man, but not at his dog." Right! But to this I would add: "Cast a stone at Juhani Jukola but not at his cat."

Eero: Help that beer-pail on over here, Juhani.

Juhani: It shall be given thee. Drink, brother, God's creation, drink, for now it's Christmas and there's plenty in the storeroom. What is lacking with us here? What should we care if all the world were to burn to dust and ashes, except Impivaara and the lands around. Here we live in clover, on our own soil, without having to bother about ill-tempered neighbours. Here it is good for us to be. The forest is our meadow, our field, our mill and our nest everlasting.

Timo: And our meat-larder.

Juhani: Just so: It is good to be here. Thanks, Lauri, for the way thou foundest us to escape from the markets of the world. Here is freedom and peace. I ask once more: what would we care if golden flames were to burn down the whole of this world, if only the northern end of Jukola's lands and its seven sons were saved.

Timo: If a forest fire once started to lick up the world, it's dust and ashes Jukola's northern end would be too, and its seven sons into the bargain.

Juhani: That I well know. But sithee, a man can think what he wants, think himself master of the whole world or a creeping dung-beetle. Look you, he can think God, devils, angels, all mankind and the beasts of the sea, air and land dead; think the world, Hell and Heaven vanished like a bunch of tow in a fire, and a darkness fallen in which no crowing cock ever greets God's morn. So the thought of a man can fly down here, and who can cast nets in its path?

Timo: Who knoweth the plan of the world? Not the child of man, who is daft and silly as a bleating goat. But it's best to take he day as it comes, let it go as it goes, whether it lead to weal or woe. We're here and that's all.

Juhani: What's wrong with us being here. What is lacking?

Timo: "Not the grace of God nor bird's milk." The storeroom's full and the cabin warm. Here too we can sprawl on straw.

Juhani: Here we sprawl like bull-calves on rustling straw. We can bathe whenever we like, whenever the idea comes into our heads, and eat when we're hungry. But now we are sated. So there's nothing else for us to do but to bless our bellies and clear the table.

Simeoni: Wait till I've said grace and sung a verse on top of that.

Juhani: Never mind this time. Why didst thou not do it before the meal? Go thou, Eero-boy, as the youngest, and draw ale from the cask.

Simeoni: Wouldst thou forbid a verse of a hymn in honour of Christmas Eve?

Juhani: We're no singers, brother mine. Let us sing and pray in our hearts, which is after all the most pleasing offering to God. But here comes the pail again, bubbling and frothing like Kyrö Rapids. Ta, lad, ta! Here goes! Take a swig, brother Tuomas, a real man's swig.

Tuomas: I'll soon do that.

Juhani: That's how a man drinks. Swigs like that will soon turn our throats into true chorister's throats.

> Well fared the men of olden days,
> The wilds did not dismay 'em.
> Driftwood kept their fire ablaze,
> Their ale the river gave 'em.

Just so. But now our drink is the brown juice of the barley, our fuel cordwood and resinous roots, and under us is a soft bolster of straw, a prime wrestling-mat fit for kings and grand dukes. A word, brother Tuomas. Brother Aapo once backed thy power and

strength as mightily greater than mine, but that I'd scarce like to
believe. What if were to try a throw? Let's try!

Simeoni: Let us behave! and spare this shining straw until
tomorrow at least.

Juhani: Now jollity is its height, the "eve is the height of the
holiday"; and straw has got to turn to litter anyhow. Does the
idea please Tuomas?

Tuomas: There'd be no harm in trying.

Juhani: Cross-buttock wrestling!

Tuomas: I'm ready.

Juhani: Let's set to, let's set to!

Aapo: Easy, lad! Let Tuomas get a firm grip of the waistband
of thy trousers.

Juhani: He may, he may.

Eero: Juho, what art thou grinning and rolling thy eyes for, like
a bull on a bench? Oh brother! See thou dost not bring shame
on thyself.

Aapo: All clear. Whose is the first throw?

Juhani: Let Tuomas have it.

Tuomas: Let the older brother have it.

Juhani: Stand firm then.

Tuomas: I'll try.

Juhani: Dost thou stand, dost stand?

Tuomas: I'll try.

Aapo: Hallelujah, boys! That's the way, like that! Ye fight
like heroes of the Faith. Juho wrestles and strains like Israel himself and "Tuomas stands an oak unbending."

Eero: "Hearing Aapo's gab unending." But look at Juhani's
mouth, it'll terrify thee. Ah! if I were to thrust even a bar of steel
between his teeth now — snap! it'd be in two like a shot. I'm
terrified. I'm terrified!

Aapo: Only a bout between men. The very beams rise and fall
beneath us.

Eero: Like the pedals of an organ; and Tuomas's slippers plough
the floor like heavy wooden ploughs.

130

Aapo: It's not with fingers of milk they're stroking each other. Lord! if this bout were on yonder hill, their heelplates would strike sparks from the rock.

Eero: Real golden sparks would fly into the forest and there'd be a jolly forest-fire. But Tuomas still stands.

Tuomas: Well, hast thou jerked to thy content?

Juhani: Try a throw thyself.

Tuomas: I'll try. But now look out, for the floor's going to whirl.

Eero: Remember, remember, Juho!

Aapo: That was a throw.

Eero: That was a swipe from "Haman's mallet", a blow from "Heaven's fiery hammer."

Timo: And there lies Juhani like a sack of malt.

Eero: Poor Jussi-boy!

Timo: 'Tis what he called himself when a little boy.

Aapo: One ought to know however, how to throw a man. Remember, Tuomas, a human body is not made of iron, but of flesh and blood.

Timo: Ay, though it does wear trousers.

Tuomas: Did I hurt thee?

Juhani: Look to thyself.

Tuomas: Get up.

Juhani: I'll get up and show thee a man's strength at pulling the bar. That's the game for measuring strength.

Tuomas: Eero, bring a stick from yon corner. Here, Juhani.

Juhani: Here I am. And now hind-paw against hind-paw and claws round the bar.

Aapo: When I yell, then pull, but without the smallest jerk. The bar over your toes, right above the toes, not an inch over on either side. Now, boys!

Timo: Juho flies up like a chip.

Aapo: Even pity wouldn't help him there.

Juhani: Go and draw ale, Timo.

Timo: Thou'rt limping, brother.

131

Juhani: Draw ale, thou accursed lout! Dost hear me, or shall I clout thy ear?

Tuomas: Did I hurt thy foot?

Juhani: Why worry about that? Look to thy own foot. What does it matter if the heel did chance to come off my boot in the wrestling like a slice of turnip. But look to thyself, thou. It seems thou winnest at wrestling and pulling the bar, but let's fight.

Aapo: We have nothing to do with fighting now.

Juhani: Yes we have, if we want.

Tuomas: I don't want.

Juhani: Thou durst not.

Aapo: Know that wrestling is play.

Simeoni: I know it for play that often gives rise to fighting and murder.

Juhani: May Tuomas win, but no other can overthrow Juhani. That I swear and will show man by man through the whole company. A little bout, Aapo! Will thy waistband hold, will it hold?

Aapo: Madcap without the slightest cause! Wait, wait, and we'll wrestle properly.

Juhani: Bright lightning!

Aapo: Wait, say I. Now, try now.

Eero: Juho dances the polka like a true lad, even if he does limp.

Juhani: What dost thou say now, brother Aapo?

Aapo: That I'm down under thee.

Juhani: Step up to thy number, Simeoni.

Simeoni: Not for a thousand crowns would I break the holy festival.

Juhani: All honour to the Christmas festival! A bit of innocent wrestling won't harm it, if only our minds are joyful and our hearts pure. One try, Simeoni!

Simeoni: Why wilt thou tempt me.

Juhani: One bout!

Simeoni: Thou Satan!

132

Aapo: Peace be with him, Juhani, peace.

Juhani: No harm in trying. Now then, one single tug at thy waistband.

Simeoni: Get thee to Hell, evil spirit. I admit thee the winner.

Tuomas: I'll believe that when I see it. I don't think Simeoni's sinews are of veal either.

Juhani: Well, let him try. Then we'll see whether they're veal or black, stringy bear's-meat.

Aapo: Leave him in peace and let the next man, more willing for a bout, step forward. Brother Timo, always a stout fellow!

Juhani: Wilt thou?

Aapo: Into the wind, Timo! Thou hast never been a mammy's boy.

Tuomas: Never, but always hearty like a man in his own home. I'll never forget the fight he put up in that matchless tussle with the Toukola men. Before he knew it he had got a grand bash on the head, but caring little for that, he turned gravely round, snatched the staff out of the man's hand and hit him back on the skull — and snap went the staff. Broke in two like a flash and down flopped the man like an empty sack. That was Timo Jukola's work. And I know he's still game to meet any man.

Timo: Come on, lad.

Juhani: Just what I want. But let me too get hold of thy flounces. Now I'm ready.

Aapo: Let Timo have first heave.

Juhani: All right. Then I'll have time to get my breath back.

Timo: How's that?

Juhani: Nay, my son.

Tuomas: A fairly stiff heave, Timo, thou brave Timo! But canst better it?

Juhani: We don't go as easily as that.

Tuomas: Timo, canst better it?

Timo: I ought to be able to. What does this say?

Juhani: "We don't go so easily, said the beggar at Hyvämäki."

Aapo: Once more, Timo.

Tuomas: Canst better it?

Timo: I ought to be able to. How's that?

Juhani: "We don't go so easily, said the beggar at Hyvämäki."

Tuomas: But it was a jerk that made itself felt.

Eero: Nothing to be afraid of; brother Juhani's voice only shook the least bit, but quite innocently.

Juhani: Upright I stand.

Tuomas: Once more, Timo.

Timo: We'll try, we'll try.

Juhani: Wait a bit! my trousers are falling!

Timo: "But now, said Kaitaranta!"

Juhani: My trousers are falling! Dost hear me!

Timo: How's that, brother!

Aapo: Is Juhani lying there again, kissing the floor?

Eero: And puffing like a bull. But it is well "he can get his breath back again."

Timo: Under me the lad lies like a wet slipper.

Tuomas: But his trousers played him a mean trick.

Aapo: That must be said in truth's name. Juhani's own trousers rose against their master and joined themselves with Timo.

Eero: That's true. So trousers off and a new start.

Simeoni: Hold thy jaw now, jackdaw! Or I'll hit thee on the nose. Hast thou not had enough of this Hell's game?

Eero: Well, let's make it a heavenly game then. Trousers and shirts off, and wrestle like two angels in the fields of Paradise.

Tuomas: Why art thou sitting on his neck, Timo?

Timo: If I had a faggot now I'd lay it along his buttocks till the room echoed.

Aapo: Why so? This is wrestling, not a fight.

Eero: Is Timo angry?

Timo: Not at all, not at all, all I say is, if I had a faggot or a round stick, I'd lay it smacking along his buttocks.

Tuomas: Let him get up.

Timo: Get up, God's creation.

Juhani: I'll get up, and know that when I have fastened my trousers it'll be thy turn to lie down and somewhat quicker than I did. I, poor boy, stumbled down by accident, which thou didst hasten to turn to thy profit, lout, boottree!

Aapo: No anger! I know that he hardly noticed thy trouser-accident before the throw was over. He did it in the heat of the scrimmage, the poor boy.

Juhani: He knew quite well, the bull-badger. But you are all like ravens at my neck. He didn't know! Didn't I roar in a loud voice: wait a bit, my trousers are falling? But he never cared, but tore with teeth and nails like a cat. Stand and burn! I'll teach thee to use a man's flabby trousers to his undoing another time, oh I'll teach thee.

Timo: I, poor boy, did it in the heat of the scrimmage.

Juhani: I'll teach thee, when I've hoisted up my trousers and pulled my belt tight as a wedged hoop.

Timo: I give a fig for the whole wrestle; once I've won, I've won, and there's nothing more to grumble at. What have trousers to do with it? In wrestling it's the man who wrestles, not his trousers or leggings or snow-socks.

Juhani: Waistbands in fist and breast to breast again! Stand and burn!

Timo: Shall I join him in this childish job?

Eero: How can he ask? Go, God's creation, while thou hast the chance.

Simeoni: Don't go, say I.

Eero: Don't go if thou fearest and tremblest.

Juhani: Fear and trembling won't help him now, but he's got to join in a new tussle and this very God's moment.

Eero: Have mercy on him, Juhani, have mercy!

Timo: Why, Eero, why? Let's try another bout then, one or two. Seize hold!

Juhani: So, my boy.

Tuomas: Have a care, Juhani!

Aapo: Carefully! That's how two hungry hawks might fight.

Simeoni: Fighting, pure fighting!

135

Aapo: Sensibly, Juhani!

Simeoni: Oh you monsters, you monsters!

Eero: Don't lame thy brother!

Simeoni: Aha! Aha! now Eero turns pale. Here's the fish thou hast angled for.

Tuomas: Juhani!

Simeoni: The whole cabin's breaking up, you wild beasts and devils!

Juhani: Vot, lad, says the Russian! Well, why art thou lying there and peering up at the ceiling?

Timo: Thou winnest me now, but wait till time has worked on us a bit. Thou wilt grow older and smaller, while I fill out and become stronger.

Juhani: Even the world will wear out once and end, let alone a sinful human being. Time wears us all down, brother mine. But get up and gulp a swig of ale into thy face and admit there's an ounce or two less strength in thee than in me.

Timo: That was seen. There I lay on all fours and thou atop o'me like a raving bear.

Juhani: Here's to us all, my bonny boys! I am second therefore in the hosts of Jukola in the matter of strength. True, Lauri and Eero are still untried, but may they know that there'd be a buzzing in their ears if it came to a trial; and Simeoni has admitted himself the weaker. But not one of Jukola's brothers is a little-finger man, that I guarantee. Let even fifty Toukola men come at us, fist against fist. Five barrels I can carry on my back, and Tuomas a bit more; five barrels if some one piles them up on my back.

Tuomas: I'd like to see Lauri and Eero wrestle in deadly earnest.

Aapo: Truly it would be a sight. One solemn and calm as a thaw in winter, the other small as a dwarf, but swift and keen as lightning. Into the wind, boys, and we'll see a scrap between a weasel and a buck-hare. Mind, I'm not calling thee a hare for thy bravery, there's no call for that, nor for thy walk, for Lauri steps out like blacksmith Könni's hoer — whose feet and hoe were

136

moved by a trickly clockwork in its belly — but to me the tussle would just look like one between a big jack-hare and a weasel.

Juhani: One breasting, boys, one breasting or a buttock-throw

Lauri: What use is a bout with Eero? You can't even get a proper grip of him, but there he wriggles between your legs like a cat, scratching and squeezing your middle so that you can hardly draw breath. He did that when we wrestled in Aro Meadow last autumn, and who won and who lay under, was beyond anyone to say. Why should I wrestle him again.

Eero: I wasn't a hair stronger than thee. Believe me if thou canst.

Lauri: I believe thee, knowing thee to be weaker.

Juhani: Let honest wrestling prove it.

Lauri: Why should I try a second time with him.

Simeoni: Let's go to bed now, you madmen.

Juhani: Nights are many, but Christmas comes but once a year, so let us rejoice now. Rejoice, thou Christmas chamber, rejoice the whole land of Israel! This night, this very second a great miracle has happened in Babylon Town. Let us rejoice! What game shall we play? Blind Man's Bluff? Slaughter the Pig or Prod the Cobbler?

Simeoni: There now! Are we to start tumbling about like wilful brats? Go away!

Juhani: A young unmarried fellow's life is a dance. Isn't it, Timo?

Timo: He-he-he!

Juhani: Isn't it?

Timo: It's like that, surely.

Eero: Just so, Jack-darling.

Juhani: Said the fox to the rabbit. Right! This life's all right; it's jolly sometimes and makes a man's heels itch. Let's dance a Russian jig; I'm quite a master at that. Look!

Aapo: Would our ale have made thee drunk?

Juhani: Empty three cans of it into thy mug and see if thou

137

dost not notice a blaze like in thy attic. But sing, Eero, while Jussi-boy dances. Out with it.

Eero: What sort's wanted?

Juhani: Any sort, so long as it rings and roars. Out with it, yell till the bottom logs rise up! Sing, thou he-badger's whelp, sing while I dance, while I buck like a goat, buck right up to the ceiling. Sing!

Eero: I'll try my best:

"Let us carol and rejoice,
Christmastide is here;
Now the vats are full of ale,
Full the tankard and the pail;
Full of ale, full of ale,
Full the tankard and the pail.

At the Anjanpelto Fair
Gin we drank like water,
With the money for the bull
A wedding-ring we bought her.
Bought her, bought her;
With the money for the bull
A wedding-ring we bought her.

Jussi, Pussi, Jukola's Jussi!"

Aapo: Shut up, Eero, and don't aggravate him.

Juhani: Go on singing, I won't get mad; keep on singing, that I needn't dance without music.

Eero: "Jussi, Pussi, Jukola's Jussi!
Jussi, Jassi, floury-snout,
Dusts the litter in the sty..."

138

Timo: He-he-he! Oh what daft words thou singest.
Juhani: Keep on singing, keep on. I won't be angry.
Eero: "Jussi, Jassi, floury-snout", I sing and snap my fingers at thee.

"Dusts the litter in the sty,
Sings the pigs a lullaby!
Jussi, Pussi, Jukola's Jussi!

Ida walked along the strand,
Wrote upon the wave-washed sand
The name of her true-love,
The name of her true-love.

When I heard my sweetheart's voice
The first time I did meet her,
I seemed in Heaven to rejoice,
No seraph there was sweeter,
I seemed in Heaven to rejoice,
No seraph there was sweeter.

Jussi, Pussi, Jukola's Jussi!

Dost thou remember
The times we have rambled
And merrily gambolled?
Fra-la la-la- laa!
The times we have rambled
And merrily gambolled?
Fra-la la-la- laa!

Jussi, Pussi, Jukola's Jussi!

Never, poor Aato
Blame little Jussi,
For well thou knowest
There's strength in our Jussi.

Jussi sits in jail,
A goatskin for his tail,
All of us brothers
Can tell the same tale.
Fra-la la-la laa!

Woe me, poor madcap fellow,
Why was I ever born?
A farm have I at home —
And sit in jail forlorn.
A farm have I at home —
And sit in jail forlorn."

Juhani: That's the way! So! There's no fetters on this fellow.
Go on singing!

Eero: "Jussi, Pussi, Jukola's Jussi!
Jussi, Jassi, floury-snout,
Dusts the litter in the stye,
Sings the pigs a lullaby.
Jussi, Pussi, Jukola's Jussi!"

Isn't that enough?
Juhani: More! This is Karja-Matti's wedding. More! More!
Karja-Matti's wedding!
Simeoni: Even the cock crows wrathfully at this godless medley
and din.
Juhani: Hold thy jaw, cock, and stop that clucking.
Tuomas: Enough of that, Juhani.
Aapo: That Turk's dance will be the death of thee.
Juhani: This is a Russian jig, isn't it, Eero?
Eero, This is a Jussian jig.
Juhani: All right then, we'll have a score or so more hops of
this Jussian jig.
Simeoni: Thou wild fellow!

140

Timo: Look, look! He-he-he! Well, may the Old Un take me!

Juhani: Out of the way! Or I'll tread thee to paste like a cossack's horse a drunken fair-goer. Hih!

Aapo: The loose end of his belt is in a fair lather there behind. It's bouncing, it is; bouncing up, bouncing down, walloping his back and his buttocks in turns. Oh thou!

Juhani: La-la laa laa! That was a dusting, he-he! That was the second time I danced in my life. The first was at Karja-Matti's wedding where there were none of the female sex except three old hags, but a rare crowd of men. But sithee, after Matti had brewed us a couple of mugs of juicy coffee-punch, nothing would do for us but to start hammering the floor-beams, we men amongst ourselves; and didn't the sinful earth sigh under us. The poor old women were thankful to be let off such a kneading; we'd have danced 'em to tatters. Lord what a time! But now clothes off to our shirts, and up on to the gallery. We're not, in any case, going to close our eyes just yet, but around a foaming pail of ale and in the light of a resinous torch will relate merry tales and legends up there in the gallery's warmth.

They undressed and filling their pail once again with ale, climbed on to the gallery. There, all in their shirts, they sat amidst their straw in the steaming heat. Busily the foaming pail went round from man to man, and in a crack in the wall a pine torch burned with a golden flame. Then a thought came suddenly into Juhani's brain and words fell from his lips which were to prove their undoing.

Juhani: Here we can truly roast ourselves like sausages in a straw-filled oven, and it is the hot stones of our fireplace that give us our warmth. Eero, pour a can of ale on the oven and we'll see what barley juice steam tastes like.

Tuomas: What silly trick would that be?

Juhani: A grand trick. Do as I say.

Eero: I wish to obey my master.

Juhani: A couple of cans of ale on the oven!

141

Tuomas: Not a drop! If I hear the tiniest hiss from there, unhappy the man who caused it.

Aapo: Don't let us waste a fine drink.

Timo: We can't afford to live in beer steam, not we.

Juhani: It would be jolly to taste it.

Tuomas: I forbid it firmly.

Juhani: It'd be jolly to taste it. Winning just now in the wrestling has lifted Tuomas's crest-feathers a lot and he now thinks he can rule this house as he wants. Remember though that the bitter spleen, once it really swells, gives its lad the strength of seven men in a fight. Be that as it may, mine eyes are surely not inclined to wait on thee.

Simeoni: The fruits of wrestling, all fruits of wrestling.

Juhani: Let's hear it splash, Eero, I'll answer for the deed and defend its doer.

Eero: It's the master's command, and I must obey; else there's a hare's passport in my fist on Christmas Eve of all nights.

Then Eero, clenching his teeth and pursing his lips in a cunning grin, hastened to obey Juhani's will, and soon a splash was heard from the oven, swiftly followed by a fierce hissing. Enraged, Tuomas flew up and dashed like an eagle at Eero, but Juhani too was quick to defend his younger brother. Whereupon a general scrimmage arose, in the confusion of which the burning torch was thrown down from the gallery on to the floor. There, unnoticed by the brothers, it soon set the straw in a lively blaze. Like a ring on the surface of a pool spreads evenly and rapidly in all directions, so the bright circle of fire on the floor grew. Ever higher it rose; it already licked the floor of the gallery before the inhabitants of the room became aware of the danger beneath them. But they perceived it too late to save more than their own lives and those of the animals in the cabin. Flames already billowed over a wide area and great was the distress and commotion. There was a general dash to the door, on the opening of which men, dogs, cat and cock charged out almost simultaneously with a fearful din. It looked as though the cabin had spewed them from its smoking maw on to the snow-

142

clad ground, where they then stood coughing as for a wager. Last to come out was Lauri, leading by a halter Valko, who would otherwise probably have perished in the flames. For already a devouring fire poured out of the narrow window-openings, and soon from both door and roof. Enwrapped in flames, Impivaara's stout cabin glowed. But on the snow-covered ground stood its garrison, destitute; even the charcoal-burner's hut which had first given them shelter had been razed to the ground, and the store-room was built loosely as a magpie's nest. There the brothers lingered, and their only protection against wind and frost was a short shirt of tow. Not even a cap for their heads or birch-bark slippers for their feet had they had time to snatch from the flames. Of all the property in the cabin there remained only the guns and birch-bark knapsacks, which had been taken into the storeroom when the brothers began their bath. In the snow the brothers stood, all with their backs towards the roaring flames, lifting and warming in turns their right and left feet; and caressed alternately by fire and snow, their feet were red indeed, red as the webs of a goose.

They enjoyed the last gift their cabin still had to give them, enjoyed the warmth of the fire; and this fire was immense. The flames rose violently on high, a shimmering light spread everywhere, and the mossy spruce on the crest of the hill smiled as sweetly as in the glow of the rising sun. From the stack of resinous roots smoke, thick and pitch-black, rose to the clouds, rolling in dark balls under the vault of the sky. But on the clearing and around it light dwelt; a ruddy day reigned in the heart of the winter night, and astounded at this phantom light birds gazed down with staring eyes from the branches of the snow-clad trees as the stoutly-built cabin on Impivaara turned into cinders and dust. Scratching their heads in rage and sorrow the brothers stood around, all with their backs turned to the fire and lifting the soles of their feet in turns towards its grateful warmth. Gradually, however, their bonfire waned, collapsed at last in a rain of embers, and the night air filled with thousands of crackling sparks. Terror-stricken, the brothers then became aware that the sky was clearing and the wind

143

veering from south to north. The weather was changing from a thaw to a frost.

Aapo: We were saved from the fire, only to fall victims to the frost. Look! The sky clears and already the north wind blows cold. Brothers, our danger is terrible.

Juhani: Death and curses! Who did this?

Tuomas: Who! Thou food for fire, thou askest who? Were I to do right now, I'd dash thee to roast in yon fiery ash-heap.

Juhani: Never could one Tuomas do such a feat, never. But accursed be the man who brought this Hell's night upon us!

Tuomas: He curseth himself.

Juhani: Accursed be that man, namely, Tuomas Jukola.

Tuomas: Say that a second time.

Juhani: Tuomas, son of Juhani Jukola, is the cause of all this.

Aapo: Tuomas!

Simeoni: Juhani!

Lauri: Softly!

Timo: Now you shall not fly at each other, you won't be let, my bantams. Ay, ay, let's all keep quiet now and warm ourselves in brotherly fashion.

Simeoni: Ye godless!

Aapo: No anger and quarreling when a miserable death awaits us.

Tuomas: Who is to blame, who is to blame?

Juhani: I am innocent.

Tuomas: Innocent! Holy fire! I'll eat thee alive!

Aapo: Softly, softly!

Simeoni: For God's sake, softly!

Aapo: Guilty or innocent, may that be left undecided now, seeing that only haste can save us. Our cabin is in ashes and we stand almost naked in the snow. For what am I to call this rag of a tow-shirt? One good thing is that our guns and ammunition were in yon storeroom; for now we have need of weapons. Teerimäki echoes with the howling cry of wolves.

Tuomas: What shall we do then?

144

Aapo: All I can think of is to hasten to Jukola, hasten for pale Death's sake. Two can always ride on Valko and the others follow running. Let us do that: run and ride turnabout on horseback. With the aid of our horse we can thus avoid having to tread snow the whole way and with God's help we can still maybe be saved.

Juhani: Our feet will be one single turnip-stew before we stand in Jukola, in the warmth of a cordwood blaze.

Simeoni: Yet there lies our only hope. So let us hurry. The wind grows keener and the roof of the sky is already clearing. Let's hurry!

Eero: Our death has come.

Juhani: There go Jukola's seven stout brothers!

Simeoni: Our danger is awful, but strong is the Lord on high. Let us hurry!

Tuomas: Guns and knapsacks out of the storeroom!

Juhani: A night of terror. Here a ringing frost threatens us, yonder the hungry howling wolves.

Timo: We are in danger, both Valko and ourselves.

Juhani: Ours is the greater danger. A naked man, I have heard, is a very tasty joint for a wolf in the winter.

Timo: And a man and a pig, I have heard, taste the same, and it's well-known that a pig is a wolf's favourite dish in winter. We've a hard knot before us; that no one can deny.

Juhani: What are we to do?

Aapo: Rush off to Jukola like sorcerer's arrows through the night before the frost turns fiery and heats our blood to ice with its burning coldness. Away to Jukola over shrieking Teerimäki! We are armed against the wolves, but not against rimebearded, old King Frost.

Tuomas: Here's the guns and bags. Gun on shoulder now and knapsack on back every man of you, and two up on horseback, while we others pound on behind best we can. But hurry, hurry, for our everlasting souls!

Juhani: The north turns bright and the stars shine. Hii, haa! But let's hurry.

Aapo: Tomorrow we can fetch what goods and chattels the fire has left us; we'll come tomorrow and fetch the cock too and the cat. This night they'll be warm enough beside yon hot ash-heap. But Killi and Kiiski can take the road with us like faithful comrades. Where are they?

Tuomas: I can't see them. Hush! let us listen.

Eero: They're off galloping far away by now. Yonder you can hear them barking behind the hill.

Tuomas: They're chasing a lynx that I suppose has passed close to the cabin, giving a scent to the dogs. Well, let them hunt as they like; we've got to forget them now and hasten off on our stern journey.

Juhani: Right! For Life and Death are now at each other's throats like two he-bears.

Aapo: Let's put forth all our strength now!

Juhani: All the strength of our souls and bodies down to the marrow.

Tuomas: Remembering that the most miserable death awaits us.

Juhani: Black death threatens us from two points. Hii, haa! its a frozen snout now or guts on the ground if this lad isn't soon on slippery straw before a fire. One of these three will have to happen before the hour is out. But dawdling here won't help, not in the least, so clenching my teeth I'll go now even through icebergs, miles thick.

Simeoni: Let us try in God's name, with His help.

Juhani: With His help. What can man that is born of woman do down here with his own strength alone? Let us be of good cheer.

Eero: Let us start off without any more delay.

Juhani: And without any fear. Let's go now!

Tuomas: All ready then. Get up on horseback, Eero and Simeoni, and start riding towards Jukola, but so that we who trot on foot after you through the snow are always at the old nag's heels.

So they set out on their journey: naked, clad only in towshirts

146

and each with his knapsack on his back and a gun on his shoulder or in his hand. In such fashion they set out on the wintry night road, fleeing from the frost which attacked them from the waste lands of the north. It came not, however, wearing its most frightful aspect; the weather on this occasion was not yet at its severest. True, the brow of Heaven cleared at times, but the sailing clouds soon hid it again, and the north wind blew tempered. The brothers, too, were friends of old with the cold, with skins hardened in many shrieking frosts; and earlier, as wilful children, they had often trampled the snowdrifts for hours in their bare feet. Notwithstanding, this journey from Impivaara to Jukola was terrible, exceedingly terrible to them. Hotly they dashed onward, with terror in their hearts. Foremost, on Valko's back, rode Eero and Simeoni, and the others followed them running, treading the backwoods' snow, which whirled around their feet. But on Impivaara clearing, near the glowing oven, sat the cat and the cock, melancholily staring at the waning embers.

Towards the village the brothers hastened; Sompio Bog already lay behind them, and they approached Teerimäki Hill, whence the ghastly howling of wolves could still be heard. In a thicket of young spruce, between the bog and Jaakko Seunala's clearing, the riders were changed: Eero and Simeoni climbed down and two others hastened to replace them. Then without delay they continued their journey; they dashed along the crest of the heath, across the Viertola road and onward through a wide, humming pinewood. And at last rocky Teerimäki drew nigh, and suddenly the multiple chorus of the wolves was stilled. Soon they stood on the summit of the hill and gave their steed a breather; the riders again dismounted and were quickly replaced by others. A while yet they stood on the snow-covered rock; the north wind blew, the dome of the sky cleared again for a moment, and the head of the Great Bear showed midnight to have passed.

But having rested, they hurried down the smooth hill track, and when this ended entered a dark sprucewood, and a cheerless scene spread around them. The moon looked palely down, owls shrieked, and here and there in the forest's sombre depths weird phantoms stood, resembling in shape gigantic bears; these were the upward-pointing mossy roots of fallen spruce-trees. Immovable, like frozen ghosts, these bear-shaped images stared at the strange procession which sped swiftly by. Immovable they stared, but between and around them a frightening liveliness soon made itself apparent in the forbidding forest. Hungry wolves circled around the brothers, approaching closer and closer. Now ahead and now behind, now flickering across the path, now on both sides of the road, their loping run could be seen. Furious, thirsting for blood, they followed the nightly refugees from Impivaara; and with a crackling sound dry branches broke snapping from the spruce-roots. Quivering and snorting the affrighted Valko ran; and the man who rode in front could scarce restrain him from breaking into a wild gallop. And ever bolder waxed the wolves. Panting in a bloodthirsty manner they flashed by close to the men; and now to the right, now to the left, the gun of one of the brothers would bang in an attempt to scare them. This, however, did not seem able to drive them far away.

They came to Kiljava's open, fire-ravaged heath, where the trunks of withered pines stood dotted here and there, seats for hawks and owls. And now the fierceness of the wolves became alarming, and the men's danger grew. Tuomas and Timo happened just then to be on horseback, but those who ran on foot behind suddenly halted and fired almost simultaneously an angry volley at their foe, who, alarmed by this measure, now retreated a space. The men dashed onward again; but soon the pursuing pack of wolves rustled once more around them, and the danger was greater than ever. Then Tuomas reined in his steed, saying in a loud voice: "Let the man whose gun is empty load it at once, and let him hurry like fire and lightning!" So shouting, he dismounted and ordered Timo to hold Valko firmly. The brothers now stood and loaded, and they felt not the cold, neither in their feet nor in any part of their bodies. The wolves too halted, about fifty paces away, and tossing their tails lustfully, stared at the men with avid eyes. And

148

naked of clouds shone the heavens, whence a bright moon now looked down on the heath.

Tuomas: Are the guns loaded?

Aapo: It's done. What is thy purpose?

Juhani: All together again!

Tuomas: Not if our lives are dear to you. Someone's gun must always be loaded; remember that. Lauri, thou hast the steadiest hand and the keenest eye, come up abreast of me.

Lauri: Here I stand. What wouldst thou?

Tuomas: A hungry wolf will eat even his bleeding brother. If we could only bring about this, it would be the saving of us. Let us try. Lauri, we'll both aim at the same time, but you others must spare your bullets. Now, Lauri, aim as carefully as an eagle and blaze away when I say now.

Lauri: I'm ready.

Tuomas: Now.

Both fired at the same second, and the wolves fled at a gallop. One lingered, however, on the scene, trying hard to follow the others at a crawl, but without success. And onward with all their strength the brothers hastened once more: six men running on foot, Timo riding on ahead alone. And thus passed a few moments. Soon the wolves halted in their flight, and returning, again flitted swiftly towards the nocturnal wayfarers. The snow foamed around them and Kiljava's naked heath drummed as they came on in a body. At fiery speed they drew level with their comrade who squirmed in his blood; they charged already past him, but turned quickly round as the tempting smell of blood was borne to their nostrils. Round they spun: tails wagged, the snow boiled and fire flashed in the night from eyes of lust and greed. Then, grinning fearfully, the whole pack sprang at their wounded brother; and on the heath arose a grim struggle and a din such that one might have believed the pillars of the earth would collapse crashing down. The ground quaked and the snow was turned to a grisly pulp as former comrades tore the son of the woods into pieces, the wolf whose blood Tuomas's and Lauri's well-aimed bullets had set flowing. Then

149

silence reigned again on the nightclad heath. Only a soft panting and the snapping of bones was heard, as with bloody faces and flashing eyes the brutes rent and devoured their victim.

But the brothers already fared far from their terrible foe; and delightfully had the murderous din of the wolves on Kiljava echoed in their ears; for them it was the sweet and ravishing message of salvation. Soon they had reached Kuttila's big meadow, round which the road made a detour over hilly ground. But to gain time they decided to cut straight across the meadow. Under their combined weight the fence gave and fell, and Valko, again with two of the brothers on his back, stepped over it, and urged on by the men's switches, set off at a trot over the meadow's smooth surface. And without delay, those of the brothers whose turn it was to tread the snow, hurried after. Across the meadow a winter track led to the village, and just at that movement a number of travellers, in three sleighs, were moving along it. But great was the alarm of both men and horses when they perceived the brothers making towards them from the north. In the light of the moon they saw seven men in their shirts, with guns on their shoulders and accompanied by a horse, hastening in their direction; and they believed a host of wicked demons from Impivaara's caves was attacking them. The tumult and din in the meadow was immense. Mad with fright, the travellers' horses galloped hither and thither, while the men shouted or prayed, cursed or raved in ringing voices. But the brothers cast hardly a glance at this confusion, only ran madly across the meadow towards Jukola, and the snow was cleft in smoke before them. They reached the fence on the other side, and under their united pressure this too gave with a crash, and soon they were all out on the hilly road again.

This night was to them of a truth a fearful and terrible night. Stoutly they ran, with twinkling feet and panting wildly, while doubt glared from their wooden-stiff glance, which was ever directed towards their former home. So without a word they dashed onward, and swiftly the snow-covered ground retreated beneath them. Until at last, having reached the crest of a hilly field, they

150

saw in the pale moonlight Jukola standing on its hillside, and almost with one voice the cry: "Jukola, Jukola!" broke from their lips. They ran on down the hill, jumped the ditch like bewinged demons, and staggering uphill again, stood on the threshold of the closed door of the farmhouse. Time to knock and wait for admittance there was none, so putting forth all their strength they flung forward, and with a crash and a clatter the stout porch door flew open. With a great banging and stamping they rushed from the porch into the house, and on like a whirlwind towards the embers in the fireplace, from which a luxurious warmth still breathed. But great was the alarm of the tanner's sleep-drunken family at this intrusion, for they believed themselves overfallen by robbers.

The Tanner: What monster enters the room of an honourable man in this fashion on Christmas night? Answer; my gun is aimed!

Tuomas: Leave thy gun in peace, man.

Aapo: Don't shoot the farm's own people.

Juhani: We come, God help us, from Impivaara.

Timo: The seven sons of the former Jukola.

Simeoni: The Lord ha' mercy upon us! Seven souls are passing to eternity this selfsame terrible moment. The Lord ha' mercy upon us!

Juhani: Fire burned down our good cabin in the forest and all our belongings with it. Here we had to gallop like hares with no more covering to our poor bodies than a rag of a shirt, a short shirt. And that was a tight place.

The Tanner's Wife: The Lord Jesus preserve us!

The Tanner: Oh you poor lads!

Juhani: Ay, is this a right state of things! Here we sit like magpies, beseeching God's mercy. Ah! I must cry.

The Wife: Poor, miserable children! Hurry, husband, and light a fire.

Eero: Oh unhappy night, oh unhappy us!

Aapo: Oh night of terror, oh!

Simeoni: Ah! oh!

Juhani: Don't cry, Eero, don't cry, Simeoni, there's no cause at

151

all to blubber, Aapo! Don't cry, don't cry, brother Eero; we're in shelter now. But it was a Turk's march.

The Wife: Oh child of man on earth, alas!

Juhani: Dear mistress, your tears and pity awaken my own tears again. Ah! But don't cry, mistress, don't cry. Haven't we escaped from the clutches of wild beasts and the cold to the warmth of Christian neighbours? And for that, thanks be to God.

Tuomas: Wretched, wretched indeed is our state. But build up a blazing fire for us, bring a couple of sheaves of straw for our beds on the floor, and put Valko in the stable and hay before him.

Aapo: Forgive us, if we beg so hard in the name of the law and our lives' sake for help and shelter. For our lives' sake, for our lives' sake!

Juhani: O angels of the Covenant of Mercy! the life left in me is all at the tip of my nose, ready to fly off, to fly off. If there be meat and ale in the house, bring it forth. Look you, this was a game, a dusting we shall never forget. Bring meat and mulled ale for the sake of our dear lives and souls.

The Tanner: As fast as we can and all we can, good friends, as soon as I have lit a light. You hapless! in your shirts!

Juhani: Not a rag on our heads or an old boot on our feet. Look at these goose-legs, look!

The Tanner: It fair makes my hair bristle. Come and look, wife.

Timo: Look at my legs too.

Juhani: What are yours to mine! There! Look, lad, at two roast turnips.

Timo: What about these!

Juhani: What are thy trotters here.

Timo: Eigh? Mine? Never mind. Just look at them. Is this human flesh?

The Tanner: Hurry, wife, and look.

The Wife: Well, good people and powers of Heaven!

Juhani: Ay, is this a right state of things? Even Tuomas's eyes are wet. Don't cry, Tuomas. What did I say? Is this a right state of things?

152

Timo: That's how we human calves are chased down here.

The Wife: How they flush and glow, flush and glow! Good people!

Timo: Like iron in the furnace, especially cast-iron. He-he!

The Wife: So red, so red! Lord Jesus save us!

Juhani: They're just "like unto molten brass," as it says in the Bible. The Lord help us poor wretches!

The Wife: Oh, poor children!

Lauri: Do as we begged you and you did promise.

Aapo: We beseech you, hurry! We'll kindle the fire ourselves, seeing that there is cordwood in yon corner, fine barkclad faggots.

Juhani: Here we are again in old Jukola, under its well-known sooty rafters, and here we stop right until May-day. May the old home be our lodging for one more winter.

Tuomas: But wait till summer comes.

Juhani: Wait till summer comes, and a cabin, grander then ever, will stand on Impivaara clearing.

Tuomas: As soon as the snow has gone, the forests and hills will soon be echoing again with the ring of axes, and the Jukola brothers will no longer need to beg for shelter from anyone.

Juhani: Grand words, Tuomas. Let's forget the accursed luck that caused our cabin to be burned down, and picture in our minds the new cabin we shall soon have put together again.

Tuomas: Know that all grudge vanished from my mind as soon as we set out on our dreadful journey, and know that when thou blewest on my neck like a swimming stallion as thou camest on behind, it cut me to the heart.

Juhani: Let us rejoice then that the journey is ended and that we are once more in a warm room. Here comes food and drink, and there two mighty sheaves of shining straw. Let us thank God, beloved brothers.

Merrily blazed the birchwood fire, and in its grateful warmth the brothers wallowed and warmed themselves. And having stood there for a while, seven men in a row, they moved to the table to enjoy the meat, bread, sausage and mulled ale, all of which the tanner's wife, a pitying woman, set before them. The master himself took charge of Valko, led him to the stable and filled the manger before him with hay. And at last, following the men's tracks, the dogs too came from their dismal journey, came panting and fawning, with joy blazing in their eyes. And with joy the brothers received them; they petted them, fed them and fondled them in every way.

But when the brothers had finished their meal, they sank down on their bed of straw, and soon, wrapped in the soft blanket of sleep, forgot the battle of life. Sweetly they slept, and for long they were warmed by the flickering fire, until it had dwindled into a heap of glowing cinders. Then the mistress closed the dampers and a delicious warmth streamed into the room from the fireplace; and having done so she lay down on her own bed, and silence reigned in the room. But outside the frost skipped crackling along the fences, the north wind blew roaring under a star-glittering sky, whence a pallid moon looked smiling down.

CHAPTER 7

EARLY in the spring, before even the cranes had arrived, the brothers forsook Jukola, and fleeing again to Impivaara clearing, began at once with all speed to build themselves a new home. Soon stout logs rested on the corner stones, and tier was added to tier. Then for many days from the break of dawn to evening twilight axes crashed and the heavy mallet thundered. Juhani, Aapo, Tuomas and Simeoni sat each at his corner, while the others shaped and rolled the logs up to the framework along sloping spars. Sweating, but always in merry mood they toiled, and steadily the house rose, and around them the resin spread its fresh perfume. But then days would go by when the brothers moved not an axe, but lay snoring in heavy slumber from eve to eve, sometimes until the morning of the third day.

Nevertheless, before the autumn sowings had yellowed in the village, the house stood completed on Impivaara clearing; on the same spot, in the same form and condition as the first; prouder even than before it stood. And now that their stout-walled cabin was ready, the brothers were able to devote themselves once more with all their might to their hunting trips. Both for the hunt and for the fishing on Lake Ilvesjärvi they equipped themselves, set out with guns and traps on their adventure, and the dogs followed them with flaming eyes. Tirelessly they roamed the wooded heights, bogs and backwoods, and cleft the bright surface of the lake, wresting a livelihood both for the moment and the coming, savage winter. And in those days many dwellers in the woods and waters gave up their lives.

But I would now like to relate of old Tinder-Matti, the brothers' sole friend in these wilds. There was an old man, by name Tinder-Matti, who lived on a hill close-covered with curlywooded birch, lived alone in his tiny hut a few thousand paces from Impivaara Height. He prepared the softest tinder in all Häme and strong and lasting birch-bark shoes, and this work of his never failed to provide him with his daily bread. In his younger days he had travelled in North Finland, whither as trusted coachman he had followed the former Vicar of the parish, who had moved right to the boundaries of Lapland. There Tinder-Matti had remained until the following summer, hunting bears, gluttons and cranes in the limitless boglands of the north. Of these excursions he had much to relate; and his memory was matchlessly sharp; he never forgot what he once heard or saw. Sharp were also his gifts of observation and his eye; through bewildering forests he wandered without ever losing his bearings. No place existed, however distant, the direction of which he did not believe himself to know, without the error of a hairsbreath, after a single visit. He pointed towards it immediately with his thumb; and it was vain to argue with him, so firmly he trusted in his own knowledge. If for instance you asked him: "where is Vuokatti Fell?" he would answer at once, butting his thumb at the horizon: "there; look along my thumb; over there, couldst shoot it. Kuusamo church is where that little dip is; a tiny cock's pace to the right runs the line to Vuokatti Fell." Similarly, if you asked him: "where is Porrassalmi battlefield?" he would again answer straightaway, butting his thumb at the horizon, "there, look along my thumb; over there, couldst shoot it." So exact was the old man, and indeed he knew accurately the forests for many scores of miles around his hut. He had tramped them in all directions, seeking now for fungoids, now for birchbark for shoes, now visiting his traps. It happened sometimes that in his wanderings he would step over to the brothers' cabin on Impivaara. And then the brothers would enjoy a pleasant time: gaping they listened to the old man's tales, mouths open, ears erect as a bat's. Once on an evening in August he sat again with the brothers, telling them about his hunting experiences in the lands of the north.

Juhani: Ah, indeed. But what happened then?

Tinder-Matti: Ay, what happened then? We went on to a great big open space, a squelching bog, and slid on our skis over that bubbling pit. We found many warm cranes' nests, shot many shrieking cranes, stuffed our bags with eggs and feathers, and of the cranes each man threw a fine bunch over his shoulder. And then we had a drink. We jogged off again, the cranes and dogs across our necks, over the quaking and squelching, bubbling and hissing quagmire; and often a man was near to sinking for good into the everlasting depths, a whining hound on his neck. But we came however to an echoing hill, to firmer ground, though drenched like drowned rats. There we camped for the night, made a leaping fire and took off our sodden coats. And nothing helped but we had to peel off trousers and shirts too, peel off like eels. Soon our clothes were steaming on the branches, cranes' eggs hissing in the ashes, and we ourselves turning and wallowing in the rare warmth of the fire, naked as midnight goblins. And then we had a drink. But how think you the time passed? How went that May night with us? There the dogs were for ever twitching their damp nostrils and glowering up at the treetops. So at last we too started peeking upwards, and what did we see?

Juhani: Tell us; a tiny-eyed little bear-pup, I'll lay.

Timo: Or Old Horny or Bogey himself, I guess.

Tinder-Matti: Neither one nor t'other but 'twas a great dark-brown monster of a glutton sat in the fork of a dried-up, whiskery pine. Heiskanen fired and missed; Little-Jussi fired and missed; I too let fly in the end, but with almost the same blessing. The glutton only swayed once and growled real fiercely, but still sat nicely on its branch. At that Heiskanen shouted: "Sorcerer's tricks,

157

sorcerer's tricks!" took a dead man's tooth from his pocket, bit it a few times and spat on the bullet that he rammed into his gun. Then he waggled his hand a while in the air, and, fearfully rolling his eyes, uttered, the little devil, a couple of strange, awful words, fired, and down thumped the glutton from the pine. But the imp was far from dead yet, and a new game began. We ourselves, stark naked as we were, couldn't well go near the raging devil; nor did the dogs seem to like it, but there they hopped and skipped a fathom or so away, while the glutton spat, spat growling at them from the bushes. Black magic, you see, was still at work. But Heiskanen began gabbling his awful words again, waggling his hand and rolling his eyes fearfully. And now one of the dogs charged right at the red-mawed monster, flew at it like a crackling rocket, and a real shindy arose. Well, son of the Lord, that dog shook the poor glutton like that, and that, and that! Devil take me, you never saw such a worrying and dusting in all your days, and that's truth.

Juhani: Ten thousand flaming devils!

Timo: That would have been fine to see!

Tinder-Matti: It was a merry game and jolly, surely.

Timo: And then you stuffed the glutton into your bags?

Tinder-Matti: 'Twas a fine old rogue for any bag; a fat rascal. Ay, and then we had a drink. We put on our coats again, dry as powder, and laid ourselves peacefully to sleep in the warmth of the dancing fire. But 'twas little the sleep we got, what with sorcerer's arrows flying all the time like fiery serpents criss-cross through the air over our reeling heads. Often enough, Heiskanen bounced up, crying in a loud voice: "Out, sorcerer's arrow, out, sorcerer's arrow!" and with a roar many of them fell, some in the forest, some in the grey bog, but still more went skimming along their smooth track without heeding his shout. And once we heard, sweeping from north to south, a damned angry and swift puffing that was followed for long by little squeakings. "What kind of a goblin was that scurried past?" I asked Heiskanen, who answered after a while in a growl: "That was the Old 'Un himself passing by." An hour went by again and another, and fire kept flashing in the mild, muggy air. Then, from the edge of the bog to the east, there came a sudden noise like the roar of mossy firs, and a moment later from the bog's western side, another noise answered, but softer, like the rustle of a young birchwood. "What roar was that over there, and what rustle this over here?" I asked again, and Heiskanen growled at last: "Th' old Spirit of the Firs spoke to his daughters." The night passed, anyhow, and in time morning dawned, and we set off again. And that very minute we saw, right at the edge of the forest, a grey wolf, the damnedest big one for size, that flew off like a stack of peas in a whirlwind. All we saw of it at last was its left hind leg, and lifting my gun I shot it right through the paw, snapped it in two like a piece of crackling, though it saved its skin after all. Broke the poor beggar's peg in two.

Timo: The devil! Paw broken off like an icicle, and lying there before you on the ground like a pig's trotter at Shrovetide?

Tinder-Matti: Well, not quite like that.

Tuomas: How did you know its paw was broken then?

Tinder-Matti: We chased it a mighty long way and saw several times that where the son of a wolf had trodden, his dragging, waggling paw had made like number tens in the sand.

Timo: Well, may the Old 'Un take me! Number tens in the sand? He-he-he!

Tinder-Matti: Plain number tens.

Juhani: That wolf had a hot time.

Tinder-Matti: The wolf had a hot time, if the men had too. But the dogs, rot them, wouldn't budge a yard from our feet, but jogged along sadlike, tails drooping, the old dogs that had always been so brave.

Aapo: What had taken the spirit out of them?

Tinder-Matti: Black magic, the bewitched spellbound vapours of which the air was full as a battlefield with smoke. Heiskanen sure did his best, shouted charms and cursed, waggling his hand, but it was all no use. And Little-Jussi, the scamp, scurried along like a ball, pounding the earth and sweating hard. For the lad had no more leg than three spans of your hand at the very most; but he'd a real badger's back, long and tough. Tough he was altogether, devilish tough, and hard as any badger. Right long he dusted after that wolf, which ran on limping ahead; but it was no use, he had to leave old wagtail to the forest. Ay; and then we had a drink. And when this was done we set off home again, carrying our rich haul. There we marched, bags under our arms, the bags full of eggs and feathers and this and that little game from the forests; our skis and the cranes on our backs, guns in fists; and the hairy glutton dangled on each of our shoulders in turn: so we fared. But at the edge of the clouds flew a little chattering snipe; I shot that and put it in my bag. Then after walking a while I saw a flying squirrel, flat, with great eyes, in the crown of a pine; I shot that too and put it in my bag.

We came at last to high open clearings, and once in the south we saw Turkkila Farm, where we had begun our stiff journey. We came to a bloodstained spot which the master of Turkkila had pointed out to us on our way to the hunt as the place where a bear had killed a fine stallion only two days ago. We gazed awhile at Bruin's bloody table and I noticed at once he had been there, likely at sunset the evening before, to enjoy the remains of his joint. I now reasoned that he would come again when this day faded, and so decided to stop and wait for him; but on to Turkkila went the others to prepare a mighty supper. There I stood then and pondered, thought hard, holding my head, how best to await my visitor on the open clearing, where wasn't a single tree to climb. But "better be smart than be quick", I hit on a trick at last, a downright good plan. Quite near I saw a tarry stump, black and enormously big, its roots lifted into the air by the spring thaws, at least a yard high. I chopped off the middle root that stuck out downward to the right, pulled it clean out and opened up the hole a bit more. Into this I crawled, and thrusting out the muzzle of my gun towards the bloody field, settled myself to wait for Bruin's coming, a stout castle over me. He came, waddling along from the plain, drove his eeth into the torn thigh of the dead stallion, and I prepared as carefully as I could to give him a dose of lead in the forehead. But lamme, anyhow! just then the little brass strip on the stock of my gun made the weeniest clink against the tin button of my coat, and he bear's sharp ear caught the tinkle at once. In a rage, he charged at me, but was met with a bang. Taking no notice he came on, shrieking on a fearful note. Then there was a crashing over my head: the roots crackled and the earth shook as the many-pronged stump rose up over me. And I, poor lad, thought my end had come, and only waited, gun in hand, when the monster's open maw would yawn before me. But the hubbub ended suddenly and all was quiet, still as the grave, and there was no tussle between me and the bear as I had expected. I waited a moment yet, but at last I peeped through the skyward-pointing roots to see what was on the other side, and there lay the bear stone dead, the uprooted stump in its arms and blood flowing from its mighty chest into the earth. But hallelujah! thinks I, standing a free man again under the free sky. For the stump had been lifted real neatly from around me.

Juhani: "Hell", said Heskuun-Jaakko!

Timo: The Seven Smiths take me!

Juhani: The funniest scrap on the face of the earth!

Tuomas: A brave scrap, a manly scrap, both on Bruin's side and yours!

Juhani: O thou big black bull!

Timo: The devil! That's all I can say. But what then?

Tinder-Matti: Well, thou canst guess what happened then, canst guess that the bang carried to Turkkila like from the bottom of a barrel and soon brought men on to the clearing like midges. And then a din and shouting arose as Bruin was carried to the house on a bending, dancing pole. There was a daddy for you: Hanging from a rafter he darkened the big room at Turkkila like a thick thundercloud does the sky. Such were that day's doings, that day's and that trip's. And then we had a drink.

Juhani: And celebrated a merry wake.

Tinder-Matti: The wake began at Turkkila and ended at the

Vicar's, ended with greasy faces and filmy eyes. So it was, and those days have been and gone. But gladly the old man remembers the adventures of the days of his best manhood and gladly he speaks of them.

Aapo: And right glad are we to hear them.

Juhani: Keep on telling them to dawn, and we'll forget there's sleep in the world.

Tinder-Matti: Well, it's time to start crawling off to my lair again; ay, it's time. God watch over you, brothers!

Juhani: The Lord preserve you, honoured Matti.

Aapo: The best of health, and welcome to our hut always.

Matti departed, axe on shoulder, to his little hut on the birch-clad leafy hill, far away from the village. But the brothers prepared for their nightly repose, for darkness already triumphed, and the failing light of evening shone sadly through the narrow window-holes of their cabin. But for long thoughts swarmed feverishly in their brains, driving away refreshing sleep. They pondered over Tinder-Matti's tales of the deserts of the north, of the bewitched air of those places and the sorcerer's arrows speeding hissing from every quarter of the dark night. And like to the sparkle of the arrows and the flaming of the guns, so flamed in their breasts a strange desire and eagerness. Above all was their lust whetted by the thought of the crane, that bird of wise and darting eye, whose austere cry echoes through the northern boglands; and to meet their thoughts came a breath of the pleasant warmth of feathered nests, a vision of gleaming eggs in nests hidden away in the bog-bilberry bushes. To hunt this long-necked prey and despoil its nests, for this the brothers now lusted. Powerfully the awe-inspiring gloom of the northern bogs fired their imaginations.

Longer than any other, Juhani lay awake in his bed. He pondered over the best way to arrange a hunting-trip in his own parish that would compare with the one newly related from the lands of darkness. He thought of Kourusuo Bog, where, although cranes there were none, there were plenty of speckly-feathered wild duck. And with the interlarded drinks of the northern hunters haunting

162

his mind with a strange fascination, he bethought him that spirits were to be had at Viertola Manor. And so he finally built up in his mind a copy of the brave hunt of the north, and having decided to carry it into effect the very next day, fell asleep at last; but in his sleep he battled long on Tinder-Matti's mighty adventure. Once he started up dreaming from his couch, crying in a fearful voice: "The glutton, the glutton! Seize the crane-necked devil!" To this shout the others, but half-awakened, answered with angry grunts from their berths; soon, however, they were asleep again. But Juhani stared around him for long before he realized that he stood not on the vapoury plains of Lapland, between the bogs, on a grey neck of land, but on the peaceful gallery of his own home. Then his mind gradually cleared, he dropped down on his bed again and slept undisturbed. But on the morrow, awakening he remembered his decision of the night and began at once to introduce the matter to the others.

Juhani: Brothers, listen to what I say and to what I would impress on you. I have remembered a place that teems with game and marvel greatly that to this day we should have forgotten Kourusuo, where waterfowl swarm in the reeds and clear pools without count or number. Let us go and hunt there and we shall bring back wild duck by the sackful.

Tuomas: I'm with thee.

Timo: And willingly I.

Eero: I too; and as we plod over the bog I shall fancy myself Little-Jussi on the Lapland marshes. I'm with thee!

Aapo: Neither will I oppose a plan that can bring us food for many days.

Juhani: We decide on the trip then. But it's a fearful way to Kourusuo, a wolf's league, and we shall be gone at least one night. Therefore, I believe a drink would do us no harm, camping under the naked sky.

Tuomas: There's spirits at Viertola.

Juhani: Good spirits too.

Tuomas: Seven spans, boys!

Juhani: Right! a span each.

Aapo: Maybe we'll leave out the spirits, to which luckily fo: us we are unused.

Juhani: Thou hast taken a dram now and then, both thou and I

Eero: Grasp, Aapo, the childish hint of the man. Permit us tc be able to say in our time: "and then we had a drink", when a. grey-haired gaffers we relate the adventures of our youth to gaping children. Allow us to imagine that we are giving young gluttons a hot time in the north.

Juhani: More nonsense! Isn't it only right and just that a man should feed his carcase. On this trip we shall often enough be treading bogs and squelching quagmires, and spending our nights wet through on beds of bear-moss. At such times a little gulp from a pocket-flask can do good, think I. We deem it best therefore that we shall not lack a drop of medicine in our bags when we set out. And now let Lauri-lad go to Viertola, our best fox-skin in his pouch; and spirits will soon be forthcoming.

Lauri set off to bring spirits from Viertola, for a cordial on the wild-duck hunt on Kourusuo Bog. About five thousand paces from Impivaara, on land belonging to Viertola, lies this bog, wide, surrounded by sombre forests. Its surface, a favourite resort of wild duck, shows in succession clear-watered pools, high clusters of reeds and hummocky islets with dying pines. Thither the brothers had decided to march to harry the creaking wild duck, hoping for a rich booty.

Lauri came from Viertola bringing sparkling spirits in a tin bottle, their father's former hunting flask. But as well as spirits he brought important news from the forest which stirred the brothers' minds to a still keener enthusiasm. He related that a bear had felled one of the best bulls in the Viertola herds, and even knew the site of the kill, which was north of Impivaara on Viertola ground, but near the Jukola forest boundary. Past this spot the brothers now laid their route, deciding not to set off until the day inclined to evening. In this way they might perhaps meet the bear, whose habit it is to return at sunset to enjoy the remains of his

164

rey. So at least they hoped. And when a hearty dinner had been eaten and the afternoon declined, they departed on their hunt, heavily equipped: birch-bark knapsacks on their backs and stiff charges in their guns. Last came Lauri, leading the dogs on a leash and carrying in his pack the seven spans of spirits. He had been ordered to halt with the dogs about three hundred paces from the site of the kill, and was to release Killi and Kiiski on hearing shouts or the sound of firing. He acted accordingly, and stopped in time at the foot of a fir to await the outcome. The others approached nearer the spot where the bull had been felled and found the half-devoured carcase on bloodstained ground in a dark clump of spruce. Hiding themselves in a low but dense thicket of young firs within reasonable firing distance, they prepared to wait.

A fairly long spell passed. But at last a stealthy shuffling and the creak of twigs was heard from the plain, and it became clear that their guest approached his feast. And so it turned out to be. Between the trees, softly and with caution, an unusually large bear drew near. But it seemed it scented danger; for grunting and turning its muzzle from side to side, it halted a long way from its victim. Long it hesitated, and it looked at last as though it was inclined to turn back, without approaching within gunshot of the men. In deepest silence the brothers waited in their thicket, until finally Timo, heedless of the others' forbidding gestures, began, creeping in a wide curve, to approach the ferocious beast. And then, thinking himself sufficiently close to the bear, he fired; but only the powder flashed in his pan and the charge in his barrel failed to ignite. Enraged, like a huge moss-covered stone. Bruin now charged at the man, who without delay threw himself down on his face, and remained there motionless. The brute sniffed at him, nosed and tugged, grunting and blowing angrily. In all likelihood Timo's doom had been sealed, if Juhani had not sped to his assistance, firing at the bear's backbone. Lower he dared not aim, remembering his brother, who lay beneath the monster. But the bullet missed a vital spot at least, for in greater rage than ever the sprucewood's king now rushed at Juhani, leaving Timo to sniff the soil. Then Juhani, his life at stake, turned the stock of his gun towards the brute's open maw, and an awful struggle seemed imminent. But now Tuomas fired, sending a fiery bullet into the animal's thigh. Afraid, he too, for his brother, he was unable to aim at the head or breast, where a wound is more likely to prove mortal. Still, the brute now tasted lead in its system, and the blood streamed down its sturdy, rounded limb. Furious, screaming terribly, it flew at Tuomas, but met with so deadly a blow on its forehead from the stock of the man's gun that, shaking its head, it was brought up in its charge. And so the combatants stood a while, defiantly regarding each other.

Then the dogs rushed forward, approaching as swiftly and silently as two streaks of lightning, until, having reached the ruffled bear, a virulent din arose. Killi raged at the bear to its face, keeping, however, a few paces distant. Kiiski stormed in the rear, even daring, now and again, a hurried tweak at its woolly hindquarters. It leapt, however, switfly aside whenever the forest's pride, like a grey-black enormous haycock, turned round. Finally, after a few fruitless lunges at its tormentors, the bear fled, with the yelping hounds at its heels.

All this occurred with extreme rapidity and before the other brothers had arrived on the site of the conflict. Meanwhile Juhani and Tuomas quickly reloaded, hoping to catch up with the bear once more. Timo, too, gradually rose from the ground and stared around him a moment as though unaware where the north was, whence the wind then blew. Heatedly the others now scolded him for the foolhardiness that might easily have cost human lives and had perhaps spoiled the chase for good. Without answering a word, Timo sat on a hummock, opening up the touch-hole of his gun and chipping its flint sharper with the back of his knife. And soon they all stood ready to continue the hunt.

Farther and farther the barking of the dogs receded, until it was almost inaudible, and the brothers began wondering whether they would ever meet with their prey again. But after a while the voices

166

of Killi and Kiiski echoed plainer, steadily approaching, and it be
came clear that the bear was completing its customary circle, and
so would return to the spot whence it had started. The brothers
arranged themselves in comfortable positions, gun in hand, to await
the approaching hunt. In a little grassy clearing stood Simeoni
and a short distance away Lauri, both stockstill, silent as two
statues. At full speed, so that the earth thundered, the bear drew
nigh, showing its open, dark-red maw. Straight towards Simeoni
the panting monster sped. The man fired, and down tumbled the
bear to the grass, only to rise again and charge at the shooter. Then
came the flash of Lauri's gun, a sharp report echoed around, and
the bear collapsed silently at Simeoni's feet. There it rested, not
a limb moving, and the blood flowed from its head and chest.

But the brothers gathered quickly round the fallen bear; and it
was an aged, huge male. They saw now that its skull had been
pierced close to the root of its ear, and that its side likewise had
been pierced. The former wound all knew had been caused by
Lauri's bullet; for an animal whose brain has been pierced falls
immediately, never to rise. Satisfied, the hunters sat round the
thick-pelted hero of the woods, preparing to drink to the kill.
Content also, with noble gaze, the dogs sat beside their fallen
enemy. The evening was fair, the wind had died down, and the
sun sank into the lap of the dark woods. Pleasant it was to rest
in so delicious an evening hour, after the wild and heated encounter.

Juhani: The first drink is Lauri's. He shot like a man, hit the
beggar in a real golden spot, and down on his palms flashed the
bear like grass before the scythe. A good gulp, my lad!

Lauri: What if I too were to let a drink slide down my throat
for once.

Juhani: Thou beginner on the path of drink, strange to its very
taste, innocent yet as a lamb.

Lauri: I know its taste, enough anyhow not to be befouled by
a bird, but how the world feels when a merry lad dances in his
cups, that I truly don't know.

168

Aapo: Think a while, Lauri, and I would sooner bid thee nay than yea.

Lauri: Here's to it!

Aapo: And let us hope that this is not the beginning of a harmful habit.

Lauri: Rubbish: Take a drop of this, now that we have reason to be a little merry like.

Juhani: There our bogey lies like a great heap of hay, and the lives of many bulls and horses are saved.

Timo: I know that next time we meet, the master of Viertola will stuff a bottle into our bosoms for nothing, a bottle or two.

Juhani: I wouldn't call that much, seeing that we have saved his herd of bulls from the monster there.

Aapo: But there's a herd for you; forty head of horns. All the summer they live in the forests, night and day, but when winter comes they draw all the manor dung into the fields. But that free life of theirs in the woods all the summer makes them nearly wild.

Juhani: God keep us from meeting them with the dogs; they'd soon make mincemeat of both a man and his dogs. Let us remember the danger Nikkilä got into amongst the Honkamäki bulls; his danger was great although the number of beasts was not as terrifying as in this glowering Viertola herd. Through his dogs, which in a scrimmage of this kind always take shelter with their master, death would have have been his lot in the end, if he hadn't come to a strong pasturage fence that stopped the mad charge of the bulls like a protecting castle wall.

Aapo: Let us be careful. A little while ago I heard something that sounded like a hoarse bellow from yon hill. To my belief they are not far away. But what is Eero up to with that boulder?

Eero: There's a badger here, in this hole under the stone.

Juhani: Would that be possible?

Eero: Surely. Tracks lead into the hole but none out, as I can see in this sand.

Aapo: Show the tracks to the dogs, and the wagging of their tails will soon show whether there are lodgers there.

169

Juhani: Hither, Killi and Kiiski!

Tuomas: They are off on their own again, and, I'm thinking, on the track of a hare.

Eero: Together we could easily lever up this stone.

Tuomas: Jobs more foolish have been tried. Give me thy axe, Juhani, and I'll cut a stout bar for each of us, and then we can all lift up the stone when the dogs come.

So they talked; and with Juhani's axe Tuomas cut a thick staff for each of the men, four of birch and three of mountain ash. But suddenly, from the forest, they heard a furious crashing and roaring, which seemed to approach them at great speed. In amaze the brothers listened, staves in hand, listened and waited for what the forest would reveal. A confused, wicked bellowing carried thence; at intervals the dogs yelped pitiably; and soon a dreadful vision broke on their sight. In mad career, ten furious bulls galloped towards the men, sweeping before them the dogs, which, fleeing for their lives, hurried to their masters' side. But at this the men's hair bristled, and cold shivers ran down their bodies. And without pausing the bulls charged at them, bellowing deafeningly; their onslaught was stoutly met, and a terrible battle ensued. With their heavy staves the brothers laid about them, splitting horned heads, and already two of the bulls lay on the field, brandishing their hooves in the air. But death seemed nigh for the brothers, too. Timo fell, and a bull bent down already to pierce his breast; but then Tuomas's ashen stave fell heavily, and falling, broke the bull's back. With a groan the beast sank lifeless to the ground, and Timo was saved. A similar doom threatened Aapo, but he was saved by Juhani and Eero. Mightily Juhani laid about the bull, hitting it with his cudgel between the horns, Eero tearing meanwhile at its tail to alter its position, until this beast too lay on the ground, brandishing its hooves. In the heat of the conflict Timo lost his staff of birch, but soon perceived Juhani's axe on the grass; snatching up this, he began laying about him with fiery energy. Right and left he smote: dreadfully the bull's stomachs opened, and bubbling water, blood and offal poured on to the earth. So,

170

pale of visage, fought the men, in the jaws of death; and the dogs too did their best, plying their teeth like iron pincers at the brutes' throats. Loud in this confusion was the din and turmoil; up and down danced the staves, high in the air flew the loosened horns of the bulls, and the shouts of the brothers, the snarling of the dogs and the bellowing of the beasts mingled in one terrific noise.

But at last the combat ended. Seven bulls lay lifeless on the field, and three fled, one with a single horn, one with none, one with a sorely battered carcase. Pale and wild of eye, the brothers stood on the bloodstained battlefield. Gory all over stood Timo, a bloody, bedraggled axe in his hand, stood like a woodcutter amidst fallen trees. Hardly could they visualize what had befallen. When they reflected upon the conflict, which like a whirlwind had come upon them, raged a moment in their midst and with equal suddenness ceased, it all seemed like a dreadful dream. Horrorstricken, they viewed the number of animals on the bloodstained ground before them: the sprucewood bear, terrifically large, and seven fat bulls. They too had experienced hard knocks in the fight, especially Aapo, Juhani and Timo; nevertheless, all of them still stood on their feet. And there they now stood, staves in hand, panting, perspiring and silently regarding each other.

But hardly had they gained their breath before a new danger approached, greater by far than the first. It was as though a hurricane had followed a squall. It semed indeed that the end of the world was now come. The earth shook as in an earthquake, the forest crashed and a mighty roaring filled the still evening air as three and thirty maddened bulls sped at them at a gallop. The brothers listened to the tumult as a harried herd of swine stands dumb in the bushes beside a fence, listening ears acock for the renewed approach of their pursuer. Thus the brothers too listened until the horde of bulls broke from the forest. At that they threw away their staves, snatched their guns, and with the dogs fled at full speed, and snorting, the bulls followed them. Towards the boundary-fence between the Viertola forests and their own the brothers scurried. A shallow pool, decked with the semblance of

171

green turf, opened in their path; but there was no time for detours, and so without hesitating they ran through it. The water roared as they disappeared in a shower of foam and spray, but almost at the same moment they emerged into sight again. Their flight reminded one of the moon's passage through the blue meadows of the sky. Not for her to move aside for the cloud which attempts to bar her path; unheedingly she sails through it and brighter than erstwhile appears again on its farther side. And her pilgrimage is grave and solemn. But the Jukola brothers ran like hares and wild goats; for death ran at their heels. A fence, new and strong, barred their path, and like fire the brothers flew over it, pausing a score of paces away on the smooth clearing on its other side to see whether the fence would save them. The raving, trumpeting herd of bulls drew near; a loud crash was heard; and down fell the spruce fence, and the bulls were nearer to the brothers than before. Ever onward sped the chase across the hollow clearing; the men and the dogs ahead, the bulls behind, snorting and kicking up clods and clouds of sand, as the winter winds drive the smoking snow high into the air. With furious speed the brothers ran, the terror of death in their hearts, for they believed that it was already the last lap of the road of their lives they were treading.

Then a cry was heard from Aapo's lips: "bags off your backs, but keep the guns!" And immediately six birch-bark knapsacks rolled to the ground; the seventh still danced on Lauri's back, for he was not yet inclined to part with his. Little, however, did this avail them; for closer and closer the terrible drumming and roaring approached. And again a despairing, shrieking cry broke from Aapo's lips: "To the Devil's Rock, to the Devil's Rock!" by which he meant a certain rock, enormously large, which stood in a sombre forest. Towards this the brothers now hastened and soon stood at its foot, and quick as lightning the men and dogs scrambled up to its crown. The moss flew far around as their hands clutched at the corners of the rock; firmer, sharper and more sure by far than ever the crooked claws of a glutton, their fingers seized on the rock. Thus they were saved from an awful death, but close had

the abyss been to them. Hardly had they reached the rock before the horde of bulls stormed around them, rumbling and pawing the earth. This rock, the brothers' shelter, was almost square in shape, a slab of stone a fathom high which stood in the forest about three hundred paces from the edge of the clearing. On this the brothers now sat, perspiring and panting fearfully after their run from angry death. Silent, uttering not a word, they sat for long. But at last Juhani opened his lips.

Juhani: Here we are, brothers, and let us thank our luck for that. For this was a march we shall remember as long as there are bulls in the world.

Aapo: Here we are, but how are we to get away? Bulls are obstinate brutes, and these here are in a furious rage over the death of their comrades, which they would now like to avenge on our dogs with interest.

Juhani: And we'd be served from the same ladle.

Aapo: But for the dear height of this rock

Juhani: It was surely a welcome find for us. In truth! Like squirrels, we scrambled swiftly up it.

Eero: "And then we had a drink."

Juhani: Just so! Thanks be to God that we still have the spirits, if it turns out that we lads have to learn to fast up here.

Lauri: I didn't drop my knapsack, I.

Juhani: Thanks to thee too, brother mine. But bring forth thy tin flask, take a good gulp at it and then set it going round. Our hearts need a little strengthening now.

Aapo: Such stuff has to be enjoyed with caution in a dangerous situation like this.

Juhani: A wholesome reminder. But take a moderate pull at that.

Aapo: Moderation's always best. Let us remember that this is our bed too, and maybe for more than one night.

Juhani: God preserve us from that! I hope hunger will soon drive away that forest of horns around us. Ay, here we sit like

174

seven owls in the woods, on this mossy Devil's Rock. How did it get that name?

Aapo: From a certain strange tale.

Juhani: Tell us it now to pass our time. For this is just the place for tales, tales and stories.

And this story of the rock was now told them by Aapo.

There once lived in his castle on the Lapland fells a mighty prince of the Underworld, the most powerful wizard in the north. He had an elk, beautiful and nobly formed, matchlessly swift at running. This lovely animal set out one day in early spring to frisk on the frozen snowdrifts, and ended by starting to run round the whole of Finland. Then many an archer, seeing the golden-pelted sweet-eyed deer, hastened to the chase with his arrows of tempered steel. But none could follow it, for right quickly it left a skiing huntsman behind. It came at last to Häme, where lived a mighty skier and great marksman. This man now scented the magnificent elk of the Underworld and set off swiftly to ensnare it, gliding on his smooth skis, a powerful bow on his shoulder. At a shrieking pace the deer galloped over the frozen snow, but at still swifter pace the archer followed. So they ran for long over plains and up and down steep hills. But at last weariness began to overcome the deer; already it panted greatly as it ran; its speed slackened and the man approached closer and closer. Then a wonder occurred that has been seen before to hold back a marksman's arrow. Suddenly the elk turned and approached its pursuer with beseeching glance and shedding quick tears. But without the slightest hesitation the pitiless man shot his bolt, piercing the beautiful animal's brow; and thus the deer from the Underworld fell, dyeing with its blood the white snow.

At that the Prince of the Underworld, pacing the dismal valleys of the uttermost north, felt a sudden pang at his heart and knew at once that his golden elk walked in danger. He hurried to the fell on which his castle stood and with his magic spy-glass began looking towards the south. And far away in a sombre sprucewood he saw his deer, which, bathed in blood, writhed in its death agony;

175

and he saw the murderer standing by his victim with rejoicing glance. Then a terrible rage possessed him; he snatched a huge, square block of stone from the wall of his castle and flung it high in the air, flying towards the archer in Häme's forest. The mighty rock sped onward with a great roaring sound, cleaving the windy world of cloud in a wide arc. It rose to the crest of the sky, sank down again, sank southward, and exactly on the marksman's brow this unspeakable weight fell, burying the man beneath it.

Juhani: And the man's death was our luck. Where should we be now without this stone? There in the forest, carrion and crow's-meat, we'd be lying.

Tuomas: We shall get our fill of this stone yet. I'll stand for that.

Juhani: May God help us in time!

Timo: We lads will have to snore in layers here, packed on each others' backs like young swallows in a nest.

Aapo: That won't do. A sleep-fuddled man would soon roll off, a prey to the bulls. So let two of us, one on each side, always keep watch over their sleeping brothers.

Juhani: Wise advice, and let us keep to it closely; this is to be our lodging for this night at least. That we can see already from the movements of the bulls. There three of the scoundrels lie, basking on their accursed bellies, puffing and chewing, the devils! But go to sleep, lads; Aapo and I will keep watch up to roundabout midnight. Go to bed, go to bed. The Lord bless us!

Aapo: Oh we miserable wretches!

Simeoni: To what pitch have we unlucky lads come!

Juhani: To misery, great misery. But go to sleep; bless your souls and bodies and sleep in the Lord's name.

So they spent their night: two always awake, while the others slept on the moss-covered rock; and long was the night. Day broke, however, at last; the sun rose and climbed up the sky, but their fate remained unchanged; always the same horns, on every side, danced around the Devil's Rock, and hunger already assailed them fiercely. Nevertheless, they still hoped that the same pitiless guest would work his will in the stomachs of the bulls, forcing them in the end to seek other pastures. Thus hoping, they awaited the withdrawal of their foes. But to their horror they soon observed that there was sufficient food for the brutes in the moist back-woods' sedge around the rock. This the bulls now began solemnly tugging, moving on no farther but that the mossy rock was constantly in sight.

Juhani: They're not even thinking of shifting. They're taking up, the Devil seize them, their quarters here until the winter.

Eero: The Devil's in their skins.

Timo: What's lacking them here? The forest gives them both food and drink; but dry moss is our bread and meat.

Simeoni: The matter is this, that we sit here for our dogs' sakes. I fear our only road to salvation is to throw down Killi and Kiiski as a sacrifice to the bulls.

Juhani: Cruel advice.

Aapo: That we shall not lightly follow.

Juhani: Not as long as Jukola's Juho stands upright.

Tuomas: Should we to save our skins cast away those who have saved our lives many times over from the murderous claws of wild beasts? And would it even help us? I doubt it.

Juhani: I too. The bulls there, having made rags of our dogs, would start nicely waiting for something else to spear with their horns. That's sure.

Simeoni: Ay, ay, but what way out shall we find when hunger begins to squeal in earnest in our bellies.

Juhani: It'll squeal at first in our stomachs, but from there it soon shoots up to the beating heart of a man, like a cat on a fat mouse, and 'tis then a strong man crumples up. Hard, hard days for a man. What way out can we find? ask I too.

Aapo: Let's all shout loudly with one mouth; perhaps the sound might be heard by some one in the forest, or carry right to Viertola and set the people there guessing.

Juhani: That's a trick worth trying.

Timo: Let's shout hard.

Juhani: Like mad. Let's all break out together into one world's marvel of a shout. All together, and its effect will be more than grand. There now, let's get up and be ready. When I clap my hands the third time, we yell, and yell like seven men. One, two, three!

They shouted together with all their might and all at the same time, until the rock and the earth beneath it rang, and even the bulls rushed startled a few paces from the stone. Fearsome was the sudden scream of the seven men, which was followed by a long-drawn quivering cry, in which the plaintive howling of the dogs was further mingled. They shouted five long shouts, and the forest roared and the echoes rolled afar. But when the fifth and hardest shout was over, they sat down to breathe a while. Having rested, they repeated the work, shouting seven times, and then began to await what the effect would be. With blackened faces and bloodshot eyes they sat on the mossy rock, and the bellows of their chests worked fiercely.

Juhani: Let's wait and see what this does, let's wait. Folk are crazy if they can't understand that a crowd of men don't scream like this except in the greatest danger. Let's wait.

Eero: But if no help comes after all this noise, we are surely dead men. The second sun sinks already in the west and our hunger grows fierce.

Simeoni: God ha' mercy on us! one night and a day and a half since our last meal.

Timo: That's so. Listen to the rumbling in my stomach, rumblings and growlings and even little pipings. This is hard.

Juhani: Hard, hard; we know it and believe it, having peeped into our own belly.

Simeoni: Long is the day of a hungry man!

Timo: Ay, it's long.

Juhani: Long and dark! Are even Aapo's brains emptied? Canst thou not remember even the caw of a crow or the chatter of a barnyard owl to tell us, sitting here on Hunger's terrible isle.

Aapo: I remember one tale that hunger brings to my mind;

178

though it won't make us forget the need for refreshing our bodies, but only remind us of food and drink.

Juhani: Thou meanest the man in the mountain. I have heard it.

Timo: But it is new to me; tell us it, brother Aapo.

Simeoni: Tell it, tell it!

Aapo: It is the tale of a man, a noble hero of the Faith, who sat for a time imprisoned in Impivaara's caves, like aforetime the Pale Maiden, although for other reasons.

And Aapo told them this tale:

Once upon a time, when the Christian Faith and heathenism still fought together in Häme, there was amongst those converted a good man, pious and eager to spread the new religion, which he practised with passion in the shelter of Sweden's arms. But those armoured heroes had to return suddenly to their own fatherland and the baptized inhabitants of Häme fell under the terrible persecution of their heathen brothers. Many were killed in awful ways, while others sought to save themselves by flight into the tortuous backwoods, the caves in the hills, in short, anywhere. This pious man fled to Impivaara's caverns; but his persecutors, following on his tracks in their thirst for revenge, soon found out where he had hidden himself. "Shut the wolf up in his own lair!" they shouted with wicked joy, blocked up the opening to the cavern securely, and left the man to perish of hunger and darkness.

A miserable end would now have befallen him, if Heaven had not worked a new miracle. Scarce had the last gleam of daylight fled from its mouth, when the spacious cave was lit by the most wondrous, silvery light; and thus in the heart of the chilly rock the man had his own mild heavenly daylight. And yet other miracles occurred. Lo! from the floor of the cavern burst a tinkling spring, the waters of which were not lessened by use; and thus the man always had refreshing drink in his rocky chamber. And from the brink of the spring rose up a beautiful, blossoming tree, bearing the most tasty fruits, that were never lessened by taking from them; and of these the man had his delicious food. Here he spent his days, praising the Lord, here his nights were spent, dreaming of the lands

180

of the blessed. And his days were as summer days, warm and filled with light, and his nights a fairy twilight. So passed a year, and Christian blood flowed in streams in Häme. But when a ghastly year of persecution had run its course and a delightful September morning shone without, the clink of hammers and iron bars was borne to the hero's ears from the cavern's walled-in mouth. Through the piled-up rocks day gleamed at last, and in a flash the marvellous light vanished from the cave, likewise the spring and from its brink the fruitful tree.

But what had caused this commotion and clatter out there beyond the cavern's opening? Outside stood a great host of heathens and in their midst a few Christians bound in ropes and sentenced to die of hunger in the dark depths of the hill. Nor could they guess that any other fate had befallen the man imprisoned a year earlier in the same dungeon. But great was their astonishment when, on the opening of the cave, the hero walked out with transfigured, shining brow. And a voice whose holy clarity cleaved to the marrow sounded from his mouth: "Greeting, friends and brothers, greeting, golden sun and soughing forest, greeting!" At that the host fell on their knees before him, praising the god in whom he believed and who had saved him from an awful death. But in a loud voice the man told them of the miracles that had befallen him in the dark womb of the hill; and with one voice the people cried to him: "Baptize us, baptize us too to belief in the same god!" Thus to the man's exceeding joy they shouted, and at once released the prisoners sentenced to death from their bonds. Then the pious hero stepped to the brink of a stream and the crowd followed him, and renouncing their paganism, allowed themselves to be baptized in the Christian Faith. But on the bank stood the erstwhile victims, singing a hymn of praise to Him who had saved both them and their saintly father from a death of agony and led the children of heathens out of darkness into light. So, looking up into the high heavens, they sang.

Aapo: Such is the tale of the devout man.

Juhani: And the heathen's baptism took place just where our wolf-trap now stands in the brook.

Simeoni: Belief can work miracles. I am quite sure that the man had neither a spring nor a fruitful tree in the cavern and that no light seen of human eye lighted up his chamber, but that a firm and unwavering belief satisfied all his bodily needs. The strength of his spirit was to him a cool spring, tasty fruit and a shining light. What was it my former comrade at the herding, Tuomas Tervakoski, said? "If thou hast the shield of belief and the sword of the spirit, thou canst go and dance a polka with devils." That was what the pious old man said.

Juhani: But a full-grown man's stomach can't live long on belief and empty air, no, rot it, it can't. And I swear he shoved tastier vittles than fruit and water into his cheek. A man's body demands it, that has grown and thriven on meat and ryebread. Ay, ay, they tell the same tale another way too. They say that five black bull's horns suddenly appeared to the man in the cavern's wall. And then when he opened the first horn, the best factory spirits, clear as water, squirted hissing out of it for an appetizer, one that would have drawn any man's mouth together. From the second horn he dragged out by the yard puckered, fat and hot pork sausage. And from the third the best new-crop porridge sputtered out in a stiff curve, and from the fourth buttermilk to wet it with, buttermilk thick as tar. And then when he had stuffed his belly as full as a tick he opened the fifth horn in a hurry and pulled out twist, best Danish roll, that swelled in the lad's cheek like a sucking leech. Could a man with no work at all want better grub?

Timo: He was in Heaven, he was. But we?

Tuomas: This makes a man's head go hot.

Timo: Makes a lad's head dizzy.

Juhani: A thousand crowns for a meal like that now! A thousand thousand crowns!

Simeoni: "Puckered, fat and hot pork sausage!" Ay, we sit in Hell's midst and hear how they rejoice and eat in Heaven. Ah! What are we to do, brothers, what are we to do?

Eero: Believe, believe!

182

Simeoni: Dost thou still talk with mocking tongue, thou monster!

Eero: The last gasp, brother mine, the last gasp; believe me. Soon I shall crumple up sighing like an emptying bladder, a bull's bladder. Ah if I had here a new-baked loaf and butter on it!

Timo: And on the butter a terribly big sausage.

Juhani: If we had here seven new-baked loaves, seven pounds of butter and seven sausages baked in the warmth of a cordwood fire, there'd be a feast.

Eero: Bright fire and lighting!

Timo: A man ought to be wise and always carry a paper of salt in his pocket. Salt binds our innards and can keep us alive for weeks without a scrap of food as big as a midge in our guts.

Juhani: Ai, boy! salt wouldn't keep us alive for long.

Timo: But Iisakki Koivisto, that matchlessly lazy man, lies sprawling for many God's days at a stretch on the boards in Karkkula's sauna, without a crumb to break his fast. And how does he keep the wretched life still simmering in him? Why the rogue keeps sucking a lump of salt like an infant its mother's breast.

Juhani: He also sits like a corn-crake in the village cornfields, rubbing the grain from the stalks into his face. Look you now, it's late evening already, and no sound of help from the world of men, and here's thirty and three puffing devils for ever walking and walking round us. But there's two of the rascals butting. Strike together, strike together and pierce each others foreheads, burst 'em so the brains spurt out of your skulls on to the field, and there'll be two tormentors less for us. That's the way! Here's a little fun to pass the time. Just so! and may the game last long and eight bony ploughs tear up the ground.

Tuomas: Stoutly they're fighting, the white-backed and the white-headed one.

Juhani: But white-head wins.

Tuomas: White-back wins.

Juhani: Here's my paw, a wager on it.

Tuomas: Agreed. Timo, judge thou.

183

Juhani: Done!

Tuomas: A span of spirits!

Juhani: It's said. Let's watch now, let's watch the lads fight. But now they're like resting a bit, forehead to forehead.

Timo: And jerking slightly, as if they didn't care.

Juhani: But now! Now they're at it at full strength. Now, Whitehead, my Whitehead, dig thy hooves well into the ground!

Tuomas: Dig deeper thou, my brave Whiteback. That's the way!

Juhani: Whitehead, Whitehead!

Tuomas: My brave Whiteback with the steely forehead! So, lad! But leave off that solemn shoving and butt thy man to Hades.

Juhani: Whitehead! The Devil cut off thy horns! Dost run away, damn thee?

Tuomas: Flight's good enough for him.

Timo: And the other tears after him like a good 'un. He-he-he!

Tuomas: Ay, Juhani.

Juhani: A span of spirits gone. Thou shalt have it when we get out of this fix. But when will that day dawn? Ah! After many years it'll happen that under the eyes of the hunt-bailiff there'll be a fine load of faggots carted from here to the village and from the village to the graveyard, a cartload of clinking, clattering skeletons of seven men.

Simeoni: And so ended our sinful lives.

Juhani: So ended our lives.

Timo: So they ended.

Juhani: Ended miserably. But open thy knapsack, Lauri, and let a drink go round.

Aapo: All right for this once, but the rest of the spirits will have to be saved for a greater danger.

Juhani: As thou sayest. But now we'll take a drink that makes itself felt and then shout like clarions.

And when each had drunk, they lifted up their voices again, shouting all together. The echo carried to the ear of the Viertola bailiff, as he walked on the barn rise, but instead of understanding the significance of the cry, he only uttered to himself with awe:

184

"The boundary-spirit cries there." But the brothers, straining their jaws towards the heavens and all agape, with mouths wide open like those of dragons or of young birds in their nest when they hear the flapping of their approaching mother's wings, still shouted madly, shouted ten times. Whereafter they sat down again on their mossy resting-place, hope dying in their hearts.

CHAPTER 8

THE third day has come round of the brother's sojourn on the rock, and there, ever besieged by the bulls, they still sit. Now and again the beasts would move farther away, but always one or another paced in sight and soon rumbled the news to its fellows if the brothers tried to break out of their prison. Now on every side, here one wrenches forest grass into its maw, curling its tongue, there another chews the cud, breathing heavily as it rests on its tubby stomach. There two contend, half in sport, half in earnest, and the rattle of their horns echoes around. There, again, right at the foot of the rock, one paws the earth wrathfully, casting soil and sods high into the air and roaring wickedly. So to the agony, the pale fury of the brothers, they linger on; and already the sturdy sons of Jukola await their death. — A moment ago Lauri poured a stiff drink down his throat, and now he does so again, which greatly surprises the others and causes them to remonstrate with him seriously.

Juhani: Has the Old 'Un bewitched thee?

Aapo: Whatever art thou thinking of? Remember that we are all in the same fix.

Tuomas: Remember that our dwelling is the width of a man's palm, on which we must move with caution.

Lauri: A man mad with anger!

186

Aapo: That won't do here.

Lauri: Let it do in the pit of Hell then. Let the old castle spin like a millstone and cast down seven unhappy lads to the brutes there. Spin, rock, from east to west, and thou, forest, from west to east! Heleiyah!

Juhani: Art thou already drunk, boy?

Lauri: Is that a question to ask? What is life and the world worth? Not a mouldy farthing. Well then, let everything go in dust and ashes the way of the wind. Clunk! A drop of this, my heart's brothers.

Aapo: He's drunk. Take the can away from him!

Lauri: It won't come in play. The can's mine; I didn't leave it on the clearing to be trodden by bulls. But you others? Ah! you all laid your knapsacks nicely on the ground like wretched gypsies when the bailiff's gun goes off.

Juhani: Give the can here!

Lauri: The can's mine.

Juhani: But I want it in my care.

Lauri: Thou wantest? If thou wantest, thou'lt get it bang in the forehead.

Juhani: Wouldst thou show fight?

Lauri: If thou wilt, even that shall not be lacking. But loving brothers never fight. So let's take a drop of this.

Timo: Don't drink, Lauri.

Juhani: Give the can here at once!

Lauri: A hiding's what I'll give thee. What dost thou fancy thou art?

Juhani: A sinful human being, true; but still thy eldest brother.

Lauri: Eldest? Well, all the more time hast thou had to sin in, and all the more thou deservest a hiding. But skool, said the Swede!

Tuomas: Thou shalt not taste a drop.

Lauri: I like Tuomas very much, Tuomas and Little-Eero. But those others there? What am I to say of them?

Tuomas: Hold thy jaw and give the can here! There, Juhani, take the knapsack on thy back and the spirits in thy keeping.

Lauri: Thou alone canst turn the will of Lauri. I love thee, thee and Little-Eero.

Tuomas: Silence!

Lauri: Men like them! What is Jussi Jukola? A chuckleheaded cock; a hammerheaded bull.

Juhani: Shut thy mouth at once that my ears needn't hear such words a second time.

Lauri: "He that hath an ear, let him hear" preaches Aapo, Jukola's holy Paul.

Simeoni: Ah thee! Art thou the former grave, solemn and silent Lauri? Can this be Lauri? This babbling child of sin?

Lauri: Art not thyself Simeoni, the mealy-mouthed "Hail-Rabbi"?

Simeoni: That I forgive thee, ever heaping, ever heaping coals of fire on thy head.

Lauri: Go to Hell, there are coals of fire!

Simeoni: Godless!

Timo: Even the hairs on my back stand on end.

Lauri: What is Timo, Jukola's watery-eyed billy-goat, bleating?

Timo: Never mind. Goat's milk is good.

Lauri: Eigh?

Timo: Goat's milk is good. I thank thee for the honour: thankye kindly! Ay, that was our share; thankye kindly! But here's another kind of truck before thee too. Look at thy honey-boys there, Tuomas and Eero, yonder.

Lauri: Eigh?

Timo: Look at thy honey-boys, Tuomas and Eero, yonder.

Lauri: Eigh?

Timo: A parson speaks thrice, but he's paid for it.

Lauri: "Another kind of truck," thou didst bleat. I know well what kind of truck to liken them to. Tuomas-lad is a noble axe, grave, manly and strong, but little Eero-nipper is a tiny, sharp and biting whittling-hatchet. Ay, that lad can whittle, whittle right smartly, throwing little jests like chips around him, the scamp.

Juhani: Good. But didst call me a chuckleheaded cock?

Timo: He called me a he-goat. Thankye kindly!

Lauri: Eero whittles jokes, but he has the heart of a man.

Juhani: Good, good! But didst call me a chuckleheaded cock?

Lauri: I called thee a hammerheaded bull too.

Juhani: Good, brother, good!

Timo: Keep quiet, Juho. Me he called a billy-goat, and I thank him for the title; for the goat is no useless animal at all. The red-cheeked young mistress at Viertola, Mistress Lydia, drinks only the milk of white goats, and nothing else. There you are.

Simeoni: Should we be men if we hooked on to the words of a drunken man?

Lauri: Thou a man? Thou? Oh little brother! bitterly wouldst thou weep if thou sawest something girls don't as a rule show to a milksop like thee.

Juhani: Simeoni, Simeoni, I'd sooner be stabbed with a knife than with such words.

Simeoni: Ay, ay, it'll be seen on the last day whom they have stabbed.

Timo: Us thou hast painted as anything between a cock and an axe, but what art thou thyself, if I ask thee sternly and take on my worst temper.

Lauri: I'm Lauri.

Timo: See, see! Plain gentle Lauri?

Lauri: Good-fellow Lauri, and nothing more, though you have been pleased to make me out and call me many things: badger, Könni's hoer, mopy, and a thousand suchlike. Hm! I've heard something of the kind from the lips of each of you. And in deepest silence I have stored up every word. Now I feel like spreading out the pile a little, I feel, devil take it! like giving each of you a thwack on the forehead, and down every man of you to the bulls like a stack of chaff!

Aapo: Is this truly Lauri, well-behaved, silent Lauri? Who'd believe it?

Juhani: Aih! brother Aapo, ah! there's many weeds in that

golden corn. I've suspected it long, but now I know the man's heart.

Lauri: Hold thy jaw, thou Jukola's bull.

Juhani: For the Lord's sake don't annoy me any further, for my blood's getting hotter and hotter! Accursed puppy, I'll throw thee down into the mortar of those bulls, and may the terror of destruction come, the last day of the almanack!

Simeoni: Woe, oh woe!

Aapo: Silence! No fighting.

Tuomas: Be sensible, thou.

Juhani: He has shamelessly insulted me. A cock, chuckleheaded!

Aapo: What about holy Paul. Keep calm.

Timo: What about billy-goat. What sayst to that? Many thousand thanks, twin-brother!

Aapo: Let us remember how close we are to the jaws of death. Brothers, there is a thought in my brain, an idea on the tip of my tongue that I believe is important to us just now: Note: this rock is a ship in a storm, the storm being that muttering, angry drove of bulls around our rock. Or shall I choose another picture? Ay, let this rock of ours be a castle, which the enemy, cruelly armed with spears, besieges. Now if the besieged castle has no chieftain, no leader in discipline and defence, mutiny and disorder will spread amongst the men, and soon both castle and garrison are lost. And that is what will happen with us, unless we arrange and provide for ourselves differently, unless we set up lawful order in our midst. Therefore, let there be one whose words of wisdom all shall listen to, and behave accordingly. Juhani, do thou now control thyself and the whole band of brothers. Know that most of us are on thy side and uphold thy authority in this besieged castle.

Juhani: What punishment shall we fix on for the one who disobeys my word, and through his evil temper causes a general disorder and danger?

Tuomas: Let him be cast down to the bulls.

Juhani: Right, Tuomas.

190

Aapo: A stern punishment, but one our situation demands. I agree to the rule.

Simeoni: "Cast to the bulls" like the martyrs aforetime; but tenderness won't help here.

Timo: May he be thrown to the bulls; let this be the law and commandment.

Juhani: Let it be the law and commandment. Impress this terrible paragraph on your hearts and live thereafter. Now my first command is that Lauri is silent and lays himself nicely down to sleep; secondly, I command each of us except Lauri to take a little sup from the tin flask to comfort our hearts. Ay, here's to us!

Lauri: And I'm to be without, I?

Juhani: Thou art to go to sleep.

Lauri: Time enough for that in Hell.

Juhani: God knows, Lauri dear, where we shall yet sleep.

Lauri: "God knows, Jussi-dear,
　　Where our skins will dry this year."
I sing like a man, hoot like a hunter's horn.
　　"I'm a loving little child,
　　　　Mother's little Jussi.
　　I'm a loving little child,
　　　　Mother's little Jussi."

Juhani: Save thy song for the present.

Eero: Save the little boy's song for me.

Lauri: Save it for Jukola's Jussi and let's begin a new one, a real big song. Let's sing and dance, heleiyah!

Juhani: See that I do not sentence thee to be cast down to the bulls.

Tuomas: Lauri, I warn thee now for the last time.

Lauri: For the last time? Well, it is best thou ceasest.

Juhani: That we can brawl like this at the very gates of Death, we full-fledged heathens!

Simeoni: God has cause to punish us thus. O punish us, smite us on this rock of torture!

Lauri: A rock of joy, this is, Väinämöinen's rock of joy, which

191

same old gaffer is said to have been the god of Savo. I once heard a right smart song of him from an imp of a chimney-sweep's boy. I remember too a real jolly sermon by that same boy, which he spouted glibly out of his red lips and grinning teeth as he stood in a smoking chimney at Kuninkala. And this is what he preached...

Juhani: Quiet now, thou raving brute!

Lauri: And now, having sung to our fill, sung together with one voice as is the custom in church, let us preach. I am the parson, this rock is the pulpit, you are the choir, and the bulls around us the congregation, solemn and pious. But first a marching hymn to accompany parson to the pulpit. Ye heard. Parson's waiting.

Juhani: Wait, wait, thou'lt soon be marched and hymned.

Lauri: Thou art the hymnleader, the old hymnleader himself, these others thy 'prentices, the half-woollen gentry, thou knowest, that fill the choir bench on Sundays and holydays, sweating and red as turkeycocks. Here they sit again like owls, with swelling lapels, hair smoothed with butter and lard, fading grey beard quaking a little. Sit in peace, however, and sing Parson-Matt into the pulpit. True, he trotted to church from Keijula tavern, but he laved his head and brushed his hair, and now, greatly moved, climbs prayerfully into his tub and sets the old women weeping like a true lad. Now, hymnleader, I roll my eyes at thee, so let her ring. "Hurry up, Harry," as the former parson shouted to his hymnleader.

Juhani: Close thy mouth right quickly, thou vagabond!

Lauri: Not so, but "Open Thou each shepherd's mouth" is what thou hast to sing. But let this be enough, be still, hearken, and purse thy mouth to a smug church-mouth when I preach. Now, chimney-sweep's boy, lend me thy mind and thy unfettered tongue. A sermon I will preach today, a speech to reach your souls, of Peter's tattered travelling-cloak and its ten button-holes. However, glancing o'er my flock, my heart receives a sorry shock, for mine eye sees only stinking nannygoats and the devil's own billy-goats. O virgin-maids, sluts and jades of Kärkölä! ye strut in silks and satins, gilded o'er like peacocks; but spit me right i' the face if on the last day ye do

192

not shout loudly for Parson-Matt to speak for you. But that's a vain hope, yea! Good morrow, old man Sorrow. I would have a word with thee: take after old man Kettula. But thou damned Paavali Peltola, how didst thou behave at building-bee last winter? Thou drainedest many glasses and huggedst the serving-lasses. But I say unto thee, young feller: take after Jumppila Jalli: or be judged in the end by Parson-Matt, the heatrens, Greeks and breeks; and then a sack over thy head and down to Hell. Open therefore in time the flaps of thy ears and hear my speech and what I proclaim and preach; for I've been boiled in many a broth, and the heart in this breast is like an old sealskin pouch. This lad has been in much and various. In Helsinki I've been bound to a trade, bound in jail, bound in the stocks and behind other locks. But best to my belief is that I am no thief, never besmirched my neighbour's well, or hugged his wife and then farewell.

I had a little sweetheart once, a little cat, a downright minx, but she escaped and ran away. Forth I went to look for her: sought through Finland's lands and lakes, round the Baltic and Germany, but couldn'd find my golden nugget. Back I came to Finland's big island and found her on a sandy ridge beyond the town of Tampere. There's my little Tettu! I cried, nigh off my head, but Tettu was touchy and said: What art thou? What earthy lump, what tarry stump? And skipped into the nearest shanty. But I, always a jolly lad, was neither hurt nor sad, but stuffing a quid into my cavern, went to the town's best tavern, where Mick was fighting and old women frighting.

A mug of ale and two spans of brandy as a chaser is a fair amount and measure for a tired man's throat and head. And now the can danced and my beard wagged, the boys all burst out singing and the old woman's daughters giggling. But I forsook the joyous scene and set off down the street. My song rang out, the windows fell bang out, and this set all the Tampere townsmen afoot. But I, always a jolly lad, I ran like a rabbit along the strand, kicking up in their faces stones and sand. I came along to Pori, they put me in a basket there and dragged me round the market square; to Uusikaupunki I roam, they called me names from every home; Turku's worst of all the pack, they stuck a knife into my back. However, I came to Aningaisten Street and there five merry jades did meet. The first she kicked me on the thigh, the second said 'let the lad go by, for he is no meddler and no broken-down peddler.' But the third inquired "what aileth the lad?" and the fourth said "let's help him before it gets bad." Well, let's go along then arm in arm, said I, but the fifth poked me furiously with her fist and howled: "Go to Helsinki!" To Helsinki I then did plod, they gave me gruel in the quod, and then they cross-examined me, and mercilessly punished me: "Go now, go thy way, thou son of a hammer!" I took the road again and went, I, always a merry lad, I, whose heart is like an old sealskin pouch. I wandered singing along the road: and so I came to Häme, popped into the Kuninkala pulpit; and then 'tis amen!

I will now announce the banns. The parish clerk and the parish midwife are firmly bent on marrying; their wedding's tomorrow, tomorrow after supper. May they join together and stick to each other like pitch and tar! The following farms are hereby set a day's work at the vicarage: Yllilä, Allila, Yli-Seppälä, Pimppala and Alavesi. A dozen boards, a box of nails, a man from each and two from the best to patch up the smaller vicarage pig-trough. From Kiiala meadow a horse has escaped, old but wellshaped, bearing a bell, ironed well, smallish, shortish, dock-tailed, white-maned. And now dear brothers, one word more, the sheep on violence sets no store, he doth not kick, he doth not gore, but alas when a savage bull is loose, he worries trees, paws up the soil and casts confounded filth and dirt over his shepherd's Sunday shirt. And then again amen once more, each to his shanty as before, I'm off to a real brick house. That was the sermon.

Simeoni: Such godless doggerel thou knowest, but canst thou read, evildoer?

Lauri: There's a question for you: can a parson read. "Here's a man can read and rant, and never falters in his chant: a hymn as tall as the cowshed wall." But a parson sings the Mess and no hymn. I'll say the Mess and Little-Eero can do the responses.

194

Eero: I'll answer if hunger'll let me.

Juhani: Wouldst thou begin larking with a madman? Thou limb! Always ready to play the puppy. Ay, that I well believe. And thou, Lauri, lay thyself quietly to sleep; finish, brother, this ranting and raving, or I'll utter the dreadful sentence, and in a trice ten arms will cast thee down to the bulls. Stop this play.

Lauri: This is only the opening dance, brother, the opening dance. Ay, let's dance, let's wrestle, let's dance a Jussian-jig till the moss flies. Look, so!

Timo: Confounded youngster! I was near to tumbling off the rock. Quieter, quieter!

Juhani: Lauri, must I now say the dread word that turns thee in a twinkling to hash? And that merciless word is this: let him be thrown to the bulls. Shall I say it?

Lauri: Say nothing, but sing while I dance a Jussian jig. Hih!

Juhani: Let him be thrown to the bulls, and may God be with him! Amen. Now it's said. Let him go.

Lauri: Let's all go together, hand in hand out of this vale of starvation — Life!

Tuomas: Let the law be fulfilled, and go to thy death.

Juhani: What the Hell, Tuomas!

Tuomas: Down from the rock, lad!

Juhani: Stop, for Heaven's sake!

Aapo: Tuomas turns pale! God help us! Tuomas turns pale!

Juhani: Wouldst thou do deeds of terror? Brother, brother!

Aapo: He turns pale like a dying man, and deeds of terror are upon us! Calm thyself, Tuomas, oh calm thyself! I beseech thee. Up all of you and help Lauri, help him!

Tuomas: Out of my way!

Juhani: No, Tuomas, no!

Tuomas: Out of my way! Thou wert the judge, I am the hangman, and may our law be fulfilled. Down from the rock without mercy, man!

Lauri: Like a log down the chute at Nukari. Heleiyah!

Simeoni: Mercy, Tuomas, mercy, mercy!

Tuomas: Not a grain of mercy!

Juhani: God keep us from killing our brother!

Timo: Ay, Cain from killing Abel.

Aapo: Calm thy mind!

Tuomas: He dies.

Juhani: May the powers of Heaven shelter us! No, Tuomas, this cannot be.

Timo: Never, never. Lauri is the brother of each of us. Stand!

Juhani: Murder is nigh. Save Lauri, save our wretched brother!

A fierce struggle now arose on the rock. And while some held the enraged Tuomas by the collar, others by his belt, some clung to Lauri's legs, others wherever they could lay hold of him, to prevent him from rolling off the rock. Like a terrible, many-headed, many-legged monster seemed the group of brothers as, entwined in one single body, they struggled noisily. Tearing at itself, growling, grunting and sighing this monster moved, whirled round, tumbled from one side of the rock to the other and back again. With drooping tails the dogs dodged hither and thither in their fear, often on the point of rolling down to destruction, intent on preserving their lives. In greater numbers than ever the bulls too gathered around the rock, looking round-eyed at the furious struggle. But a general weariness brought peace at last on to the rock, and panting, the brothers rested on the moss, now ground to a fine powder. Then Simeoni lifted up his voice and preached, rolling his eyes fearfully upward towards the heavens.

Simeoni: Wild beasts and devils are Christian folk become. So punish us, O lord! Strike hither with thy lightning, pound to mash and offal the seven sons of sinful Zion!

Aapo: Ay, Tuomas, there'll always be five to one here; that thou knowest. But may there be peace now; and keep Lauri still until he falls asleep, poor wight.

Tuomas: Curse! I'll cast every man of you down if I want, and I shall want if the flame of my anger grows hotter. But quietly, boys, now, quietly and nicely! For my blood boils and at such moments the slightest thing looks to me like death and the horrors of death. So — nicely now!

Juhani: Tuomas is a dangerous man. Be thou my comrade, man, who flyest out at me every day and hour, rather than thou, man, who art enraged seldom but powerfully, putting at such times my miserable life in danger. Ah! this was a wicked game.

Simeoni: Whip us, punish us, Power on high!

Timo: Shut up, Simeoni, I beseech thee.

Simeoni: If I am silent, this stone shall speak and cry out. Whip us, chastise us!

Juhani: Don't call down worse things upon us. This is plague enough.

Tuomas: There he preaches like a madman, his hands crossed, the eyes in his head like those of a death-owl. Hold thy jaw at once!

Timo: Shut up, Simeoni, I beseech thee; and let us all live in peace. Look at Lauri-lad; he droops already and falls asleep, the poor lad; he sleeps. Ay, for God's sake let's live in peace and patience till we can march home again from here.

Juhani: Home! We shan't even reach our funeral home, an honourable graveyard; but here we shall sleep at last to be picked clean by ravens and eagles. I shall die this minute, on this very spot; oh, well, I die then. Was this life? What was it worth?

Timo: Ay, was this life? What was it worth? A question.

Juhani: Thou knewest not, dear mother, into what misery thou once broughtest forth seven little nippers.

Timo: Thou knewest not.

Juhani: Oh, what if we were to take one more drink, drain the last drop from the bottle. There, Tuomas, take a sup and let her go round.

Tuomas: I don't want your spirits!

Juhani: Ha-ha! Now Lauri's forgotten Jumppila Jalli and Kuninkala's pulpit and all that. Well, well, thou didst indeed rave, rave and rage on the very brink of life and death. Terrible, when I think of thee gone before thy Maker drunk, with eyes aslit.

Timo: Thou scarest me! Before God drunk!

Juhani: Before God drunk, with eyes aslit. That's a bold thought.

Simeoni: Thou canst well say so.

Juhani: It was perilous near it didn't happen. But there he lies now pale. Ah! my eyes brim over, for my soul mourns over him, and I would hide that wretched, poor and suffering brother of mine in the deepest chamber of my heart.

Aapo: In his sleep he can forget this hunger of ours, this murderous worm.

Simeoni: The third day! Ah, let us sink down in death.

Eero: For die we must, though meat, living meat walks before us.

Simeoni: It is this meat that kills us!

Juhani: This very day, this hour and minute! Ay, this hour.

Timo: Let's kill the meat, shoot every horned brute, and have fresh meat in stacks. Five rifles are loaded, and there's plenty of ammunition in Lauri's knapsack.

Juhani: There's an idea!

Aapo: That will save us!

Eero: In truth, 'twill save us!

Juhani: Ah! how shall we reward Timo?

Simeoni: Thou angel of God!

Timo: Meat, fresh meat! And nothing else. He-he! There's dozens of newly-cast bullets in Lauri's knapsack, and even more charges of powder.

Juhani: Just as thou sayest, thou peerless boy! Here's bullets and powder, more than enough. The bulls number thirty and three. Hm. We dolts and idiots! Why didn't we think of this idea before?

Aapo: In truth I did think of the same trick once, but the stuff in Lauri's knapsack never entered my mind, which is why I never spake my thought to you, for five bullets, five bulls.

Juhani: Something of the sort crossed my mind too, but without getting further. Three and thirty bulls. Good! Listen, you good-for-nothing sons of Kaura-Matti! if we shoot now like men, we can pierce the heart or brain of a bull with every shot, and the road to freedom lies open, open. Ah thee, Timo-lad!

Timo: Hey, didn't I say it. And there's nothing else to do. And well thou knowest it. Are we to perish here like rats? Bonny lads have no time for that. Hey, hey! I said it.

Juhani: Now a flash and thunder and the road to freedom is burst open!

Aapo: Ay, Juhani! True, this road goes over bleeding corpses, but it can't be helped.

Juhani: It can't be helped, so let the red-black blood flow around the Devil's Rock. We lucky badgers! soon we shall be gorging meat like wolves!

Aapo: But how shall we pay for forty bulls?

Juhani: It is a matter of life and death, in which case the law is on our side. We'll make meat, and the potbellied master of Viertola can cart away his meat, if he likes. It doesn't concern us.

Aapo: What'll happen afterwards we'll see when the fated work is done. But when the great murder is over, there's another task to be done at once. Note this, as soon as the last beast is stretched on the ground, we must start flaying them; and one of us must bear the mournful tidings to Viertola manor.

Juhani: Important advice. Flay them, skin them, before the hide sticks to the flesh. Let it be so, and then who will can take the flesh and skin, the guts and all else within. The ox on the bench and the skin off him! Each of us has a knife at his belt that can cut; here's my sheath-knife, sharp as a serpent's tongue. Ay; let's start the bloody work. Let the man whose firelock is empty, load it again with a trusty charge; and then the bloody, bloody work can begin.

Aapo: But brothers! we can wrestle with hunger an hour or two yet, especially as our salvation is now sure. Let's try once more the power of six men's throats and then wait an hour, the last hour of our captivity.

Juhani: True, hunger pinches us, but let us do as thou sayest. Let's shout, and and maybe we can get out of the trap without shedding a drop of blood. A vain hope, however. Well, well, we can wait a bit longer; for the terrible key to our freedom is in our fists. So let's yell with all our might again. I beseech you all, do it, for it is my command. Tuomas, silent as this rock, set thy trumpet roaring, too. Do it, I beseech thee, for it is my command.

Tuomas: Don't babble. I'll do as our common law demands.

Juhani: Be ready then. One, two, three.

They lifted up their voices, shouting seven times, and their cry and the howling of the dogs was borne afar. Wheareafter they sank down to wait again, although hunger assailed them fiercely, for now the certainty of salvation infused new strength into them. Of their number, one, however, brother Lauri, felt neither the pangs of hunger nor the joy of hope. Snoring and pale, he lay at the others' feet. The brothers waited an hour, waited a second, and the sun of the third day already approached its setting.

Then Juhani, hearing a faint growl of thunder from the southwest, shouted in a high, deathlike voice: "Now, boys! The Lord help us, and Amen!" And at once the gory, firespitting ga ne began.

Clouds of smoke hid the grey Devil's Rock; but from the smoke death flashed and crackled on every side for the bulls. Now here, now there, a horned beast, pierced by a bullet, suddenly bounded groaning from the ground and fell, collapsing with a mighty puff. A beast whose brain had been pierced subsided quickly with scarcely a kick, only stretching out its legs into four stiff bars; it yielded up its life, and from the wound blackish red blood spurted high into the air and from the air in a curve to the ground. But one hit in the chest, if its heart was unscathed, raged for long, galloping hither and thither among those death had still spared, until at last it too tumbled headlong to earth, where for a while, rumbling, it whipped the air with its legs. Haste, confusion and a horrific animation quickly spread among the rest as, scenting the steaming blood of their comrades, they gathered into one turbulent mob. Tongues hanging, rolling their eyes and filling the forest with a fearful bellowing, they sent dead twigs, sods and soil flying high over their backs.

But on the rock, wreathed in smoke, the brothers stood, pale phantoms, shooting, loading and firing again without pause, and ever more bulls fell staggering to the ground. Their guns flashed and banged, but sterner still was the crashing and fire on high, where the thunder rode over mountains of cloud. The smoke and the dark clouds of the heavens spread a sombre twilight around the Devil's Rock. The screams and trumpetings of the bulls, the howling of the dogs, the crackle of muskets and the growl of thunder echoed in this gloom, and in the spruce-tops a storm-wind roared. Direful was the hour; the air hot as blood. Even Lauri now woke to semiconsciousness, opened his eyes, but saw only a ghastly dimness, and in the dimness shadowy figures standing around him. He heard a matchless din, heard it beside him, heard it rise from the ground and fall from the skies, and in the unrest of his blood he seemed to feel everything whirling swiftly downward. A dismal thought entered his mind, and he said to himself: "Now we're sinking into the bottomless pit, we're sinking; well, if we sink, we sink, what help is there for it?" So saying, he shifted his position, closed his eyes and fell again into a deep sleep.

But like an arrogant castle, the Devil's Rock cloaked itself in smoke and aped the tongue of the thunder. Around it blood flowed in streams, and a hundred hooves strained skyward. Thunder rolled in the clouds, which now began to rain heavily, pouring water into the roaring wilds. But the murderous work was over; not a single horn pointed upward. On the field lay three and thirty of the Viertola bulls, altogether lifeless or still kicking; and here and there could be heard the rattling breath of a beast in its death agony. And down from the rock stepped the brothers with their dogs and scuttled to cover at the foot of a dense spruce. The thundercloud still rained torrentially, and the shaggy forest sighed. There they stood, gazing on the rich harvest of death spread before them; and in many gurgling rivulets bloody water flowed in all directions from the Devil's Rock. But when the rain had stopped, they emerged from their shelter and with distorted faces, speechless, walked among their victims, looking about them with terrible glances and ever and anon shaking their heads.

Juhani: Here's meat.

Timo: And blood.

Juhani: And blood too, in truth. Around this rock even pepper'd grow for ten years at a stretch after the manuring the soil has had. — But let's strike a light and make a fire, so that we can roast ourselves fresh meat. Ah, roast meat will taste well, that it will, in our mouth now, boys. Fetch wood and resiny chips, brothers; I'll strike a light; and do thou, Timo, hurry off to the clearing and bring the axes and knapsacks we dropped there in our hour of danger. And then, when we've eaten, we'll all set to work together, start "undressing the skins", as Old Man Krööni, that redbeard, used to say. He rests in the bosom of the earth now, and best for him to be there. Here the poor old beggar starved like a stray cur; not a friend, not a kinsman, not a roof over his head; even the empty honour of a good reputation had been struck off his papers. He crumpled up in Kolistin's barn, and now all lies forgotten under the sod. — That's good, Eero, fine resiny chips, and here's Simeoni with dry faggots, so we'll soon have a lively fire blazing. Do thou, Tuomas, cut a few mighty slices from the haunch of that mottled one. Ha-ha! I could pounce like a cat this very minute on a raw, bloody joint.

Tuomas: A mite of patience yet, and our joint will taste all the better.

Juhani: Just so. But let's be thankful that we belong to a family, a family and a race used to fighting hunger. But for that we wouldn't be hustling around like this. That I wager.

Soon seven magnificent steaks were roasting in the flames. They remembered, therefore, Lauri, though they had no wish to disturb his slumbers on the rock, where he still lay, without waking even when the rain poured down on him. Timo had set out on his errand and found the knapsacks on the clearing, found also an axe on the bloodstained field where the bear and seven bulls lay dead. He returned with the knapsacks on his back and the axe under his arm, and then six round loaves were handed out and the meat taken from the fire; and the dry bread and roast meat dipped in salt were ground fine between the men's teeth. But when they had nourished themselves, the dogs and the men, a leaden lethargy suddenly made itself felt in the brothers' limbs. Weighed down by a heavy, overpowering drowsiness they sank down, eyes closed, one after the other to the ground. Up on the rock Lauri lay snoring, down at its base the others around their campfire, as the sun died and the September day darkened into night. So amidst their victims, the slaughtered drove of bulls, they slept; and fierce Killi and Kiiski kept guard over the camp.

At last, when the night was some way advanced, they woke from their slumber and felt again in their limbs the old vigour. They rose to their feet and began to build up their fire with black, juicy, resinous tree-stumps, that in its red blaze they might see to flay their rich bag of game, but Eero was sent off without delay to inform the steward at Viertola of what had happened. Up danced a dark red flame, lighting up the ground and the rugged forest. Eero marched off to the manor; the others began with all energy to flay the beasts they had felled.

Lauri, too, woke from his long deep sleep and stared squinting around him, stared for a while without comprehending what he saw. A burning pile of stumps lit up the dark calm night, and on every side lay bulls weltering in their blood, tongues hanging out, swelled stomachs upturned. Two had been transformed into beef, a third was just undergoing the same change. And there were his brothers, some flaying, some steadying carcases by the leg; one was smashing thick bones with an axe, another was stacking meat in a mighty pile at the foot of a spruce. All this Lauri's lack-lustre eye took in; and at last he understood. He looked down, and there on a mossy hummock beside the fire was a loaf, and on the loaf a hunk of roast beef. At that a fierce spasm shook his stomach, and climbing down from the rock he sat down in the warmth of the fire and seized the bread and meat. First, however, he bared his head, crossed his hands, and rapidly nodding his tousled head said grace, and only then did he begin to eat a tasty supper. There, eyes sullen under a sullen brow, he sat and ate in silence. There he sat, drying his clothes in the glow from the resinous flames, while the others, a few paces away, toiled rapidly, for they had to flay and cut up a bear and forty bulls.

203

Eero bore the news to the steward at Viertola, the steward in all haste to his master, and a loud outcry and feverish bustle ensued; and Eero scudded off at greater speed than he had come. Screaming and blazing with anger, the master of Viertola called together all the men he could muster. Then, in furious haste, he set out for the Devil's Rock, accompanied by ten brawny men, and nearest to the master strode the broad-shouldered steward, in his fist a fear-inspiring tarry rope-end. They pushed grimly onward and at last drew near to a place where a ruddy light could be seen to gleam fitfully. And in this light they saw seven braves, seven nerve-racking phantoms of the night, and gory was the task at which the phantoms laboured, bloodstained knives in bloodstained fists. Some were flaying, some steadying the carcases, one smote asunder the sturdy bones of a flayed bull, another spread hides to dry on the yielding branches of a spruce. There dogs too were flitting, enjoying the offal the slaughterers scattered around them. Soon, however, Killi and Kiiski noticed the approaching strangers, and barking angrily charged at them, whereupon the brothers hastened with stern commands to pacify them. Then the angry lord of Viertola Manor stepped forward; bathed in perspiration the potbellied, goggle-eyed master strode forth, backed by ten strong men.

Aapo: Good evening, master!

Juhani: God help us! here's been a terrible game.

Viertola: Has Hell broke loose? Forty bulls killed! Death and torment!

Aapo: Seven men's lives were at stake.

Viertola: I'll teach you, you Jukola robbers and bandits! At them, men, and beat them until they lie in their blood like my fine cattle. At them, men!

Aapo: Softly, master!

Tuomas: Softly, softly!

Juhani: Halt, master, with thy men, halt! and remember what becomes thy peace.

Aapo: Let us talk over a case of hard fortune sensibly.

204

Juhani: There is one common law for all of us, before which we stand as equals. From the womb of a woman thou camest as I came, and as naked, just as naked, a lad not an inch better than I. And thy noble birth? Our old filmy-eyed cock can do a little trick on that. The common law! in this case it stands strongly on Jukola's side.

Viertola: On your side! Have you the right, accursed, to kill my bulls on my own ground?

Juhani: Have you the right to let loose bulls that might cost a man his life?

Viertola: They were on my own land and in a fenced pasturage.

Juhani: Then we'll set this in the scales. The piece of boundary-fence that the bulls, to our great worry, broke down, belongs rightly to Viertola's section. But now I'm minded to ask: why does a wealthy manor set up such a poor fence that a beast can break it down at one rush?

The Steward: A fence as dense as a horse's mane, thou scoundrel!

Juhani: A fence that a bull pushed out of its way like a blade of grass.

Viertola: What were you doing in my pasturage, my pasturage, you rogues! What?

Juhani: We chased a bear, a dangerous brute that would soon squash both thee and thy bulls. We killed the preying bear, and thus did our country a great, a public service. Isn't this a public service: to weed wild beasts, bogies and devils out of the world? Look you to that. The law is strongly on our side, though I were to rot.

The Steward: Keep thy mouth shut, thou rogue, and don't talk nonsense!

Viertola: They're minded to make a mock of us now, the scoundrels. Beat them! At them!

Aapo: Softly, gentlemen, stewards and grooms, and remember how we have been tortured on the rock, and that every one of us will soon be mad with fury.

Juhani: Truly said. Mad with fury, mad with fury! Ah! the

205

thoughts of a man in that state whirl swiftly round, he clenches his heart hard as a rock and then a single flash, and earth and heaven squeaks. Ah! here we've been tortured three days and three nights betwixt life and death.

Tuomas: But now we have eaten bloody meat, breathed murder's bloody vapour, and here we stand, bloodstained knives in our blood-drenched hands, bloody up to the elbows. May the Lord move you to take heed of our words in time, else we'll make this night a hell of horror. Take heed, take heed of our words!

Eero: And a warning from the bulls there.

Juhani: O God, grant them this moment eye-salve, and strength to their hearts to keep them from teasing us further! Give wisdom to their brains and make them take warning from the unhappy bulls there, for we are still in a state to make mincemeat! Give to them wisdom, Lord, lest we become their high priests and with these bloody knives wed them to one flesh and one blood with the unhappy bulls, and make a shrieking hell of this nightly forest. O Lord, protect that big-bellied master of Viertola there and his over-bold men! Have mercy on them, Almighty Son of God!

Tuomas: Here we stand, come forth if ye are minded.

Juhani: Here we stand, come forth if ye are minded.

Viertola: Good — good! Brag and boast now, but the time will come, I believe, when the law will decree otherwise, and then the tail of your pride will droop, and even your miserable home will go, down to its rotting foundations. Away, men! I leave you forty bulls as your prey now, but every one will yet be torn from you to the very last hoof. Let us go!

Juhani: Take away your meat and offal before they spoil. They're nothing to do with us; we only hastened to flay them before the hide stuck to the flesh.

Viertola: All's well! Home, men, as I command.

And with his men the master of Viertola departed, still fiercely threatening and cursing; but the brothers set themselves to their butchering again. And the following day the forty bulls had been flayed, and the brothers returned to their home, carrying the

206

enormous grey-black bear on a pole. The flesh, hides and offal of the bulls they left in the forest, with two of the brothers, however, to guard them. And thus ended the hunting-trip that was born of Tinder-Matti's tales of the lands of the north, and planned, in the beginning, as a hunt for wild duck on Kourusuo Bog.

CHAPTER 9

IT IS a morning in September, a few days after the brothers' adventurous journey had ended. There on the clearing they now sit around a boiling cauldron of meat. For two days they had watched from a distance over the meat in the forest, but as no one came to remove it, it began to look as though it was to be left to form a mighty carrion-heap. Whereupon they decided to make use of the great stacks of meat in the forest and to live nobly for a while around reeking flesh-pots. They bore the carcases to their storeroom, which became filled with meat, while the rafters disappeared beneath hanging hides. And now, spluttering and foaming, a gigantic cauldron of meat boiled on the stump-covered clearing near the house, boiled almost without cease from morning to night, and, glutted, the brothers' stomachs laboured. Around it they spent carefree, merry days; now eating, now relating tales and legends, now sweetly sleeping again, heads pillowed on hummocks, and the hollow clearing echoed with their snoring.

The morning was fine, and limpid and blue stretched the sky, while from the surrounding forests the booming of the fresh north-east wind could be heard. Around their fleshpot the brothers sprawled; some sitting on stumps, some on the dry surface of the clearing, enjoying an abundant breakfast. There the dogs, too, lying on their stomachs, gorged themselves on the fibrous, powerful flesh of the bulls. Cheeriness and a deep-rooted calm shone on every face.

Timo: Thanks to the master of Viertola for this meal too.

Juhani: All thanks and honour to him!

Aapo: We shall count this feast dear yet. Viertola will certainly not leave matters as they are.

Juhani: The law is on our side; this the master is bound to see and to leave the law alone. Let's eat meat, brothers, and may it lie lightly on our stomach, for our backs are free. But more exercise, boys, more exercise and marching is what we want; beef is strong food.

Eero: Let's join hands and dance a brotherly ring-dance; let's buck and-jump, and I'll lay our tummies shrink.

Juhani: We're not going to skip here like hawks in summer, but will join in some other game. Ah! where are the madcap days of my boyhood now? Brothers, let us hit the whirling disc once more as we used to on Toukola's dusty highways. Here's a smooth clearing for us; such stumps as are in our way we can tear up by the roots, and on yon side we can take the smooth surface of the heath to lengthen our playground with. Let's form two sides, and each of those on the losing side must swallow ten pounds of ox-flesh this evening.

Tuomas: Agreed.

Juhani: Ten pounds, brothers?

Eero: Just so! Ten pounds as punishment for those whom the tough disc sweeps before it.

Juhani: Three a-side would be fairest, but there are seven of us.

Lauri: I'm out of it. I'd sooner hunt for useful timber in the forest than run and sweat like a hairbrained nipper. Play your game, I'm off into the forest with an axe under my arm.

Thus speaking, they ended their meal at last and set out to prepare their playground. They shaped it to run across the clearing and for some distance farther along the heath on the clearing's eastern edge. And a few hours later they stood ready for the game, sturdy birchwood staves in their hands; and they stood divided into two sides: Juhani, Simeoni and Timo on one side, and Tuomas, Aapo and Eero on the other. The disc began to fly between them, and the forest echoed far around as the staves smote the hard wooden wheel as it sped humming backwards and forwards.

But deep in the backwoods Lauri walked, an axe under his arm. Slowly he marched, looking carefully around him, and ever and anon his progress was halted as his eye caught nodes, forked stems, twisted trunks and tousled wind-tangles high in the crowns of dense birches and pinetrees. He came to the tall stump of a storm-felled spruce; he regarded it thoughtfully for a while, then began to chip a hole in its side with his axe. This accomplished, he thought to himself: happen next summer a redstart or a little mottled wood-pecker'll build its nest in that hole. With this idea, he marked the spot carefully and continued his journey again. But having wandered a while, he saw a hanging birch, from the trunk of which an enormous node protruded, rotund, big as a Christmas cake. He chopped it off and took it with him, deciding that it would make a capacious scoop. He set off wandering onward again, but soon his sharp eye descried on the edge of a tongue of rock a marvellously twisted juniper. Now what would that make? he pondered, and striking once, twice, with his keen axe, he felled the juniper. He lopped off the branches, regarded it smiling for a moment, and resumed his journey, taking the juniper with him. He heard the cow-bells from the villages and emitted a fearful yell to scare away wolves from the neighbourhood. He yelled, and the echoes flowed around in friendly answer. So he marched on until he finally reached the heather-clad ridge of a hill, where he saw a large windtangle dancing in a pinetree's crown, rocked by the cool north-easter. He felled the pine, chopped off the tousled crown and sat down to contemplate his find.

For long he sat there, thinking and examining the wind-tangle and the node and the richly twisted juniper. "How had Nature formed these things? What had bent the juniper into all those twists and bends?" And sinking down to the ground, he leaned his head against a deserted, grass-grown ant-heap. Thence he stared

210

at the tree-tops, at the slow-sailing clouds, pondering over the build of the earth and heaven; and from afar, from Impivaara clearing, the faint clash of the disc-players' staves was borne to his ears. Feeling at last a desire to dispel all thought from his brain he decided to go to sleep; but sleep seemed loth to approach him. But what did Lauri usually do when the Goddess of Sleep chanced to prove coy? He would either fancy himself a little mole that digs deep down in its peaceful underground manor, to sleep at last on a bed of finest sand, or he would imagine himself a thick-pelted bear, resting in his rough mossy cabin beneath the spruce-roots, over which the blizzards of winter go roaring. Thinking thus, he would nearly always find sleep soon closing his eyes. And so it was now, as he fancied himself a little mole, burrowing deep in the womb of mother nature.

He slept, but in his sleep his mind went on weaving his fancy. His whole body, so it seemed to him, shrank swiftly to that of a fine-haired mole; his eyes became exceedingly small, and his palms swelled to enormous gloves, until he was a mole, burrowing beneath the pine-roots, deep under the heath. There he burrowed and dug, digging himself finally upward along the rotted pith of a tall pine until, when he reached the topmost stem of its crown, he found himself sitting in the middle of a wind-tangle in a soft, mossy pen. "This is a good place to be in, here I will live for ever", he thought, peering with little mole's eyes out of his tiny chamber window. And he saw beneath him a sombre world wrapped in the cheerless grey of the autumn eve. He saw Impivaara's beetling height, and in measureless distance that tore at the heart, he saw amidst the twilit forests the melancholy cabin, and he saw his brothers, hitting the disc with the Vicar on the misty, echoing heath. And a desire to weep bitterly assailed him, but the tears seemed loth to come and only rolled restlessly at their source. Towards Impivaara he looked: and over the clearing and for some distance along the heath oxhides had been spread, blood-bespattered, fresh, in a long row, along which the disc danced humming. With staves of birch, bent near the handles, the brothers bravely

211

smote, but the Vicar, with his sword of the spirit, smote still more bravely. And this sword of the spirit was beaten of toughest iron, of old horse-shoes; so boasted the Vicar himself, as he proudly waved his weapon in the air, waved it and beat it against the oaken shield of faith that dangled on his left breast.

With sweating brows they battled; backward and forward flew the disc beteen them, and a great din and crashing was heard afar. But at last the Vicar noticed that the disc was no ordinary disc at all, but a red-backed a-b-c-book, which the brothers were using as a disc. And at that the Vicar became incensed; he cursed and swore, shouting a thousand maledictions on the brothers' heads. With his sword of the spirit he pointed east, west, south and north, and shouted in a loud voice "iiyah, iiyah!" And from every quarter black clouds approached in whirling tempests, approached mournful Impivaara at terrific speed. Came whirlwinds in their thousands, and around the brothers they all crashed together, sucking up the brothers into their embrace. And soon six brothers spun high in the air on the wings of the winds, head-over-heels in a confused jumble. So, wrapped in dust and vapoury clouds, they whirled giddily round, spun as a warping-mill spins when sped by the spinner's nimble hand. Terrified, Lauri in his mole's attire looked on from his wind-tangle, up in the crown of the bowing pine. He saw emerge from the revolving mass, now a man's hand, now a chin like to Juhani's mighty chin, and then again a coarse shock of hair would flash by his glance. Then the Vicar suddenly smote his oaken shield of faith with his sword, and at once the pillar of cloud moved; it began speeding towards the pine-wood where Lauri rocked in his high cradle, and at this his mole's eyes opened wide. The raging whirlwind flew past him, however, and suddenly sounding, and as suddenly dying away, the brothers' pitiable moans and yells were borne to his ears. Past him it flew, with fear-awakening speed: the forest roared like a thousand rapids, roared and crashed, and the pine in whose top Lauri sat in his wind-tangle fell crackling; at which the man, horribly scared, woke from his dream. Shrieking loudly, he bounded up from his hummock, shouting in a voice nigh to weeping: "Help, O God, the child of Man!" For long he stared around him without immediately recollecting where he was. But at last his thoughts settled down in their former channels again, especially when he saw beside him his belongings: the twisted juniper, the globular node and the windtangle, frilled like the Turkish Sultan's turban.

He began at last, axe under arm and the collected spoil on his shoulder, to walk towards Impivaara, resolving nevermore to picture himself an animal, God having once created him a thinking human being. Thus meditating, he fared onward, noting yet beside the stony path a little birch that pleased his eye. "Now what would that make, — a good fastening-pin", he decided, and striking once with his axe, he now had the makings of a good fastening-pin on his back. With this addition to his load he resumed his journey; and a while later he stood on the heath, watching, morose and silent, the brothers' merry pastime, the fiery speeding of the disc. Hard they smote and ran, and the winners were Tuomas, Aapo and Eero, who had already driven their opponents to the eastern end of the ground. Then when the playground cleared for the game had been won, the parties changed ends, and brothers Juhani, Simeoni and Timo began retreating homeward, although resisting with all their might. Difficult was it to meet Tuomas's stroke as the disc flew shrieking and dancing forward; difficult for the disc on its return to spin past Eero without being met by a stroke of his staff. And so they battled and perspired, yelling at the top of their voices, and silent, Lauri watched the struggle, with his booty from the forest on his back; Killi and Kiiski watched too, ever sitting near Juhani and now and again opening their jaws in a gaping yawn. The autumn sky stretched bright above them, the fresh northeaster hummed in the pines, and in the forest, perched on the side of a withered spruce, a redcrested, yellow-eyed woodpecker hammered, sounding ever and anon its beautiful high-pitched call.

Juhani: Let the wheel come and he'll feel my stick on his forehead, just to let him know where he comes from.

213

Tuomas: See that: there's a stroke that'll sweep you down to Lake Ilvesjärvi.

Juhani: That I'm not inclined to believe. Ay, here it lies, little brother, nicely. But God's lightning! look to thy shins, lad, now. There!

Tuomas: Hit back, smite it, Aapo!

Aapo: Flew like a swallow humming past me. But Eero's staff will ring again, that I know. Just as I said! Well hit, Eero, good!

Tuomas: Honour to Eero, high honour!

Juhani: If it wasn't for that cursed infant there at your tail end, you'd be deep in the forest by now, poor fellows!

Tuomas: Step out to the disc, man, and don't stand babbling there like a child.

Eero: Heleiyah! Past him again.

Aapo: Not a single staff could touch it, not one.

Tuomas: No more than they'd hit a shooting-star in the sky. Well, brothers, what do you say?

Eero: They've little time even to whisper a word, running with drooping tails after their lost sheep.

Juhani: What is Aapo thinking of over there? See to it, lad, that thou hast not slaughtered my disc, so tough and hard.

Tuomas: It bounced off the road into the heather yonder and stopped, to my mind, near that little fir. Good morrow, Lauri! Why art thou standing there so sullen and silent?

Eero: What news from the forest, Lauri?

Juhani: Ask him. There he stands like the former Heikki Pajula, that man from Myllymäki, with a bunch of old boots on his back. But Aapo, Aapo, thou dratted loon, what art fumbling at there.

Timo: Hurry up, hurry up, brother Aapo.

Juhani: Peering and seeking there like a cat after its kitten. "The wind it blows and the tree-tops sway..." Move a little out of my way, Kiiski-boy, or thy paws'll be in danger. Dost hear me? Get out of my way.

"The wind it blows and the tree-tops sway,
My love's voice echoes from far away."

Ay, ay, poor Kiiski, pity won't help here. And well thou knowest
it. Yonder thou canst sit and yawn as seems best to thee. Hey,
my pet, hey-hey-hey! There thou canst sit in peace and watch the
disc fly. But the Devil's loose if that disc isn't found! Every
man looking for it!

Eero: Here the thing is.

Tuomas: Place it there in the vice of my finger and thumb.

Aapo: And let them have it from a man's hand.

Juhani: Just so! And here's a man's staff to meet it.

Tuomas: Out of the way, or I'll give thee a horn on thy forehead.

Aapo: It flies past him.

Eero: Oh, my poor Juhani-brother! why dost thou whip the
empty air like that?

Juhani: Strike at it, Simeoni: knock it down so that the earth
rings! Oh thou butter-fingered dolt! Now Timo-son, see that thy
staff clashes! The Devil in thy skin! Thou deservest five brace
of stripes, old slowcoach!

Tuomas: Keep on marching! There's no help for it.

So the strenuous game ended at last, and the sun sank westward
into the bosom of the mossy pines. Perspiring, the brothers now
marched home, both the victors, Tuomas, Aapo and Eero, and the
vanquished; and last of all came Lauri, a mighty burden on his
shoulder. Arrived in the home yard, a cauldron full of meat was
set on a fire and there allowed to cook. Then they began their
meal together; but Juhani, Simeoni and Timo had to swallow a
fearful quantity of beef, ten pounds, according to the common
decision when the game was begun. Without any mercy they had
to fulfil their task, Tuomas standing threateningly over them.
Nobly they chewed and swallowed, though their stomachs rose in
revolt and their eyes became shot with blood. At last Simeoni and
Timo completed their measure and then, puffing and with hid-

215

eously contorted visages, made for the cabin without delay and dropped down on their rushy couches to sleep. But for some time yet Juhani lingered over his enormous meal, though he chewed and munched diligently. Silent, staring stiffly downward at the forest, he sat on a stump and ate, filled with wrath, particularly as Eero's uncontrollable giggling was wafted to his ears. Finally he too swallowed for the last time, and his features swelled and darkened terribly, but down slid the piece at last from his throat, only half-masticated. And then hastily, puffing, grinning piteously and holding his stomach, he staggered to the cabin and fell down to sleep on his bed of rushes, and others followed him to their night's rest.

When at last they woke in the morning from their deep sleep, juryman Mäkelä, accompanied by a witness, stood in the room. Sent by the master of Viertola, he came to command their presence at the Assizes to answer for the killing of the bulls. Without a word, staring, the brothers heard the juryman's command, then finally they got up and dressed themselves, the confusion of sleep gradually leaving them. Wrathfully Juhani scratched his poll and uttered in a growling tone:

Juhani: This is a hard case, for there were seven lives at stake. And what are a thousand cattle compared to one man?

Mäkelä: The bulls wandered peaceably on Viertola land, in a fenced enclosure.

Juhani: But a bear, which is the enemy of cattle and man, the foe of all authority, does not wander as peaceably when it comes on Viertola soil, but will eat up both master and myself, and Mäkelä too; and we are all, I hope, dearly-bought souls. Look you to that point. Ai, ai, Mäkelä! there's many a point, pitfall and paragraph stored away back of my teeth, and with these I'll stop up Viertola's mouth nicely yet. I'm in no mind to blab all of them now, but before the judge I can let out one thing and another, as matters demand, aye, matters and circumstances.

Timo: We're not exactly children in matters of law. Didn't we, Lord ha' mercy, come forward like real gentlemen in that mighty

216

lawsuit that Kaisa Koivula started to get support for her child? I still remember how they shouted: "Juhani, son of Juhani Jukola and his younger brother Timotheus!"

Juhani: Timo, shut up, shut up this minute like a young mole. Yes, Mäkelä, the matter is as I just said.

Mäkelä: You will not even try then to repay Viertola the damage voluntarily?

Juhani: Not a penny, not a penny, not a single Crown's penny! We have justice on our side, and the victory'll be ours at last, though I were to rot.

Mäkelä: Yet I've heard that meat is eaten here every day as though 'twas always All Saint's Day. What is the meat you gorge so unstintingly?

Juhani: Beef, beef, the juicy meat of Viertola's bulls. And it isn't exactly our habit to gorge, but to eat ordinary-like, as much as a hungry Christian belly will hold.

Mäkelä: So you touched the meat anyhow, with which, as you yourself said, you have nothing to do.

Juhani: The meat would otherwise have spoiled and spread the itch and scab, plagues and sores over the whole of Finland. We saved the country from this ruin. And again, should you ask us why we did not, for the greater freedom of our skins, bury the meat in the depths of the earth, — which would be a truly daft question — but if you were to ask us why, we would answer thus: We did not want to commit so great a sin as to rob our Fatherland and those set in authority over us of such strong, juicy fare as beef, especially if we remember that this year too so many lads have been forced to chew pinebark like goats.

Mäkelä: Well, in truth, you did right in taking what Viertola proudly refused. That is the answer to that question; but to come to the kernel of the case, the payment of damages, I'm afraid it'll be taken from you in the end.

Juhani: Not in play, not in play. Sooner both house and lands can go, down to the last corner-stone.

Mäkelä: I have done my duty and given you my opinion of the case. Farewell!

Juhani: Give us your opinion of another matter. What is the Vicar thinking of us nowadays?

Mäkelä: In that matter the world chatters fearfully, but there's no trusting in what rumour chooses to whisper. But one thing I can assure you is true, namely, that the Vicar is in lively correspondence with the Bishop regarding you and that soon fifty cossacks will be sent to the parish at the Bishop's request.

Juhani: Good!

Mäkelä: Ay, fifty horse and men.

Juhani: Good! Finnish lads have broken cossack pikes before now.

Mäkelä: A sorry matter all the same. Still it's not as bad as rumour would have it. Could this be true now? "A company of cossacks, a dusting company of lanced cossacks, with knouts and all." Ay, why should any one believe such foolish rumours. There'll be fifty of them, no more.

Juhani: Let 'em come.

Mäkelä: Dost thou say so? Rascal! And here I'd give five crowns to escape them, to escape the shame of it. What nonsense! The military to our parish for the sake of seven men? Nonsense, nonsense! But such is our Bishop's plan.

Juhani: All's well!

Mäkelä: Ill, ill, devilishly ill. But fare ye well now!

Juhani: God protect you, Mäkelä! and thou, Taavetti Karila, go in God's·name and peace.

Tuomas: Would there be any truth in it?

Juhani: Think, lads! Forty bulls and a company of cossacks! Take me to thy bosom, Ilvesjärvi!

Aapo: I doubt greatly...

Juhani: Forty bulls and a battalion of cossacks, knouts and all, goggle-eyed knouts! Take me to thy shining bosom, lake!

Aapo: Calm thyself, man, and stop raving.

Juhani: Thou heardest what he said?

218

Lauri: He lied. I saw that from his eyes, although the old chap tried to look grave. He lied; that I'll swear to.

Aapo: A great rogue, that Mäkelä. Let cossacks be set afoot for Karja's robbers and Nurmijärvi bandits, and not for honourable men, without a single mark in their papers yet. But Mäkelä's a great rogue.

Tuomas: And yet always a man of honour.

Aapo: A man of honour, honesty itself, but he can jest whenever he is so inclined, and so finely, finely, that you'd never notice what he was at before you're kicking in his net. Ah! if there were a cold heart and an evil mind in that breast, he'd beat the Devil himself in plots of darkness. But now he desires and does only good, though he does play pranks now and then right madly. Ah thee! how well thou didst arrange thy words and sentences in this tale too. It was hardly that I wasn't taken in a little myself.

Juhani: I, poor lad, was scared almost to death at the prattle of that great rogue; but now I see that it was all pure lies. Cossacks to this place? What next? He-he!

Aapo: But it was a big enough shock on a fasting stomach. Hasten now, Lauri, and make a fire under that oven-stone; for my belly says that meal-time draws nigh.

Lauri went out on to the clearing, kindled a blazing fire, and after a time the others came out of the cabin, placing themselves around the stone; and once more a cauldron of meat was cooked for breakfast. They began their meal, but for Juhani, Simeoni and Timo beef had lost its flavour that day.

Eero: Eat meat, boys. Juhani, have some beef.

Juhani: Eat it thyself.

Timo: The fatness of these bulls doesn't please me, however much I try.

Simeoni: I feel a shudder go through my sinful frame whenever I turn my eyes towards the pot yonder.

Timo: Shall I ever eat fresh meat again? Perish the thought!

Juhani: To swallow ten pounds of beef into one's stomach. Ten pounds! Why, it's like a wolf. But now I've had enough, and the

219

path of my life is closed, now my appetite for meat is gone. For it's meat, meat, that we have to depend on down here. But the cauldron there is as though full of black toads to me now. Ah! a little more and I'd cry.

Timo: What's the use of crying? Believe me, I haven't wiped my eyes since at mother's grave-side; when the old girl was hidden in a hole in the earth, then I blubbered a bit, sure. At other times, when hard luck seems to threaten a poor lad, what I always think is: nothing fiercer than death can come of it, anyhow. Why be cast down? Time will bring new advice.

Juhani: Right! That's something I'll show you just now, I will, Nick take me! In this skull of mine a spark of an idea lit up just now. Ay, ay! Even a thick head, even the thickest head isn't quite the stupidest thing. Ay, ay! The spark of my idea is alight.

Timo: What kind of spark?

Juhani: Ay, ay!

Timo: What kind of spark?

Juhani: Maybe every screw is in its place here. Ay, ay!

Timo: Hast thou found a way out?

Juhani: Here, Lord love us, we have resiny stumps around us in thousands like black goblins.

Timo: Ay, that we have. But what blessing is a resiny stump to us?

Juhani: Oh poor soul of little faith. From the stumps we can boil hissing tar, from the tar pitch, shiny black lumps, for which we can get money. It's a trick I know as well as Rajamäki's Mikko. But thanks to Eero, who sang of him yesterday, and thus brought this stump-idea into my head; for there's no other way for us to make money. Even the game in our forests grows less and less, and turned into money wouldn't bring in enough even for bread and other grub, now that I have, as it seems, said an eternal farewell to meat. But now tar and pitch will repay everything. Let us take after Mikko, take after Mikko.

Timo: Let's do so. But then we ought to add Mikko's other job to it, if our new life is to keep us in bread. I myself know that a cat is put into a leather sleeve and a dog into a sprat-barrel, to get a proper hold of them, but there's lots of other wisdom needed too. And the job is looked on as in some way shameful. Let us remember that too.

Juhani: Go to Hell with thy gelder's knife! I'll burn tar, I will, and boil pitch; and thou'lt see yet how money can be made from chunks of pitch. Aapo, what dost thou think of my idea?

Aapo: I've turned it over in my head, and it's not without sense, but it isn't going to bring in enough bread. Still less can we go to law with rich men on the strength of our lumps of pitch. And woe to us if we lose in this matter in the end!

Juhani: Ay, ay, but what are we to do? Every man seeks his right down here.

Aapo: Let's come to some agreement and leave the law aside.

Juhani: Boy! how are we to appease the fiery master of Viertola and pay for his bulls?

Aapo: Pitch won't be enough for that, nor tar nor game, which grows less at an alarming rate. But look now, how one idea springs from another and one word from another. When thou spokest of resiny stumps, there came into my mind the boundless backwoods of Jukola, its dense birch-woods, pine-woods, and spruce-woods. In a few days seven men could fell many acres of forest for sowing. We could burn the undergrowth and branches and sow the ground, and later reap and take the harvest to Viertola as the price of his bulls, leaving, however, a part in the storeroom for our own needs. And that means bread for those whom meat and blood terrify. And to come back to Viertola, if the first crop is not enough to pay for the bulls, why a second will do it, and in any case a third. But until grain waves in our new clearing, we can squeeze mother nature with all our might; and for you three, meat will yet taste well. We can go on thus for two years; but when a heavy-eared harvest stands in our clearing, then we can build frames for our ricks and hammer together a threshing-barn, and well, that'll be like working on a real farm. But if we decide to begin such a task, one or two us must go quickly to talk over the matter with Viertola,

221

and I do believe he'll be appeased and agree to await the harvest from our clearing; for they say he is on the whole a worthy fellow.

Tuomas: That's advice worth thinking over.

Juhani: Sure, 'tis worth it. It's advice from a man's skull and not from the little knob of a daft woman.

Aapo: Let us think this over, and tomorrow what's decided is decided.

The day passed, night came and another day dawned and the brothers decided to follow brother Aapo's advice. Two of them, Juhani and Aapo, set out to speak the language of peace with the hasty master of Viertola. And soon the dreaded master was all mildness and was pleased to await compensation for his loss from a mighty clearing. And why should he not have agreed to a plan by which many and various profits were offered him from the stately Jukola forests. Highly satisfied, the brothers returned from the manor, to bring home the glad tidings.

Two days went by again and a third, and the brothers set out for the forest in a body, with gleaming axes on their shoulders, while, burdened with a brush-hook and an old broken sickle, Eero brought up the rear. A wide hill-side of dense pines, sloping southward and topped by a grove of tall trees, was fixed on for the clearing. Whereafter they began to fell the forest; axes clashed, the forest rang, and with a great crashing pine fell on pine. Always in the van hastened Eero, cutting down the tough pliant shoots with his hook. So fell many an acre of luxuriant forest, and all around spread the fresh perfume of new chips and of green, coniferous branches. And soon on the sunny slope, Impivaara clearing lay ready, enormously large, so that its like had hardly been seen before. And the work had been accomplished within five September days. Whereafter they reposed sweetly in their cabin again, snoring for three nights and three days. But when their bodies were sufficiently rested, they fared forth to hunt in the yellowing forests. Over echoing hills they wandered; they strode through dismal backwoods, thinning with well-aimed bullets the herds of Tapiola for provision during the coming winter. Greatly, however, had the game begun to diminish in the lands around Impivaara; and it was high time for the brothers to seek new fields for the supply of their daily bread.

Winter came, snow hid the ground, keen winds circled round the clearing, sweeping up drifts against the cabin's walls. But within the cabin, the brothers wallowed in the stifling heat of the platform, resting from the many labours and dangers of the preceding summer. Diligently they bathed, whipping their limbs in the grateful heat with soft bunches of twigs. Roaring the steam rose from the hot stones, spreading in rolling clouds through the room, to escape at last through the cracks and disappear in the cold, shrinking air, under the melancholy, pallid sky. So, stretched on their rushy coches, the drowsy men lived through their days and nights. There on many a winter night they looked through their tiny window on the flashing, livid northern lights. At such times an arc of light, visible afar, shone on the mountain's rim, beyond the bearded spruce. There, fluttering and silent, the play of light was lit and extinguished and lit again; fire pursued fire, stretching from the pale gateway of the north up to the dome of the heavens, and at times a faint light quivered over all the sky. From the platform of their cabin the brothers watched the play of light, marvelling and speculating hither and thither over the origin and cause of this solemn spectacle. But they conjectured and pondered in vain.

Now and again, however, they went out when the brief day dawned into the playground of the winds, fared forth on well-greased skis across the rime-clad forests. And as luck stood them by, they bagged now a lively heath-grouse, now a grey-clad squirrel, now some other denizen of the woods. In the back-woods they chanced on the round tracks of a lynx that ran in a pretty line along the crust of snow, and at once the ardour of the dogs rose to boiling-point, showing that the animal could not be far away. Soon the whining bark of Killi and Kiiski was heard and the sound of the chase moving swiftly onward; and swiftly the brothers hastened on behind. Through the forest they swept, out of the

223

forest up a stony hill; and from the crags the snow and moss was whipped high up into the air. Ahead fled the lynx, its eyes brightly flashing, bright as two mirrors held up to the sun. The screaming fury of the dogs pursued it, and with the swishing of skis the seven men. Now along Kamaja's lofty ridge they sped furiously, headed towards the southwest, whence the dying star of day glowed through the spruce to meet them; and on the right the low-lying northward lands rang with the chase, and on the left the low-lying southward lands echoed the sound, as Killi and Kiiski gave mouth to their fire-breathing eagerness. But suddenly the medley of sound was still as the crook-clawed lynx, just when the danger was greatest, climbed swifty into the top of a tree. The spruce took it lovingly to its bosom, helpless, however, to ward off the pursuing death. The dogs raged, looking with burning eyes lustfully upward, whence a low growling was heard; and wrathfully the spruce shook its mane, threatening the pursuers. Then with a violent crash and din the brothers came into view on their skis, with cheeks glowing like fire and heaving bosoms. And Tuomas said: "Keep back the dogs now, brothers, from starting a dangerous fight, in which their bellies would soon be ripped open." And at his words the others quickly seized the dogs by their furry coats, while Tuomas aimed his gun and fired. Down from its shelter tumbled the lynx, bleeding, and immediately the screaming dogs began struggling wildly to be at their prey, though without succeeding. The lynx lay on the snow-covered ground, kicking and squirming, its sharp claws raging madly everywhere around it, until a second ball, piercing its brain, cut short its agony, and it lay still. Threateningly the spruce shook its locks once more, scattering downward from its crown a shower of glittering snow to hide its dying son, as in the hot stream of its blood the keen life fled from its heart, to dissolve in a vapour into the air. And thus ended a mighty chase on Kamaja's spruce-clad hill, whither Impivaara showed faintly in the northwest, with the stump-covered clearing palely gleaming at its base. Thither the brothers now merrily bent their steps with their spoil.

So in the rime-clad forests they ski'd up hill and down, ski'd over level plains; and the men's open and bronzed breasts shone afar. And so they passed their time; for the most, however, in the cabin's warmth, while the rayless, drowsy sun lingered in the sweltering lands of the south. Far indeed had it travelled, the burning source of life; one day it hardly lifted even its brow from the blue bosom of the forests. But with that it turned again and began once more its journey northward.

Summer came, the clearing was prepared for firing; the logs were rolled away, and in the calm, hot days a mighty sea of branches dried, and the time for burning drew nigh. Without sending word to their neighbours, without informing a soul, the brothers set out to burn over their clearing. Fire was set to the brushwood and a great flame rose roaring towards the heavens, and soon the brown smoke rolled right to the edge of the clouds. Onward spread the fire, and in the bright light of the sun the litter burned to ashes. But the mere branches and litter of the clearing failed to satisfy it ,and with a thunderous noise it charged at last into the pillared halls of the pines. Then the brothers, terror-stricken, hastened to fight the unfettered element with all their might: they swept and smote at the heathery ground, and their brooms of spruce whizzed and whined through the air, as they fell heavily on the ground, setting all the sandy hill-side booming. Yet the raging flames seemed little dismayed at this; they sped, still hurrying swiftly, onward. Cried Juhani at last in a loud voice: "trousers in hand, every man; wet them in the spring and beat the fire with 'em!" Hastily tearing off their trousers, they dipped them in a brimming, cold spring and began beating, whipping the burning surface of the heath. High into the air flew the hot ashes and the soot, the earth thundered as though a host of riders had galloped at full speed over it; and at length confusion seized the angry flames. Black as niggers and bathed in perspiration, the men collapsed weakly on to the ground, puffing, sobbing after their heated game.

But the clearing had burned cleanly and was sown and ploughed, harrowed with a primitive wooden harrow with the combined strength of seven men, and finally a stout fence was built up around it, and before the coming of winter an excellent young crop had sprouted there. And in the fence suitable openings were left, in which heavy snares were set, to the death of numerous hares.

CHAPTER 10

DAYS passed; summer and harvest-time came round again, and in the clearing swayed a crop, brilliant and magnificent, the like of which had scarcely been seen before. In the heat of a blazing sun the brothers reaped their field; and soon the sheaves too disappeared as they were removed into the cabin. There in the heat of the platform the grain was dried, threshed against the wall below and winnowed. And in the end the clearing lay quite naked, despoiled of its grain, of which the greater part was at once taken to Viertola, twenty barrels being retained by the brothers for their own use. With this grain about half of the brothers' debt was paid; but the master of Viertola promised to wipe off the whole of it if the brothers would allow him to use their clearing for one crop of oats, give him the logs for a big new barn from the Jukola forests and return the forty ox-hides. And the brothers agreed to the bargain.

They were now released from an awkward situation, which had helped, however, to store their granary with more grain than they needed for the coming winter. But it led to other more far-reaching results as well. This same grain, fine first-crop grain, suggested to Juhani the idea of distilling spirits, an idea that was soon approved by Timo. The others were against the enterprise in the beginning, but finally the will of Juhani and Timo prevailed. Juhani described how spirits, enjoyed with skill and in moderation, could bring joy and happiness, especially to them, young ravens in the dismal forests. And they set to work and fashioned a small distillery in the ditch by the wolf-trap and to it brought the old Jukola still; for the tanner lacked means to distil spirits for himself. And now smoke began to rise towards the heavens from Impivaara ditch; and richly the still yielded clear spirits.

And then the brothers began to enjoy themselves, tippling from morning to eve, and their time went by like the flow of a river. And already after the lapse of two or three days a ceaseless, humming music, like the sound of a distant bassoon, echoed in their ears, and the world span merrily round before their eyes. Attired only in their shirts, they lolled in the cabin, whence a fearful din and singing was now constantly heard, broken now and again by the dull thuds of a wrestling bout or the clamour and banging of a fight. Often, at such times, the stout door of the cabin would suddenly fly open and a man gallop out as fast as he could with another hard at his heels. Round and round the cabin they would scud, short, homespun shirts waving and brown limbs twinkling. So they would run until a collision occurred or the rest of the brothers stepped between to restore peace and harmony. Then they would enter the cabin in a body, friendship would be drunk again and a merry song sung together.

Lauri alone kept apart from this riot. Remembering his wild spree on the Devil's Rock, he had taken a noble and sacred decision never to let intoxicating liquor pass his lips again, and this vow he kept. Now he strode the forests in silence, studying the bends in tree-trunks and seeking useful timber for household purposes. He also worked steadily with his traps in the clearing and would often return from his outings carrying a young hare in his distended bag. Once, having gone out to examine his traps, he chanced to see a brown animal in a snare. Highly satisfied, he said to himself: "Thanks be to God that I have caught a fox!" but soon a rough, snarling cry was heard from him: "Viertola's tabby cat and the Devil!" With this shout he cast the cat angrily into the forests, set the snare again and went on to his other traps and gins. Thus he spent his days in the cool woods, while the others gambolled with shrunken eyes in the scorching cabin.

Michaelmas drew nigh, and the brothers felt like enjoying this holiday in high fashion. A rich load was haled together to be taken to town, and with the proceeds titbits were to be bought for the coming feast: rum, bottled beer, eels, salt herrings and wheaten bread. Great was the bustle around the cart one fresh autumn morning. Sacks were lifted and stored, ropes bound and strong slip-knots tied. Everything was done lightly, done at fiery speed; for each of them, with the exception of Lauri, had poured a mighty morning drink down his throat. Soon the load stood ready in the yard, and Simeoni and Eero began their journey to Hämeenlinna, with a barrel of rye and ten cans of spirits on the cart and old Valko between the shafts.

But in the cabin the merrily roaring life continued; spirits were drunk out of a tankard, and day followed day. A week went by and part of the next, but there was no sign of the travellers from town, and finally the brothers began to speculate hither and thither as to the cause of this delay. And while they still speculated the tenth day dawned, and still on unknown paths Simeoni and Eero lingered.

The sun rose and in the cabin merriment was at its height; mighty words were bandied as each boasted of his powers. Lauri alone sat silent in his corner, whittling a gun-stock of curly birchwood. Big phrases filled the air. "A lad like the corner of a house!" "Feet skyward when a real man hit out!" "Do you remember, brothers, how sweetly Kolistin's Antti got it from this hand, there under his jaw? It was a man's blow, and the ground shook and Heaven echoed when the big fellow fell." So they competed in boasting, ever and anon pouring the pearly liquid in the tankard down their throats. But suddenly a violent quarrel arose between Juhani and Timo, and the eldest brother was soon highly incensed. For this time Timo did not seem in the least inclined to give way,

230

but supported his argument firmly with proverbs, quotations from the Bible and badly-limping metaphors. And at this Juhani's gorge rose, his eyes flashed fire, and at last, suddenly refraining from speech, he dashed like a baited bear at his pig-headed brother. But Timo fled; out on to the clearing he ran in his shirt, and after him Juhani, similarly clad. A few paces from the threshold, however, Juhani came to a halt; but Timo, in the belief that his enraged brother was at his heels, ran dodging along the stump-filled clearing. And then, feeling his pursuer's fingers at his neck, he opened his mouth and emitted a hoarse squawk, looking stiffly behind him. But his eyes grew round when he saw Juhani standing far away from him, near the cabin step, scratching his neck and staring at two wretched wayfarers, who with lagging footsteps approached the house from the edge of the forest. The other brothers came rushing out, flushed as though they had come from the sauna steam, hastening to patch up matters between the quarrelers. But soon their eyes too were fixed upon Simeoni and Eero, who returned at last from their journey in miserable condition.

Valko, now only skin and bone, walked unspeakably slowly; its head hung down almost between its fore-legs, its mournfully drooping lower lip brushed the ground. The men too were a sorry sight. With filthy faces and garments they sat on the cart like two crows in the rain. Simeoni had had his cap stolen, Eero his stockings and top-boots; all that was left of the money was six kopeks, which had remained unnoticed in Eero's vest pocket, and with this money was a crumbled biscuit. Where and how had they wasted the price of the load? It had been spent in Hämeenlinna on gin and wheat-cakes; and thus with empty hands and aching heads they drew near to their home. Dumb, struck with astonishment, the others viewed the sight which had burst upon them, and in that gaze Simeoni and Eero read their awful doom. And Simeoni deemed it best to make off while there was still time. He sprang down from the cart, leaving both his brother and the horse to their fate, and disappeared into the forest. Eero thought of imitating him, but hoped to be able to absolve himself from all blame and prove his own innocence. And with this idea he decided to keep on to the end.

Reaching at last the home-yard, he took on a deeply dejected air and without a greeting, without saying a word, began to unharness Valko. But now came a furious questioning about the success of the journey and the fate of the money received. Eero confessed everything, reminding them that Simeoni had had the care of the money; that Simeoni had commanded and he as the youngest had had to obey; that Simeoni was older than he and therefore more experienced and wiser than he, a young thoughtless lad. Thus he defended himself, but the others knew well that he too was not guiltless, his debauched appearance bearing witness to his guilt. They deemed it right, therefore, to punish him, and that without delay. Tuomas now seized him by the collar, set him, lightly as a doll, outstretched on the ground, while Juhani took a pine-branch from the dung-heap and laid on with it across Eero's thighs; heavily the blows fell, and the lad under him squealed shrilly. When this was done, Juhani cast the rod angrily away, saying: "God grant that this was the last time I need punish thee, and may this thrashing awaken a new heart in thee! That's what I hope, but I'm afraid my hopes are vain, for a good child chastiseth itself, but a bad one even punishment can't help." So saying, he walked moodily into the cabin and made for his bed of straw. But as he passed the oven he noticed the cat, which sat sleepily on the oven-top, and taking a piece of bread, he chewed it to a pulp and gave it to old Matti, who, purring and with half-closed eyes, enjoyed the gift. Then, still with bitterness in his glance, he climbed on to the platform, rubbed his stomach once, laid himself down on the straw and covered himself with a warm rug.

Eero's thrashing had been watched by Simeoni from the darkness of the forest with dread; he well knew that his own lot would have been worse at the hands of his enraged brothers. So thanking his stars for the protection afforded him by the spruce, he withdrew farther away from the light of the clearing and vanished into the forest's sheltering bosom. But dark and desolate as the gloomy woods around him was his heart. For long he walked the mossy backwoods, until he came at last to a rocky, bilberry-covered neighbourhood, and mournfully the yellow birches sighed in the dismal wind. Whither was he to wander in the bewildering halls of the forest? Whither could a man betake himself when life was cheerless and dark, and dark the night of death?

But in the yard, near the cabin door, the brothers laboured, feeding the weary Valko with breadcrumb, and rubbing down and grooming it. Furious even in his misery, Eero sat on the step, grinding his teeth, and up on the platform Juhani lay under his rug. But when Valko had been fed and let out to pasture and the cart pushed aside against the wall, the brothers entered the cabin, thinking with aching hearts of the vainly-awaited titbits. Eero too, came in at last, silent and with glowering eyes. Whereupon Juhani, lifting his head from the rug and peeping over the edge of the platform, delivered himself of the following speech: "Dost thou still glower, thou bullock? Wast not beaten according to thy desert, billy-goat? Devil! if we had given thee what thou deservest, thou wouldst scarcely crawl into the cabin on thy own paws. Believe that; and thank thy luck that thou gottest off so lightly. It will be different with Simeoni. Ah! may he anoint his back with bear-grease before he dares to open our door. He deserves it, truly he does! Sell the spirits, and then when the tavern-keeper has had good time to blend rotten punch of it buy it back many times dearer; and then to soak all the rye down to the last grain, in a word, all he could pry loose from the cart, in this same chicory-water and dear, ah so costly syrups, squander it on brandy, syrups and wheatcakes and biscuits. Who would have believed it of Simeoni? Was this his piousness? Was this the end of all his devout prayers? Yet we needn't be over much surprised at all this. Godly men, more's the pity, usually have the same strong longing for liquor, especially for dram-drinking behind the cupboard door. This in all my stupidity I have noticed. Think, for instance, of the master of Härkämäki, who is looked upon as a religious man; yet this same nabob walks his days drunk as a king, flushed like a glowing coal from morning to eve. See him as he goes out of his room, from his book of homilies and hymnbook. First he'll steer his way to the cupboard, where a little trick takes place, a movement of the arm. And now we step out, toddle towards the stable, and the groom, poor lad, knows he is in for a sermon, long enough and good enough. But even the worst parson's sermon ends at last; the door creaks, and sideways like a crab, the old boy now marches to the cowshed. And there the poor rag of a maid is on hot coals, while the mastera scolds, scolds, clucks and cackles. Ah thee, old fellow! Ay, but even a famine year has an end, so on we go to the house. But here's where a row arises, a sermon hotter than the hottest for the mistress and daughter, one that last an hour or two. Even the mistress sometimes snaps back, snaps and scolds, but the poor girl is dumb and a tear drops from the poor body. Oh thou crosspatch! At last, however, the preacher's throat seems to get dry and hoarse, so off we go to wet it at the cupboard; and then hymnbook in hand to singing till the door-posts shake. So passes the man's day, ay, his week, until on Sunday he jogs off with his daughter to church, jogs along in that trap of his, a skull-cap on his head and his coat-collar sticking out behind. There he now sits in the Lord's temple, with pursed-up lips and eyebrows halfway up his forehead; he sits there, clearing his throat like the most godly, as solemn, grave and unwinking as a newly-gelded ox. He squats there like a boundary stone in the forest; but when he comes home from church and reaches his own yard, he rushes like a tempest, a fire-spitting tempest, straight to the cupboard in his room; and now the old man drinks until the bottom of the bottle shows. So hard can a man drink who is known as a pillar of the world; in such lust, in such lust does a converted man walk down here. And that's what I believe will happen to Simeoni too, if luck should at any time set him in Härkämäki's shoes. True, a better spirit has worked without cease on Simeoni for years, that can't be denied, even if he has often fluttered the wings of his soul a bit too much. Ay, ay, but in many things he is still altogether a child of this world, as big a sack of sin as I or many other, and plays tricks for which a good hiding is the only remedy. And now he's played us a real fiendish trick. Obeying the whispering of Satan, he drank up our fine load and left us without a crumb of relish for our feast. Hrrh! it makes me grind my teeth. Well, his back will warm for this, until the cabin rattles." Thus spoke Juhani, peeping over the platform's edge; then he sank down on his couch and slept. The others too lay down to rest, and they slept soundly until the morning.

But of Simeoni there was no sign, not even after several days and nights had passed. And this caused the others some anxiety, anxiety mixed with grief, especially after Eero had at last told them of his real condition. For when Eero's sulkiness had abated a little, after the elapse of two or three days, he grumblingly told them of the state Simeoni had been in on their return from town. He had frequently spoken of certain little, inch-high beings, who, as he had said, swarmed around him in thousands. This Eero now told them in a low and grumbling voice, and his tale altered the brothers' feelings towards Simeoni. Filled with gloom, Juhani set out to seek his lost brother, wandering far afield and calling him by name. Under a hill he met Tinder-Matti, who sought, axe in hand, for fungoids, with which he had already filled the bosom of his shirt. Matti recalled how on the previous evening he had heard mournful sounds and wailings from the forest, and the voice had reminded him of Simeoni's. This pricked painfully at Juhani's heart; he hastened home, weeping tears over the unhappy fate of his brother. A search-party was now organized. Each of the brothers was to set out alone and in a different direction; the one who found the fugitive was to take him home, and then, mounting to the top of Impivaara, inform the others of the find by blasts on a birch-bark horn. Eero brought out his horn from its hiding-place in a dense thicket, a mighty horn of birch-bark, two yards long and audible afar, and sank it for the night in the purling brook in the wolf-trap. Having been made in the spring when the sap was at its richest, the hooter was now badly shrunken and dry.

Early the next morning they set out on their search. The cabin

235

formed the centre from which six men set out in different directions like the spokes of a wheel. And now a din arose in which shout merged into shout and echo pursued echo in the measureless depths of the forest. Farther and farther the din receded as the circle grew apace. And this circle thou couldst have drawn if, standing on the summit of Impivaara and listening to the shouts around thee, thou hadst drawn a line from shout to shout. They fared on in every direction, each along his own radius; and the weather was clear and calm, the September sun shone mildly. Shouting loudly, Juhani marched crashing up hill and down. But his ear caught no answer from the lost one; and midday drew nigh. At last, however, his throat tiring not, but roaring incessantly like a brazen trumpet, he heard a strangely weak and hoarse answer. And this voice seemed to come from a gap between two mossy crags, shadowed by a tall spruce. To this spot Juhani hastened and there found the missing man, found him in pitiable condition. Like a ghastly phantom, with arms crossed and eyes wide open like an owl's, his hair sticking up, he sat under the thick spruce. There he sat, swaying his body, while from his lips issued the soft and trembling notes of a hymn-tune. Juhani began to question him about his condition, but receiving only muddled and fantastical answers, he hurried his precious find home as fast as he could. And when he had got his brother safely into the cabin and fastened the door, he quickly climbed the hill, the mighty horn in his hand. Calm, blue in the distance, the wooded earth spread around him, and on the edge of the west the sun bathed the old shaggy spruce on the hillside in its gold. Juhani lifted the great trumpet to his lips, but no blast issued from it; from the yawning maw only a few hoarse croaks came. He blew once again, yet the clear notes still clung to their prison. Then swelling out his chest once more, he blew a third time, his cheeks bulging terrifically, and now the birch horn shrieked and brayed with solemn voice. Far out in all directions the echoes rolled, and soon merry answers began to be heard from the east, west, north and south, faint and dying in the eternally distant blue haze. And now an hour went by, a second, and

237

a third, and then the brothers began to appear in the yard, entering the house one by one. And at last they all stood around Simeoni, eyeing him with pitying glances as he sat on his stool like an owl on the roof of a barn, staring stolidly back at them.

Juhani: Simeoni, brother!

Tuomas: How art thou?

Timo: Dost know me? — not a created word. Dost thou know me?

Simeoni: Ay, I know thee.

Timo: Who am I then?

Simeoni: Ha! Jukola's Timo. Ay, shouldn't I know him?

Timo: Right! I am Timo, thy own brother. The danger's not as great as it could be, boys.

Simeoni: Great and awful is the day that approacheth, and its name is the terror of destruction.

Aapo: Why dost thou prophesy so?

Simeoni: He said so.

Juhani: Who?

Simeoni: He, he, my companion on the journey.

Eero: What, I?

Simeoni: Not thou, but the horror who hath led me. Oh brothers! I could tell you things that would raise your hairs on end like the bristles of an angry boar. But give me a little drink first to strengthen my heart; and let this be the last drink I ever swallow down my throat.

Juhani: Take a drop, God's creation; here, darling brother.

Simeoni: Thankye kindly! Now I'll try to tell you what I have seen and heard, tell it as a warning to us all. Hear me: I have seen him.

Juhani: Whom in wonder hast thou seen?

Simeoni: The Master himself, Luciferus himself.

Aapo: That was only in a dream or a fever of the mind brought upon thee by overmuch strong drink.

Simeoni: Truly I have seen him.

Timo: What shape was he?

Simeoni: The image of foolishness, but, sithee, a fox's tail wagged behind him.

Timo: Was he big?

Simeoni: About my height, though he could change himself at will. When he first appeared, he entered the thicket in which I sat as a gust of wind. "Who's that?" I shrieked; "Friend!" he answered, and taking me by the arm, told me to follow him. Not daring to kick against him, I followed, believing it best to do as he said. And then we went on together a long time over a thorny, stony path; and he changed into all kinds of things on the way. Now he would run before me in the shape of a little kitten, mewing and looking back at me so stupidly. At times he grew into a fearfully tall man, his head reaching right to the clouds. From there he shouted to me: "Canst see my head?" and I, speaking the whole time to please him, greatly admired his length, saying that I could hardly make out his middle. Whereupon he twisted his mouth into a triumphant grin and looked seachingly at me. He played many other tricks and finally led me up a high mountain; there he bowed down before me and said "Get up on my back." I was terrified, but dared not refuse, and climbed obediently on to his back. I asked him, anyhow: "Where are we going?" and he answered: "We're going up." Then he began puffing mightily, sweating and wriggling his body, while I danced hither and thither on his back, up and down, like the monkey I saw dancing a few days ago on a dog's back in Hämeenlinna Market. At last two speckled wings burst from his shoulders and when he had waved these a few times we began shooting up into the sky, towards the moon, which shone over us like the bottom of a copper cauldron. We shot up towards it, and the poor earth fell away behind us into giddy depths. At last we reached the moon, which, as our blind uncle told us, is a great, round and shining rock island in the air, and there I saw wonders and marvels, wonders and marvels! Ah! a sinful tongue cannot relate them.

Tuomas: Do the best thou canst.

Juhani: The best thou canst, brother, even if not as well as the great importance of the matter calls for.

Simeoni: I will try. Ay, we came to the moon, and Satan took me to its farthest edge, to a high hill with a still higher tower standing on it, built of leather, boot-leather. Up into this tower we marched, he ahead and I behind, and we climbed those twisting stairs for a good long time. At last we stood at the very top of the boot-leather tower, and then I saw many countries and seas, great cities and marvellous buildings in the depths below. I made bold to nudge Satan in the ribs and ask him: "What is that down there?" Snapping and looking fiercely at me he answered: "Sacramento, lad! what have I to do with thee? That's the world from which we set out. Look and search." That's what he said, and with a sigh I began to look and search carefully; and I saw the whole circle of the earth, the Kingdom of England, Turkey, the town of Paris and the land of America. Then I saw the Grand Turk rise and work terrible havoc; anl in his tracks walked the great horned Mammon, driving the race of man from end to end of the earth like a wolf does a flock of sheep. He went on driving and sweeping them before him until at last he had choked the whole world and the land of America. Seeing this I asked again, nudging Satan in the ribs: "Is the world destroyed now, where I come from?" He answered fiercely: "Sacramento, lad! what have I to do with thee? This is a prophecy of what is to come. Look and search." And sighing deeply I looked and searched. But once more I made bold to ask: "When is this to happen?" And with a horrible roar he answered again: "It will happen just as soon as two leather trumpets appear to us through the wall, right in front of us." And then he whistled long and hard. Ah! if I could only tell you.

Juhani: Do it, if thou but canst. Oh what marvels and wonders thou hast seen! This means something, and likely as not, our doom. God's wrath, if not the end of the world is upon us. Is this in reason: walk with the Devil in the moon?

Simeoni: And in a leather tower!

Juhani: A boot-leather tower. What a thing!

Timo: A boot-leather tower!

Juhani: Ay, a tower of boot-leather. Ah! But tell us every-thing; for even if I do feel a shuddering in my spine, this shaking must surely do my sinful heart good, that is so hardened, so tough, that nothing less than the wooden mallet of Hell or the fiery bolt of Heaven could move it. Let it thunder and rain, brother, let it rain even scorpions; for that's what we need. Ay, what happened then?

Simeoni: Listen, listen! Satan whistled shrilly, and as he said, two leather trumpets appeared, two fearful horns came bursting through the wall. They began to bray horribly and shriek like maddened lions, began to pour out smoke, the smell of pitch and sulphur gas. And soon we both started coughing, Satan as well as I, coughing, retching and holding our ears, while the two trump-ets blared on. And still the noise grew, the tower shook, the great boot-leather tower shook and at last fell to pieces with a great crash, and we followed in its fall, in a cloud of strips of leather. Where Satan got to, I don't know, but I fell head over heels downward, down from the rock, down at last towards the earth on a piece of leather about two yards wide. But the leather, which was of the moon, drew moonward, while I, being of the earth, drew earthward; so it was said; and as the weight of my body was bigger than the pull of the leather, I floated downward, but slowly, as though sailing on an old crow's back. All to my good; for without this leather boat of mine, my airship, I'd have fallen like a bag of offal to the earth, now that I no longer had Satan's wings under me. Slowly, slowly, I now sailed down towards my dear earthly home, and at last came down at the foot of a spruce near to the place whence I had set off with Satan. I still held the piece of leather in my hands, and now noticed these words on it, written in red letters: "To the Jukola brothers, with a fistful of greetings! And when a fiery sign, or like the glowing tail of an eagle is seen on high on the edge of a cloud, lo! the end is nigh unto the day on which this shall happen. Given in Boot-leather Tower on nearly the last day of what is almost surely the last year." So it stood on the leather table, which I now loosened from my hand, when it started shooting up towards the moon again. This was my journey, awful and of a truth true.

Juhani: Marvellous, strange and terrible all at the same time.

Timo: Thou hast learned to read on these strayings of thine, anyway.

Simeoni: Don't think it. I am just as stupid as ever.

Timo: Perhaps thou hast caught the trick of it. Try, here's my a-b-c book.

Simeoni: Ay, what else. It's as though I were looking on Russian or Hebrew. Then I knew much owing to the power of the spirit that is now dark to me again, and I am once more the same poor human, the same sinner, a great sinner. And my head spins, for the day has come! My head goes round, for my eyes have beheld Luciferus himself. Ah, how hairy he was.

Juhani: Oh we poor lads, oh!

Simeoni: A thousand times oh! My head spins, spins! I have seen Luciferus. It spins!

Juhani: Pray to God, brother, pray to God!

Simeoni: Let's all pray together. I have seen the hairy might of Luciferus! Let us all pray!

Timo: Why not, if it's needed? Why shouldn't we pray?

Juhani: Pitiful this is, ah, oh!

Timo: Don't cry, Juhani.

Juhani: I would weep blood if I could; here we have lived like Kalmucks, drunk spirits like Mahomets and Turks. But now may a new chapter follow that verse, a different life, or soon the awful anger of Heaven will fall on us like a mountain and press us down to Hell. Ay, we lads have been warned by signs and miracles, and it's the worst of devils for us if we don't heed these signs in time.

Lauri: It's the very worst we have to expect; for I too have something to tell you. Listen: once while you were hitting the disc on the clearing, I walked in the forest, looking for useful bits of wood for tools, and while I slept on yonder heath I had a marvellous dream. I watched as though from the top of a tall pine you playing fast and furiously with the disc on the clearing here along fresh oxhides. And guess with whom? Brothers, it was with our own hot-tempered Vicar you hammered away. But what happened? The Vicar noticed at last that it was no ordinary disc, but a red-backed a-b-c book you were hitting. This made him fearfully angry, and waving his sword he shouted in a loud voice: "Iiyah, iiyah!" and at once a terrible hurricane arose which sucked you up like chaff into the power of the winds. This I dreamed and this dream must mean something too.

Juhani: Surely it means something, foretells some Hell's polka for us; that we needn't doubt. We have been warned from two quarters, and now if we pay no heed, fire, pitch and little stones will soon rain down on us they once did on the towns of Sodom and Gomorrah.

Aapo: Don't let us be too terrified, all the same.

Tuomas: I won't say for certain, but what Simeoni has seen is perhaps all sprung from a drink-ridden brain.

Juhani: What art thou saying, man? Wouldst thou bring Heaven's great works to naught?

Timo: Don't speak against God's works and miracles.

Simeoni: Ah! I have been in the moon and seen Luciferus, of which my soul is now in great dread. Woe is me and woe is us all!

Tuomas: Woe, indeed! But take another drink and then go to bed.

Simeoni: Ay, do you think it would help?

Timo: There's no spirits left.

Tuomas: That alters things.

Simeoni: Thanks be to God that it has all gone, that horrible poison. And now may never another drop of that drink pass my lips, this I promise and swear.

Juhani: A curse on this Hell's ale!

Timo: It was perhaps a bad thing that we began to distil the stuff.

Aapo: Whose wish was it that we should do so? Answer me, Juhani and Timo.

Juhani: The spirits tasted well enough to thee too, brother, that they did. And secondly, what's done is done, and moaning and lamenting won't bring it back. Ay, what's gone is in the wolf's mouth; but let there be a new law from now onward. Now to the brook! with the back of my axe I'll knock that Devil's copper bull, that accursed vat into a thousand dents, and scatter the still like a rook's nest.

Simeoni: Do that, brother, and Heaven will rejoice.

Juhani: I'll do it.

Aapo: Why should we smash property that we might honourably sell?

Juhani: But see this point: the man to whom I sold my still, what would he make with it, what kind of water of health, eigh? The same sort, the same sort, the same Hell's lawyer that has dashed us to the very brink of ruin; with this still of mine I could bring the same misery on many others. But from this sin let me be far, when I come at last to the judgment of the Lord. Let's squash the vat and break up the still.

Aapo: Let's sell it to the Crown for them to mint money of.

Juhani: It'll do for coin just as well if it is knocked flat. Here's my axe; take thy axe too, Timo, and come with me to the wolf-trap. And tomorrow being Sunday, we'll all go to church. To church we'll go, to pray on our bended knees for the deathless, miserable and only soul of us; it is necessary enough. To church, the lot of us, else the Devil'll baste us. To the wolf-trap, Timo!

Juhani and Timo now marched down to the brook, and soon they had battered the vat to a shapeless mass and destroyed the still. And that night they rested in deepest sleep, and waking early on the morrow, began to prepare themselves for church. They set out: Aapo with their father's old hymnbook under his arm, Simeoni carrying "The Voice in the Wilderness," Juhani and Timo with their a-b-c books in their hands. And as they walked they conversed as follows:

Simeoni: Ah! the nearer I come to the Lord's temple, the more does the storm in my mind calm down and my heart seem refreshed.

A wise man walketh in the counsel of the righteous, but fools and the blind wallow in the filth of sin. Oh, when I look backward, like a terrible Hell, ringed by the blue flames of alcohol, does that unhappy trip to town seem to me.

Timo: Therefore, brother, never do it again. I beseech thee. Is this a right thing to do? Pour dear tavern gin into thy face night and day, night and day, and on top of that soak hot syrups like fine gentlemen. Well, well, let this be no blame, only a brotherly warning.

Simeoni: I did wrong, and we all did wrong in starting to brew spirits and drink them. But now, let us all decide never to touch such drink that can change a man into a beast.

Juhani: Into a real pig; it brings its man even lower in the end than a grunting pig. On this very spot we shake the hand of liquor in firm farewell and beg him to depart from us for ever and a day in the name of our Lord. Ay, Aapo, tell us the tale of the pig that we once heard from our blind uncle; tell it as we walk along.

Aapo: I'll do that willingly. Oh! may it awaken in us a still fiercer disgust for that confounded brawl-water.

And Aapo spun them this tale:

It was Sunday morning; in a mud-pool a pig wallowed in the rays of the summer sun, watching the folk go past him to church. With envious, aching heart it looked upon the noble, beautiful form of Man, remembering its own bristly body. And what more, a light so stern shone from the brow of some passers-by, that the pig's glance recoiled from them in astonishment; and great was its anger against God for not having created it a man. And when at last it had grumbled and complained to its fill, it stretched out its trotters, closed its little viper's eyes and slept. When it awoke, a companion lay by its side, a drunkard who had rolled in his cups into the puddle and was on the point of choking in the mud. The pig saw his danger, and taking mercy upon him, dug its sharp teeth into the man's collar and dragged him on to firm ground. But having done this work of mercy, it stared at the man, grinned horribly to itself and said: "Thou miserable man, thy appearance is so disgusting that I cannot bear to look upon thee." So saying, the pig went away grunting and began rooting in the earth.

Juhani: That's a fine tale. Over yonder lies Jukola Farm, and well for us that our road leads so far aside of it, or else the sight of our former home might crush our hearts. A good thing too that Toukola village and our enemies there are far behind. Otherwise, I'm afraid that if we were to meet them and they grinned the tiniest bit, I'd be at their throats at once like a cat. I haven't forgotten the beating they gave me, nor my vow of a terrible revenge.

Tuomas: Two things have not left my memory either.

Simeoni: We must forgive and forget.

Juhani: All right; if they are humble and come to pray for forgiveness from me, bearing witness that they have done wrong, why, I'll forget everything willingly. I'll even shake paws with them, with tears in my eyes. But as long as they are unminded to give way in this, and still nag, then I too will clench my teeth, clench them till the sparks fly.

Thus speaking, they approached Tammisto Farm. A crowd stood in the yard, both men and women, and a voice was heard afar that counted: "For the first, second and third time," and went on: "Does no one else want to bid?" It was an auction held by the Sheriff himself. He sat beside a little table near the porch, entering in his book the names and addresses of purchasers and the prices obtained; and just at that moment the farm cattle were under the hammer. The brothers were highly astonished and wondered why this work was being done on Sunday. But, in the giddy toils of intoxication, which make a man's time fly, they had lost count of the days of the week. It was actually a Monday, an ordinary weekday, on which the brothers, believing it to be Sunday, had gone marching to church.

They looked around them for Kyösti, their faithful friend. But he was not there; he walked far away in the fields, staring gravely at the soil in silent meditation. At last Juhani asked the man nearest to them, why a public auction was being held on Sunday, the Lord's holy Sabbath. At that, laughter and giggling spread like a forest fire

246

through the whole crowd, and now the brothers guessed how matters stood. Bewildered, silent and blushing, they stood for long, listening to the taunts and mockery of the crowd. A group of Toukola lads then approached them, asking them about the new religion of Impivaara, about its calendar and what this eighth day of the week was called there. The brothers listened to all this, but suddenly their anger flared up and the storm was loose. Like unleashed hounds they sprang yelling upon the Toukola men, and a terrible struggle broke out in Tammisto yard.

Simeoni was loth to join in the game, and so the books were left in his care; holding firmly to these he watched with agonized countenance and pitiably restless glance the varying phases of the battle. But seeing Aapo sorely pressed by three lusty foes, noting with aching heart his wretched brother turn pale and his glance rove vacuously amongst the tree-tops, while blows, stinging blows rained on him from every side, Simeoni laid down the books on a near-by rock, hastened to Aapo's assistance, and was soon lost to sight in the billowing waves of the fight.

The auctioneer tried at first to stem the onrush of this angry flood, but realizing his powerlessness, he stepped aside in time and watched in amazement the unbounded strength shown by the brothers. Strength so herculean, such whirlwindlike speed in its application, had never before been shown by the brothers. A secret and long-nourished lust for revenge felt the breath of a sudden wind and was fanned by it to a raging, terrific holocaust; and an unheard-of din and thundering was the result. Women fled, pale and trembling, from the field, carrying or leading by the hand their little panic-stricken children. Mad with fright the farm cattle, the big bull and the solemn cows, rushed hither and thither, while all around echoed shouts, bellows and lamentations, as the Jukola brothers smote, and the men of Toukola smote back, the men of Toukola and their many friends. Clenching his teeth, ashen-grey of face, Juhani struck out right and left, hammered lustily at the host of his foes, his jaw quaking in an ecstasy of fury. But like a rock sturdy Tuomas charged, and wherever his mighty fist fell, a man, was sure to collapse, even two at one blow. It was seen that when he struck out, the man hit fell with such force that in falling he knocked down the man beside him. Timo hewed away like a brawny woodcutter; and his coarse, brown cheeks, blazing with rage, shone afar. Nor was Eero an easy task for a man in this fight. True, he rolled with some frequency under the others' feet, but was ever quick to struggle up from the heaps of the fallen, and blows rained from him like stars from a revolving fireworks. Maddest of them all was Lauri; pale as an angel of death he lashed out, and before him all fled or were broken.

People watched this fight with terror. Everywhere ghastly, livid faces were to be seen, faces with fearfully working nostrils, here bleeding, there bespattered with earth. Behold the sombre glow of anger in their eyes, the passion which rushes heedless upon its prey, undismayed though the heavens rained fire and brimstone. All this they saw, and heard a howling and clamour as terrible as when a pack of wolves fights murderously in the dark woods on an autumn night.

So they fought in Tammisto yard, and ever hotter grew the struggle. Already a man lay here, another there, shedding his blood on the sandy ground. The brothers' dark-red blood flowed too, for the men of Toukola were striking now with their knives; but the brothers had no knives at their belts, for this was to have been their trip to church, to God's holy temple. Now, feeling their hot blood flow, they seized the poles on the hillside for weapons, or broke off rails from the nearest fence, and with these charged madly at their foes; soon, however, they were met by similar weapons on the enemy's side; and now staves and cudgels began to fly crashing round the men's heads. And even now it was uncertain who would win, who would have to give way, vanquished. Nobly though they battled, the brothers had an overwhelming foe to meet, and furiously their blows were returned.

But then a man drew nigh who at once turned the scales in the brothers' favour. From the fields, running, scrambling and bellowing as he came, stout Kyösti Tammisto drew nigh. With a mighty staff in his hand, he dashed into view like a grey phantom of terror, his hair sticking up in a goblin-like crest; like a thunder-bolt he fell on the Toukola men in the rear, throwing their ranks into confusion, and causing the brothers' ardour to rise. Bellowing and rolling his eyes he struck out wickedly, struck like a witless fellow; the brothers laid on from the other side with redoubled strength, and at last their enemies fled wildly, those whom the staves had not already stretched out on the ground.

The brothers, too, then hastened away, beginning to run towards their home and shouting to Kyösti to follow them. But he recked nothing of their cries, only raged ceaselessly in his yard, raged and yelled; and dreadful was his appearance. The brothers sped already along the dry, smoking surface of a lane; they had reached a little bridge between the fields, when they heard Kyösti's voice behind them. Halting and looking back, they saw a wild figure with a staff on its shoulder approach them at a run, bellowing and waving its hand at them; and soon Kyösti, terrible to behold, stood beside them. He sweated and panted, and what with defiance and fury his eyes squinted in his head. In vain they tried to make out his muddled speech, in which a loud and long-drawn cry of "Ala-mulloo, ai alamulloo!" frequently recurred. They entreated him to come on with them to Impivaara and not to return into the wolves' jaws, but he stood moveless, muttering to himself and staring. Suddenly, however, he looked sharply at the brothers and said: "Go home now!" after which he turned away from them. The brothers turned round too, and began to make off in the opposite direction. But a moment later they heard Kyösti's thickened voice again, and looking round, saw him stand in the lane, shaking his hand and his head. Once more he shouted in a high-pitched voice: "Go home now!" Whereafter he hurried off the way he had come, and the brothers hurried in turn to their cabin in the woods, many of them with great bumps on their foreheads and blood-dripping wounds in their arms. Looking stiffly before them, they stepped furiously out, in their minds the freezing gloom of death. So ended the fight in

Tammisto yard, from which many were carried swooning away, and many received wounds that were to disfigure them for ever afterwards.

CHAPTER 11

EVENING has come of the day on which the fight had raged so fiercely at Tammisto. The brothers sit in their cabin, having anointed and bandaged their wounds as well as they could. They sit, night, black and everlasting, in their hearts, and their glance, directed downward at the floor, is full of fury. They think of what they have done and know the punishment that threatens them; they ponder over their unhappy, hopeless situation, and an awful silence reigns in the room. Finally Simeoni started the following conversation.

Simeoni: Brothers, brothers! say a word. What are we to do to escape the clutches of the law?

Aapo: Ah! not a single road of escape is left to us out of this fix, not one.

Juhani: We're trapped now, trapped! All is lost, all hope and happiness!

Tuomas: The Devil'll get us without any mercy; so let's take what we have earned with eyes shut. We disturbed a Crown Servant in the midst of his hurry, and that's a serious thing; we turned men into cripples perhaps, and that's a worse thing. Ha! maybe we even knocked the dear life out of someone, and then all's well; we'll be shut up and can eat the Crown's carefree bread.

Simeoni: Oh we poor boys!

Timo: Poor sons of Jukola! And seven of them! What shall we do now?

Lauri: I know what I'll do.

Juhani: I do too. Knife to throat, every man of us!

Timo: For God's sake!

Juhani: My knife, my shining knife! I'll let blood in waves!

Aapo: Juhani!

Juhani: Let the blood of seven men flow into one single pool and let's drown together in this Red Sea, like every manjack in the Old Testament once did. Where's my birch-handled knife that atones for all, the atoner of all?

Aapo: Calm thyself!

Juhani: Away out of my way, thou, and away out of this accursed life! My knife!

Simeoni: Hold him!

Aapo: To me, brothers!

Juhani: Out of the way!

Tuomas: Steady, my lad!

Juhani: Let go, brother Tuomas!

Tuomas: Thou sittest down quietly.

Juhani: What good will quietness do us when all is lost? Art thou minded to take forty brace of fresh birch-rods quietly?

Tuomas: I'm not.

Juhani: What wilt thou do?

Tuomas: I'll hang myself, but not before.

Juhani: Let's do now what we shall have to do in the end.

Tuomas: Let's think it over first.

Juhani: Ha-ha! It's all no use.

Tuomas: We don't know yet exactly.

Juhani: The law's waiting to lay its gloves on us.

Simeoni: Let's leave Finland and go as herds to Ingermanland!

Timo: Or as doorkeepers to St. Petersburg town.

Aapo: These are childish ideas.

Eero: Away off to sea to cleave the waves like our grand old uncle used to! Once we get away from the Finnish coast we are free from the hand of the law, and can then try to reach the Englishman; a man's worth something in the masts of his ships.

Aapo: There's advice worth thinking over.

Tuomas: It might perhaps be that, but remember: before we could reach the coast, we'd most likely have the Crown's engagement-rings on our wrists.

Timo: Aa! Even if we get away from Finland with whole skins, when should we be in England? It's millions and thousands of millions miles there. Aa!

Aapo: Listen to a word: let's join the wolves ourselves, and it's little we need fear their teeth. Let's march to the army and enlist for a few years. Ah! it's a hard way out, but still perhaps the best in this mess. Ay, let us set out for that famous and great big battalion at Heinola, that marches and drills all summer on Parola Plain. This is an idea worth weighing, seeing that the Crown looks after its own.

Juhani: I'm afraid, brother, thou hast found the only way. The barracks have saved many a wild lad from prison before this. Think of Karila's farm-hand, that great rogue, who once got it into his head to thrash his master a little; it would have gone ill with him, if the rascal hadn't suddenly had a grey coat on his back which saved him. Let that be settled! And now off to barracks! Why, our father's uncle died in the wars, the Kyrö War, where they say a five-fathom log floated in blood. Our own uncle too died in the wars, fell on the coast in North Finland; and so it has gone with many another, both kinsfolk and neighbours. We too know how to fall, to fall like devout heroes. Better death, better to be in Heaven than here amongst such wild beast of men. I can't help crying. Ay, much better there than here. Oo-ay, much better.

Tuomas: Brother, in this way thou canst set us all wiping our eyes.

Simeoni: O Lord, look down upon us and let the sun of Thy mercy shine!

And their conversation ended in tears, in a general, choking fit of weeping; not a single eye remained dry. But the evening drew on, night came, and from weeping they all sank at last into a deep sleep. The next day they took up the matter again and sought sweating some plan that might save them, and meanwhile their eyes kept close watch on their surroundings, in order that any approach of the forces of the Crown might be observed in time. Thus they kept watch and pondered; and the barracks, though dreadful enough, began to seem the likeliest sanctuary. They decided therefore to set off together to Heinola and to enlist for six years. And when the next day dawned, they embarked on their long journey with downcast minds and troubled hearts. They strode on, forgetting that for their purpose passports and parish reports were necessary; strode on, first towards Jukola, meaning to beg the tanner to take charge of their animal friends and keep an eye on the cabin.

Reaching the Viertola road, they met the Sheriff, who, with his man seated behind him, drove rumbling towards them. The brothers were taken aback, believing his errand to concern them. They were on the point of running away, but then stepped forward, sure in the belief that no two men would ever be able to arrest them. They were mistaken, however, regarding his errand; other matters had set the Sheriff driving round the parish. Moreover, he was a fine fellow: brave, high-minded and always merry. He had been greatly amused by all that was told about the Jukola brothers and their life in the forest; and he was their well-wisher, a friend and not an enemy. And now, having come up with the brothers, he began in a pleasant voice:

The Sheriff: Good-day, good-day! Whither away with such long faces? Answer me, and don't look at me like that, like backwood's wolves. Whither away, with those knapsacks?

Juhani: We have a long journey before us.

The Sheriff: Is it to Hell ye're off then? Hey?

Juhani: Do you want anything of us?

The Sheriff: What would you have to give me? A man can ask without wanting to buy. Well, well, your eyes are glowering and glaring at me; if I wasn't used to looking the Devil himself in the face, my heart might even start beating. Ha-ha-ha! What the blazes is the matter with you?

Juhani: One thing I ask you: will it be a Crown job?

The Sheriff: Will what?

Juhani: Hm. That, that.

The Sheriff: What, thou tousled-headed loon? What?

Juhani: That shindy at Tammisto Farm.

The Sheriff: Ahaa! That game the other day. Ay, there's something I want to say to you about that now.

Juhani: Was anyone killed?

The Sheriff: Thank thy luck that there wasn't. But, thunder and lightning! you drove away a Crown Servant from his work and even upset his desk, think what that means.

Juhani: God ha' mercy! It's just what we have thought about a lot, and have come to realise what it means for us. Ay, the Devil'll get us, and so we have chosen the Devil's part. Know that it is to Parola's big battalion that our road now leads uphill and down so that the sand rattles. There's the last pass to which we can flee in our danger and distress, what with people, those raving devils, worrying us on every side as though we were young wolves in a trap. We're off to Parola! and woe betide the man who tries to stop us; for the Crown needs men, war is brewing, so we have heard. Soon we shall wear the Crown's armour, and touch us then, if you dare, you Satans. Hii, haa! I could bite the world in two, bite it in two like an eel; a bit more and I'd weep for very rage and sorrow; weep and shake my fist. We're off to Parola! There's men like young ravens there at Parola.

The Sheriff: You owls and boobies! would you leave your own cabin on your own soil and go off to the whizzing rods at the barracks?

Juhani: Better there anyhow than quarrying rock in prison; and as for that, the brown skin of a Häme man is an inch thick, as they will see.

The Sheriff: Quarrying rock in prison! Why?

Juhani: You yourself, sir, are minded to drag us there in clanking chains. And why? Because of that unlucky tussle in Tammisto yard, because we dusted the backs of those Toukola lads a little, a dusting which, God help us, we were thoroughly egged on to give. And now the idea is to make a Crown job of it, make a bull out of a fly, as the proverb says.

The Sheriff: Now thou liest! Go to Hades, man! I have other and more serious work than that.

Juhani: Even if you were to grant us the freedom to go to Hades, which we do not yet believe, the Toukola men are still at our throats with the law behind them. We unlucky lads struck the first blow, and that makes our case bad; but they won't either escape without "pay up, please." There are wounds enough on our side too, on which the scab has scarce had time to form, and they prove something, these wounds do. Hrrh! But even if we hold our own against the Toukola men, there's still a day of judgment awaiting us every year: Bible-reading Day. The Devil! I say like Paavo Jaakkola, that fine lad: "This life would suit me if it had one day a year less, if it wasn't for that accursed Bible-reading Day." And he also said: "It isn't the pain, but the shame," as he did once after one of those hair-pulling feasts, in which his own crop had been badly milled again. And what happened to him the next year at the same feast? Ay, the parson made him sit under the table like an owl in full view of his young and pretty sweetheart, who stood in the porch; she fainted when she saw it, the poor body, tumbled head over heels on the floor like a young duck. It was a sad case; after that Paavo took to drink, was jilted by his sweetheart and drank all the harder, and ended his days as a miserable knacker. That was bonny Paavo's end, a man by no means thick-headed, indeed not, for he was one of the wisest and deftest of men; only his stepmother had surlily thrust the book upon him in the beginning, and so reading-day became a day of terror for him. And is this either a right state of things! Mikko Kukkoinen, a man big and stout as a chopping-block, broad in the cheek like old mother Tuhkala's cat, but not what you would call a good reader, shied like a lamb when he heard in his tool-shed the sound of the parson's sleigh-bells on reading-day. So awful is this day, this feast of sweating and hair-pulling. And once we too will be taken there by force at the Vicar's command, and from there to the scaffold of shame, the stocks; but from all this the grey coat of the Crown can save us, to all this we now say an eternal farewell.

The Sheriff: You brainless goats, what fool's plans are you hatching? Well, go, go, march on as far as the Crown's sandy field will take you. What in fury have I to do with it! Our reckoning is discharged as regards Tammisto, that I say and will swear to, you loons! Discharged! and even the mouths of the Toukola men are stopped. Ho! I did that the same day the fight took place, as soon as I was satisfied that no lives had been lost. The rogues threatened to have the law of you, though they had boiled the soup themselves. But then I put my own weight in the scales, and the Toukola men shut up like moles; I have a good many hooks of my own fast in them with which I could drag them into a tight fix. And now they are silent and hold good with what they have got. And as for your matter with the Vicar, I only ask you: has he troubled you lately in any way?

Aapo: That he has not done, to our great wonder.

The Sheriff: And never will any more; remember who says it. For who brought this about? Who other than that old Sheriff of ours. And you, you ungrateful imps, you now say that he has evil designs on you. Somehow, I've been foolish enough to be tickled by the life you young cubs lead. Ha-ha-ha! Well, well, always room for a joke, a clean joke. But let this be clear: peace be with you on my part and on the Vicar's part as well; he has begun to understand that a coat can't be made out of birchbark. Well then, there's no danger at all, boys, none at all, although you do deserve a good thrashing, you confounded mules. But go home now! At once! say I. Ay, ay, left turn there, left turn and quick march home, Impivaara Company! Home, you rascals, and God be with you. Gee-up, White-mane!

So saying, he jerked at the reins, and the Sheriff's white-maned gelding, famous all over the parish, broke into a trot. Rattling they sped away; the hat of the Sheriff's Man on the back seat shook, and the dust rose in clouds behind them. And like seven images of salt, the brothers stood by the roadside, watching this departure. Silent and wondering what to think of it all, they stood and stared after the cart until it was lost to view in a turn of the road.

Timo: How the Sheriff's Man has aged since we last saw him in Kuokkala woods with our mother and all the village folk!

Juhani: What dost thou, Aapo, think of this fine speech of the Sheriff's?

Aapo: I should think him an honest man and that he spoke from an honest heart, but let us be on our guard, for there's no trusting gentlefolk.

Juhani: We'll keep ready to gallop off to the wolves' home. The Devil's in him, he's trying to entice us into a trap.

Tuomas: He wants to fool us into going back home, ready for him when he comes back from Viertola with a crowd of men, for everyone knows it isn't wise to pounce on Jukola's troop without enough men. He'll come back and collar us nicely if we go home and wait for him.

Juhani: Ha! that's what I think too. He's out hunting, out on a mighty chase, and we are the game he is after. Very likely terrible things have happened, things from which even the barracks couldn't save us. And now there's nothing left for us but to become outlaws and make off into the woods at once! Off the highway, lads!

Aapo: Ah! what are we to do?

Juhani: Everything's done already; here are seven bandits. But let us try to be as kind, as merciful robbers as we can, and always ask politely beforehand for something to still our hunger with: ay, and then if kind words won't help, we can try force, though even then we can stop short of bloodshed and murder. Let's go now.

Simeoni: Juhani, Juhani, what art thou saying?

Aapo: Ah! where are we wretched brothers to find shelter?

Juhani: Where bandits do! Let's move on.

Tuomas: Hold thy jaw, thou raving madman! I'd sooner march

258

to the eternal colds of Siberia than eat a robber's bread. Thou maniac, wert thou in earnest, or was it only a senseless joke? What am I to think of thee?

Juhani: Oh brother! this meeting has addled my brains, and I hardly know what I say or do. The Sheriff was here and vanished again in wind and cloud; but that seems long ago to me, it was long ago, long ago! Yonder he vanished, where my thumb points, like Tinder-Matti's thumb. Vanished in smoke, and in the midst of the smoke the white mane of a war-horse flickered. But that was long ago, long ago!

Tuomas: There now!

Aapo: What now, what now?

Tuomas: You see, brothers, that even Juhani isn't always to be shot from the branch on which he seems to be sitting.

Lauri: What art thou rolling thy eyes and twitching thy head and breathing through thy nostrils for like that? Ay, I will say. Be thankful that thy brains are sound.

Tuomas: Ay, let him hide his foolishness best he can. But what the Hell are we to do? Say, Aapo.

Aapo: I don't know.

Eero: Listen, brothers. We don't know yet for certain whether the Sheriff had a fox up his sleeve or not.

Lauri: I believe he had not; for I looked him carefully in the eye and there was no treachery there. And think it over. Why should he have come all this way without assistants, when there were villages and farms enough on his path? Why should he go past Impivaara right to Viertola Manor, where he has less help to expect than in the big villages he has left behind him? Strange! Then from Viertola he would come all this long way back with a crowd of men to our cabin. Nonsense! This doesn't fit together with the wise and cunning ideas our Sheriff has always had.

Aapo: It doesn't seem to, that I too can see, but still we mustn't trust him too much. Thou believest that thou hast thought out a matter real cleverly, yet it often happens, it's often the case, that the truth is just the opposite to what the best and wisest brain had made out. And we have cause to be afraid. Our crime is great in the eyes of the law, very great; and remember how very, how exceedingly friendly the Sheriff was towards us.

Tuomas: It wasn't the language of truth, but gall boiled under its honey. But what are we to do now?

Eero: Let us do this: go home, but not stay a minute in the cabin, only leave the door ajar, so that it would look as though the family were quietly at home; but we'll all go and hide ourselves in the caves and gullies of Impivaara; sprawl there for two or three days, keeping a close watch on the cabin. And then if we see the Sheriff come near the house during that time with his men, we'll always be ready to escape to the hills and forests. But if nothing happens in these three days and nights, all danger will be far from us.

Tuomas: That's advice and good advice.

Aapo: We'll follow it.

Tuomas: Let's turn back then; come, Juhani, and put away that sulky look.

They set out once more towards Impivaara and soon reached their own yard. Acting on Eero's advice, they opened the latch of their door and then climbed the height, where they hid themselves carefully in comfortable crannies between the rocks or under the dense spruce that covered the hill-side terraces. Lounging there, they kept a searching eye on the cabin, the edges of the stump-covered clearing and the dark line of forest. During the three days and nights they rested there, they kept watch in turns, eating from the birchbark knapsacks and slaking their thirst at a clear spring, which welled up on the summit of the height and flowed down in waves along a rocky road. Joyously the little brook gurgled while the long day held, gurgled all the moon-lit night, ever sounding in the watchful ears of the brothers.

But when the sun of the third day hastened to its setting, the brothers strode down from the hill and with rejoicing hearts took possession of their cabin, for now it seemed to them that their fears had been groundless. Even yet, however, they were not quite satisfied, but kept casting cautious glances out of the window. And the next day a spy was sent out; Aapo went to bring confirmation of their safety. He lingered in the villages and farms a day and a night, and when he returned the message of peace could be read on his brow. And now all seated themselves round the big pine table, while Aapo, at its head, began to relate all that he had heard.

Aapo: Brothers! He is a peerless fellow, that Sheriff of ours; he has done as he said, and our case is as he said it was. The Toukola men, in spite of their spavined legs, the big bumps on their foreheads or the holes in their bodies, say nothing of going to law or of revenge by their own hands; and all this the Sheriff has done with his terrible threats. And what do you think is the Vicar's idea of us? Ay, the old man has made peace with us, eternal peace; for he is now firm in a belief, which the Sheriff has argued into him, that hardness towards us would only bring about our everlasting doom. And another thing: when old Härkämäki, a rare old fellow after all, happened to mention us one day to the Vicar, saying in a growl: "Who knows but that those lads turn out real students one day," the Vicar replied that his joy in the Lord would be exceedingly great if one day the Jukola brothers were to come before him, reading passably well by sight and knowing the ten commandments and the confession of faith by heart. These were indeed melting words. All this and much beside I heard from the mouth of many men, the most trustworthy being Kyösti Tammisto, who never smiles and never tells a lie.

Juhani: Sheriff, thou bonny man, I would charge into blazing fire for thy sake! May the black bellowing bull take me! I can hardly believe it.

Aapo: Everything is as I said. We must now admit that gentlemen are not altogether such rogues as people think. Think of Viertola too, who came round so quickly and agreed to our offer on every point. While our Vicar, if we regard him without spite, straight from an honest heart and mind, rises in our eyes to noble heights, that I know. He is a fiery but true worker in the Lord's vineyard, and has already done a mighty lot of good in the parish.

261

He has closed many a wicked tavern; forced many a man and his former mistress to wed properly; and many neighbours who were always after each other's blood he has enticed into sweetest friendship. And what has been his aim in all his work on our behalf? To make respectable Christians of us. Now he has taken his hand from us, but utters at the same time so beautiful a hope that the memory of it nips at my heart.

Tuomas: And now to reading, now a-b-c-book in hand and the alphabet in our heads even if it has to be hammered there with a mallet.

Aapo: Now thou hast said something which, if we carry it out, will bring us new happiness. Ah! what if we were to start this great work together, without resting until it is done!

Juhani: I understand. We are to pounce tooth and nail on the alphabet, without flagging until we are under the cock's tail. Right! Soon we shall perhaps decide something, and once we decide, we'll carry it out too, though we sweated blood. I have a hard head, hard enough, but there's one and another thing in it, some real nimble works too. Shouldn't I with daily practice be able to keep step with a five-year old tit of a girl? Why not? Hard work helps even with the worst of luck.

Aapo: Oh Juhani! my heart is uplifted by thy words, so full of manhood and sense.

Juhani: Hard work conquers even the worst of luck. Ay, if we once start on the job, we'll stick to it with clenched teeth. But the matter needs thinking over, wisely and from the roots upward.

Aapo: We're going to try, for it is a mighty matter. Note: If we cannot read, even a lawful wife is forbidden fruit for us.

Timo: What! Is that so too? Well rot me! Then it's worth trying if this trick is perhaps going to help me to get a good wife, if I should ever be so mad as to want one. But who knows what'll come into a lad's head. Only God knows that.

Juhani: Let us think the matter over wisely; we have such hard heads.

A few days were suffered to go by, and then one evening the

matter was taken up anew, and they now decided to begin studying the alphabet in earnest.

Juhani: In two years from now may the whole a-b-c be in my head; that's said. But I'm sorry for Timo; his head's harder than mine, twice as hard.

Timo: Never mind, even if it is twice as hard. Thou'lt learn in two years, and that'll be four for me. Ay, only patience is needeh for that.

Juhani: Hear him; that joke wiped a good many days off the reckoning, a whole year. But, lad! we're in the fiend's sleigh. There's going to be more than one sigh squeezed out of us, and the a-b-c-book will be pulp before it's in our heads from back to back. God help us!

Timo: I'm going to learn my a-b-c.

Juhani: I'm going do it too, even if it felt and tasted like chewing little pebbles and raw potatoes. I'm going to do it because our Vicar is so kind and merciful towards us that I'm quite sorry for him. But where can we get a good and gentle teacher?

Aapo: I've thought that out too. I look to thee, Eero. Ay, ay, thou hast a sharp head, that can't be denied. But thank God for this gift and go out for a few weeks into the world, with food on thy back and thy a-b-c-book in thy bosom. Go to the Sheriff's Man, that fine wolf-catcher will teach thee. He is a clever fellow, and I know he will not deny thee his teaching, especially if we promise him a fine patch of forest for sowing and a jack capercaillie or two for a roast. Then when thou hast learned the chief points of ordinary reading, thou canst return and teach us.

Juhani: What? Is Eero to teach us? Hm! Eero! Well, see that it doesn't make thee proud, Eero; that I say.

Eero: Never! A teacher must always set a good example to his pupils, remembering the day of stern reckoning when he will have to say: "Here, Lord, am I and those Thou gavest me."

Juhani: Hark, hark, did it prick thee? But this is what is going to happen: thou wilt teach me when I want and keep silent as a roach when I want, and I learn from thee only when I want. That's

263

that. We'll keep thee in order all right, that thou knowest. But maybe this plan will do.

Tuomas: The best plan Aapo has ever invented.

Juhani: A thousand crowns for this plan!

Aapo: Eero, what is thy own idea of the matter.

Eero: I'm willing to think it over.

Aapo: It'll work, work beyond any doubt. But now I am going to row forth with a bigger idea, an idea that stands for itself. Brave boys and brothers! Let's help to make Impivaara a fine new pioneer farm, make a farm in the forests with the strength of seven men. Ay, your eyes grow round and you stare at me in wonder. I'm not surprised. But just think it over: our living grows harder to get day by day; only seldom now we hear the bear whistle and rarely does a capercaillie start up crashing before us. Let us note another matter too, note that "it is not good for man to be alone". That is what we shall once think; but the savage in the forests has to keep far from the bridal bed, the man who can hardly fill his own rumbling stomach, let alone those of a wife and children. But if we clear these wide backwoods into meadows, hoe this sloping sunlit clearing into fields, and around this house, around its echoing yard, gradually build stables, a cowhouse, a barn, a storeroom and other buildings as they are needed, that will be a different matter. Then we shall have a big farm, Impivaara Farm, a farm in better condition than our birthplace, Jukola. And before that day comes when old Jukola will be ours again, the meadows here will be green, the rich fields wave with corn and each evening a herd of lowing cattle draw near us from the forest.

Juhani: Thou speakest finely. But think, brother, we have one farm already, though rented now to a stranger. In a few years time we shall have it back.

Aapo: But before those years have gone we shall be idlers without like, hardly bothering to lift our feet from the ground, while our farm will be about as wasted as it used to be. I have heard that the tanner is a shiftless fellow, a poor body, and that no change has taken place yet in Jukola, either in the fields or the meadows.

264

And even if that were not the case, it is always better to have two farms than one: Jukola and Impivaara. Our reputation would also rise greatly in the sight of men, and for wife there'd be many a bonny daughter of Häme to chose from. To work, brothers! To work with all our strength; for such a life would be worth the labour, and we have seen that mankind is not such a rogue as we have thought; nay, I would say that the world is towards us as we are towards the world, and that the one who "always suffers wrongs" had better look into his own breast. We have often been scurvily treated; granted! but in reality only by those Toukola rascals, and I think that even they have had some cause for it. However that may be, peace and harmony are best; and we can always have peace if we only want. Listen, we shall work here for a time like all honest people do, and when at last we go back to Toukola, our former enemies will look upon us with a bit more respect than before, and if we then give them friendly looks on our part, a bright day of general forgiveness will soon dawn. I admit that it will have cost us much, much work and teeth-clench-ing hardship, but without these there's no harvest to be had down here. And one more thing: set plainly before the eyes of your souls what will be our final victory: we shall be men, friends with everybody, owning two farms, our future a "Cape of Good Hope"; and our graves on the misty coming shore of life will not seem a home of terror to us, but a place of delightful rest, a shadowy porch to the halls of the blest.

Tuomas: Thou speakest prettily and rightly, and I'm with thee for one. Brothers, let us listen to him, for this is a mighty matter; it gives us a new birth, raises a new dawn over the edge of the forest. I'm with thee!

Timo: And I too.

Simeoni: God has heard us and our lives grow lighter. I'm agreed to Aapo's blissful plan.

Eero: I agree too, for it is a manly step we shall be taking.

Juhani: Should I not do the same, I, your wretched eldest broth-er? I agree, and shall always call this day a day of joy. Weren't

266

fetters or the Crown's grey coat and the roll of drums almost upon us? Whereas now we are far from things like that, here amidst our own forests. So at midnight our sky was suddenly lighted, and this light, let us hope, will once drive away all clouds and "God's candles shine", as the shepherds sweetly sing. Ah! God and the Sheriff have done their best by us; we will now try to do our best by them.

The next day they sent brother Eero off to his studies, well equipped. With a birch-bark knapsack on his back, a bag over his shoulder and an a-b-c-book in his pocket, he set off on foot to the Sheriff's Man's home. The others equipped themselves with hoes and spades and began to hoe a field of the clearing around their cabin. Day by day, the area of ground broken up into clods increased; and an eternal grave was dug for the whortleberry bushes and cudweeds. But when they had hoed an enormous patch of the clearing, enough tillage to keep seven men, they left the clearing for the forest below, and began to clear a meadow amid the century-old spruce which dozed there, wrapped in cloaks of moss. Then the axes echoed again and with a crash the spruce fell on the moist ground. They peeled the trunks, gathered the branches in heaps, ready to be hauled to the yard in the winter, and carried the logs up to the old clearing to be used for their coming barn and cowhouse. While doing so the men stepped stolidly out, keeping time, the log resting on six stout shoulders. And when they reached a certain mound, at a word of command from Juhani they would simultaneously cast down their load, and the log would fall thunderously to the ground, and the earth would boom and the forest answer. So from day to day their meadow grew in extent, stretching ever farther southward from the forest's rim, while the timber for their new buildings grew in proportion.

Eero too worked hard to learn the art of reading, and his skill increased with great rapidity. Every Saturday evening he would return home with empty bag; and on the following Monday he would set forth again, a bulging knapsack on his back and a bursting bag over his shoulder, set off for school with his a-b-c book in his bosom. Thus the autumn went by, winter approached, and the brothers left both fields and meadows to rest until the following spring and hastened to gather food for their cattle and for themselves. In the dark autumn woods they trudged in all directions with their dogs, reaping a bloody harvest; and down on the edge of the bog a high hay-rick grew again for Valko's use.

Winter came; on Christmas Eve Eero returned home, sufficiently learned in the opinion of the Sheriff's Man to be capable of teaching his brothers. Remarkably easily he had learned. He read fluently by sight and knew the a-b-c book by heart from back to back, and the Lesser Catechism as well. And then when Christmas was over, lessons began. Eero sat as teacher and his brothers as pupils, all shouting as with one mouth the names of the letters as the youngest brother called them out. They would all shout together, and the spacious cabin would echo. Hard and agonizing was this work to them, full of agony especially in the beginning; sorely they all sighed and sweated. Hardest of all worked Juhani; for very zeal his jaw would shake, and dozing Timo who sat beside him received many an angry poke of his fist whenever his poor head drooped. An added trial was that Eero did not always take his high calling with due gravity, but frequently allowed stinging little quips to pass his lips. For this he had received many warnings from the brothers, but the game was dear to him.

Once on a winter day, when a biting frost prevailed outside and an almost rayless sun shone over the southern rim of the world, the brothers sat hard at work in their cabin, a-b-c-books in their hands. The devoted, but monotonous sound of their reading might have been heard afar; it was the second time they were going through the alphabet.

Eero: A.

The Others: A.

Eero: B.

The Others: B.

Eero: Ay, A is the first letter of the alphabet and Z the last. "A and Z, the beginning and the end, the first and the last", as

268

it says somewhere in the Bible. But have you ever happened to see the last as the first, Z as A? It certainly looks a bit funny to see that little thing, the one that always used to be at the tail end, suddenly cock of the dunghill and all the others looking up to him with honour and respect, as at something fatherly, even though they do it with somewhat bulging eyes. But why do I turn to matters with which we have nothing to do just now. Ay, go on reading.

Juhani: Do I catch thy meaning? I'm afraid I do. But teach us nicely now, or the Devil'll get thee.

Eero: Go on nicely with your lesson now. C.

The Others: C.

Eero: D.

The Others: D, E, F, G.

Juhani: Wait a bit; I, poor boy, have lost my place. Let's start again at the beginning.

Eero: A.

The Others: A.

Eero: A, B, C, "the cow ran up the tree". What does this sentence tell us, Juhani. Canst thou explain it?

Juhani: I will try to discover its meaning. Come out with me a little, you others; there is something important we must talk over.

So saying, he went out into the yard, and the others followed him; and with beating heart Eero began guessing what this withdrawal might portend. But in the yard the brothers discussed the best way of keeping down Eero's cruel bent for joking, which caused him to jest with the a-b-c book in his hand and thus mock not only them, but also God and His word. And they concluded that he had earned a good whipping. They entered the cabin again, and the fresh birch-rod in Juhani's hand struck the soul of Eero with dread. Tuomas and Simeoni seized the lad firmly; and then Juhani's rod did its best. Eero yelled, kicked and raved, and when at last he was free, looked around him with terrible, murderous glance.

Juhani: Now then, take the book in thy hand again and teach us properly, thou rascal, and remember this hiding whenever thy blackguard tongue feels like talking mockingly. Ah indeed! Did it hurt? Ay, ay, thou hast got what I prophesied thee years ago. For "evil is the mocker's reward in the end", that thou now knowest. Take the book, say I, and teach us in a sensible and proper way, thou rascal.

Tuomas: Stop grinding thy teeth, and sit down nicely at the head of the table there and do as we bid thee. And do it without grumbling, or the stick'll dance in my hand, and that'd mean a worse blizzard than a minute ago.

They began reading again; but it was in a very surly and biting tone, accompanied by baleful glances, that Eero read out the letters to his brothers. And thus a stormy atmosphere reigned for long over the school-table at Impivaara, until time, after a few days had passed, again softened down Eero's wrathful mind and countenance. Thus the brothers laboured to attain skill in reading, and their work prospered, although extremely slowly in the beginning, especially for Timo and Juhani.

CHAPTER 12

SPRING came and work in the fields began. The brothers ploughed and harrowed their field, cleared meadowland in the backwoods
and worked at their new cowhouse on the echoing clearing. Such
toiling was exceedingly irksome to them in the beginning; but, by
compelling themselves to keep at it, they were able in the end to
work all through the week from morning to eve. And so their
cowhouse was completed, their field transformed into a plain of
finely-sifted mould, and ever bigger grew the new meadow in the
forest. Full of tree-stumps and hummocks, but productive of much
hay, the fine new meadow spread before them. Then sowing-time
came round; the brothers sold another patch of their forest and
bought rye with the money. And Tuomas sowed the new field on
Impivaara, strewing three barrels of rye into its dusty plots. And
soon a promising crop had sprouted and flourished mightily in the
fresh September winds.

But the birches yellowed, the aspen stood in its purple garment,
and the dank fogs of evening hid the new meadow in their gleaming embrace. Autumn had come again, and the brothers were alive
to the winter's needs; and they had now three heifers and one
young hornless bull in their cowhouse. Work in the open was
over, for everything lay under the drifted snow; but in the cabin
toil of another kind began: the struggle with the alphabet. Dilig-

ently the brothers worked again at their reading, and their skill increased, though slowly. They could read fairly well by now, and were trying to learn the paragraphs in the a-b-c book by heart; jabbering and mumbling to themselves in every corner of the room, they strove to reach the cockerel at the end of the book. And one after the other they arrived at their goal: first Lauri, then Aapo and Simeoni and finally Tuomas, while Juhani and Timo toiled far in the rear. At last, even Timo was in haven, but still Juhani sweated, sighed and puffed angrily over his confession of faith. It cut him to the heart to be the last, but the others' pity could not aid him, but only his own diligence and application. He read perhaps a little better and with greater speed than Timo, but at learning by heart Timo beat him.

Those who already had the a-b-c- book tucked away in their memories, now decided to keep holiday for a few days and enjoy a backward glance at all the toil and trouble endured. Gun in hand they ski'd around the forests, and their bullets felled white-furred hares under the snow-clad trees, felled a male capercaillie as, with ruffled feathers and heavy with the cold, it sat on the branch of a bearded spuce just where a sombre forest and an echo-ing heath met. Meanwhile Juhani sat in the cabin, stripped to his shirt and oozing sweat, sat behind the table, a-b-c book in hand. Greatly enraged and tearing his hair, he fingered his stout-leafed book. Many a time, grinding his teeth with rage and almost shed-ding tears, he would bound up from his stool, snatch the chopping-block from its corner, lift it on high and dash it fiercely to the ground; and at such moments the cabin shook and the man's skimpy shirt fluttered. Thus, at intervals, he would vent his rage on the chopping-block; for only with much toil did the alphabet take root in the man's head. But he would always sit down again at the table corner and go through a stiff paragraph anew. And at last, as spring came round, he too knew his book from cover to cover; and his glance, as he closed it, was proud.

The snowdrifts melted, flowing down in water to the meadow and from there to Sompio Bog; and now the brothers set to work to build their barn; they laid its foundations some distance from the cabin on the smoothest part of the clearing; and again the clash of axes and the thud of mallets echoed far around. And when the sun rolled over the sky at its highest, when the forests and meadows were green and the ear was on the rye, the barn stood ready on Impivaara. Nature wore then its fairest summer raiment, the scented field bloomed, and the hopes of the men of Impivaara were at their highest. But the wind suddenly veered round to the north and blew thence strongly a whole long summer day, making the air cool and chilly. Tirelessly it blew, until at last with the fall of evening it was still and sank down to rest. Like a grave, so cold and silent was the night, and on the bosom of the field a grey frost lay like a choking nightmare on the blooming breasts of a young maid. And the next day the sun looked down with mournful eye on the deeds of night, on the rime-covered, frozen, sprouting corn. The brothers too emerged early from their cabin; they saw with horror the ruin worked by the frost, and their minds grew dark. Two or three days later they saw the flourishing crops white and withered.

Juhani: There went our hopes, our golden harvest. The stalks are there, but the ears hang dry, without sap or life. Ay, boys, next year's food has been snatched from us.

Tuomas: A hard blow, especially if we think how scarce game has already become. Didn't we course the forests like lynxes last autumn, and hardly got our winter grub.

Juhani: What's to be done then? We can't simply leave our field altogether, the field which we dug with so much toil and sweat from the hard surface of the clearing.

Tuomas: That we will not do, but will sow the field again next autumn, knowing as we do that frosty and frostless years come in turns here and that on the whole there are more frostless years than of those damned rime-whiskered ones.

Aapo: I believe we shall perhaps have a visit from the frost every spring, so long as Sompio Bog down yonder is a home for frogs and whortleberries. Ay, I fear so. Therefore, if we wish to save our field from frost from now on, we shall have to drain the bog, lead the water and moisture under it away, by clearing it and digging drains. And then we shall be hitting two birds with one stone: at one stroke we shall be protecting our field from the frost and making new meadow-land for ourselves.

Tuomas: That, I should say, we are all agreed is best. That's what we shall have to do, if we mean to build up a farm for ourselves out here in the wilds.

With spades and axes on their shoulders they set out one day for the bog. They dug the main ditch first, straight and deep, and then led smaller drains into it; and soon high ridges of moss, mud and clay rose along the sides of these ditches. Here grew stunted, dwarfed birches; these were felled and gathered into heaps for burning the next summer; and so new meadow-land was added to Impivaara Farm. Thus they laboured for many heavy days from early morning to late eve. And at length the greatest part of dismal Sompio Bog lay ditched, and day by day its surface now began to dry. But sowing-time had come, and again Tuomas sowed the field, and soon the grain had sprouted. The brothers spent the winter as they had done the last, practising reading; and finally the Lesser Catechism had been memorized. And Eero, Lauri and Aapo stopped not even here, but continued their studies ever further afield towards the last page of the Catechism. With hungry stomachs they sat by their books for days at a time; for game had been scarce that autumn and they had had less time than before for hunting. They scoured the forest even now on their skis, but little was the gain from their labour.

Came at last the verdant spring, and the rye grew thick on Impivaara field. But once again the wind veered suddenly to the north, whence it blew fiercely all through the summer day, until at evenfall it was stilled and sank to rest. Like the grave, so silent and cold was the night, and on the bosom of the field a grey frost lay, breathing a chilly death. And early the next morning the brothers came out of their cabin and looked terror-stricken upon the havoc wrought in their field. And soon the crops, newly so flourishing, gleamed white and withered. The men now pondered what to do and what step to take next, and deemed it best to drain Sompio Bog thoroughly, whence they knew the frost rose on to their fields. This they decided to do, and on the misty bog they grubbed and dug while hot summer passed, often prey to a depressing hunger. At such times the day of labour was heavy; wearily they returned to their home only when the sun was setting, and black lines of pain and fatigue ringed the lips of the pallid men.

But by the approach of autumn the bog was ditched from end to end and its surface had been transformed into a dry carpet of grass; and now the brothers had a fine new meadow, flat Sompio Meadow. Once more the field was sown; new plots were hoed for spring-sowing the next year. The supply of game, however, had been greatly affected by the coldness of the spring, and smaller than ever was the stock of winter provision the brothers were able to collect. Bitterly were they therefore assailed by hunger this winter, when the snowdrifts hid the ground a fathom deep and the frosts were severe. Walls crackled, stones and rocks split into two, and little birds fell down like snow-flakes, fell dead from the sky. A wayfarer would often see the saliva freeze into a ball of ice as it fell from his mouth, and when it reached the ground, roll tinkling along the smooth sleigh-tracks. On one such day, with the north wind shrieking under a pale, bright sky that sparkled with cold, the brothers sat in their cabin in perspiring heat, talking over their situation and the means by which a moaning stomach might be satisfied.

Juhani: This won't do. Over a day has gone by since I last ate. And what tit-bit was it I ate then, and how big a chunk? A thousand blazing imps! it was the two dry, resiny legs of a squirrel. A full-grown man's belly hardly notices a meal like that. What dost thou say, Tuomas?

Tuomas: Tighten thy belt.

Juhani: Look! I'm as small in the middle as the most gracious lady, small as a brown ant; but this trick won't help us for ever. It won't help long, so whatever it is we have to do, let's do it and soon. My heart chokes, brothers, my heart chokes and dismal melancholy makes my mind sink.

Simeoni: It there any other way out for us but the highway, the beggar's long and stony field?

Juhani: Let that be our last road to salvation. Oh, my breath seems to come from an empty barrel. Isn't there a single trick or wheeze left for Aapo's brains to find out?

Aapo: What can we build up out of nothing?

Juhani: The whole of this world was created out of nothing. So why couldn't even a little bit of chaff bread be made out of it?

Aapo: Ay, if we were almighty beings.

Juhani: Ah! if we were only their errand-boys, we'd be skipping about in those golden halls, and manna, boys, pure manna would be our grub, and we'd be drinking honey like water from a river. That's the kind of time we'd be having, and we'd listen spitting to some poor beggar from the earth tell us of seven wretched brothers down there beside muddy Sompio Bog, dawdling in a smoky cabin on each others necks like bats in a hollow pine and hungry as wolves.

Eero: Why fancy such things. Let's go to Kuokkala's backwoods and search the part we left so easily last autumn a bit more carefully.

Juhani: The bears have gone to Hell from there, that's almost sure.

Eero: Almost! What foolishness to sit here hungry with crossed arms, when we might be getting ourselves a fine joint.. There's not much hope, but let's try, let's comb those woods, and even if we don't find a bear, we might find some other game. And even if that fails, there's Kuokkala Farm nearby, where we can at least borrow a loaf each and perhaps a bushel or two of peas. We've got to turn to others for help in the end, if all our own attempts fail. But we'll only borrow and pay when we can.

Thus spoke Eero, and at last the others deemed it best to follow his advice. With their guns under their arms they set out with their dogs to ski to Kuokkala backwoods. Smoothly the skis ran over the hard snow, but panting and much slower than before the brothers made their way; the former strength of their knees seemed to have vanished. Finally they reached the intended woods and began skiing hither and thither in all directions, seeking, though vainly, for a bear. Evening drew nigh and the brothers lost hope, but at Eero's exhortation they decided to search once more the surroundings of a certain wooded rock. When they came to this spot, a violent barking was soon heard and out of a dense grove of spruce a bear dashed forth and hastened away, the snow eddying in his tracks. He ran twisting among the trees, and the brothers followed by devious ways on their shining skis, and the keen frosty air rang hoarsely with the angry yelping of the dogs. At last a shot was heard from Tuomas's gun, and bleeding, the bear crawled on the snow. At it charged the dogs; a man drew nigh with his bear-spear, and there with hardly a struggle the bear met its death at the man's spear and the dogs' teeth. Down on its palms it dropped and blew out its life into the bloody snow. But hardly had this happened and the brothers gathered round their kill, when a new furious barking and yelping was heard from the forest. Two year-old bears, fleeing from the dogs, shambled out of their lairs, a few hundred paces from the winter lair where the first bear had been found. And now a fierce struggle arose between the shaggy cubs and bold Killi and Kiiski, which endured, hot and bloody, until the brothers had come to the dogs' help with their spears. Soon they had felled the furiously struggling bear-pups and put an end to a fight in which the fur flew fast.

But now evening had fallen; the rich prey was borne to the foot of a spruce-covered, mossy rock and a fire made. And on the windward side of the fire beds were made of moss-covered branches and a screen of twigs raised on poles to prevent the wind from fanning the blaze and to allow the flames to burn steadily. Then the brothers began preparing a tasty supper; they scored and flayed the big bear's magnificent thigh, and cutting tender slices from this, roasted them in the fire and joyfully filled their hungry stomachs; nor did they forget Killi and Kiiski. And soon they slept on their mossy beds, after their weary bodies had been nourished and the dread of starvation driven away for many days to come. Sweetly the dogs too rested, after running long and hard; muzzle on paw they rested, now and again opening their eyes, which with a noble calmness were directed towards the bloodstained carcases on the snow. There they all rested while the camp-fire blazed and the stars twinkled; but around them frost crackled in the dry spruce and cold, sighing winds sang in the austere forest. And when morning dawned the brothers set off to ski home with their burden; and their burden was heavy, but pleasant.

The following spring came early and fine. The brothers fished diligently on bright Lake Ilvesjärvi; and in their nets or on their hooks many a bull-necked roach and golden-ribbed rudd was caught. On the bank, in the shelter of a scented bird-cherry, they sat out the dawn of many a pale summer morning, pulling out with their hooks the shining denizens of the lake. Wild duck flew creaking over the oily surface of the water, and the brothers' bullets dropped many of these in their flight. Beautiful was the spring both on the banks of Ilvesjärvi and in the meadows and fields around Impivaara cabin, where a splendid crop flourished, growing in the gleaming sunshine of day and the gentle coolness of night. This year too the fierce north wind often raged, bringing a chilly and windless night; but deep at the bottom of Sompio Bog lay the frost, cocking its ears, but powerless to lift its head above the grassy carpet. So grew the grain in the fields and the hay in the meadows that sunshiny summer, and sometimes a gentle rain refreshed the perfumed ground. The meadows were mown and the fields reaped in blazing sunshine; and in high towers the ricks on the meadows and the stacks by the cabin rose heavenward. The richest harvest was reaped that summer, which the brothers ever afterwards remembered as "the golden summer."

But when the grain had been reaped and the autumn sowings were over, the brothers set forth one Saturday morning on a long-planned excursion, intending to go to the vicarage to be examined by the Vicar. In fatherly, gentle fashion they were received by the

Vicar, who to his exceeding joy soon found them to be irreproach-
able readers, some of them even highly commendable readers;
Lauri he declared to be the best reader in the big village of Toukola.
He also found their conception of dogma to be fairly clear and
honest. And so, when they returned home a week later from Communion Service, each carried in his hand a leather-bound New
Testament, a gift from the Vicar for their diligence. Satisfied,
though with solemn air, they entered their cabin, which Kyösti
Tammisto, their cattle-tender for the past week, had swept and
garnished with leaves. And when they had eaten and Kyösti had
gone, they sat down apart to pore over their Bibles; and a deep
silence reigned in the room.

So passed the pleasant summer, autumn came fresh and cool,
came winter and a new happy summer. And the years which now
followed brought happiness and prosperity to the farm. Industry is
the spring of happiness, and the brothers toiled industriously, with
the result that the fields grew apace, grain gathered in their bins,
horses in their stable and cows under the beams of their cowhouse.

Old wall-eyed Valko still stood in the stable, but on each side of
him a sturdy foal stood in its box, one bought from Tammisto, the
other from old man Kuokkala. Neatly the foals munched the clean
meadow-hay, and with childishly carefree glances would tease now
and again the old veteran between them, trying to pass the time of
day with him over the low partition. But crusty-tempered and with
hanging ears Valko stood there, its drooping lower lip among the
hay, as its old worn teeth ground bluntly at its provender. Ten head
of cattle stood in the cowhouse. Wert thou to open its door, eight
guileless and solemn cow's faces would stare at thee, and two bulls
like two mighty tree-tumps. The eldest of the two has already been
sentenced to lose its liberty next spring, and to submit to the fate of
a draught-ox, but the youngest there is still to hoof it in the pastures
at its own will. So stood matters in the cowhouse, where Simeoni's
blameless hand worked the hardest.

Gradually all the buildings needed on a farm grew up in Impivaara yard. Thus a fine sauna was built where yard and field met,

279

and after that the platform vanished from the cabin, together with the stone-covered fireplace near the door, and in its stead a chimneyed stove was built of the kind usual in farms. A stout floor was laid of split logs, which reached the whole length of the room, instead of stopping half-way as before. Three large windows replaced the former apertures in the walls. And now looking southward from the room, thou sawest the farm fields and a big meadow below these, with another bigger meadow farther down, formerly Sompio Bog. Across the fields and meadows the farm track led towards the church and their former home; it led from the meadow into a dense spruce-wood, then along the heath to the top of Teerimäki, which rose majestically in the south to the rim of the clouds. Looking westward, thou sawest behind the fields mossy tongues of rock, with here and there a low, but thick pine, in whose swaying crown the sun often shone on summer evenings. The cabin's northern window looked boldly at Impivaara's steep side. So would the world have shown itself to him who looked at it from the windows of the spacious cabin. But if he had opened the cabin's heavy door and looked eastward and northeast, he would have seen the stony, stump-covered clearing, and at its rim a heath and an echoing pine-wood from whose bosom the sun rose into the sky in summer. Such was the face of nature around Impivaara, which was now fast becoming a prosperous farm.

Rumours of the change that was taking place in the brothers and through them in the fields and yard of Impivaara, soon spread through the parish. At first they were discredited, but the rumours proving true, they awakened wonder; and gradually the brothers began to gain in honour and respect. They, however, seldom left their own lands; they were unwilling to see their birthplace until the time came when Jukola would be their own again. They had made such a promise, and therefore they avoided seeing the beloved fields of their home even at a distance.

Came the last summer of the ten years for which Jukola had been given to a stranger to till; and the brothers were entitled next autumn to take over their old home again. In June came a clear and warm Sunday. Through the open door of the cabin the bright sun-light flowed in, drawing golden patterns on the leaf-strewn floor. At the table Tuomas and Simeoni sat in silence, each reading his New Testament; Juhani, Timo and Eero walked in the fields viewing with delight the flourishing beauty of the summer; Lauri wandered silently in the woods and Aapo had gone to visit Kyösti Tammisto. Blue stretched the sky, a faint west wind breathed in the air, the birch gleamed on the hill in its new cloak of green and a white-foaming rowan spread its perfume far around. In the fields wave gently pursued wave, and the rye flashed in the rays of a fiery sun, which already hastened up to its midday height. But soon the brothers came home again: the walkers from the fields, Aapo from Tammisto and Lauri from the bosom of the heath. With a hidden smile on their lips they drew near to their noble dwelling, which smiled peacefully in turn at the comers, and on its sunlit roof danced the silvery heat of that day. With contented hearts and open countenances they entered the leaf-strewn, spacious room.

And when they had eaten, they sat down again, each where he listed and thinking his own thoughts, or looking at the open book before him. Beside the back window, which opened westward, Aapo sat, fussing with his pipe, and one saw that his thoughts were busy with some important matter. At last he opened his mouth and a conversation ensued.

Aapo: I met the tanner at Tammisto and spoke with him about our common business. He has got a job as miller and would be willing to leave Jukola already at the beginning of next September, of which I gave him good hopes.

Tuomas: Best for him to get out of our way quicker than usual; for his hand has not uplifted Jukola, but pulled it down all the deeper; and of his rent he has not paid us a single grain.

Aapo: All of which the law might sentence him to pay, but how is he to do it?

Tuomas: He'll always lack the power to do that, unless he pawns his miserable soul.

Aapo: The law might make him work off his debt, but the rag has a sickly wife and a lot of mewling children.

Juhani: Let the poor lout go in God's name. Ay, his score with us can be wiped off. He has had hard luck too during these ten years; that we can't deny. But even if the best of luck had hugged him, he was never born to build up a farm; a bonnier boy's needed for that, but there's as little sign of that in him as in an old glove. Let him go therefore and clatter away at his mill, and we'll show people that Jukola can be made into the grandest farm in the parish.

Aapo: It's always nobler, anyway, to see before us a farm, whose ploughed fields and cleared meadows we know to be the work of our own hands. Three of us can stay to look after this new farm, while the others dig and plough on Jukola's soil; but at all bigger, urgent tasks we'll set to work together with the strength of seven men, both here and in our former home. And soon we shall have two fine farms and two crofts, all of the best, and there'll be property, land and room for each of us separately when the final division is made, and all of our futures settled. And let's hope that everything will be for the best in the end. Ay, all will be well at last; if only commonsense and justice are always our guiding stars down here while we tread the path of life.

Timo: A lot depends on the wife and her work under the rafters, whether the good man's labours outside, in sun and rain, are to bring riches or poverty in the end.

Aapo: Hark at Timo! He speaks like a man of experience. It's just as thou sayest. The wife either raises a household to power and glory, or tears it down right to the foundation-logs. I'm not speaking, mind you, of a farm whose master is quite crazy, who can waste the fruits of years in one moment; such farms I do not mean, for even the wealth of a manor wouldn't help there, or the toil of a wife, even though she were as nimble as a weasel and as close as an old Jew woman. But take an ordinary farm and an ordinary spendthrift master, and look you, if the mistress of that farm is tight-fisted and saving, the farm'll stand in spite of every-

282

thing. On the other hand, a farm where the mistress is wasteful is soon lost beyond mercy, lost even though the master were to fight against it like ten men. True, a master may get royally drunk and fight in the village, for which the law salts his back according to his deserts; yet we can regard such shipwrecks as little sores, as bleeding wounds in a human body, to which I now liken a farm. But a wife who is wasteful is the daily worm in a farm's body, its canker that wastes all its juices and at last undermines and ruins the whole building. I remember a story I once heard from our grandfather, that ever wise, cautious and far-seeing man. And this is what he told me: There were once two brothers, both as sober and hardworking, each with a farm equal in every respect to the other's and each with a wife and children. One remained always prosperous, but the other became poorer day by day, and many were the guesses made at the cause of this difference in the brothers' households, without anyone finding the real reason. Then one Saturday evening our grandfather had some errand to both of these farms. He came first to the rich brother's house, where the wife, having finished churning, was sharing out bread and butter to the children; from there he went on to the poor brother's house, where the wife was also giving the children of her churning; but look you, the woman put at least twice as much butter on the bread as her neighbour did, and now the old man had found the reason for the riches of the one and the poverty of the other. For just as the poor man's wife used twice as much butter, so, though almost in unseen ways, twice as much of everything else slipped through her fingers. And thus she would have needed two such farms to keep level with her neighbour's one farm. So said an old man famous for his wisdom.

Juhani: He judged the matter rightly. A bad and wasteful wife is the devouring rat of a household and as ugly to behold as an old boot in a puddle.

Aapo: Let marriage therefore be, as it ought to be, the most serious step in our lives. For a bad wife is a man's ruin, while a good and loving wife is his greatest joy, his best friend, his honour,

283

who makes his home a haven of joy and peace. And let him cherish such a wife as the apple of his eye, as his soul's dearest treasure. And I also believe there'd be less, much less, bad wives, if husbands were always to correct the mistakes of their young better halves with kind words and loving glances, taking great care never to harp in a nagging spirit on the example of "my neighbour's good wife" and to let that "good mistress, my dear dead mother" rest in peace in her grave. Ay, brothers, perhaps all of us will soon have wives beside us and little nippers around us, and that is why I am not speaking so much because of a passing whim, but of set purpose, meaning to sow these words in the bottom of your hearts.

Juhani: Thou hast done everything well, and hast given us much valuable advice. Truly, thou hast led us in the night of these forests with a father's mind and tongue. Brothers, let us thank Aapo, he has done a great work.

Aapo: Go away! Why talk nonsense. Oh — well! Ay! We're here anyhow now and together we have fought: struggled, strained and wrestled to escape from the tangled backwoods of hard fortune to a free and open clearing. Look! the weather is bright and calm, the sun's beginning to sink and the carp will be spawning now in swarms amongst the reeds of Ilvesjärvi. Let's go and lay our osier-nets and we shall have a tasty breakfast tomorrow.

They went down to Lake Ilvesjärvi to lay nets for the gold-ribbed carp, which spawned merrily just then, setting the lake's reedy margin flashing. Simeoni and Timo stayed at home to look after the cattle; and lowing and with a clatter of bells the crooky-horned cows returned from their pasture along the heather-clad heath. And on the stump-bestrewn, dry clearing they milked the chewing cows and drove them into the pen, where they sank down one after the other on their couches of spruce-twigs. But yonder on Ilvesjärvi's calm surface the others rowed their bluntnosed log punt, sinking the osier-nets into the bright depths of the lake along the many-tongued edge of the reeds; and in the crowns of the pines in the northwest a fiery-red sunset glowed.

284

IT is a pallid day in September, the day on which the brothers are going to take possession again of their former home, which they have not seen during the course of nine years. On the road that leads towards the village across the fields and the two meadows, seven men now journey, leaving ever farther behind them the new farm on Impivaara, where Tammisto's Kyösti is to tend the cattle for a day or two. In the van Juhani, Aapo and Tuomas marched side by side; willingly they stepped out and on their faces dwelt a calm joy. Following them came a loaded waggon, drawn by two young mares and steered by Lauri from his seat on the ribs of a small ale-barrel. This barrel was full of ale, specially brewed for a homecoming festival at Jukola. Then came Simeoni and Timo, each leading a lowing cow as a beginning for the coming herds in Jukola's cowhouse. Last of all came brother Eero, guiding by a rope a young hammer-headed bull, to whom had been entrusted the aggrandisement of the farm stock. Gladly the young steer followed the cows, stepping out behind them with a quite arrogant bellowing. Merrily pranced Killi and Kiiski too, now ahead, now behind, now bounding along on each side of the party, merry, though already grey of coat. They were the only animals of those born at Jukola to return to their former home. Valko was dead and slept sweetly in a deep grave behind Luhta-meadow's fence; dead, too, and buried was the old hoarsely-mewing cat, Juhani's beloved Matti; and at last even the proud-necked cock had died and was buried. Another cock now crowed lustily on Impivaara's rafters, from the stove another cat peered down, and two handsome young horses now drew the brothers' load at a hearty speed towards Jukola.

Onward they journeyed; they emerged from broad Sompio and entered the depths of the forest. The weather was clear and still: the sun shone mildly from a pale-blue, smiling sky. They came to Seunala Matti's clearing, then to the road that led from Viertola to church, across which they kept on uphill, along the sandy heath and through the pines. And at last they stood on Teerimäki's crest, whence their road ran in a smooth track down the rock. But on the ridge of the hill, from which one could see far in every direction, the brothers halted for a moment to rest their horses. They looked to the southwest, and in the distance the Jukola of their childhood gleamed. But soon a tear dimmed their eyes and a curious languor filled their bosoms as the bubbling water fills the lungs of a drowning man. They looked again to the southwest, and on the sloping surface of a hill Jukola loomed like a darkling past. From it they looked at last back to the north, and amid flourishing fields of sprouting grain the new farm at Impivaara seemed to smile merrily, and above it towered the steep height. So they stared, now to the north and now to the south, now all around, with eyes deliciously moist. But Juhani drew ale and the foaming tankard was passed from man to man.

Juhani: We shed tears, but these tears are pearls of bliss and joy; so let us drink and be merry.

Aapo: Thanks to the Creator that we now stand here as children of joy! Lucky we, who in one happy hour found out what became us and brought forth good fruit before our dreadful sentence was written on the wall. This, and God's guiding haand, has led the path of our life upward to these noble and joyful heights on which we now stand as conquerors. Ten golden years have passed since with hate and fury in our hearts we fled into the darkness of the

286

forests. We did that. But I believe if we had gone on idling in the south yonder, in the bitter air of persecution and wrath, it is as sons of sorrow we should now be walking! Lucky for us therefore that we left the village and our neighbours; for now a great change has come over us. Here we stand, casting·the mild eye of peace over Toukola village yonder, and there behind us we have a noble support to our backs.

Ay, yonder's the former, beloved Jukola, yonder Toukola village, yonder the church-tower and yonder again mighty Impivaara. How clearly the changing scenes of our life-journey rise before me from the bosom of the past ten years. Look how that road has run. At first, though greatly unworthy, we tried to approach our Christian fellows, making our unhappy journey towards the solemn tower yonder on the edge of the sky. It was a cruel, accursed journey, but it was, too, the powerful spur that forced us into the depths of the forest. Yonder to the slopes of that steep grey hill we moved and built ourselves a strong shelter. But envious fire burned down our house to dust, and we lads had to gallop back to Jukola like young wolves; and that was a hard game. Even of that we recked little, but went back into the woods and built ourselves another cabin, stouter than the first.

There we could freely devote ourselves again to our favourite work; and the dogs raged, the firelocks banged and the quick blood of the backwood's children flowed in streams. But there a hard fate suddenly raised us on to that terrible Devil's Rock, to a trial grim and ghastly. Somewhere over there lies that rock of hunger, agony and blessed fortune, yonder where the misty edge of the forest dips down and that sparse-branched spruce lifts its crown high above all others. There lies the rock that brought us sorrow and agony, but which we might also call our rock of joy. For note: from that rock, ever onward, we can follow the birth of this hour of joy and peace, on Teerimäki's summit here. The rock in the dreadful backoods gave rise to the first great clearing, which in its turn gave us a rich store of grain. But out of this — sadly, sadly enough — was born that drunken festival of mournful memory. But never mind. This riot of drunkenness stirred up hell and all its devils as a terrible warning to us to strike out in some new path. From two directions we were warned: by Simeoni's weird vision of the spirit and Lauri's remarkable dream. And well for us that we heeded these grave hints from a hidden world! Like men we then decided to forsake for ever intoxicating, accursed liquor, in which decision I hope we shall nobly stand.

But we had still one downright ugly blow to meet. And this was caused as much by heavy drinking as by that wicked and obstinate temper of ours that had even then not been sufficiently broken, but deep down went on fanning its lust for revenge. We faced a day of angry screaming, of wolfish tearing, of crackling staves and bloodshed on Tammisto Farm. So were we punished for our indulgence in drink. But it was then, on the very day of punishment, that our luck began to turn. Behold, when we stood already on the brink of black despair, our merciful God lit up the world for us; and this he did through that splendid Sheriff of ours. But we ourselves, what did we do? Like men we took the road of self-denial, of toil and labour. True we had yet many troubles and hardships to meet, but we bent all their necks, forced our way onward by main force, and here we now stand. Thanks be to God who has led us, thanks also to ourselves who were willing to seek wisdom in time, thanks to our mother who reminded us in the days of our childhood of God's will and law! One and another of her sayings sank into the depths of our hearts, whence a warning voice ceaselessly whispered in our ears, whispered even during the wildest storms, and the ship of our lives sank not in shipwreck.

Juhani: Ah, if mother were alive now and walked yonder in Jukola's yard, seeing her sons approaching, she'd hurry to meet us right to the rise in Oja-meadow. But the old dame sits in the halls of Heaven now, waiting for her children. We're coming, mother, with God's help we'll be there yet. Well, let's set off again, brothers, on our way, set off down the rocky road.

They trudged down and came to a dark forbidding forest, whence they emerged at last on to Kiljava's fire-ravaged, lofty heath, where hawks sailed shrieking through the air under a limpid sky. And already they fared on the rolling road that led past Kuttila's spacious meadow.

Juhani: Boys, boys, I can feel the smells of our old home, sweeter than the scent of Virgin Mary's bedgrass, in my nostrils. Boys and brothers, bred and born of the same mammy, listen to one great word: let us invite every blessed man and woman, buck and bitch, we meet on the road before we are home, to a mighty homecoming festival.

Aapo: We'll do it.

Tuomas: It's said.

Timo: We'll invite the lot, from the Governor down to Beggar-Mary; that is, if we meet them.

Juhani: From the Governor right down to Toukola's youngest infant; and a merry feast it'll be, truth it will. And then we'll pound a jig with the daughters of Toukola, jig until Jukola's planking thunders and the bark peels off the roof! True, matters are so that only Aapo can dance the quadrille, and we others only the polka, but that we dance like men. So let it be polka, nothing but polka. But where can we get a real, rattling player and a willing wench to brew coffee?

Aapo: There'll be a way out of that fix too.

Juhani: Ay, somewhere in the world. Sure there's a way to settle that somewhere. We haven't lacked ways and means even in the hardest cases, but everything has had to bend or break, or twist or turn as we have wanted. Everything has had to give way, and ten years have gone in a flash. Trala, ra, ra, trala, ra! I haven't tasted coffee since at Karja-Matti's wedding, but we'll have some today in honour of the festival, and drink a true brotherly health, all seven of us, seven bonny lads. And first of the lot, always first march we three here: I, Aapo and Tuomas, Impivaara's Life Guards battalion. Stout fellows, though, all of us. Even Eero is no longer amongst the smallest in Finland, not by any means. But slowly he grew from his perch, devilish slow. However, he's made a passable man both in soul and body. And it was the power of the years in the forest that did it, with our help; only a couple of little hidings from the hands of us others and the fellow was as though oiled. Hey? What dost thou say thyself there behind?

Eero: All true so far as my body goes, but in my wretched soul, I'm afraid, there's plenty of that accursed Old Adam's gall left even for you, the gall that so often gets loose and turns the whole world topsy-turvy. Even now it works in my eyes, as I look upon you in the first row from behind. How like a goggle-eyed stable-goat beside a solemn gelding Juhani pounds along there beside Aapo!

Juhani: Ay, Eero, my son. But today spirits of joy and merriment swarm in the air. So what do I care? I only sing.

> Frala, la trala, la!
> How can I be so merry?
> How so content today?
> Frala, lala, lala, lala,
> Frala, lala, la!

Who's the man stumping towards us on yonder clearing?

Aapo: The old man himself, I do believe.

Tuomas: Of a truth! Well, goodday to him!

Juhani: The hymnleader! The same hymnleader!

Tuomas: The same, the same. Goodday to him, eh!

Juhani: Son of the Lord! The same old rogue, knotty stick in hand and the former Vicar's long-peaked cap on his head. Well, may the big black bull take yourself! The same old rogue, the same old rogue.

Timo: Our schoolmaster.

Juhani: But how was it he schooled us? Ay, ay, now's the time to ask him.

Simeoni: Let him go by us with honour.

Tuomas: He has to be asked to the home-coming, as we agreed.

Juhani: The Devil! We have to do it. But I feel like reminding him a little of olden days, for there's still a little sting against

290

him in my heart. I'll remind him of one thing and then he can join us if he is still so inclined. He has taught me. Good! Maybe I can teach him a thing or two in my turn now, maybe I could put a cunning little question to him out of my Testament.

Timo: I'll ask him something too. There's a catchy riddle here, under the roots of my double teeth, and we'll see how he explains it. I'm not angry with him at all; for isn't my hair as thick as ever it was; but we'll see how he opens the knot I'll give him to open.

Aapo: Shut up, brothers! and let us treat him with respect, show him that we come back to the village different men from what we were when we left it. Let us always behave wisely.

Juhani: As far as wisdom goes, it's just what I want to do my best at this very minute, by casting him offhandlike a few little questions from the depth of the Bible. I've read my Testament from cover to cover and understand it too, I hope. But tell me, Eero, what shall I ask him, thou knowest, simple-like?

Eero: Ask him how five men and two fishes could be fed with five thousand loaves.

Juhani: Hold thy jaw, thou Loppi's devil, thou gabbling goblin from Kylmänoja! I'll teach thee. Am I likely to ask and explain a matter the archbishop himself doesn't understand. But I know what to ask him; and here the old man is.

Tuomas: I warn thee: treat him properly.

Juhani: I know how.

The Hymnleader: Goodday, goodday, boys!

The Brothers: Goodday!

The Hymnleader: Changing quarters, I believe.

Tuomas: Something a little in that style.

The Hymnleader: Is that so, is that so? Hm. Well, well. It's sure beginning to blow. Do you think it might rain now?

Juhani: It might maybe do that too.

The Hymnleader: It's blowing quite heavily.

Tuomas: Heavily, ay, heavily.

The Hymnleader: So it is, ay. Hm, hm. And so this is how the lads are moving.

Juhani: Ay, slowly does it. But has the hymnleader a scholar or two at his table-corner these days?

The Hymnleader: Not now.

Juhani: Not one tousleheaded brat in the door-corner?

The Hymnleader: He-he! No, my son, no. Hm. Well, well. So this is how ye're moving now. Eh, well, welcome to your old home again!

Juhani: A thousand thanks, Mister Hymnleader. We come from the backwoods as you can see, and our foals there have a thumping load to pull, its weight bigger by seven New Testaments, seven gifts from England. And I do believe it's the deepest, the hardest parts in this book that tell in the load the most. What if we were to try to lighten the load a little, ease out a few knots, kinks and twists? Can you...

Tuomas: Juhani!

Juhani: Can the hymnleader answer me one question, a question that has set the brains of many pondering. Tell me: what were the names of the sons of Zebedee?

Timo: "I and thou one, Post-house Antti and Jussi two; how many of us are there?" a man from Loimaa asked me once, and I now ask the hymnleader the same.

Juhani: Let Timo keep his bread-trap shut. Ay, Mister Hymnleader, what were the names of the sons of Zebedee? That's my question; listen hard, boys!

Timo: I and thou one, Post-house Antti and Jussi two, how many of us are there? That's my riddle; listen hard, boys! How many, my master?

Hymnleader: Two, my boy, certainly not four: ay, little son, two, only two. He-he!

Timo: Ah! there's where we are caught. That's what I said to the man from Loimaa. But not it! In that crowd there's four of us, Mister Highly-learned Hymnleader.

Juhani: Canst thou not keep thy damn jaws shut until thy eldest brother has done his bit? Ten thousand flaming imps!

Timo: For the love... for the love of the Lord don't poke me in the face a second or third time. Thou bully! Am I a calf before thee, a calf or a bullock? Not I, not I, I'm a right hot-tempered man if I once really lose my temper.

Juhani: Keep thy mouth shut now and listen. What were the names of the sons of Zebedee?

Hymnleader: A guileless question. But our old Vicar once asked of me: "What was the name of the father of the sons of Zebedee!" and guess, brother Juhani, what I answered in giving him the right answer? Ay, permit me to ask: what was the name of the father of the sons of Zebedee?

Juhani: Ah... Ah... Eh, indeed. Is that name too in the Testament?

Hymnleader: Truly 'tis there, it's in the question itself.

Juhani: So-o... ay, to be sure... hm... so it's in the Testament? But—that's just what I meant to ask you, but in my flurry asked it a little the wrong way. I've heard that riddle, but never bothered to seek out the answer to it in my Testament. You see, I'm no great book-learned or schoolmaster, I don't belong to the clergy like for instance a hymnleader. He belongs to it, but to the tail end of the order, that same tail that was once in a tight place with Old Man Viksari, the bottle imp.

Timo: It was the verger, or waker-up, who called himself the tail of the clergy and dusted Viksari a little.

Eero: It was the hymnleader.

Juhani: Hymnleader or verger, verger or hymnleader: all I wanted to say was I haven't the honour, I haven't the right to crow in church like a cock in the morning on a rafter or to twist the scurfy polls of little boys. And if you've a mind to hear the whole truth from my lips... D'y'know what Old Man Kork from Estonia said to the Sheriff of Hämeenlinna?

Hymnleader: Why, what did he say?

Juhani: "Go to 'ell, thou tamn man!" Hmmh! Whose fist think you would dance highest here? Hey? Look here, gaffer! and take note how the face of the world changes in ten years.

Aapo: Juho, Juho!

Tuomas: Now, brother, I too will have my say; and for thine own peace' sake keep quiet. May the hymnleader forgive them; they do not understand. Take no notice and be so good as to come with us to a little home-coming at Jukola; for this day is to us the day of days.

Hymnleader: I thank ye, but my time will hardly allow me to accept of your kind invitation now.

Simeoni: Come and build up peace between us and the men of Toukola; do it for God's sake.

Aapo: We pray you, come and build up peace. Is not such work a duty to you, seeing how your calling is of the Church? So beware lest not only God is angered with you, but likewise our excellent Vicar when he hears that you were unminded to act as peacemaker in such an important matter as this. Consider this point.

Hymnleader: Be it as you will. I'll follow and try my best to shake up the Toukola men's hearts, and with the power of the Lord and my own speech bend them to brotherly harmony. But let us first speak out our minds. I see in your eyes a glowering, though perhaps a little faded hate for me, and know the cause of it. Ay, I was a strict teacher to you, strict and stern, that I'll admit, and bitterly have I already repented it. But I myself was once taught in the same strict way, in the same hardhanded way, more's the pity! But what did I mean with my strictness towards you? Your own best, your own best; know that. And you can be sure too, that at this very minute, even though my mind was somewhat startled when you came marching towards me, my soul rejoices as I look on you as men and know all your deeds and struggles while ten of our dear Lord's years have rolled by.

Aapo: For this praise we thank you.

Tuomas: We know you for an honourable man and know that Juhani and Timo will beg your forgiveness for their unfriendly words.

Timo: I'll admit he's an honourable old gent, even if a hard schoolmaster.

294

Juhani: The hymnleader admitted to not having done quite rightly by us, I make the same confession on my own part, and our relations are square, especially as I agree that we were wooden-headed scholars, against whose hard heads the breastplate of his patience was broken. And who'll guarantee, who'll guarantee, I ask, that this hair-pulling and curl-dusting didn't do us some good? There's no saying at all.

Aapo: Except that all is forgotten. So let's all march on together. Be so kind, Mister Hymnleader.

They set off on their journey again, plodded along the hilly road, which to the brothers, however, was beautiful and dear; for crowding to meet them came the clearings, rocks and stumps of their childhood; and against their bosoms breathed the fresh west wind. But suddenly they heard a fearful din, and the Rajamäki Regiment came marching into view. They saw Kaisa's visage and blazing eyes under an old black nightcap; between the shafts the old woman tramped, scolding and cursing. But Heikki had now outgrown his hobby-horse, Mörökölli his bottle-cart, and beside their mother they marched, each helping at his shaft to pull the waggon. Mikko himself, a black felt hat on his head and a mighty quid in his cheek, pushed as was his habit with his stick behind. He was followed by the twins, riding their hobby-horses, and last came Mikko's youngest, dragging a bottle-cart behind him in the dust of the village road. And on the waggon was a sack of pitch, the horn-bag and a calf-skin pouch in which were the knives of Mikko, Heikki and Mörökölli, and there was also a violin, wrapped in Kaisa's old red shawl.

Thus the two strange processions moved to an encounter, and then a turmoil and tumult arose. Unwillingly and snorting, the young horses from Impivaara approached the regiment. Killi and Kiiski, the bristles on their necks standing high, raged and bellowed loudly; and the twins and the youngest ran roaring to the waggon for shelter. Kaisa cursed and scolded her offspring furiously; but Mikko brandished his staff at the hounds, lunging and gibbering frantically. The parties came to a halt, and for a long while each regarded the other stiffly; the Rajamäki family staring with astonishment, the brothers greatly taken aback, as they remembered their recent decision on the road. At last, however, brother Aapo stepped forward.

Aapo: Peace to you!

Mikko: The same to you, but call off your dogs a little.

Aapo: Killi and Kiiski, quiet!

Juhani: Greeting, thou Rajamäki's Mikko! How art thou and what news from the world?

Mikko: Mixed, both good and bad mixed, but always, dog take it, the good has outmeasured the bad, and this rackety life has suited me, that it has.. Ay, boys, there's always a bit of a job and work in the farms and villages. Ay, ay, there's no danger for Mikko at all so long as there's jobs to do in the world, even if he has to tramp and babble at every farm, tramp from village to village looking for work and bread. No worries at all for Mikko.

Aapo: That we well believe; and may your trade prosper ever better and better. But now, Mikko, an idea came into our heads, and we've a mind to keep you company for more than one minute. Ay, listen to one word.

Mikko: Ahaa! I can guess your idea, when I remember that fish we cooked once under Sonnimäki Heath, the fish that still sets you belching. It's a good thing for us that we are on a public road and that we have a good witness here in the hymnleader. So move a bit to one side, kind friends and neighbours, a bit to one side.

Aapo: Listen a moment!

Kaisa: Out of the way, you devil's prey! We want to be pushing on. Out of the way, or the hangman'll have you!

Hymnleader: A mistake, thou respected Rajamäki family, a big mistake! Hear what I say and sacredly affirm. Ah! the life of the Jukola brothers has changed, both in soul and body. Changed, so God help me! Know that they have plucked the sweet fruit of repentance and conversion and now return to the home of their birth as sons of joy and glory, burning to gather the whole world

296

to their bosoms. Wherefore they invite you also to a merry home-coming, to a feast of reparation in old Jukola. Such is their heart's striving towards you in this their hour of jubilation. Believe the word of your hymnleader.

Juhani: It's just as hymnleader says!

Aapo: Mikko and Kaisa! we wish to show ourselves men and to do men's works, forgetting the past. But what said Mikko of our kettle of fish on Sonnimäki? Why, kind friend, we boiled that ourselves and we ourselves had to swallow it. Just so, and I remember another thing from that Sonnimäki evening. Didn't thy wife foretell us dark days of ruin? That she did, and rightly she foretold. The storms came and whipped us sorely, sorely, but the storms and clouds have passed again and a fair day dawns. Well, come and prophesy for us once again, and we hope your eyes will see brighter visions. I have heard you read fortunes best in coffee, and there'll be no lack of coffee this evening at Jukola.

Juhani: Coffee and ale!

Aapo: Coffee and ale! So come and foretell happy days for us.

Mikko: Kaisa can tell fortunes in coffee and I'll play the fiddle to heighten the feast; that suits very well.

Aapo: Quite well.

Juhani: Thou stout Mikko.

Mikko: I'll play you a merry march as we come to Jukola.

Juhani: Thou matchless Mikko! Play, play till the world rings, play, God's creation.

Aapo: Everything suits excellently.

Juhani: Fits like a key in a lock.

Mikko: Round with the waggon, Heikka and Matti boys! and thou Kaisa, cast that scowling temper from thy face to Hell and make a nimble rightabout towards Jukola.

Kaisa: Ay, faith, I'll rightabout thee in a minute. Even if I were to be mad enough to start tramping back again on my old legs, would I let myself be trampled by their skittish asses on the road there? Let them swagger on ahead, we'll crawl behind.

Mikko: Right, Kaisa! Let them go to the fore, brothers, let 'em gallop on with the speed of a comet, we'll whizz after you like a smoking tail. That old woman of ours is a rather hot-tempered woman.

Juhani: But there's a wife you all the same.

Aapo: A grand wife.

Mikko: The Devil that's so; I dare to say it. She's my wife.

Juhani: A wife like spades are trumps.

Mikko: That she is. A hot-tempered dam, a hot-tempered dam; but once the old man really raises his fur, then even mother herself has to purse her mouth into a pretty little pout, has to, no help for that. But I'm a gentle old cove just the same, I am, and let Kaisa do the ordering. And why should I worry about that so long as everything pans out? Heleiyah! boys! Here we come along behind like the cobbler after the tailor to Heaven. "After him though the Devil squeals", said the cobbler, pulling at his wax-thread, with his teeth agrin. Ay, ay, march on and let her bang!

They set off again all together, and the wind grew into a storm, the birches hummed and bent, and the sun now shone cheerily, now disappeared from view into the bosom of the delightful tatters of cloud which, driven by a north wind high up in the sky, scurried swiftly towards the distant curving rim of the sky. They wandered uphill and down, and both the wandering and the storm were pleasant to the brothers as they drew nigh to their home hill in the southwest.

They met on their way an old man, black-haired, crusty old Kolistin. His grey, bushy eyebrows, like two owl's wings, almost hid his surly eyes. In his time he had been a famous shot and had felled many bears and wolves. But then a severe illness had affected his hearing, and now he could hear only shouted speech, screamed loudly into his ear. This unlucky event closed the path of bear-hunter to him for ever, whereafter he had taken to trapping. Every autumn and winter he laid his numerous traps in the forests, to the death of wildfowl, hares and squirrels. He was a solemn, obstinate, sharp-tongued old man; looking at life from his own

298

standpoint only, he lost his temper easily. This was the man who trudged towards the brothers along the hilly road in this evening hour on a September Sunday.

Juhani: Greeting, thou old one!

Timo: Greeting, granfer, greeting!

Juhani: Halt, hale honoured sir!

Old Man Kolistin: Eigh?

Juhani: Greeting from the forest-world.

Old Man: What dost thou want?

Tuomas: Shout in his ear, and loud.

Juhani: Here we are you see!

Old Man: So, Devil take you, you are, and may the old man of Heaven help us in the villages from now on again.

Juhani: What?

Aapo: Now the old boy isn't in a good humour.

Juhani: What dost thou mean?

Old Man: Thou canst guess. Ay, ay, yes, yes, yes, there's different times coming for us now. That's clear.

Juhani: Brothers, this cuts at our honour.

Aapo: Never mind that, but ask him to come with us to Jukola.

Juhani: However and in any case, old man, thou being such a grand old man, we now ask you to come to Jukola to partake of a real rowdy home-coming with us.

Old Man: Why hast thou come, dolt? Why didst not stay yonder in the caverns of thy mountain right to thy miserable death? Why didst come?

Juhani: Eh, what? Is this the thanks for my invitation?

Old Man: I go hot with rage and fury when I think of my traps. Curse! there's more than one fat capercaillie will leave my snare for another's bag from now on. You blackguards! there was enough sneaked from them without you coming.

Juhani: Didst thou call us thieves?

Old Man: Did I, did I? Thou canst understand a hint, understand it well, e'en though thou art a stupid cuckoo, a staring young capercaillie.

299

Juhani: Dost thou call us thieves when we invite thee to a feast?

Old Man: What dost thou say? Speak louder, speak up like a man and don't screech and squeal there. What didst thou say, boy?

Juhani: 'Twas to a feast I asked thee; for all of us are in a way thy godchildren.

Old Man: Thou my godchild?

Juhani: I and these six brothers of mine here. So come to our feast, godfather.

Old Man: Hold thy tongue! I am not thy godfather.

Juhani: That thou art for sure.

Old Man: I am not thy godfather, no!

Juhani: Truly thou art.

Old Man: Hold thy tongue, say I.

Juhani: Truly thou art, unless Granny Pinewood lied.

Old Man: Who?

Juhani: Granny Pinewood, the common midwife of this village.

Old Man: I give a fig for Granny Pinewood, and I am not thine nor those others' godfather. I thy godfather? Ha!

Juhani: Ha: Eigh! Is that it? I tell thee I was not borne before the parson a full-toothed, blind-eyed puppy, no! But however that may be: I ask thee to the feast.

Old Man: But I won't come, no, but forbid thee to ask me.

Juhani: I ask thee notwithstanding.

Old Man: But I won't come, thou devil-possessed! Hold thy jaw!

Juhani: I ask thee still.

Hymnleader: Boys, boys, let the old man go in peace.

Mikko: Let him go in peace for us. A simple and surly old man; looks into your eyes like a poodle; let him go. Quick march, old man!

Juhani: But it seems to me, however, as though from the bottom of those simple, grey, glowering eyes something a little foxy-like doth peep; and he has made my gall swell somewhat. I ask thee to a feast, to a roaring riot. It's to pour ale into thy face I ask thee. Thou art a good old soul, anyhow.

Old Man: What dost say? Shout louder.

300

Juhani: A good old soul, though somewhat curious: but that sin has always been the besetting sin of the deaf.

Old Man: Eigh?

Juhani: Curious, inquisitive, old rag; otherwise a good old sort.

Old Man: Blockhead, shameless blockhead! But can, can, can there be brains in a young capercaillie's skull? Not an inch. Ho! here's a whole swarm of them starting up at my feet, a swarm of capercaillies...

Juhani: Seven young capercaillies, for example.

Old Man: What didst say?

Juhani: Seven young capercaillies.

Old Man: I don't care how many of them there are; there they stare down at me from a birch-branch. There one of them glowers at me like a bull at a new gate, and he won't take heed until the gun bangs, but then he's fast. In the same way seven loons now glare at Old Man Kolistin for all the world like seven owl-eyed young capercaillies. Louts! What, what do you want of me?

Juhani: I want to tell thee with solemn mind and tongue that I am no thief nor young capercaillie nor lout, and I say at the same time that a certain old crust, a confounded old fellow, who is standing not so very far from me, not many versts of this sandy road away, that this man, this shameless old crosspatch is a great scoundrel and blackguard; and I say it with all respect.

Old Man: Who, who, thou daft young cuckoo on the top of a withered pine? A... a... a... am I a blackguard before thee? Say! Who, thou young cuckoo?

Juhani: What the hell shall I blow down his accursed ear?

Aapo: Don't blow anything else, but let's be off.

Juhani: Not just yet; for he's a rascally old chap. But what devil's mush shall I blow down his ear?

Eero: Let me try. Hold this young bullock for me.

Juhani: Yes, blow a hot word or two down there.

Old Man: Who? Hey?

Eero: "Cuck-whoo!" said the little cuckoo on the top of a withered pine. "Cuck-whoo!"

Old Man: There's a cuckoo for thee!

Eero: Thou devil-possessed!

Juhani: See the devil! What a bang!

Eero: A big bang that set my ear singing.

Aapo: Well done, thou Kolistin's ogre, well done!

Eero: To Hades with the fellow! I saw sparks.

Juhani: Old man, old man! Note what thou hast done: banged a respectable man with thy fist on the cheek right in the midst of the highway and on the holy Sabbath. Ai, ai, old man!

Aapo: Well done, thou Kolistin's barn-gnome, well done!

Old Man: What art thou jabbering at there?

Eero: Well said, thou Kolistin's old mule, well said!

Old Man: Hold thy jaw, thou too, weasel. I'll, I'll teach boyₒ to jump on my nose. Kolistin's old man isn't the fellow to think long before he lets fly.

Juhani: I'll let fly at that ragged collar of his and drag the old crust with us to an ale-feast without mercy. Heigho! old man! Now we're off!

Old Man: Go to Hell thou!

Juhani: Come and drink ale till thy belly splits!

Old Man: Let go my collar, or I'll bash thee in the face. Let go, thou Devil's Jew, let go!

Juhani: A bucket of ale!

Tuomas: What fool's trick, Juho, is this again?

Aapo: Leave the old man to himself.

Juhani: God preserve us! he has rated us like dogs. What shall we do with him? An old sinner like him. But let him come to the celebration at Jukola and drink ale in his anger. Ay, old fellow, my heart won't allow me to give way, no!

Old Man: Loosen thy claws!

Tuomas: Art thou minded to release him? See now, how nicely thou unloosest him. Go, old man!

Juhani: Ah! I would have carried him to a merry feast, carried him like a little baby; for my hairy bosom flashes sparks. Son of the Lord! from whose snare have I snatched a bird? A bird or a hare?

Tuomas: Hold thy tongue!

Juhani: Am I a thief, I?

Hymnleader: That he never said, my boy.

Juhani: That was what he hinted at, anyway. Ah, if only the snows of twenty or thirty years had been off his crown, ah son of the Lord!

Tuomas: Go, old man!

Old Man: Blockheads! A... a... a... am I a hobbyhorse in your sight, you drab-haired wolf-cubs that someone ought to bash on the skull? But I'll, I'll, I'll teach you yet, I'll, I'll teach you yet, louts!

The crusty old fellow, old Kolistin, left them at last; but for long he muttered in his anger, spat and muttered to himself as he tramped along the hilly road. The brothers too set off on their way with their company, the hymnleader and the Rajamäki Regiment, which brought up the rear. But when they had journeyed thus a while, they met two women: Granny Pinewood and her nimble, plump daughter Venla, marching rapidly onward, on whortleberries bent, with white baskets of birch-bark in their hands. This encounter greatly embarrassed the brothers, and they regarded the approaching women in deep silence, coming to a halt, however, before them; and now on each side a protracted staring followed, both parties gazing round-eyed at the other. Until at last Aapo stepped forward, informed them of the firm resolve taken on Teerimäki and begged them to come as guests to the home-coming celebration. Doubtful what to do, the mother and daughter stood there, grinning in secret at each other and primly pursing up their lips. But after the hymnleader too had begged them to give ear to the brothers' invitation and to take over the post of coffee-maker at the feast, they decided at last to join the merry company. And thus the Jukola brothers already had a mighty mediator and peacemaker for any encounter with the men of Toukola in the hymnleader, willing coffee-makers in the old woman and her daughter, and in

Rajamäki's Mikko they had the right man to play a merry home-coming march and to fiddle for them in the coming dance with the maids of Toukola. Meditating over all these advantages, they marched with increasing, prouder speed towards their goal, and stood at last on the sandy crest of Jukola's north field. Before them they saw Brook Meadow, behind that the home fields and, rising above these, Jukola farmhouse itself, ravishingly mournful. Silent and with moist eyes the brothers stood on the green, reverberating mound, looking at their home; and the sun sank westward. But ever fiercer blew the north wind that roared in the pines on the stony hill to the south of the farm.

Tuomas: Yonder is therefore Jukola.

Juhani: Art thou Jukola?

Aapo: Thy bearing has somewhat slackened and moss has stuck to thy brow, dear home.

Juhani: Moss has stuck fast to thy golden brow, honoured mother Jukola.

Timo: Welcome, Jukola, thou who sittest, squattest before us, beautiful like once Jerusalem.

Juhani: Art thou Jukola? Thou? Ah! I can't help a big tear rolling down my rough face, so fiercely my heart foams and boils. Oh! everywhere, wherever I let my eye rest, the kind smile of a friend looks back. See how lovingly even the black window-hole of the cowhouse smiles at me. Greeting, thou star of hope, greeting!

Eero: Greeting, greeting, thou black star of hope!

Juhani: Greeting, thou sweet dunghill under it, fairer than hills of happiness! Ah!

Timo: It surely is beautiful, but why hasn't that dung-heap been carted into the fields many a good day ago? Ay, ay, that pile there proves, announces and betokens deep-rooted, altogether hopeless laziness on the part of the tanner. Is this a right state of things: a dung-heap squatting in the yard in September? I'm greatly vexed with this tanner. Well, well, thou'rt forgiven, especially today, which is Jukola's great jubilation.

Juhani: Greeting, drab dung-heap, greeting! say I in spite of all,

304

without minding what it witnesses and portends. Greeting, Jukola, with thy heaps, fields, meadows, fair as Heaven!

Timo: Heaven is fairer, anyhow.

Juhani: Hold thy jaw! This is the fairest paradise.

Simeoni: Don't talk sin.

Juhani: My tongue utters what my heart whispers.

Lauri: I would say something too, but this wonderful hour has quite fettered the former nimbleness of my tongue.

Juhani: Unloose thy tongue, with heart and lung, yell out the bliss that is in thy bosom! The mountains rattle, the forests roar, silence seizes Heaven for half an hour, a half-hour brief and holy. There's poetry for you, made up by Juhani Jukola in his joy.

Aapo: But may this be enough here, and let us hurry on.

Juhani: Ay, let us push on to the very end like a spawning shoal of roach into the farthest corner of the seine. Let's go now before our honoured guests tire of our mighty spasm of joy. Jukola yonder is not their home, and for that matter they have seen it later than we have. You, hymnleader, you, Granny Pinewood with your daughter and you, honoured Rajamäki family, do not be offended at this.

Hymnleader: No need to beg that of us. We can well understand what this moment means to you; it is a high and solemn hour, full of intoxicating joy.

Juhani: Beautifully said, a blissful remark! Let's go now!

Tuomas: Let the guns bang and Mikko strike up!

Juhani: Ay, what if we were to have a little music now. One volley, brothers, one mighty volley. All together!

Mikko's fiddle emitted a shriek and almost at the same time the guns of Juhani, Tuomas and Aapo banged. The spirited steeds before the waggon leapt high, the cattle galloped panicstricken in all directions, tails in the air, one here, one there. But not one of their guides released his hold of the halters in the game, neither Simeoni nor Timo and least of all Eero. Clenching their teeth they followed, half-dragged along, each after his own beast, and the dry sand rose in great clouds. And the cattle had to come to a halt and turn with their man on to their right road again. So fared the procession downward, disappeared for a moment in the hollow of Brook Meadow, emerged into view again, climbed the long steep hill and entered through the gate of the home field. Grandly Mikko played his fiddle, madly Killi and Kiiski raved with joy and defiance, their barking answered by the yelping of the tanner's lean, poky-chinned mongrel that limped from behind the house corner, a trembling weakling. The din brought out all the folk from Jukola into the sloping, stony yard. But seeing the Rajamäki Regiment approach the house, the children fled swiftly back again into the living-room, and loudly whimpering, hid themselves, some in the bed under the counterpane, some on the oven-top among the clanking timber set there to dry, all with terror in their hearts. With the same fear the mongrel too was suddenly quiet, and hooking its tail between its legs, crawled into hiding under a bench in the corner. But there was now enough noise and bustle in the yard. The shouts of the men, the clamour of the hounds, the lowing of the cows, the bellowing of the chubby little bull and the shrieking note of the fiddle all echoed in one warring discord as the wandering company drew nigh to the house; and with a mighty roaring the north wind rattled the close-set pines on Kivimäki Hill. The brothers, their only feeling a languishing kindness, went forward to greet the farm-folk in the dearly-beloved yard of their birthplace. And when hands had been grasped and the cattle and the load stowed away, they stepped at last in a body into the airy living-room of the farm.

But off to Toukola marched the hymnleader and Aapo, to invite the men there to a feast of reconciliation and a merry homecoming, the men who had lived so long in hate and persecution with the Jukola brothers. And when the invitation which the hymnleader announced in fitting words had spread through the village both to men and women, they hurried back to assist the others in arranging the feast. The floor of the pleasant living-room at Jukola was cleared, foaming ale in capacious tankards was borne to the tables, and beside the fireplace the willing Venla hustled with her mother.

The smoke from the coffee-fire rolled in clouds under the sooty rafters, the roasted beans broke crackling into fragments between the teeth of the coffee-mill, and on the fire steamed the tanner's wife's coffee-pot. And now the yard was swept, cordwood was borne from the pile into the room, fir-twigs were hacked to decorate the floor, and a multitude of other tasks done. And beside the window, on a broad bench, merry Mikko sat, letting his fiddle squeak every now and then.

But what can Granny Pinewood be whispering so eagerly with Juhani yonder in the porch, and why does Juhani stand so dumbfounded, with eyes wide open, solemn as on trial? The old woman is informing him in roundabout fashion that on their side there is no longer any obstacle to a union with Venla. And at this the lad is struck with wonder; he puffs, sighs, sweats and tears lustily at his neck-hairs, and at last begs the old woman to grant him a moment to think it over. The old woman leaves him with shining face, but out into the yard staggers Juhani, steps aimlessly like a homeless brownie, without knowing whither to betake him. There behind Jukola's walls he wanders backward and forward, sweats, sighs, glows and steams and tugs lustily at his neck-hairs. But at last he hurries back to the porch, opens the creaking door and utters in a sobbing, almost tearful voice: "Would the hymnleader mind coming out here a little behind this corner, and thou too, Aapo, dearest brother!" They comply with his wish, and soon all three stand under Jukola's wall, meditating over the matter which Juhani has told them. There they ponder, discuss the matter and finally decide that Juhani is to take Venla, who is after all a good girl. Then, impetously and with firm step, Juhani enters the house and seizing Venla's hand, says: "Be it said." Whereupon Venla is stricken with shyness, hides her face and smiles, but allows, however, her hand to rest in Juhani's bunchy fist. This fills the mother's heart with delight and she gives them her maternal blessing; the hymnleader wishes them happiness and prosperity and in a short speech reminds them of the most important duties of the wedded state.

307

Juhani was thus engaged, the old love re-lit in his bosom. But greatly the bridegroom puffed and sweated, looking ever and anon in secret on his bride. And suddenly he hastened out to look at the horses in Brook Meadow, and there looked upon the two young mares from Impivaara, but seeing them saw them not. Even two cranes on the distant edge of the meadow would have been as two horses to him. So whirled his thoughts around his bride, whom he could not as yet bring himself to believe he owned. For him the day was a day of marvels. Soon he was rushing back again, lusting to look on the features of his Venla. Swiftly he strode, and already in the field he heard a fiery Polish march from Mikko's fiddle. At that his mouth twisted suddenly, a tear moistened his eye, which he dried with his powerful fist, and it seemed to him as though he were amongst the joys of Heaven. Reaching the yard, he saw not before him the Rajamäki twins, who, sitting astride their hobby-horses, galloped madly across the yard; his eye saw not Mikko's youngest on the steps with his little bottle-cart. With firm footsteps he entered the room, and in his glance was a secret, glowing triumph, an eternal solemnity.

But little by little the lads of Toukola gathered on Jukola hill. Between the woodshed and the stables a cluster of them already stood, pipes in teeth, examining sleighs and carts and the tanner's spring-trap, bought at Hämeenlinna market. They stood there, examining and criticising for a fairly long time, to saunter finally across the yard towards the farmhouse, first one, then another. Here they lined up standing against the walls on either side of the stoop, and a few penetrated into the porch and listened to the clatter and chatter within. Until after a time the door opened and Aapo came out, inviting the guests to enter.

The Toukola men stepped inside, crowding together to the left, between the door and side-window. They stood there solemn of face, each holding his cap to his lips. Amongst them Kissala's Aapeli was seen standing at an angle to the door and casting backward glances at it, and Kuninkala's Eero, his eyes boring into the floor. Near them beside the window sat Mikko with his fiddle, turning the quid in his cheek and spitting. His youngest, the apple of his eye, leaned on his knee. But in front of the table, a knobby stick in his hand, stood the hymnleader, ready to launch on a speech that would pierce his hearers to the marrow; and his air was forbidding. Clearing his throat and rubbing his chin with his thumb and forefinger, he glanced, glaring sternly, to the right at the men of Toukola, glanced to the left where the Jukola brothers stood, silent and staring down at the floor, between the table and the northward side-window. Near the fireplace were the tanner's family, Granny Pinewood with her daughter and Kaisa Rajamäki, who, snuffbox in hand and snuffy of face, sat on a stool, swaying to and fro. In the corner between the fireplace and the door, hard by the chopping block and water-tub, were the Rajamäki boys; there they stood, Heikka, Mörökölli and the twins, staring in amaze at the hushed congregation in Jukola's living-room. But beside the table stands the hymnleader. Utterly solemn and silent he grips his chin, opens at last his mouth, only to hold back his words and again clear his throat. He darts a new terrific glare to his left, another to his right, grimacing as though he were chewing dogweed. But at last the following speech issues from his lips.

"The Devil, who goeth around like a raving lion, puffing poison into the world, hath lighted a flame of hate and anger also in the hearts of these neighbours. It flickered at first faintly in the dry brush, but soon spread and grew into a terrible forest fire. At first like to a little fly, it waxed and swelled as a bull that is being fattened, hiding with its thick smoke the light of the heavens. Thus was power given to the black fiend, and with raised fists they charged at each other, to part at last after fearful fighting with bruises, gaping wounds and lumpy foreheads. Oh what misery! The heavens sighed, the hills and valleys sighed, and the brainless beasts of the fields groaned, but Hell and darkness rejoiced. Many a man thought, shaking his head, now will fetters soon clank, the rods of justice whistle and our lads go marching away from the beloved land of their birth to the icy plains of Siberia. Thus many prophesied, but wrongly they prophesied, for which let us render

309

thanks and glory to Zebaoth. For see the wonderful trick played by fortune: these brothers left the abodes of men, their neighbours and fellow men, and trotted off into the night of the forests, and again many did think: thus, thus are robbers born, seven blood-thirsty wicked bandits in the forests of Finland. But to Zebaoth be the thanks and glory that they showed these prophets a nose a fathom long.

"Whether 'twas the Devil who led them into the woods, as he once led the Tuusula parson, or whether a higher power drove them thither like John the Baptist into the wilderness, that I will not dwell on now. But there the Devil tried his utmost against them, to turn them into the path that leads to destruction. With poisonous spirits, yea, with hot syrups he tempted them; he led them, as they themselves have related, upwards to giddy heights, to the so-called Boot-leather Tower, and there showed them the sphere of this world, showed them the whole in fearful disorder, hoping to scare the wits from their brains. Such was his purpose, only his own plan turned against him, to hit him in the face with shame and hasten the footsteps of these boys into the right path while there was still time. They began a strenuous struggle, stepped forth to battle nobly with their own hearts, with deep-rooted laziness, with the hard unfeeling earth, cold bogs and quagmires, and by the steadfastness of their wills and the help of the Lord Zebaoth they conquered. Eiyah! Here they are back again with their fellow men, not as robbers, but as men of worth. With a loud solemn rumbling they came with their swiftly rolling chariot, drawn by two young and spirited mares, and in their train were lowing, seal-ribbed cows and a bellowing bull-calf of the hornless breed. So they arrived, not from the caves of bandits, but from a pioneer farm built up with their own hands, Impivaara's grand farm. Eiyah! Through them has Zebaoth been brought to glory, but the horned Satan of Hell to shame.

"Here they now stand as men deserving of praise, holding out to their former enemies the hand of friendship. And you, good men of Toukola, need no longer deem it a disgrace to call the Jukola

310

brothers your friends: for they now spread around them the light of glory and not the besmirching filth of shame. Accept therefore the overflowing goblet of peace and beware lest ye cause them to hold out their hands to you in vain, if you would escape the wrath to come. Lo! the sun is sinking, looking back with eyes fainting with love at the rainbow which glows in the east. Lo! it is the sign of the Covenant of Mercy of the Lord, now a mighty token to former enemies to make peace, to join in loving brotherhood and to deal the Devil and his angels a harder blow than ever right in the face. This is the will of God, and it is likewise my will and he who now refuseth to open his heart and ear to our word, may he be anathema maranatha, and Devils roast him in the end in Hell. Hear me, Zebaoth, hear me, Lord on high, Hosianna!"

Thus spoke the hymnleader, and greatly were the women's hearts moved. The tanner's wife, Granny Pinewood, nimble Venla and Rajamäki's snuff-faced Kaisa snuffled in uncontrollable weeping, snuffled with a sound like to the sound of new, four-woven sheets being squeezed in the soda-tub by the washer's hand. And facing each other stood the men of Toukola and the Jukola brothers, and in sign of forgiveness wrung each others hands hard. Heartfelt, guileless and solemn was this reconcilation, though hands were sometimes held out stiffly, though glances shot with sullenness were still exchanged. But from the head of the table the hymnleader looked on with a blissful smile, as he sat there with a tankard of ale and a steaming coffee-punch before him. And in the room ale was handed round in white tankards, handed round from man to man and soon from woman to woman. For already a crowd of Toukola maids had gathered in the room. To them, as they whispered amongst themselves by the chopping-block and the fire-place, Mother Pinewood's nimble Venla served coffee. Nor were they too forward to accept the refreshment offered, but only after the bearer had obstinately renewed her invitation two and even three times, did manners allow them to partake. Nor was Mikko forgotten this evening; ale in abundance and even spirits were borne to wet the musician's whistle. Whereupon he began spitting mightily into the screws of his fiddle and tuning that treasure of many glueings. And from it flowed at last a perfectly enchanting Swedish quadrille. He fiddled away at this for a while, but as none came forward on to the floor, he stayed the strains of the quadrille and loosened a merry and sturdy polka. This he ground out devoutly and long, and still not a single pair whirled polkaing on the floor. And at this the old fellow was finally greatly hurt, and letting his bow rest altogether, he twisted his quid and, spitting, began to twang the strings of his fiddle.

The folk sat in silence. Near the back-window sat Aapo, looking now and again closely at a certain round-faced, brown-skinned, but grave and blue-eyed maid who talked in whispers with Venla, a meek simper of innocence and shyness on her lips. With great curiosity Aapo regarded her, searching hither and thither in his mind, but the name of the maiden eluded him. At last he asked the hymnleader, nudging him in the ribs, and swiftly the hymnleader answered: "Why, 'tis Konkkala's Hinrikka." Whereupon Aapo's forehead cleared and after a while he uttered to Mikko: "Give us a quadrille." Mikko began again, and Aapo now approached the coy daughter of Konkkala, begging her for his partner. The maiden followed him and placed herself at his side, but shyly, smiling and blushing furiously. Couples gathered on the floor from other directions too, and at last, to the squeak of the Rajamäki fiddle, a Swedish quadrille was danced in the spacious room. Merrily the fire blazed, a torch flickered in its holder and the broad-beamed floor shook thunderously as with grave and solemn faces the measure was danced in an awful silence.

But beside the table sat the hymnleader, and he had with great satisfaction drained two hot coffee-punches and three drams of spirits cold. He sat, watching with a smile the young people dancing on the floor, and a becoming flush had appeared on his cheeks. But when the interminable quadrille was at last over, the hymnleader stood up and announced his intention of going. And having partaken of a farewell dram and delivered a valedictory speech, he departed gratified from the house of Jukola. He refused the cart which was thrust on him with great tenacity, and set out on foot, his knobby stick in his hand. He was accompanied across the yard by Juhani, who hastened to open Jukola's weather-worn, tottering gate for him. And there for a while the mighty conciliator stood, looking upward towards the star-filled sky and holding converse with Juhani of winds and weather. Finally he took his leave, and deeply Juhani bowed, scraping his foot so that sand and little pebbles rattled on the cowshed wall. Then Juhani returned to the merry company, muttering to himself: "he has done a great work." But on towards the village, a knobby stick in his hand and a black peaked cap on his head, the hymnleader trudged smiling, and on his cheeks two delicate roses glowed.

Hour by hour the sounds of rejoicing and the dance in Jukola farmhouse rose higher, reaching at last an uproarious revelry. Feet were flung about, now in a quadrille, now in a giddy polka, dance after dance without pause almost, and under the young men's heels the floor thundered and the stout planks yielded billowingly. Ever the fire burned merrily, ever Mikko's fiddle squeaked gaily, squeaked until the rafters rang and the sooty ceiling quivered. From man to man the foaming ale was passed, from woman to woman the steaming coffee, and in the coffee-grounds Rajamäki's Kaisa foretold happy days for the brothers right to their graves.

Thus they made merry at the brothers' homecoming; thus the toast of peace was drunk from dripping tankards, and not until dawn had come was the feasting ended.

CHAPTER 14

ALMOST ten years had thus elapsed since the brothers moved to the wilds of Impivaara, now transformed into a prosperous farm. But soon old Jukola too, backed by seven sturdy men, had risen to equal rank with it, if not to higher. And the day came when the dear home of their birth was divided into two farms. The original Jukola, their home and mother everlasting, was left in Juhani's care, while Aapo took over the other half, which stood, in itself an excellent farm, near to their former home. Impivaara too was divided into two holdings, the masters of which, by mutual consent, became Tuomas and Lauri. Timo was given the croft known as Kekkuri, and Eero the one called Vuohenkalma, to be ruled and enjoyed by them and their heirs without tithes or tax until the day of their death. All married, with the exception of Simeoni, who, desiring neither wife nor farm, settled down as bachelor uncle on Juhani Jukola's farm. It might be added of them that they lived and toiled, each in his own sphere, like good men and true; and the homeless beggar praised both the farms Jukola and Impivaara and the crofts Kekkuri and Vuohenkalma for their hospitality. And except for Simeoni and Timo, it might also be said that they had forsworn for ever the use of treacherous liquor. Simeoni, that decent fellow, sometimes strayed into the tempting paths of drunkenness, and the same hapened now and again to Timo, though much more seldom, perhaps once or twice a year.

When juryman Mäkelä died, who stepped into his shoes? Jukola's Aapo, always a man of peace and justice. Who, when the old Sheriff's man left this earth, was promoted to this honour? Eero Juhani-son Vuohenkalma, a keen-witted man, skilled in reading and writing; even a newspaper came hurtling to him once a week from Turku.

Juhani took to wife Granny Pinewood's Venla and with her enjoyed pleasant days, though faint murmurs of discord might indeed have been heard now and again from the house. For Venla, although she was a passable housewife, was a bit of a chatterbox and quarrelsome. Often she would nag and scold at her husband for hours at a stretch, at that lout, that owl, as she was wont to call him. But Juhani too could lose his temper, and then he raged furiously, telling the "female, to whom God had given a weaker brain than a man", to shut up at once. So he would carry on, banging his fist on the table and booming like a thunderstorm. Until at last Venla would pretend to be mildly alarmed and suddenly cease answering him, grinning meanwhile in secret at her hussy of a maid. They would laugh slyly by the fireside while Juhani preached from his seat on the bench beside the table and, often with tears in his eyes, murmured against Him who had "given and assigned to him for ever" such an impudent and disobedient wife. Nevertheless, a great commotion was once brought about by that Aapeli Karkkula. While Juhani again squabbled with his wife, he began, the madman, sitting slightly drunk on the side-bench in the farmhouse, to meddle between man and wife, and held forth strongly on Juhani's side. Juhani preached lustily, calling his Venla "the Devil's own shrew", whereupon Aapeli, the stupid fellow, believing he was acting real wisely, also began calling her a harridan, a she-tramp and beggar's brat. But before long Juhani's eyes narrowed, and dashing up like a baited bear, he sprang at the astonished Aapeli, who skipped out like a hare, with Juhani pounding at his heels. The door crashed, the porch thundered, and on

315

the steps the dogs, panic-stricken and dismally howling, rushed aside with hanging tails and looked back in amazement as the men ran madly across the stony yard. Ahead galloped Aapeli Karkkula, grunting with terror, behind him Juhani tore on at a trot; but in the spacious living-room Venla and the maid laughed until the room echoed with the merrily tinkling sound. Failing to overtake Aapeli, Juhani turned back from the gate, grumbling to himself and promising to teach that impudent Karkkula puppy in the future. Entering the room, he smote the table with his fist, saying: "Scold me but not my wife! She is a wife the like of which there is only one in the whole kingdom of Sweden." Thus he prated boastfully; and indeed one could not well have belittled the woman for her housewifery. True, she drank coffee all too copiously, of which Juhani was frequently heard to complain; but the wife cared little for this and allowed her plump-breasted coffee-pot to bubble as before. And gladly her husband too accepted a steaming cup from the chubby hand of his helpmeet. Also, when away in town, he would always remember to buy his Venla a bag of coffee and a big chunk of sugar.

Venla presented her husband with sound and sturdy offspring. Only, in the beginning these matters did not turn out altogether as Juhani would have wished. The first fruit of his love was a sly-eyed girl-child, at which the father was much put out, vexed because no lusty male-child had been given him. But he hoped that next time at least he would have better luck. A year went by and part of a second, and Venla gave birth to a child again. This infant, wrapped in a white cloth, the mother-in-law now bore to the grimly waiting father, smiling a honeyed smile. Believing his hope to have been fulfilled, Juhani was delighted and asked: "Boy or wench?" "Look for thyself, little son", the old dame answered him. He looked, only to shout: "Take yours brats to Hell!" Being left alone, however, he muttered after a while: "God bless my infant, anyhow." Another year passed and another, and Venla gave birth to a son, the very spit of his father, a big, hulking boy. Then there was much rejoicing in the house of Jukola, and even Venla seemed dearer to Juhani than before. And now all the women fell to choosing names for the lad. One wanted him to be Frans, another Florentine, a third Erik Translatus, while Venla was for Immanuel. Then Juhani stepped forward and at Venla's bedside declared, pointing with his hand: "No, my Venla, no; Johannes is his name." And so the little fellow was christened after his father. Greatly did his father love him, calling him now his "tit", now his "little crow".

Juhani's family life was for the most warm sunshine, with little interludes of wind and storm. And even when clouds did appear, they soon vanished and gave way to fine weather. But with the villagers and his neighbours his relations were not as good. Quarrels would often arise, fierce little disputes over such things as boundary-fences, straying horses, untended swine and other matters. And Juhani was ever quick to settle these quarrels with his fist, so that the face and hair of his opponent were in constant danger. Often heated lawsuits seemed imminent, but then brother Aapo would hasten between and try, in his capacity of juryman, to coax the would-be litigants to reason with his conciliatory tongue. Nor was Juhani slow to come round, especially when he perceived that he was in the wrong. In everything connected with his farm he was a good worker. His farm-folk could not have found fault with him, neither in the fields, the meadows nor in the forest, in a tussle with an unruly log.

Once at haymaking time in Vehkala meadow — a meadow set in a gloomy spruce-wood — Juhani showed himself a real terror before both God and Man. The wide meadow had been raked and the haymakers already crowded round the barn to enjoy their dinners. But the master viewed with dread the sweltering, flame-tinted clouds that voyaged threateningly over the sky. Behind the barn was the stump of a birch, and at the foot of this, unseen of all, Juhani fell on his knees and prayed God to spare the juicy, sweet-scented hay of his meadow. Thus in secret he prayed; but hardly was the meal over than a roaring cloud sailed into view from behind the spruce-tops and, darting down flames and thundering,

317

began pouring down rain in torrents. In a twinkling the hay was wet through, before a single haycock could be raked together. Rakes in hand, the haymakers fled swiftly from the field to the shelter of the barn, but soot-black in the face with rage, Juhani remained standing in the space before the barn, cursing horribly. There, while the heavens crashed, he stood and swore, beating his right fist against the palm of his left hand. He cursed furiously, bending down the depth of a span each time the word "Devil!" burst from his grinding teeth. Looking up, he cried again and again in a squealing voice: "What have Heaven's dung-carts to do with my hayfield?" His wife called to him in reproach from the barn: "What horrors art thou uttering, thou sack of sin?" But the man cared nothing, only shouted in a still more terrible voice at the dark gloomy clouds: "I ask again firmly, is this the time for Heaven to cart its dung when I am already making my hay?" And at this the wives and maidens in the barn, hearing the wild language of the man, prayed earnestly to God on his behalf, with hands tightly crossed. They prayed; and each time the lightning flashed a prayer, sighing and heavy, issued from their lips, and their knees bent lower. The children, gentle and meek of eye, hid their faces and wept in their mother's bosoms or in the folds of her dress, wept and sighed. Many a little one, seeing the earth and heavens bathed in fire, in flashing, flaming fire, and hearing the dreadful thunder echo around, believed the Day of Judgement had come as the rain fell heavily and the forest soughed mournfully around them. But Juhani, seeing what the women were at, went on increasing the enormity of his curses; and ever louder the women raised their praying voices.

Among the women in the barn was Seunala's young and slender daughter, Anna of the shy glance, whose eyes shone like two stars under her pallid, gleaming brow. Often, so it was said, had this maiden seen marvellous visions, during which her spirit walked in the light-filled homes of the blest and the gloomy valley of the damned, and of these she had many wonders to relate. Often too she had foretold great tribulations for the children of mankind:

wars, famine, plagues, to be followed by the end of the world. She it was, a maiden always grave, silent and gentle, who suddenly, while Juhani cursed in the sodden hay, sprang out of the barn, fell on her knees on the ground, and heedless of the pouring rain and the cross-fire of lightning, prayed in a high, almost shrill and screaming voice. She prayed to God to spare the unhappy, blinded man and to keep the flaming hammer of His wrath from striking him. So, looking up into the heights, she prayed, and a wondrous light burned in her eyes, and on her brow shone a heavenly fire. And behold: Juhani was silent, though his eyes still glared angrily sideways at the maid. Until at last, when it seemed to him that the maiden's mission dragged on too long, he seized her by the arm and led her back to the barn, saying: "Go in, rag, go in now, and don't get thyself wet there without cause, for I need no one to pray for me." The maiden entered the barn, but immediately fell down on the hay and prayed without cease in a crying voice; and hot tears welled from the women beside her. But outside, leaning against the wall, stood Juhani, and something akin to repentance could be read in his face, though the anger still surged in his bosom.

Soon the rain and lightning moved on; and the next day the hay was gathered in Vehkala meadow, gathered in blazing sunshine. But the master of the house was no more to be seen there. Where was he now? The voice of Seunala's daughter echoed in his ears and gave his soul no rest. And so, early in the morning, he set off for the vicarage in sombre mood, and repenting, confessed his sin to the Vicar, his curse against God and Heaven. The Vicar admonished him at first in grave tones, but soon began to speak words of consolation, and Juhani returned home with his mind at peace. But after this scene in gloomy Vehkala meadow a certain change became apparent in Juhani's character and deeds. On his head appeared a round hat like a pot, the collar of his coat rose upright, while its skirts vanished, leaving behind only the snippets affected by Pietists in various parts of Finland. Thus clad he walked about, and to church he walked oftener than before. Awe-inspiring in his solemnity, he sat in the place kept for him beside the solemn master of Härkämäki, now and again clearing his throat in imitation of his companion. And after this the storms in Jukola farmhouse and in the fields grew rarer and at last the current of Juhani's life flowed in an almost undisturbed stream towards its calm evening.

Simeoni lived, a bachelor, on Juhani's farm, receiving his food and drink from the farm and toiling untiringly in its service from morning to late evening. His nature was frugal even to parsimony, and his frugality grew from year to year. With the close attention of a miser he watched over the fortunes of the farm and the work of the men and women on it. His lips first formed a saying that still lives and provokes laughter amongst the dwellers around Jukola and Toukola. One day, as he sat by the chopping-block whittling a breadplatter for Venla while the farm-folk were all at table with a heaped-up bowl of pork-stew before them, he saw fit to remind them that "a tiny bit of pork-stew makes a lot of bread go down". This he said, whereupon both men and women burst out laughing and even Juhani, after first laughing a little, found cause to rebuke his brother for over-great stinginess. But to this Simeoni only replied: "I exhorted you to temperance, warned you against making gods of your bellies, which is a sin, a mortal sin. And who is unnaturally stingy here? Not I, but that Kuninkala's Kalle might be who brewed the spirits for his own funeral when he felt his end was nigh from a consumption. The lad knew himself to be the best distiller in Toukola, the one who always got the most clear spirits with very little grain. And so it was now. In the cold sauna porch the miserable wretch sat beside his still, coughing and sniffing, his nose sharp as a gimlet and the eyes in him like two glass balls. There he sat while the spirits were carried into the house in kettlefuls. At last he too crawled up the steps into the porch, from the porch into the house, fell down neatly on his bed and a few hours later lay stiff and cold. That, good people, was miserliness, a miserliness that never left its man even on the edge of the grave, and that I call unnatural miserliness."

320

Thus he would defend himself, and never admitted to being a miser.

Nevertheless, he retained the goodwill of both master and mistress; for he was a faithful and trustworthy guardian to have on the farm. Without anxiety they could stay away from home, if only they knew that Simeoni was in charge.

Once, on an evening in the Christmas holidays, Juhani departed with his wife and his two youngest children on a round of visits to Impivaara and Tuomas and Lauri, and Simeoni was again left in charge of the farm. The road was good and the journey progressed pleasantly through the forests, under a cloudless sky. Little "tom-tit" sat, solemn and chubby, on Juhani's knee, while the youngest child of all, a girl fresh and gentle-mannered, rested in its wrapping of a white fleecy shawl on Venla's breast, enjoying its warm nourishment as the sleigh slid tinkling over the snow-covered clearings, hastening from Jukola towards the fields of Impivaara. Evening fell, and the men and maid-servants at Jukola went off to the games at Toukola, leaving Simeoni to manage the household alone. Two were left in his power, the two oldest girls of the family, one nine, the other seven years old. These two had not been taken along with their mother and father, and their uncle would not permit them to go to the village with the others, at which both were mightily aggrieved. Simeoni, however, cared little for their opinion, and decided instead to make use of his power to enforce on them his own ideas of what was fitting

It became pitch-dark, and still no fire blazed in the fireplace, as usual in the evening. At this the children fretted and began clamouring fiercely for light and a fire. But their uncle paid no attention to these demands, but lay peacefully as was his habit on the top of the fireplace, his long coarse hair hanging down from its edge. He lay there speaking words of wisdom to the girls. "A fine thing, indeed, to be always baking these bricks. Ho, ho! we're not, I'm thinking, in Vantaa ironworks. Know, you hussies, that wood is dear; and tell me what we shall burn when the forests have all been cut. Heather, eh? Ay, that's what'll happen if we don't look ahead of us in time. Less is enough for this sinful wretched body, enough, I should say, for two idle scamps like you. Get under the rugs, there's warmth for you. Ho indeed! A fine thing that would be." So spoke Simeoni; but the children, saucy minxes unused to giving way to their uncle, nagged back at him, argued quite fiercely with him, snapped and at intervals bared the white rows of their teeth at him, mocking and jibing in their anger. And when this failed to help them they at length dared to lay their claws on the old fellow's scraggy hair, which hung over the stove-top. These locks they now seized and managed to tug fairly well before the poor man had time to climb down. But at last he was on his feet, and seizing a sooty stick from the corner, he hammered with it on the floor, threatening to sweep the legs from under them. Whereupon the scamps skipped out of the room, and Jukola's tough-grained door sang as the little rascals bolted.

But a moment later they had the boldness to enter again, and in fierce tones demand their supper. Simeoni let them rage and scold for long, but at last he rose and taking a splinter from the rafters split it and lit one half. In the light of this wretched torch he ladled out gruel from the pot for the girls, but not much, only two or three ladlefuls. He set the bowl on a stool and bade the children eat; meanwhile he covered the pot with the lid of the baking-trough and for further safety put the heavy chopping block from the corner on the lid. The children, however, were dissatisfied with these rations and demanded more; they wanted at least a piece of bread; and little Venla, a sharp little puss, wept music-ally. Simeoni bit off a piece of bread hardly as big as a man's thumb and handed it to the girl. But seeing its smallness, she would have none of it, and angrily thrusting out her hand, knocked the bread out of Simeoni's hand into the corner. And now the man too lost his temper; pursing his lips tightly together, he twitched her by the hair with two fingers, saying: "Thou baggage, dost thou mock at the dear gift of God? Ho indeed! A fine thing."

At that the girl began to weep harder, but Simeoni cared not a whit for that, but merely began at last to make a fire. With a few paltry embers he built up a wretched blaze, saying in a scolding tone: "Hold thy tongue now, or I'll take a stick from yon corner and thrash thee properly. The little imp, to throw God's gift out of my hand into the corner. Oh well! Be without bread now and lap up thy gruel nicely like thy older sister is doing. And it's quite enough for a child's supper. We haven't the means to feast and live like rich men do. Shut up, thou wretch. Ay, a fine thing that'd be." Thus he spoke, sitting on the hearth and coaxing his unwilling fire of embers; the old fellow never saw how the little minx, spoon in hand, made angry faces at him and wagged her little jaw in time to his words.

However, neither the girls' tears nor angry words helped, and they had to be content with their uncle's rations. And at last an overpowering sleep laid the children in bed, and soon they were sleeping soundly under the soft sheepskin rugs. Meanwhile Simeoni's fire let the cold into the house instead of warming it; nor would he wait for the fire to burn out. Thinking to himself: the dear wood will do for tomorrow, he began to extinguish his feeble, dispiriting evening blaze and closed the dampers tightly, despite the acrid smoke that streamed into the room from the air-hole. Relighting his skimpy torch, he ate his supper: a small piece of mouldy bread and seven dried-up sprat's heads from an oaken bowl. Eagerly the burning eyes of the dogs watched his meal, the movements of his hand from bowl to mouth and mouth to bowl, but not a crumb was left over for them. And having eaten, he crossed his hands, fell on his knees on the hearthstone, and weeping burning tears thanked David's Son for having in His boundless mercy always fed him, a sack of sin. And then, rising, he opened the door and began shooing out the dogs for the night, "to guard the house from thieves". He said this, although as far back as anyone could remember thieves had been unknown in Jukola. A fierce wintry wind had risen outside and the dogs were little minded to exchange the rustling straw of the room for the cold out-of-doors; and thus a tumult ensued in which the dogs, however, got the worst. Squealing, with drooping tails, they fled at length before Simeoni's weapon, the sooty stick.

This accomplished, he carefully closed the heavy doors of the porch, a burning splinter between his grinning teeth. Coming back into the room, he held his torch to the left and looked at the girls, who dreamed sweetly in their bed under the warm rugs, cheek against cheek, glowing like two newly-blown roses on a summer night. The man gazed upon them, gazed smiling and tucked the woollen edge of the rug closer to little Venla's throat; and as he moved away to the hearth, he uttered in a fond, mincing tone: "What's to stop you from sleeping, with your bellies full of gruel." And having said this, he prepared for his own nightly rest. Once again he fell on his knees and clasping his hands firmly together and shedding hot tears, thanked the Lord, David's Son, for all the good they had enjoyed, praying for His sheltering hand to be held over the farm also during the coming night. He prayed on his own behalf, on behalf of the little ones in the bed and for all on the face of this earth. Then he lay down on his beloved stove-top, and with the embers gratefully warming the soles of his feet, fell asleep.

Cold was the room, cold and cheerless, when the men and maid-servants came back from the games at Toukola somewhere about midnight to sleep, and the next day they glowered angrily at Simeoni. And when the master and mistress returned from their visits, all began fiercely complaining, both the children and the grown-ups. But Simeoni cared nothing at all, and only whittled beside his chopping-block, remarking in an idle tone: "We haven't the means to live like gents, that you all know. To live like gents on this farm."

Such was Simeoni's life in his old home, on old Jukola: toiling diligently and always on the watch inside and outside the house. Yet days would come when nothing on earth moved him. He came back from the village on these occasions thoroughly drunk, came back a merry fellow, who blustered loudly and pranced backward and forward on the floor, to the amusement and laughter of all on the farm. But the next day he would be very ill in soul and body. Sighing and with hands crossed, he would lie on the sooty oven-top, and a great repentance would gnaw at his heart. Then came an event which caused these drunken hours and long days of atonement to grow much rarer. Juhani once brought him an expensive gift from town: a big, stiff-backed Bible weighing almost a stone. Simeoni's joy and delight was great; and for this kind deed he never wearied of thanking and praising his brother. And after that he forgot the tempting glass almost entirely.

Each Sunday and on week-day evenings he was now seen sitting beside his Bible, studying the Word; and thus he seldom fell in with strong drink. Nevertheless, this was still to happen one All Saints' Eve. In merry mood the man blustered, strutted and danced around, only to fall asleep at last on his stone; and the next day he again knew black repentance in his bosom. And what did he do then? Standing at the head of the table with the Bible open before him, he called together the farm-folk from the oldest down to the youngest. And placing two fingers on the Book and rolling his eyes heavenward, he swore a sacred oath never more to taste strong drink, not another drop as long as he lived.

A year went by and a second and even a third, and Simeoni held firmly to his oath. Once again, however, he was to fall into this besetting sin of his, and this fall caused a great commotion on the farm. A perjured, soul-less worm, the poor man now regarded himself, having broken a vow made with two fingers on the Book. He therefore decided to shorten his miserable days. Swiftly, but with firm footsteps and ice-cold mind, he left the house, climbed to the stable-loft and tying the old speckled mare's blanket-strap round his neck, fastened the other end to the highest rafter under the roof. And there he calmly set himself hanging, to sleep the sleep of death; and stiffly the man's eyes stared before him, his cheeks swelled out with terrible speed and his hands clenched into iron fists. But the measure of his days was not yet filled.

Juhani's mother-in-law went to look at her hen's nests in the loft, and seeing a man at the end of a rope she at once raised the alarm with her shouts and squeals. Juhani hastened without delay to the place of danger and saved his brother from the very jaws of death. With one jerk he snapped the strap and groaning and uttering cries of surprise, carried his brother into the house, and around them swarmed the women and children, weeping, crying out and striking their palms together. Into the chamber, on to Venla's yielding rug, Juhani bore his brother, and soon Simeoni had come to and sat gloomily, sighing and peering down at the floor, on the edge of the bed. With a smoking cob between his teeth, Juhani then hastened to Aapo, walking rapidly and groaning, to tell his brother of the awful event and to ask his advice regarding Simeoni. He himself thought a little thrashing, given secretly and in all moderation and silence by his brothers, to be followed by a few stern godly words, would be best for the man. But Aapo dismissed the hiding as unnececcary and harmful, and decided to use only the power of the word on him. And when he too had lit his pipe, the two brothers set off from Aapo-Jukola over the fields to Juhani-Jukola, to talk wisdom with Simeoni, that child of sorrow.

Aapo shook the hand of Simeoni warmly in greeting, and refilling his pipe, began with solemn mien and voice to pronounce judgment, followed soon by words of consolation. Simeoni listened for long without saying a word, only peering dismally down at the floor. But Aapo, ceaselessly relighting his cob, waving his hand and looking out of the window went on increasing the power of his speech. And the words fell from his mouth like a glowing golden rain. And suddenly, bitter-sweet lines appeared round Simeoni's mouth and the man's throat burst into a mighty sobbing. Juhani's jaw trembled too and hung aslant, and soon he too was weeping, and even in Aapo's eyes a moist gleam could have been seen.

Thus was Simeoni's heart turned once more towards life and hope. And it was with a face beaming with gratitude that he squeezed Aapo's hand in farewell. He thanked God too for the new mercy shown him; and little by little he relapsed into his for-

326

mer ways on the farm. And thus pious Simeoni, never draining another glass, lived out his peaceful days, now whittling beside the chopping-block, now, pipe in mouth, hacking pine-twigs in the fresh-scented yard, now sitting by his Bible, studying the Word.

Aapo ruled over the other half of Jukola, over the farm now known as Aapo-Jukola; his farmhouse stood only a few hundred paces from his former home. He had married Hintrikka Konkkala; a mild and gentle woman in every way; a busy housewife and good-tempered helpmate. Aapo was content with her, though he deemed it best to give her now and then strict instructions and advice in the care of a household. To these she would listen in silence or laughing, her eyes twinkling, her simple merry laugh. Aapo would also instruct the maids and little servant-girls, when their work happened to offend his eye. The oldest maid once received a stern lesson from him while she swept the floor. For Aapo, being of the mind that she swept too stormily and left dust in the corners, suddenly lost his temper and snatching the broom from her, began with nimble movements to sweep the room anew from the rear end to the door. But halfway across the floor, he thrust the broom at her again, saying: "That's how a good girl should sweep." Whereupon the mistress, who had watched from the fireplace Aapo fussing broom in hand with the maid, laughed her guileless, melting laugh, laughed, screwing up her eyes and laying her hands on her knees. For which Aapo, as soon as he had left the maid to her work, cast a sternly reproving glance at her. Yet he was always fair and honest with his men and maids; this they would all admit with one mouth.

He practised the art of healing, too, as he had learned it from an old medical book which he was always studying. Very often his remedies proved successful, though many of them were of his own invention, concocted of herbs. He was especially famous at curing erysipelas, fainting-fits, mumps and the itch. At massage he was unexcelled; many were the men whom his hand had treated and who had found in it alleviation. Stomach-aches and the gripes he would often cure merely by massage. And as danger knows no laws or rules, it happened more than once that women too had to submit to treatment by Aapo's palm, when colic pains and retchings tore ceaselessly at their stomachs.

There was one woman, the wife of the rag-gatherer, old Matti Tervakoski, who suffered from an obstinate nightmare. It rode her in the most exhausting fashion for weeks at a stretch. Sometimes when it failed to afflict her, she had hopes that she had been saved from this nightly tormentor. But then it would return and the old woman would writhe again in the grip of her persecutor. She sought help from wise women and from doctors, but always in vain. Then at last a rumour of Aapo's great skill and power of curing diseases reached her ears, and once more she fared forth to seek relief. Bundle on arm and knitting in hand, she walked the long weary way to Jukola, but once there, she was freed from her trouble for ever.

As a juryman too, Aapo was the right man. Grave, often with his hand behind his ear, he sat on the court-room bench, carefully following the course of a law-suit. There, holding his head manfully erect, he would sit, a faint smile of self-satisfaction playing occasionally over his lips. His judgments were always wise, impartial and just. Of this the Judge was aware, and therefore he always listened patiently to his somewhat long-drawn speeches, as, spreading out his hands, he held forth on the case in point.

Thus he lived in his peaceful home, a good master, and the good father of sturdy children.

Impivaara, the part first cleared, was ruled over by Tuomas, a man broad-shouldered and strong. No brave dared preen himself in the presence of the master of Upper-Impivaara. Great was his strength, and his whole being bespoke power and authority. In working his farm he never had recourse to shouting and bluster; yet he kept good order and upheld the fear of God both in his home and out in the fields. He was the most generous of all the brothers, and always treated the suffering children of hard fortune mercifully and with kindness. Not for him to question, or to probe the origin of the misery of those seeking his help. He would not upbraid the man whose own folly had brought him to the beggar's staff. He gave to all, gave without discrimination, thinking: at least thou art unhappy. Tenderest was he to little beggar-girls, who, with shy glance, walked the path of mendicacy in fear and trembling. Two such wanderers he had taken into his care, and these were brought up and cared for as lovingly as his own children, bouncing boys every one of them.

His wife was Härkämäki's only daughter, a grave and noble woman, worthy to be the spouse of the mighty hero of Impivaara. Robust, at once quick, grave and calm, was she in appearance and character. Her bosom swelled proudly; her plait, thick and flaxen-yellow, danced pleasantly on her strong shoulders under her neckerchief, red-checkered on a white ground. Peace dwelt ever on her brow, and in her heart the fear of God, strict and whole-souled. This was the mistress of Impivaara, the noble mother of the children on the farm, their own and those adopted. Often her eyes, fine and charitable, would dwell dreaming on a delicate girl-child, saved once from orphanage and destitution.

Thus the days of Tuomas's life passed calmly by, towards the calm haven of death. The life of man is often compared to a stream. But Tuomas's life, from the time when he took over Impivaara to the moment of his death, I would compare to a mighty river which fares majestically, calmly onward towards the boundless eternal ocean.

Two or three gunshots east of Tuomas's farm, Lauri's new farm stood on a heath; it formed the other half of Impivaara and was called Laurila. Here dwelt a silent man, who tilled his land with energy, toiled busily in his fields, but with greater eagerness walked the backwoods and bogs.

He had chosen his wife from Kuokkala Farm. Of the Kuokkala twins, Lauri had espoused one and the other had fallen to Timo's lot, to be mistress of Kekkuri Croft. There was a woman for thee, Lauri's wife: a broad-bosomed wench; short she was too. Her shrill voice carried far, like the piercing note of a clarionet, especially when, brimming over with wrath, she stormed at her husband; at such moments her brown eyes emitted sparks.

Silent, whittling a piece of wood, Lauri would sit, heedless though his wife raged and blustered like a tempest. And this tried the woman's patience so that her gall would rise still higher. Yet it could happen at times that the man's patience gave out, and then it was not good to look him in the face. Even the wife would be suddenly silent and slip out best she might, to hide in some corner of the cowhouse, in some sheltered nook or cranny. There she would linger a while in hiding, peeping cautiously out at intervals to find out how the storm she had awakened was progressing. So she would stay away until the man's wrathful mind was appeased. Yet it was seldom that quiet Lauri was thus aroused. Often, when his wife raged and fumed again, he would go out into the forests, a pipe between his teeth and an axe under his arm, and look for useful bits of timber, birch-bark for shoes, and fungoids. Gladly he lingered on these trips, searching, looking around and meditating. And not until long after sunset, when all others rested, would he trudge home in the mild half-dark of the summer nights, with a burden of roots, twisted tree-trunks and a mightly ball of birch-bark on his shoulder.

It often happened at such times that on his homeward way he would meet his sturdy bull, Hälli of the broad back, bound in passionate thoughts for the village; come face to face with him in the mists of eve on the sandy road; see him approach with baleful eyes. But then steel met steel; yet Lauri, roaring in his hoarse voice and brandishing his axe, would always force the obstinate brute to turn in the end. And then they would march back to Laurila, Hälli ahead and Lauri behind. Hälli tried to turn to the right, but at once Lauri would be there, brandishing his axe; once more Hälli would try to the left, but again from the left Lauri's axe threatens him. And so the bull would deem it best to march off home, shaking its head angrily and blowing out the mighty passion of its heart through its nostrils.

They would pass the home of Tuomas, where the maid would

330

hear in her bed the thud of footsteps, swishings and tappings, from the sandy road. "Who is out so late?" she would think, and rising up sleep-befuddled in her shift, she would go to the window, peep out and see her neighbour's bull go marching gravely and solemnly by with its master. In front the bull, unwilling, behind it the master, every now and again brandishing his axe and carrying on his shoulder a bundle of wood and a ball of birch-bark. So they would vanish at last from the maid's sight. Then the bull would open its maw and sing in its wrath a fearsome, screaming song, and the heath would quake and heaven and earth echo. But then Lauri would say: "Ay, I'll give it to thee. Art thou angry? Aha! rascal, march nicely home now; even Kaura-Matti's tricks wouldn't help thee here. As thou knowest." So he would say as he strode on, with the bull marching before him and blowing a proud triumphant march, which echoed in the silent night to far distant villages.

Lauri would shut up Hälli securely in the yard to keep the farm's own cows company, and then enter the house, where a supper grown cold awaited him. In the house all slept already; only the mistress lay fretfully awake in her bed in the chamber, waiting for her husband. When he had eaten Lauri would at last enter the chamber, and at once a sharp gale would blow to meet him. From her bed his wife would scream and rave passionately at him, crackling with fury like fire in a dry juniper bush at her husband, at "that lout's accursed idling in the depths of the forest". Silently the man would sit, undressing himself, and then, lighting his cob, lie down at last beside his wife, who still scolded and flared up at him. But when the pipe had been smoked to the end, Lauri would lay it carefully on the floor, twitch the coverlet a little higher and then utter in a firm tone: "Be quiet now, bless thyself and sleep in God's name while the weather's good; mind that, while the weather's good." And at that the nagging wife would be still, though her heart still heaved in her bosom; until, having angrily jerked the coverlet more to her own side, she would fall asleep like the man beside her.

331

Thus until the dark nights came Lauri lingered in the forests on these pleasant outings. And of all that he saw there worth noting, marvelling at or thinking over, he seldom said a word to anyone during the week. Only on Sundays and generally at the breakfast table would he relate a thing or two to his farm-hands.

Once when he returned from the forest, his mind worked harder than ever, thinking, meditating; but what it was he pondered over so deeply no one knew. Silent and increasingly morose from day to day he moved in his yard, snapping viciously at both men and women, which had seldom been his habit earlier. A cloud of deep or vexing thoughts hid his brow without cease and cast dark shadows in the hollows of his eyes. Such was his appearance a whole long week. Came Sunday at last, and Lauri sat at table with his men, but in complete silence. At last however he opened his lips and said to the others: "Men, I have one thing to ask you; explain it if you can. Five days ago when I walked over the smooth rise in Koivisto meadow, in the new snow that hid the ground thinly with its woolly garment as it does now, I saw tracks that my brain cannot make out. Curse! for days and nights already my thoughts have coursed hither and thither, in all directions, seeking an explanation to this matter. But listen: in the meadow I saw tracks, the tracks of a full-grown man, which I followed, idly walking. But suddenly these tracks broke off, and from this point, continuing over the rise and down into the thicket, the tracks of a fox began, clear fox-tracks, of which there had been none on the ground up to now, not one. Where had the man got to? He had not turned back, either to the right or the left, no, but he must have gone up to Heaven and a fox come down from there to continue his tracks in the snow. Oh can the man have carried a fox on his back, and then at the spot where his own tracks ended have climbed on to Reynard's back and ridden him through the thicket on to the church road? Impossible; yet I can see no other way of explaining this matter. What do you say, men? Are there still magicians in our village? Had the man changed himself with the Devil's help into a fox?" Thus he spoke, and the farm-folk listened in astonishment, nor could any of them explain the riddle; one and all ended in believing that a wizard must have walked in Koivisto meadow.

But in Lauri's heart there was no peace; having eaten, he set off tramping again towards Koivisto meadow. Reaching the rounded rise he noticed the same phenomenon again: human tracks changing into those of a fox in the newly-fallen snow. Beside himself, he shouted in an angry voice: "Is the very Devil at his tricks here?" And shouting thus with twisted lips, he kicked at a dung-hill that showed faintly through the snow, whereupon the gleam of bright steel flashed from it. In an instant fine dung and chaff flew into the air, while at the same time the shining arcs of a wicked fox-trap closed on his leg, squeezing it mercilessly. And at this Lauri's eyes opened wide; he bent down hurriedly to release his aching, swelling calf from the obstinate irons, and with a shrieked curse cast them from him to the ground. Now he knew what kind of traps had been set in his meadow, but of the puzzling change in the tracks he could still make nothing. He began wrathfully walking homeward, limping badly and clenching his teeth each time he put his foot to the ground. And soon he felt the need of some prop to help him on his way and began seeking a likely staff in a thicket by the church road. In a bush he saw two birchwood poles, and when he had dragged these from their hiding-place he found them to be two stilts, both of which had exceedingly natural fox-paws carved at their lower ends. And now his face brightened and all was clear to him. He understood now that some trapper, wishing to avoid anything that might breed suspicion in a fox, had used these stilts each time he had been to examine his traps. By this means he left behind him not human tracks, which the cunning Michael of the hills would naturally avoid, but those of a fox. The matter was now clear to Lauri; and with a lighter heart, albeit with aching calf, he limped away, using one of the wooden legs as a crutch.

And now it chanced that Kolistin, that crusty old fogey, visiting the squirrel-snares which he had set between poles stuck upright in the meadows and the fences of the fields, saw Lauri's tracks in

333

the open meadow and began to ponder deeply. "Here's a man and a dog gone by, but — what am I to think of such wonders? — a one-legged dog. The Devil and a marvel! A one-legged dog has hopped beside its master across this stump-besprinkled, God's own meadow. What in damnation am I to make of such a marvel? Are wizards and Lapps about? Eh?" Thus he pondered as he stood on the clearing, tearing at his rough black locks, rolling a quid between his front teeth and knitting his grey eyebrows in a terrible frown. Soon, however, he walked on, but still without comprehending the miracle on the clearing: a one-legged dog that hopped beside its master. He brooded over the matter long and deeply without a word to anybody until on his deathbed, when he asked his gentle daughter-in-law what she thought of this marvel, which gave him no peace even in the jaws of death. But the woman, with tears in her eyes, only shouted in his ear an entreaty to dismiss all such thoughts from his mind and to think only of his everlasting soul. To this the old man made no answer, but continued to stare before him; and thus he took the strange mystery of the heath with him to the grave unsolved.

Lauri's leg soon healed of its bite and he toiled on his farm as before, now in the forests, now in his roomy farmhouse. Such was the life he led with his sturdy wife and children. And as long as they remained in their mother's care, his children never lacked a shirt or stockings, their daily bread or the whip.

Timo ruled over Kekkuri Croft, and his wife was the second of the Kuokkala twins. Both in character and outward appearance she was the spit of her sister: a plump-bosomed, tiltnosed, brown-skinned woman. She was said, however, to posses a somewhat softer heart than her sister, the wife of brother Lauri. Greatly did Timo love her, even though his hair sometimes flew in the lusty grip of his hot-tempered mate; for it was not good to oppose her in anything. Timo tried, indeed, to do his wife's will in every way, and life went on well on the farm. One matter only would now and then disturb the peace of their household. Timo had the habit, a deeply-rooted habit, of drinking himself into a rowdy state of intoxication once a year, about the Feast of Halloween, on which occasions he would linger in the village for a day or two in the company of his boon friends. But then a rare commotion would arise when at last he saw fit to return home.

One Sunday on the confines of October and November the man had again strayed from the straight path and joined in a merry carouse with Kyösti Tammisto and Karkkula's Aapeli. In the cool attic at Tammisto they drank from a black, shining bottle, talking with great gravity, singing and embracing each other lovingly. Thus they spent two days and two nights, cheering and singing and staring carelessly with bemused eyes out of the windy windows of their eyrie. They stared over the dung-covered yard, over the straw-littered cowhouse, over a stony hill, over fields and meadows right to the distant bog called Lemmilä, over which, high under the clouds, the wild swans flashed, wheeling hither and thither on their migration to the lands of the south. Uunheedingly they stared, gazed with watery goat's eyes, prattled foolishly and wagged their heads, in which a delicious heat and giddiness made themselves felt; far away were the cares and sorrows of ordinary wretched mortals.

But at last the third day dawned, and the friends woke with aching heads from their chilly couches. Finished were both money and drink, and no way was left of inducing housewives to tap their casks. Silent and with disordered countenance, Timo finally started to trudge homeward; with lagging footsteps he passed along the lane, walked mournfully up the hill, his thoughts dwelling on the hot-tempered mistress of Kekkuri. His homespun trousers had a miserable droop to them, and between his trousers and the red-striped waistcoat he affected his shirt stuck vacantly out; his eyes bulged, little and bloodshot, as, with his hair in a thousand tangles, he marched on towards Kekkuri; and the open breast of the man, gleaming and red as the scoured side of a copper kettle, glowed afar. In gloomy humour he walked, and the forests, hill and valleys glared angrily at him. Yonder the yellowed birch bore stern witness to his sin; the dark-hued spruce loudly proclaimed it, and like a black, vicious imp a tarry stump stood by the roadside; Nature, formerly so loving, now turned a strict step-motherly countenance upon him. Yet on trees, rocks and stumps he looked but little, but kept his gaze directed ahead, remembering the hot-tempered mistress of Kekkuri. On those who chanced to meet him on the road, young or old, man or woman, he hardly deigned to cast a glance, and indeed he would have been hard put to do more on this trip, even if the Grand Duke of Finland himself had walked past him. Silent, brooding with a faint smile on his home, his wife, the farm-folk and his children, he marched on, and every now and again a sudden, but soundless sigh would burst forth from his breast.

Finally he reached his yard, and here he halted to consider whether he dared enter the house, and whether there were any means left under the sun by which he could appease even slightly his infuriated mate. There he now held his head, held it a long time, looking hither and thither, until at last an idea flashed into his brain and he said to himself: "I have found a way." And at once he began piling up an armful of cordwood from the pile. And then, with a mighty load of wood in his embrace, he staggered towards the house, hoping by this trick to please his firm-willed wife. With a great scraping he mounted the steps and entered the porch and from there shouted in an innocent tone: "Open the door ... open the door, you children there, the boy or the girl." And presently his son, little milk-bearded Jooseppi, came and opened the door, and in stepped Timo with his load, looking straight and unwaveringly before him. And when he had dropped his load with a great clatter in the corner, he said: "The cordwood pile seems to be going down a lot; but what of it; there's plenty of forest on Jukola." And having said this, he made bold to cast a swift glance at his wife: but there a thunderstorm, threatening and heavy with wrath to come, met his gaze.

It was a dreadful moment. Hardly had the wife shrieked out the question: "Where hast thou been, thou devil-possessed?" before a slap fell on Timo's cheeks, a fiery slap right and left. But soon the sound of slaps ceased and an awful silence followed, during which Timo's hair was milled with such fury that the world span round before his eyes. At last he lost his temper and seizing his wife's arms in his brawny fists, he thrust her down on a stool and there held her quiet for a while. And with his hair terribly tousled, red as a turkey-cock in the face, Timo then spoke to the furious woman: "What now, if I were to give it thee from a real man's fist, thou slut, thou she-ass's colt. Dost think thou canst dare to treat me like that? Oho! that's where thou art mistaken. There aren't many fellows I'd let touch my hair, let alone any old woman. For, devil take me, I'm a proper hot-blooded fellow, as, more's the pity, is so often seen and heard nowadays. Ay, ay, take care I do not wallop thee a little even now." Thus he threatened, without however fulfilling his threat. Perhaps he had not the heart for it. For he still loved his wife greatly. But in a black rage his wife screamed: "Let go, thou accursed man, let go this minute!" This interruption took Timo aback and he pondered for a moment whether to let go his hold, or to restrain his mate a little longer. Once again the woman shrieked and louder; and Timo loosened his grasp; but at once the man's hair was in a mill again. Whereupon he lost his temper again and completely this time, and deciding to leave his wife to the Devil, began marching proudly out. Slow, however, and difficult was his progress from the room; for the woman flapped at his neck like a little brown hawk on the back of a ruddy male capercaillie, setting the feathers flying all around. But without heeding this, he tore his way out of the room, tore himself out by force, but not until the porch steps were reached did his wife release her hold, promising to give her husband a good lesson yet; and down the steps Timo came gravely, saying as he went: "That's how I teach 'em, women!" He strode away from the house and disappeared behind the hops, but once there, he grinned cunningly to himself and returned quickly to the stables, where he climbed into the loft. He thrust down a couple of armfuls of hay to the horses in their stall, dropped down on his yielding, rustling couch, and having meditated a while on his wife's "violent heart", fell into a heavy sleep.

Night came, a cold and frosty night, but of Timo nothing more was heard. Greatly anxious, the mistress lay down on her bed, thinking gloomily of her husband's fate. "He had gone, maybe, the wild fellow, and hung himself; or perhaps thrown himself in a temper into the bottomless well in Nummenniittu meadow; or had fallen asleep in the forest, and was sure to freeze the nose, nails and limbs of him, the poor lad." Fancying these things, she soon burst into a fit of passionate weeping as she lay there on her bed without her beloved husband. She sighed and sobbed for an agonized hour or two, her restless ear ever alert for sounds in the gateway or porch. But the night wore on and on, and there was no sound of approaching footsteps. Finally she rose, dressed herself, and lit a richly-punctured tin lantern with the intention of going out to seek the lost one. She dared not, however, face the night alone; she had always been much afraid of gnomes, ghosts and all kinds of spooks. Their own sauna had a special terror for her, for had not recently the old pensioned soldier, foam-bearded Iisakki Honkamäki, died there? She roused, therefore, her maid Taava for company on her search. Taava rose and dressed herself, but it was in peevish and irritable mood that she followed her mistress into the cold, dismal night. They searched first the sauna, then the barn, but without result. They came back into the yard, and there on the edge of the field the wife fell to weeping and calling loudly on her husband by name. She shouted lustily, and the forest and the barn on the open clearing echoed. At length they heard from the loft a kind of rough, hoarse growling in answer, and to this spot the women now hastened. Up into the loft, lantern in hand, the wife climbed and there found Timo; raising himself sleep-drunken on his rustling couch, he stared bewildered at her, as an old goat scared out of its senses by wolves is seen to stare. It stops not, the crazy animal, to seek shelter with the man who has saved it from the wolves, but suddenly, unexpectedly, sets off at a run after the wolves, stopping now and then, stamping its feet and looking quite ferociously around it. So Timo too now

338

stared at his own wife without recognizing her; some remainder of the after-effects of drink still worked perhaps in his brain.

Wife: Why dost thou sit here? Come in; God's creation, thou hast no need to scorch thyself here in the grip of the frost; that I will say. Come in, Timo.

Timo: Who art thou then?

Wife: Good Lord preserve us! Art thou so far gone as not to know me? Ho-hoo! There now, that's how sin and the Devil lead poor souls astray. Ho-hoo, ay!

Timo: What art blubbering for there? Who are you anyway?

Wife: Ah indeed, ah, oh! Timo, Timo!

Timo: Eigh?

Wife: Dost thou not know me? I am thy wife Ulla.

Timo: Ah! Ay, that's right.

Wife: Come in and don't hang about here in the cold stable loft. Oh thou miserable man!

Timo: Ay, a fine fuss because the master sleeps in his loft. Shut up and don't talk so childish there. What's harming a man here?

Maid: They won't, drat them, let a poor maid rest her nights in peace, but here she has to be nosing round corners looking for a drunken swine.

Wife: Hurry now. Give me thy hand and come down nicely.

Maid: Give me thy hand! I'd drag him down by the leg like a sack of chaff.

Timo: What's Taava snapping at down there? Shut up, wench, there's nothing the matter with any of us.

Maid: I'd matter him.

Wife: Hold thy jaw thou, and take this lantern. Canst thou not get down from there?

Timo: I'll be down in my own time; go on ahead to the house, you two.

They entered the house, the mistress ahead and the maid behind, and last of all came Timo. Muttering wrathfully to herself, the maid hastened to her bed, while the mistress began nimbly preparing supper for her man. On the table she set out butter, round loaves, beef-stew and big potatoes in their skins; and with pleasure Timo tackled his meal. But sore of heart, his wife tearfully watched him from the other end of the table.

Wife: I will say; why canst thou not stop properly at home, strange fellow, when thou knowest what a hot-tempered Gypsy-Kaisa I am. Now I've been at thy hair again. What came over my claws, what came over an old woman's claws? I've been tearing at thee again.

Timo: Ay, to be sure, a fine to-do for pulling the master's hair. What art thou blubbering for so childishly when there's nothing the matter with anybody. But it was a hot tussle, all the same, and thou gavest it me with a man's hand. He-he! The Devil anyhow! Go and draw some beer.

Wife: What cause hast thou to hang about the villages and village taverns night and day, night and day? Is this a right state of things?

Timo: Well, I won't say that it mightn't have happened about once a year; ay, it has, it can't be denied.

Wife: Where hast thou frolicked now, and with whom? Say? Who were the rascals?

Timo: Ay, I had my companions, that I had.

Wife: Where hast thou wallowed and with whom? Tell me at once.

Timo: Why, with Tammisto's Kyösti and Karkkula's Aapeli in Tammisto attic yonder.

Wife: What did you drink?

Timo: Only spirits, nothing dearer. Ay, where would the likes of us get rum, rum and liquors.

Wife: You godless! If death were to strike thee now, thou'dst sink down to the lowest hell without help or mercy.

Timo: It isn't often, God knows, that anyone is ready. But what's to kill us here, in our best years. Shut up about dying and draw me some beer.

The wife drew brown, foaming beer for her husband from the cask, and having eaten a meal suited to a full-grown man, Timo

340

emptied almost the whole tankard. Whereafter both withdrew to their night's rest.

But another side of the mistress's nature should also be shown. On Sunday or holy-day mornings, before setting off to Communion Service with her husband, she always wept stinging tears and begged each member of the family for forgiveness, beginning with her husband and passing down to the shepherd boy. And with his mouth in a contented simper, Timo would go out to hurry on the harnessing of the horse, walk there happily, his shirt collar high up his neck, raised there by the nimble hand of his own wife. And to his farmhand, who harnessed the horse in the yard, he would say contentedly: "Eh, but that wife of ours is a good wife, that she truly is, no one could deny it. Where should I be, poor beggar, with all my brats without her, the wife of wives? Dog take it, three hundred roubles wouldn't pay all I'd lose if this woman were to die; even four hundred wouldn't do it. Believe me, Kaapolad." Thus he would say, and with all that he said the wily Kaapo was quick to agree, although each time he was on the other side of the brown gelding, a roguish grin spread over his countenance. But at last the mistress would come out in her new rustling skirt and gleaming linen, her eyes swollen by weeping; she would approach the cart, climb gravely into it and sit down sighing in her seat. And behind her on her right, reins in hand, Timo would seat himself, glowing like the full moon in late summer, glowing, smiling and happy, full of blood, health and vitality. He would jerk slightly at the reins, smack his lips once, and immediately the swift gelding would be trotting along the church road. Soon they would be lost in the shady opening of the birch-wood, and for a brief while a sandy smoke would glitter over the sunlit road.

Eero, youngest of the brothers, lived and toiled on Vuohenkalma Croft, on a stony hill beside the church road. He was the wise and active Sheriff's man of the parish, who caused many a wolf, lynx and bear to lose its life in a well-baited trap. He was much in demand by the Sheriff as an assistant, for all the matters entrusted to his care were wont to turn out exceedingly well. His skill in writing and reckoning also brought him much work, and likewise income. Yet these never tempted him to neglect the tilling of his land, and his farm was ruled with discipline and a fiery energy; no one was allowed to dawdle in his yards. Ever his eye swept searchingly around him, like the sharp eye of a hook-beaked hawk that spies out the land from the branch of a withered birch in a clearing in the bright summer sunshine.

On Sundays or holidays he either studied his newspaper, or wrote the news or described parochial happening from his own parish for the same newspaper. And gladly the editor accepted these writings of his, whose contents were always to the point, their style pithy and clear, often showing genius. And with these interests his outlook on life and the world broadened. The country of his birth was to him no longer a vague part of a vague world, of which he knew neither the site nor the character. He knew well where lay the country, that dear corner of the earth, where the Finns dwelt in toil and struggle, and in whose bosom the bones of his fathers rested. He knew its frontiers, its seas, its secretly-smiling lakes and the pine-clad ridges that run like stake-fences throughout its breadth. The whole picture of the land of his birth, its friendly mother-face, had sunk for ever into the depths of his heart. And from it was born in him a desire to help the happiness and prosperity of his country. By his strenuous and unresting efforts a kind of elementary school was built in the parish, one of the first in Finland. And other useful institutions, too, he brought into the district. And in all his work in the house his eye dwelt constantly on his eldest son, whom he had decided to educate into a man of knowledge and skill.

His wife was Seunala's slender daughter, the flaxen-haired, shy-eyed Anna, she who had seen the wondrous visions and in delirium prophesied many miracles. She was now mistress of Vuohenkalma, a free and prosperous croft; yet her dominion was not over wide. Much more than on her did the care and guidance of the household rest on the master's shoulders. In his pocket clinked the keys of the flour-bin; he it was who settled and measured out the rations for man and beast and paid both serving-maids and men. Often the little mistress would walk dejectedly, stand near the fireplace beside her cauldron, silently meditating. But when she bent down to the baby in its cot, her eyes beamed with a wondrous light. She rejoiced when the infant tumbled and gambolled sturdily in her lap. And to nourish him with the milk of her breasts, to nurse him, clothe him, and, as she would say to herself, "make of him an heir to the city of peace of the blest", was all she needed for her modest glance to glow.

Once in the summer, on a Sunday evening, when the sun drooped to the northwest and air and forest were still, she sat alone with her child, sat on a bench beside the table. Eero paced his fields and meadows, and all the servants had gone to the village. A rapturous peace reigned without and within the croft's Sunday-swept room, and decked with leaves the floor smiled up at her. Peace and silence prevailed; only the distant tinkle of cattle-bells was heard now and again from the birch-clad hill. On the bench sat the young mistress and talked to the child who like a radiant morn looked up at her from her lap. "Tell me; my little one', she said, humming between speech and song, "tell me, my little one, how didst thou know thy way home? — I came along the Turku road, tripped o'er the ox-paths of Häme. — But how didst thou know thy home, little one? — By the grey dog beside the gate; I knew the house by its precious well, and were there not the Vicar's horses in the shed and a barrel of ale in the barn? — How didst thou know thy darling mother, how thy father? — Mother poured out wort by the blazing fire, she poured and sang in a ringing voice, a shawl at her throat, a shawl like snow and the bow of Heaven. How did I know my father? He carved away at the shaft of an axe, whittled beside the golden window. So thou foundest thy way, so thou knewest thy home, knewest thy father and mother. But where is thy father now, say where, and whether he thinks of us? — Surely he thinks of us, and should he forget thee, I will never forget thee, not in the tides of time, not in death, thee, the bright sunshine of my soul and its languishing eve, my joy and sorrow tender. But why my sorrow? Ah! this world is false and stormy, and many a sailor has sunk for good in the eternal depths of its seas. Tell me, my child, my summer-bright, tell me: wouldst thou not sail away from here to a haven of everlasting peace, while the white pennant of childhood still flies clean? On the shore of a misty, tideless lake stands the dark manor of Tuoni; there in the heart of a shadowy grove, in the bosom of a dewy thicket a cradle is prepared for thee with snowy linen and wrappings. Hear therefore my song: it wafts thee to the land of the Prince of Tuoni. O hear the song of my heart!

> "Grove of Tuoni, grove of night!
> There thy bed of sand is light.
> Thither my baby I lead.
>
> Mirth and joy each long hour yields
> In the Prince of Tuoni's fields
> Tending the Tuonela cattle.
>
> Mirth and joy my babe will know,
> Lulled to sleep at evening glow
> By the pale Tuonela maiden.
>
> Surely joy the hours will hold,
> Lying in thy cot of gold,
> Hearing the nightjar singing.
>
> Grove of Tuoni, grove of peace!
> There all strife and passion cease.
> Distant the treacherous world."

So she sang to her child; and the harp rings not as sweet as her voice rang then in the Sunday-swept room. But when she had ceased singing she gazed for long in silence at the heavens; up into the holy, giddy heights she looked; and pure and clear was the sky,

347

not a single wisp of cloud showed under Heaven's curving dome; only a summer swallow, scarce visible to the eye, glittered there, flying hither and thither, light and happy as the thoughts of a Sunday-child. So she sat, and her cheek, tanned by the sun, drooped to the drowsy infant's temple; but the blue eyes still stared upward into the blue heights, and peace shone on her brow.

Her husband returned from the woods and in the yard heard his wife's song, and never before had it echoed so divinely in his ears. He entered, and striding across the room, sat down beside his wife; it was a mark of friendship he seldom showed her. Swiftly the woman turned to him, laid the child in his lap and, pressing her forehead against his breast, burst into passionate weeping. But at that the man threw his arm round her and stroked a lock of her flaxen-yellow hair that had fallen behind her ear. There in the calm Sunday evening they sat on the white bench beside the white table.

So lived and laboured Eero, youngest of the brothers, on his croft; and I have now related a fragment of the life of each brother, from the eldest down to the youngest. And I have yet to relate of a Christmas gathering at the house of Juhani Jukola. For the brothers had decided to foregather once again on the Christmas straw in their former home.

All arrived with their wives and children; and there was a great hubbub in Jukola's spacious living-room as the numerous host of children tumbled and rolled in the rustling straw. There, round the fireplace, sat the group of wives in cheery conversation, and Kekkuri's buxom mistress, the doughty wife of Timo, stood meekly stirring Venla's cauldron, which for very fullness boiled over in white foam. There also, at the foot of the blaze, hymnbook on knee, Simeoni was to be seen, ready to begin the common Christmas hymn. But at the back of the room, round the table sat the other brothers, talking of byegone times, of days in the night of the forests and on Impivaara's stump-besprinkled clearing, under the crannied, roaring height. And memories of past dangers, battles and toil, merged pleasantly together in their minds, as the forests,

346

valleys, mountains and high heaths all merge together in the misty blue of distance. All blended into a dark, delicious dream that awakened a faint repining in their bosoms. Thus they gazed back on days that had flown. So, on an autumn evening, when Nature has lain down to rest and the friendly grove stands yellow, may a cowherd look from afar at the beloved clearing where he had laboured through the summer, grumbling, bathed in sweat. The day had been hot and sultry, thunder rolled in the distance, and gnats and gadflies befogged the air, driving the cattle to a galloping frenzy. But before night had fallen he had gathered together his cattle and marched merrily home with them to the tinkle of bells. Such days he now remembers and smiles. So also a mariner growing grey on shore recalls to mind past storms at sea. Clouds wrapped the vessel in darkness, the foaming waves threatened death; but before night the wind had died and the wave was stilled and slept, and from the brightening west the sun shone out again, pointing the road to haven. This storm the sailor now remembers with silent joy. Thus the brothers too remembered departed days, sitting round Jukola's table on a pleasant Christmas Eve and speaking amongst themselves.

But the cauldron was lifted from the fire, a cheery blaze built up of cordwood, and now in its flaming light a solemn chanting began. And at once a hush fell over the babbling children; the brothers too round the table ceased talking as Simeoni struck up a beautiful hymn and the women, hymnbooks in lap, joined their voices to his. Sweetly the song echoed in the roaring of the fire, and sweeter than any other, the pure and gentle voice of the modest Anna could ever be heard amongst the rest. And when at last they ceased singing, they gathered round the supper-table, and presently sank down amidst the straw on the floor to their nightly repose. Early the following morning they woke, woke to set out for the transfigured church, which with its thousands of burning candles glittered like the starry heavens. Then when the day had fully dawned, they came back racing amongst themselves and spent a merry Christmas in Old Jukola.

But here my story ends. And I have now told of seven brothers in the backwoods of Finland; and what more could I relate of the day of their life and its course here on earth? It rose steadily to its noontide height and sank steadily downward to evening rest amidst the passing of many thousands of golden suns.

THE END